HIDDEN

HIDDEN

Emma Kavanagh

CENTURY

1 3 5 7 9 10 8 6 4 2

Century
20 Vauxhall Bridge Road
London SW1V 2SA

Century is part of the Penguin Random House group of companies
whose addresses can be found at global.penguinrandomhouse.com.

Copyright © Emma Kavanagh 2015

Emma Kavanagh has asserted her right to be identified as
the author of this Work in accordance with the Copyright,
Designs and Patents Act 1988.

First published by Century in 2015

www.randomhouse.co.uk

A CIP catalogue record for this book is available from the British Library.

9781780892047 (hardback)
9781780892054 (trade paperback)

Typeset in Sabon LT Std by Palimpsest Book Production Limited,
Falkirk, Stirlingshire
Printed and bound by Clays Ltd, St Ives plc

Penguin Random House is committed to a sustainable future for
our business, our readers and our planet. This book is made from
Forest Stewardship Council® certified paper.

For Matthew. Always.

Charlie: Sunday 31 August, 10.33 a.m.

I can smell the blood. It is all that I can smell. It coats my nostrils, my lungs, it stains the inside of my throat. It is on me. It covers my hands, has turned my white blouse crimson, and I do not know how much of it is mine, how much comes from the dead.

The bodies litter the hospital lobby like autumn leaves blown inside on a gusty day. There are so many of them, the floor has vanished beneath them. Now, everywhere I look I see the casualties lying at uneven angles. The coffee shop, the one that was so busy just moments ago, before the world ended, now stands empty. Round metal tables have tumbled to their sides, tubular chairs overturned and scattered. Those who could run, did. A bullet has pierced the sandwich display, sending finger-cracks racing along the glass. From somewhere beyond sight comes the smell of burning bread, a toasting sandwich abandoned in the exodus. Beyond that, the automatic main doors to the hospital stand open, bringing inside a gust of warm wind. I look at the doors, study them without seeing, obliquely wonder why it is that they do not close. They should have closed, shouldn't they?

That is when I see the security guard. Ernie is stretched out on his back, a plastic coffee cup still clutched in his hand, the coffee seeping out to form a pool that mingles with the blood. His head is pressed against the right-hand door, and it would seem that he slept, but for the hole where his face should be. His cowlick, the one that he laughed at, the one that he complained his wife hated, is stained a red so dark that it is almost black.

I look away, trying to breathe, trying not to panic. Look down at Aden. He is lying on the ground beside me, has curled inwards around me, so that his chin brushes against my knee. I am holding Aden's hand, so tight that it seems it must be hurting him, although he never murmurs. He has not opened his eyes, his lips are slack. Blood leaches through the dark of his uniform, puddling on the floor, into my skirt. I press my other hand against the hole in his shoulder, feeling warm blood ooze between my fingers. And I pray. I don't remember the last time I prayed, but today I pray. Please God, let him live.

My hearing is beginning to repair. The yawning silence ebbing away, sounds beginning to creep back in. Of course, as soon as they do, I wish they would go away again. Because now I can hear the whimpers. I don't know where they are coming from. I had thought I was the only one left alive in this hell. I'm not sure, but then I think the whimpers are coming from me. Behind that, carried in on the breeze, I hear what I first think is screaming. I wonder distantly what it is that is making the outside world tear itself apart, when the worst that can happen is here, where we are. But then the sound solidifies and I realise I am hearing sirens and that the cavalry are coming.

I look up, think to shout for help. And that is when I

see her. Imogen looks different. The way she is wearing her hair, I haven't seen it like that before. But then, what does it matter how her hair looks, now that she is dead?

Imogen lies spreadeagled at the edge of the lobby. Looks as if she is making snow angels in the heart of winter. But instead of snow she is surrounded by blood that was once hers. She has tumbled backwards, blown there by the gunshot to her chest. Copper-red hair falls across her eyes, a single strand snaking its way across her chin, trapping itself in the gloss pink of her Cupid's-bow lips. Her mobile phone lies in her wide-open hand. For a moment it seems that she can see me, her gaze fixed on me, pleading. But there is nothing there. Her overlarge green eyes are vacant.

I stare at Imogen, and stare, and my brain seems to be standing on quaking ground, because now I recognise her, now I don't. And then I think that it must be the sheen of death on her. This is why she looks so alien to me. So other.

A feeling is rising through me, and I think it must be panic. I fight against it, push it down. There is only me. There is only me amongst them all. I cannot let go.

Okay, Charlie. Take it slowly. My father always said that the only way to climb a mountain is one step at a time. So I focus on my breathing again, slowing it. I know that my lungs are pumping, my heart is beating like a drum, and I am absurdly angry with them both, willing them to calm the hell down. I cling to Aden's hand, so tightly that it seems his skin has become a part of mine, and I breathe in, holding a blood-stained breath in my lungs, and think that I am at the bottom of the pool, and there is nothing more to it than that. Just an easy dive, down into the piercing blue deep. And any second now I will skim the bottom, then I will turn, arching my body up towards the light.

And then I will break the surface. And this time the air will be clean. Bloodless.

I remember the doors, swooshing open onto the still August air. The sun on the linoleum. The barrel of the gun. The shape it made as it faced me. The endless darkness hidden inside. The certain knowledge that I was going to die. Then Aden. That look, from me to him and back again. Then the gun, swinging around, finding him.

Then a voice, low-sounding of whisky and darkness, breaks into my reverie. 'You okay?'

I start and release a sound, one that I have never heard from myself before, a kind of a cross between a yelp and a sob. Aden's face is creased in pain. Eyes open, so slowly. He lies there for a minute, as if he cannot believe that he is alive.

I wait for him to look at me. At least I give him that, before I throw myself at him. I can feel his breath on my cheek, hear his heart beating on mine. I'm dimly aware this is unlikely to help his wounds, but I cannot seem to stop myself, and after a second, as he presumably works at convincing himself that he isn't dead, I feel his arm wrapping itself around me, pulling me in tighter.

'You're alive.' His voice is rough, low.

'You too.' He smells of soap and gunpowder.

'How bad?'

I know what he's asking. I know what he wants me to do. But I stay, cradled against him, until I absolutely, completely have to move. Then, with my one good arm, I push myself up. His shoulder is bleeding. The wound looks ragged, terrifying even, and I have no idea what will come next.

'You'll live,' I lie.

He grins, a fleeting smile so out of place in this setting, yet as welcome as a long drink of water on a burningly hot day. I know that he knows I'm lying. 'Such a bedside manner. I meant the others.' He gestures with one hand around the lobby, wincing, trying to look past me, but I don't move. Ridiculous as it may sound, what with who he is and what he does, but I don't want him to see. But I know that he won't settle, not until he knows.

I don't have to look up. I see them anyway. I will see them every time I close my eyes for the rest of my life.

There's the elderly lady with the navy-blue raincoat, taupe slip-on shoes, yards away from us. Her head is rested on her arm, and it seems that she is merely sleeping. Just got tired and fancied a nap. The blood pools around her, turning her blue coat black. There's a man, about my age, perhaps late twenties. He is slumped against the opposite wall, one partner in a pair of bookends. Only his chin, with the carefully trimmed goatee, is tilted forward onto his chest, his hands resting, palms up on his lap, as if to say: look at me, I won't hurt you. His brains splattered across the wall that supports him.

And him, the one who did this. He is lying amongst the casualties. As if he is one of them.

'It's bad, Ade. It's really bad.'

2

The Shooter: Sunday 31 August, 10.25 a.m.
Day of the shooting

They don't see me. No one ever sees me. Their eyes skit across me and away, like I've been greased and their gazes just can't get any traction. I am, to all intents and purposes, invisible.

They cluster around the hospital doors. The smokers who just need one last fix. An achingly thin man sucks on a cigarette, the red glow creeping its way down towards yellowing fingers. He doesn't look at me, even though I am right in front of him. He has a far-off gaze, and all that exists for him is that cigarette, the metal strut that supports his IV bag. He's leaning on it, a hobo against a flimsy lamp-post.

I have parked in the car park today, for the first time. I have been here before, and the times that I have been here before I have come through the woods that back onto the hospital, have left my car on the other side of it, on Mullins Road. But not today. Because today it doesn't matter where the car is. I will not be returning to it.

I step into the hanging cloud of cigarette smoke, standing

stark in the stagnant air. The gym bag is on my shoulder. The weight of the gun makes it heavy, pulls me off-centre, so that I'm leaning into it. I hold on tight to the strap. Cigarette smoke catches in my throat, makes me cough, and I glance at the man, so old that he looks like he has lived a thousand lifetimes already, and I think about killing him. He is wearing a hospital gown, white with blue checks. It hangs just above his knees, his legs jutting out beneath it, two lollipop sticks, his back warped into a question mark. Still he has not noticed me. I would laugh if it wasn't so damned pathetic. My step slows. I feel the weight of the bag. I could do it. Could turn, pull the gun free, level it at his blank, empty face and pull the trigger. It wouldn't be the first time. My hands twitch, aching for the feel of the roughened grip, cold metal, the kickback as it hits the palm of my hand. The swell of relief that follows.

But, with one final look at the man as he sucks on his cigarette so hard that his cheeks plunge inwards, I turn, keep walking. Because there is a plan. I must stick to the plan.

The hospital doors swoosh open, stale thick air, a plunge into a stagnant pool. There is a burst of sound in the lobby, voices. Somewhere a radio is playing. The Beatles. She loves you. The irony hits me along with the heat, and I step onto the slick linoleum. Breathe. The coffee shop is busy, people lining up at a metal-strut counter. The security guard, his grey hair sticking up at odd angles, belly hanging low over his trousers, holds a paper cup, curls of steam climbing from it. He looks up, and for a moment I think that he has seen me. But then his gaze trickles away, back towards the clear-domed stand where the muffins are kept, and his tongue snakes out, wetting his lips. He reaches down, a movement that looks fluid and practised, adjusts his utility belt, mouth curling like he thinks he's Batman.

I wait in the sun-dappled lobby, the doors hanging open in my presence. I'm not sure what it is that I am waiting for. Is it for the security guard? Am I thinking he will stop me? I study him, his back turned to me now, can see the awkwardness of his movements, that arthritis is setting in, that in truth he isn't stopping anyone. I stand there, a boulder in a stream of people, and I look for a feeling – any feeling. I'm not sure why. After all, lately my life has revolved around running from them. Yet now, here at the end, it seems to me that they have vanished. That the sea of emotions, always raging, always yanking at me, threatening to pull me under, has suddenly stilled, like it has frozen in an instant. I prod at it, a tongue into a cavity, but I can find nothing. Just the relief of the coming silence.

I turn, feet squeaking against the linoleum floor. Look to the signs. I don't know why. I have, after all, been here before. I know my way to Ward 12.

I pull the gym bag higher up onto my shoulder. Or, at least, my hands do, although they feel like someone else's hands. My feet begin to move, someone else's feet. It occurs to me that nothing is yet set. I could always change my mind. But I won't, I know I won't. Because beneath the frozen sea the waves are still raging, and I know that I cannot survive them again.

I glance back, out into the car park, through the pall of smoke, my last glimpse of sunshine. I think it is because I want to say goodbye. But instead I see a figure, hurrying towards me. And she is not like the others. She sees me. Is looking straight at me.

Charlie pushes her way through the crowded smokers.

And I hang there, like I am frozen. She knows. I don't know how it is possible that she could know. But she knows. I see it in her face, eyes wide, frightened, jaw set, even in the movement of her hands, like she is reaching for me, like if she can just get to me in time, then she can stop me.

I turn, breaking into a run. I don't know why. I could just shoot her. But for some reason the thought never occurs to me, and so instead I run, because there are things that I must do before the end.

They are all looking at me now. They stare at this crazy man running through the hospital. Suddenly they all see me, give me a wide berth, which suits me fine. I make for the stairs. Can hear Charlie's voice at my back, calling me. Wonder what the hell she is thinking. That she thinks she is capable of stopping me on her own.

I am almost there, am reaching for the stair doors, when they swing open.

Imogen steps into my path. She doesn't see me. Is looking down at a phone in her hand, is texting, sunlight catching on her red hair. I sway. Because she looks so much like the other one. The image of her dances in front of me, shifting like a hologram, so that now I see her, now I don't. Then, all of a sudden, she stops shifting, the figure coalescing so that my brain can make sense of what my eyes are seeing, and I feel a breathtaking sense of familiarity. I realise then what it is that I have done.

Now everything I thought I knew is gone. Because I've already killed her once today.

My fingers move. They move without me, travel to the bag that is slung across my shoulder, reach in for the gun. Pull it free.

Time has stopped now.

I hear a voice behind me shout a warning, dimly recognise it as Charlie. Hear, from everywhere else it seems, a scream, an intake of breath that sucks all of the air from the room. And now the woman before me looks up, pulls her gaze from her phone. Sees me. Sees the gun. And I can see it – the moment of her death – reflected right there in her eyes, as she realises what I am about to do. She opens her mouth, like she thinks that it can make a difference.

'I . . . your text. I didn't see—'

But I have stopped listening. I know that I do not want to hear what she has to say.

I pull the trigger.

3

Charlie: Monday 25 August, 11.30 p.m.
Six days before the shooting

They move with care, black figures dipping in and out of the flashing blue disco-ball lights. The police cars are parked at odd angles, as if some giant wave has picked them up, thrown them there, so that now they lie prostrate like fish on the sand. I listen, straining against the distant thrum of traffic, the odd car still making its way down the eastbound carriageway, the lights looming, slowing as the drivers ease off the accelerator. It seems that I can see the drivers craning their necks, peering at the scene before them. Just a little something to break up a dark journey. I can just about pick up the distant thrum of conversation from the police officers on the ground, the outer edges of it, its rhythm. Then someone laughs, a high-frequency jab that shatters the quiet night air. The movement of the figures changes then, a flock of birds, heads turning in unison towards a source of alarm, and the laughter stops, the laugher swinging his head, looking up to where I stand, watching. He stares at me for a minute, then looks down, shaking his head.

I tuck my hands into my jacket pockets, lean back against

the car. It's cooler now, a breeze springing up across the sea, whipping my skirt around my bare legs, sweeping across Swansea Bay after another long, corpulently hot day. They are already calling this 'The Year of the Heatwave', are lining it up alongside the years of the more traditional British summer rain, proof positive of global warming, our fast-approaching doom. The temperatures began to climb more than a fortnight ago, at first sitting snug at a pleasing twenty-three degrees, before shooting upwards, and upwards. Yesterday it was thirty-two degrees, today thirty. The dense heat has settled over the city, a looming dome, pushing back the sea air until it seems that nothing is moving, that when one breathes, one pulls in nothing but hot dustiness. Tonight, for a change, the sea air is winning. I turn my face to the breeze, can taste the salt in it. It tugs at my hair, whipping it around my face, the strands dancing in front of my eyes. I brush my hair back impatiently, wish I had thought to bring a band. I'm rarely that organised, unfortunately.

The gathered police officers have carried on their conversation, albeit in a lower tone. It sounds like bees, buzzing just at the limits of my hearing. I should go home. I know I'm not supposed to be here. They know I'm not supposed to be here. But I stay, leaning against the car while my hair tangles in front of my face, because even standing here in the midsummer heat on the side of the M4 is better than going home. Especially tonight. I lean forward, peer down the bank. Can just about make out the rough shape of the body from here, a once-human form, roughly covered with a sheet. Spare a moment to wonder at the grotesqueness of my life; that this, with its death and its blue flashing lights, could come as a relief, a way to forget this day and this date.

One of the figures stands a little away from the others. I can't see him properly, not well enough to make out his features. But I can see the way his back is curved, that there is a strange up–down motion in his shoulders, and I know that he is trying not to vomit. I wonder if he is new. If this is the first dead body that he has seen. Another figure detaches itself from the pack, walks along the grassy embankment that runs beside the now-closed motorway. Stands beside him. I strain to listen, wondering what he will say, if he will offer words of comfort or – I roll my eyes, even though there is no one there to see – if he will take the piss.

I've worked with the police for a long time. My money is on the latter.

They stand like that for a moment, then the second figure claps the newbie on the back, turns into the light. Looks up at me, his face briefly illuminated by the swirling lights. I wave. I swear I can hear the sigh from here. He turns, begins the long trek up the steep bank to see me.

I shouldn't be here. Lydia, my editor at the *Swansea Times*, would like it, but I have learned over the years that the acceptabilities of human behaviour should rarely be judged based on the approval of one's editor. Had I been a normal person, I would be at home now, surrounded by a loving family, a couple of . . . I don't know – cats, maybe? I prefer cats to dogs. They are more self-sufficient. And I appreciate their disdain, the way they are able to look at people in a manner I have only dreamed of. Had I been a normal person, the last place I would want to be is standing above the motorway watching as the police peel a body from the tarmac. But then I have never pretended to be normal.

My mother wanted me to stay. I'd love to think that was because she had remembered, that she worried about me going home to an empty flat on today of all days, but that thought doesn't sit easily, doesn't gel with my stiff-upper-lip mother, who flits through life, never dwelling on its darkest passages. I had gone for our weekly dinner, just her, me and Ed – my old stepdad, as he keeps jokingly referring to himself. At least, I hope he's joking. My mother had cooked a leg of lamb, some nice spring veg, which we ate in silence – distantly moored boats in a too-big harbour. She never mentioned the date, and so neither did I. Just ate my lamb and kept my mouth shut, like a good little girl.

'I've made up the spare bed for you. Why don't you stay? It would be like old times,' my mother had said as I pulled my jacket on, collected my keys.

I didn't answer for a minute, pretended to be struggling with the strap of my handbag. Wondered briefly which old times she was referring too, and why the hell she would think I would long for their return. 'I should go home. I have to be in the newsroom early in the morning.'

She had nodded, grace in defeat. Has never really recovered from the shock of her daughter choosing journalism as a career, a high-flying job at the *Swansea Times*, instead of something stable, respectable. Accountancy perhaps. Sometimes I can hear her thinking the word 'hack', even though it is not something she would ever say. My mother is above such language. She leaned in, standing in their Anaglyptaed hallway, gave me the merest facsimile of a kiss, her cheek, doughy with pressed powder, lightly touching mine. Her perfume lapped against me, the same one that she has worn for ever, sweet and cloying, the smell of my childhood bedroom and stuffed animals and a funeral home with a bright mahogany coffin.

I had been driving along the A-road, still a good ten

minutes from home. Was driving absurdly slowly, because better here, in this car, with the illusion of forward motion, than at home in my sparklingly empty flat where all life has ground to a halt, caught on the thorn of this day – the anniversary of my father's death. Then I had seen the lights, had offered up a quick prayer to the gods of crime-reporting, had pulled in, movements clumsy in my haste.

The figure pulls himself up the last few steps with an effort. 'Charlotte Solomon, do you ever sleep?' Del has put on weight since we were in school together, has rounded out across the belly and the jowls. He is sweating with the climb, beads catching in the street light, rolling down the deep notches that have begun to form along the sides of his nose, down to his mouth. I think that if I listen hard enough I will hear the plop as they fall onto his fluorescent jacket.

'Rarely. How are you, Del?'

His name isn't Del. It's Peter. But his father was a market trader and we went to a school more known for its television-viewing than its creativity. Hence, Del-boy.

He grins down at me, pulling at the collar of his shirt. 'Fucking roasting. You see that climb?'

I glance down the bank towards the motorway and the body, back up at him. 'Mmm. Steep.' I move my stance slightly, tucking in behind him so that he blocks the breeze. There are often advantages to being five-foot-two. Wind cover not least amongst them. 'So . . . wife okay?'

'Yeah.' He won't look at me, because he figures that if he doesn't look at me, then he won't crack. 'Due any day now. Like living with a bloody bear.'

'I'm sure she feels so sorry for you, Del. I'm sure she'll be telling you that, as she is giving birth to your child.'

15

'Yeah, well . . . you know you're not supposed to be here? Right?'

Yes.

'No? I was just taking some air. Why shouldn't I be here?' I peer down the bank again. 'Something going on? Besides, isn't this Traffic's patch? What's a uniform sergeant like you doing here?'

Del looks at me, shakes his head. 'You're a pain in the arse, Charlie.' Stuffs his hands in his pockets, hunching down low like he's cold, even though I can still see the sweat coursing off him. 'There's a vacancy come up in Traffic. I'm thinking of transferring over. You know, fast cars and all that jazz. Of course, I pick tonight for my ride-along.' He looks back down the bank, voice dropping. 'Bloody typical. Look, you know I can't talk.'

'I know.'

'The thing is . . . Fuck!'

That's when I realise that there are tears mixed in with the sweat.

'Shit, Del. I'm sorry.' I reach out a hand, awkwardly pat him on his luminous arm, wish like hell I had just got in the damn car. 'Ah . . . You, ah, you okay?'

Don't tell me, don't tell me.

He shakes his head, brushing a hand across his eyes, up over his forehead. 'God, it's hot.'

I nod, happy to pretend right along with him.

'I . . .' He glances around him. I feel absurdly like I'm in some low-budget film noir. 'I'm not telling you this. Okay?'

'Okay.'

'I mean . . . I'm not – it's not cos you're a reporter. It's just, y'know, cos you knew her an' all.'

My stomach flips and suddenly I'm sixteen again, and

the phone is ringing, cutting through the early-morning darkness, and I am trying not to fall down as I hear the words – Your father is dead – and my world unravels around me. I cough, clear my throat. 'Who, Del?'

He looks down the bank, not at me, voice dropping to an almost-whisper. 'It's Emily. Emily Wilson?'

I stare up at him, take a step back, trying to reorient myself. 'You're kidding?'

Del shakes his head. 'Wish I was.'

We grew up on a narrow street – Emily raised four doors down from me, the houses bunched together like they are sheltering from some incoming storm. In the summer, the trees that line one side take over, drooping heavy branches over the skinny road, so that it seems like you are running through a tunnel. In the winter, the leaves die back and you can see the sea. Just about. It is a street built for a different time, before every family had two cars, satellite TV and conservatories. Our childhood games revolved around the cars, the way they parked, tilted like a row of drunken men, half on the pavement, half off. We would play hide-and-seek behind them, would kick footballs, waiting to see how long before an irate owner came out to scold us. Emily wasn't a huge fan of that game.

I don't remember a time when I didn't know Emily Wilson. Can bring to mind now a yellowing photo of her in a dungaree dress, her hair in bunches, clapping as I blow out candles on a birthday cake shaped like a donkey. You could say that we were friends, but that as a word seems incomplete. She was a part of my childhood, like the trees or the iron railings that lined our road at its steeper excesses, the ones that we would tumble over – in our minds the Olympic gymnasts of the future. She was always there.

I stand there, shivering now, follow Del's gaze down towards the blue lights and the tarmac. 'Is she okay?'

The words have left my mouth before I realise that it's a stupid question. That I haven't seen an ambulance. That there is nothing here but death.

Del shakes his head.

I stare down at the motorway. This really is a shit day. 'Do you know . . . ?'

'An accident. Driver said she came from nowhere.' Del shrugged, trying to be a policeman again instead of a kid who has just seen his classmate dead. 'These things. They happen, I guess.'

We both stand there, nodding, even though I'm not sure what it is that we are agreeing to.

'You seen her recently?'

I shrug. 'I don't know, maybe like a year ago. We . . . we grew apart.' When my father died and my world fell apart and the For Sale sign went up, and suddenly my mother and I are whisking away, living in Mumbles, because, darling, that's where everyone wants to live, and the teenage me screeching that I don't give a shit where everyone wants to live, that it's not what I want. But it had all changed anyway, and there was no choice, and so we left. I didn't see Emily much after that.

Del isn't looking at me. He is staring out across the dancing blue lights. 'I bumped into her, couple of months back. She's a nurse.' Caught himself, looking back down at where her body lies. 'Was a nurse. She was taking care of that Lowe boy. You know, the one from the shooting?'

It feels like the breeze has chilled, and I start, look at him. My mouth opens, but before the words can come out, a sound breaks out, an inappropriate musical tone, breaking into the night air. We both turn, staring down at the body – Emily – watch as figures move towards it, towards Emily's ringing mobile phone. Then, before they can reach it, it stops, and the silence returns, deeper now.

I shake my head, trying to regain my train of thought. But it is gone, lost in the thought that someone is calling Emily, that she will never answer again.

'The driver . . . ?' I ask.

'Gutted. Couldn't do anything about it. Didn't see her till it was too late.'

I nod. Thinking.

'You know,' Del glances back at me, 'I'd get into a lot of trouble . . .'

'I'll sit on the name, Del. Until its official release.'

He studies me. 'Yeah?'

'Yes.' I cross my arms, fix him with a look. 'I wouldn't burn you, you know that.'

Del studies me for a moment. 'You still single?'

I grin. 'Why Del, are you flirting with me?'

He pulls a face. 'Yeah, cos that's what I need. Another bloody woman on my plate. No, I'm just saying . . . I could set you up.'

'Yeah, whatever.'

'No, seriously. That guy down there,' he points down towards the murky figures who knot around the police cars, 'he's single. Nice guy.'

'You mean the one who's up-chucking on the hard shoulder?'

He winks at me. 'That's the one.'

I laugh. 'Thanks, Del. I think I'm okay.'

'Well, if you're sure . . .'

I watch the figures. I can see heads glancing up towards

us, know I have to tell him to leave because soon he'll be in trouble. I pause for a moment. 'Del?'

'Yeah?'

'What shoes was Emily wearing?'

Del gives me a long look. 'Seriously, Charlie. My wife's a thousand months pregnant. That should tell you that I'm not gay.'

'Ha-ha. Rapier wit. Just . . . was she wearing heels?'

'I . . . yeah . . . I had to collect one from . . . Yeah, she was.'

I look. From left to right. Down the precipitously steep bank. 'Then let me ask you this. How the hell did she get there?'

He frowns. 'How do you mean?'

I flick my fingers along the westbound carriageway. 'It's three miles to the nearest exit.' Back along the eastbound. 'Two that way.' Down towards the embankment. 'This is pretty steep all the way along. So how the hell did she get here? I mean, say she did walk. It would have taken her a while. You would have had reports of someone walking along the M4.'

Del nods, thoughtful.

I fold my arms across my chest, suddenly cold. 'Unless, she was dropped off here. Unless someone left her.'

4

Aden: Monday 25 August, 11.30 p.m.
Six days before the shooting

Aden tried not to breathe. Kept his tread soft, heavy boots crunching lightly against fallen leaves, ground that had not seen rain in far too long. A breath of air, the first of a stiflingly hot day, wound its way through the darkened trees, making the leaves whisper and dance. Beads of sweat worked their way from beneath his ballistic helmet, trickling down, along the sides of his face. The sub-machine gun heavy in his hands.

He could see the lights in the distance, the orange glow of the hospital car park bisected by the black of trees. Could just about make out the boxy outline of the hospital building, low-slung, the occasional splotch of white light from unshielded windows. The odd flutter of movement as dark figures passed before the light. Aden thought about how easy it would be to shoot them. Pick a spot, somewhere in between the trees, somewhere with nice clear sight-lines, drop to one knee, steady, steady, making sure that your target – the splotch of light, the figure within – sat central within your scope. Squeeze the trigger. He could feel it, the movement of the cold metal, the recoil, the boom that seems to come from far away. And then, seemingly all at once, the shattering of glass, the figure folding into itself, vanishing from the light.

Two nights in a row, the same call to the control room. Man with a gun seen at Mount Pleasant Hospital. They had been kitting up, still in the station when the orders had come through, Aden just about ready to head out, Rhys running in, late as usual, having to throw his kit together just so they could make it out of the door. Tonight, thought Aden. Tonight he would find him. Aden gathered his breathing, adjusted his grip, slick with sweat now, his gaze playing against the dark shapes of the trees, the shadows that seemed to form an army. Listened.

There were footsteps behind him. And for a second, just a second, Aden's heart stopped. It was as if he had forgotten about Rhys; the darkness and the shadows and the chattering leaves had convinced him that he was out here all alone. He paused in his movement, spared a glance back over his shoulder at where the younger man stood, his weapon held high and level, ballistic helmet pulled low over his brow. Rhys's face was set, lips pulled so tight that they seemed to vanish, his gaze sweeping across the trees.

It was the boy's second week back. Boy. Rhys Malloy was hardly a boy. Not really. Maybe ten years younger than Aden's thirty-four. But Rhys seemed like a boy. With his wide eyes, olive skin, the kind of looks that the ladies went nuts for. Aden knew this – they told him. The female officers he shared coffee breaks with, went through training with, bumped into in the gym. They all had the same question. When's that hottie Rhys coming back?

Aden caught the younger man's gaze, held it. Okay? A silent nod.

Aden turned, shifted his grip on the G36. Flicked the narrow torch that he carried at the trees. Where are you? Where are you, you bastard?

Aden measured his step, keeping his tread cautious on the uneven ground. The man had been seen running through the hospital corridors, had vanished before security could get there (and for this Aden offered up a silent prayer of thanks), out through the sliding doors, the puddled light of the car park. Into the woods. Was he waiting? A dark figure sitting up against the shadow of a tree, watching their torchlight dancing towards him, his weapon raised, his finger on the trigger. Aden's heart thudded in his ears, and he shook his head slightly. Calm down. Concentrate. Then something else, a memory of rain and blood, breaking through the way it always did. Aden gritted his teeth, forcing his breathing to slow. Not now.

Then Aden heard a sound, one that seemed to come from nowhere. It filled the air, getting louder and louder. A bright beam of light swept through the trees, breaking up the darkness. The trees looked like sheepish adults caught in a game of musical statues. Tuk-a-tuk-a-tuk-a-tuk-a. Aden looked up, shielding his eyes from the downdraught of the helicopter as it swept overhead. The light marching from left to right, right to left.

This would be it. If he was in there, if he was hiding, this is when he would run, flushed out by the chase. Aden felt his finger hard against the trigger, scanning the treeline. Waiting. Aden tried not to think about the last time, with its driving rain and the darkness that was so absolute, trying not to think about the blood and whether the trigger would move. It was just like training. That was all.

Then, after minutes or hours, a crackle of static, the radio sparking to life.

'Yeah, Whisky Tango Three Eight, we got nothing up here. No visual. No heat signatures. Your boy's rabbited.'

Again.

Aden stopped, sighed. He lowered his weapon, thumbed the radio. 'Okay, roger that, Hotel Lima Nine Nine. Thanks for the help, guys.'

'Any time.' Then the helicopter lifted, the wind dissipating as it climbed, and suddenly the light was gone.

'Shit!' Aden could feel the adrenaline roller coaster begin to enter its downward slide – so many chemicals, nowhere to go. He kicked at a fallen branch, a lacklustre effort that made him feel no better.

Rhys had lowered the G36, pushed his helmet back. 'Thought we'd get him tonight.' He looked to Aden like a little boy home from school.

Aden stood, eyes roaming across the darkness, the trees that seemed now to be crowding in, closer than they had been before. Where are you, you little bugger? He let his gaze run from the brightness of the car park, hugging the side of the building, closer, closer, turned, peering through the trees. There were more lights through there. Street lights, little orange dips of colour.

'That's Mullins Road, right?'

Rhys looked, gaze following Aden's nod. 'Yeah. But the other ARV has swept it.'

'Maybe he's leaving a car there. Ducking through the woods, out that way and into a car,' said Aden.

'Maybe,' shrugged Rhys. 'There's no CCTV there, though.'

Aden glanced back at him. 'There's not?'

Rhys shook his head. 'I worked a couple of cases there

when I was in uniform. Residents were always complaining that the cameras hadn't worked in years. And you know how that goes.' He sighed, shifted the weight of the weapon. 'You want to head back?'

Aden stood, staring through the trees at the street lights beyond. 'Let's just pop into the hospital for a second.' He could see Rhys's expression, see his fight between deference and confusion, and Aden grinned. 'You're allowed to say it, you know.'

'Um, okay. Why? Aren't CID going to do the follow-up now?'

Aden nodded. 'Yeah. But I'm curious. Let's just go and have a look.'

The light of the lobby was jarring after the darkness. It was quiet, few people moving about this late at night. But Tony Waterton stood at the centre of it, G36 held loose in his hands, his face set like he was ready for war. He looked at them. 'Nothing?'

'Nah.' Aden shook his head. 'We're just popping up to the ward.'

Tony gestured across his shoulder to the toilets. 'Just waiting for Kate. We'll do another sweep inside before we head out.' He shifted the gun. 'See if we can flush this bastard out.'

'Call us if you need us.' Aden turned to the left, pulling at the door that closed off the stairwell, and took the stairs two at a time, his gun jostling against his hip. 'It was Ward 12, yeah?'

Rhys trotted to keep up. 'I think so.'

'So, I meant to ask, how are you doing? Being back, I mean. You finding it okay?' Aden didn't look at Rhys, instead studying his boots, the tread against the steps.

'It's . . . it's fine. A bit . . .'

'Bit of a shock to the system?'

Aden glanced across, saw Rhys's nod, the downturned eyes. It had been almost a year. A year in which Rhys and Tony stepped out of their lives, back into uniform – not that you've done anything wrong, mind, it's just procedure; just a couple of months while the IPCC investigates. A couple of months that grew and grew, until in the end it seemed that the two were never coming back to Firearms. And everyone said, everyone knew, that they had done the right thing, that they had done the only thing they could do, that by pulling the trigger they had saved their own lives, and Aden's too. But this was the way it worked, whether you were right or not. And Aden was lucky. That he hadn't had to go through it. Because, after all, he hadn't pulled the trigger.

Aden tugged at the door, harder than he intended to, studying the ward signs up above, anything to distract himself from that night. Took a right. The security guard stood before the doors of Ward 12, his arms folded, face grim. He had to be approaching seventy. His gut lolled over the top of his trousers, his blue shirt straining at the buttons, a grey cowlick, curling above his forehead. Aden fought back the urge to shake his head. If the gunman came back, this guy would be the first one down. 'All right, mate? Firearms police. Need a chat with the witness.'

The man nodded, slowly, eyes taking in the uniform, the weapons. 'See some ID?'

Aden heard Rhys sigh behind him and fixed a smile on his own face, pulled free his warrant card. 'PC Aden McCarthy, officer number 492. This is PC Rhys Malloy, 1077.'

The man took the card, studied it for longer than was

necessary, then, without looking at them, reached behind him and gave the ward door three sharp raps. A moment, two, then the intercom sparked to life. 'Yes?'

'Got police here for you. Need to see the witness.'

A pause and then a long buzz, the door swinging inwards. 'Gentlemen.'

Aden nodded, pocketing his warrant card, and slipped into the ward. The nurse was waiting for them, standing by the nurses' station, her hands dipping into and out of one another. She looked young – too young surely to do a job like this – broad across the middle, long blonde hair pulled high into a chunky bun.

'Did you find him?' she asked.

Aden shook his head. 'No, I'm sorry. You're the witness?'

The girl nodded. 'Chloe Chambers. You know this is the second time, right? That he showed up at the door last night, too? Scared Emily half to death when she saw that gun, I'll tell you. What does he want with us?'

'I don't know yet. You get a good look at him?'

Chloe chewed her thumbnail, shook her head. 'I'm sorry. It was dark. He had like a hood up, so you couldn't see his face. I'd say he was – I don't know – maybe six foot, slim, I think.' She studied him as she spoke, hands flailing. 'I'm sorry, I really am. Maybe Emily . . . but I don't think she saw much more than I did. And that's what's so scary, you know? You just think: well, it could be anybody.'

Aden frowned. 'Emily. She's the one who reported him last night?'

'Yeah. It spooked the hell out of her.' Chloe folded her arms across her chest, shuddered.

'Is Emily here?'

The nurse shook her head. 'She's off tonight. I can try

calling her . . .' She didn't wait for an answer, but reached behind her, punching a quick series of numbers into the desk phone. Long moments stretched out, then Chloe shook her head. 'She's not picking up. It's late. I guess she's probably sleeping.' She replaced the receiver and glanced behind her to where her patients lay. 'It's just . . . it's scary, you know? The patients on this ward, they're very sick. And you just think: how much worse can it possibly get for them?'

Aden followed her gaze, looking beyond the bright light of the nurses' station, into the darkness of the ward. For the first time he noticed the beeping of machines; that Rhys was standing with his back against the door as if he was prepared to bolt. Aden glanced over his shoulder, could see the beds in darkness, the soft glow of lights, the dance of figures, medical-staff shadows moving from bed to bed, the huff of respirators. He let his gaze trickle around until it found him. Dylan Lowe lay stretched out on his back in a single bed, in a room of his own. Machines surrounded him, his hair longer now than it had been a year ago, brushed back out of his face. The light in the room was dim, but Aden could just about make out his face, looking so much older than he had on that night with the darkness and the rain and the blood. Could just about see his eyes, the way his vacant gaze hooked on the ceiling above.

And, with a crashing sense of horror, Aden understood just what it was that the gunman had wanted.

5

Imogen: Monday 25 August, 11.30 p.m.
Six days before the shooting

Imogen listened. It was, after all, what she did best. She listened to the hum of the refrigerator, the growl of passing cars – one, two – casting shadow and light across the bedroom ceiling. She listened to Dave, his breathing steady and deep. Every now and then he would let loose a snore, a low grumble that welled up from his belly, building, building, then falling away into nothing. Imogen clutched the thin sheet between her fingers, even though it was a hot night and the sheet stuck to her skin like it had been glued there.

Her engagement ring was visible, even in the darkness. It caught the orange street light as it crept its way in through the curtains that never seemed to close right, a beacon in the darkened room. A single diamond set in white gold. The band narrow and plain, the diamond that her mother had described as modest. Although surely diamonds by their very nature were anything but modest. A solitaire. Such a strange name for something that joined together two people. For life.

It had been a year now. A year almost to the day. There had been no bended knee, no champagne or beds covered with the petals of blood-red roses. But then, that had never been Dave's style. He had asked her over breakfast. She had just taken a mouthful of toast. With peanut butter. She remembered that, remembered the way the peanut butter stuck to the roof of her mouth, stoppering it up.

'Look, I've been thinking. It's been a long time. Us. We've been together a long time.'

Eight years. They had been together for eight years.

'I mean, it's probably time. Don't you think?'

Imogen had stared at him. There were toast crumbs, resting on his lower lip. Had felt like her brain had split itself in two, the part that understood what it was that he was saying – that this moment, the one she had waited for since she was a child, had finally arrived. And the other part, the part that couldn't stop staring at the crumbs.

'So . . . will you?'

'Will I what?' She had watched as the crumb tumbled from his lip, landing on his forest-green tie. It left behind it an orb of grease.

'Marry me. Will you?'

Dave faced away from her, the wall of his narrow back slicing the bed in two. Imogen turned her head slightly, watched his outline in the darkness. The narrow points of his shoulder blades jutting out, almost to his ears, sleeping like he walked, shoulders up, head pulled in like a turtle retreating into its shell.

Imogen couldn't remember saying yes. She had said yes, of course she had. They had, after all, been together for eight years. And she loved him. He was the only partner she had ever known. She studied the outline of the ring, the way it distorted the shape of her hand. She had said yes and they had kissed and a new future had unfurled itself before her – a simple white dress, a small reception, a honeymoon somewhere warm, then babies that grow to children. One, two, perhaps even three.

A year ago now. Imogen studied his back, his shoulders and, lifting her fingers, trailed the tip of them along the curve of his T-shirt. Dave gave a small grunt, shifted in his sleep, and she pulled her hand back.

'So? Are you ever going to get around to it?' Imogen's mother had leaned back in her deckchair, had been sipping something dark, exotic-looking.

It had been a thrummingly hot day today, wicked blue skies, not the merest whisper of a cloud. Her mother had called. You must both come over, we're doing a barbecue. Your sister and Amy will be here. I won't take no for an answer.

'Get around to what?' Imogen hadn't looked at her mother, had watched her niece instead. Amy, two years old with gossamer strawberry-blonde hair, lips strung into a Cupid's bow, a little swimsuit, pink striped with a narrow frill. Imogen's father had blown up the paddling pool, had carefully filled it with lukewarm water, and Imogen smiled as Amy shrieked with delight.

'You know what.'

She did. She did know what. It had been a year after all and, as her mother often reminded her, she wasn't getting any younger.

'Mum. Leave her alone. They'll do it when they're ready.' Mara had winked at Imogen. 'Plenty of time to be old and boring and married.'

They were identical twins, Imogen and Mara. The same

and yet different. Same copper-red hair, same narrow nose, same Cupid's-bow lips. But Mara was beautiful. A terrible thing to think about one's twin, but true nonetheless. There was an ease about her, an effortlessness that Imogen had never been able to conquer. Her hair shorter, cut into a sleek chin-length bob, whilst Imogen's hung just beyond her shoulders, never seeming to look quite the way it was supposed to. There were curves to Mara, her small breasts neat and shapely, her hips rounded, where Imogen was all angles and corners, thin, her stomach concave, ribs that protruded, so that when she looked at herself naked – something she very rarely did – Imogen was put inevitably in mind of a toast-rack.

'I don't know, Mum. We haven't really thought about it yet. Like Mara said, there's plenty of time.'

How to say that they had never talked about it? Not once. That the engagement alone had seemed to be a fait accompli, sufficient by itself. And that, as time had worn on, Imogen had stopped glancing at bridal magazines and flower displays, and that now, when she thought about weddings and the future that seemed to sit there, just out of reach, her stomach would ravel itself up into a tight little knot.

Dave shifted, the bed-springs aching with his movement.

She looked back down at the ring in the darkness. She wanted to be a mother. It was all she could remember ever wanting. Mara would talk about becoming a doctor, a lawyer. For Imogen it was simpler than that. For her, it was a child, dimpled hands that would wrap themselves around her own. Her own green eyes looking up at her. A husband who would look at her like she was the sun and the moon. Mara had got there first. The husband – Jack, a chief inspector in the police force. The baby. Imogen studied the outline of the diamond, feeling the weight of it multiplying with the future it promised, wanting that child so badly that it felt like a two-day hunger.

Imogen looked at the clock – 11.30 p.m.

She wondered distantly if she should get up, if some warm milk might help, pump her body full of tryptophan, quiet her seemingly relentless brain. She could take a sleeping pill, had a prescription in the drawer for times like this – seemed that there had been innumerable times like this, when her mind would swim and swim, and sleep would just drift ever further away. But then she might not wake, even though the alarm was set and it usually roused her. And she had clients back-to-back all day tomorrow, and if it didn't go off . . . She looked back at the clock. She would close her eyes, would really try. She really needed to sleep.

Then the phone rang, cutting through Dave's snores. For a moment Imogen thought it was a dream, that she had in fact fallen asleep. Then came the realisation, like falling off a cliff, that it was real. Her heart began to thunder, because no one calls at 11.30 p.m. with good news.

Imogen pushed the sheets away, swinging her bare feet onto the carpeted floor. Four paces to the phone. Who was dead? Her mother? Her father? Two paces. Dave groaned loudly, turning in a creak of springs. Imogen reached out, gripped the handset.

'Hello?' Her voice came out, quiet and small.

There were no words. Just a sound. Ragged breath, something that sounded like a groan.

'Mara?' Imogen could hear it in the breath, that little hiccup on the out-breath. Would have known her twin, even in silence. 'Mara, what is it? What's happened?' Listening as her sister sucked in a deep, shaking breath.

'It's Amy.'

'What is? What happened, Mar?'

'She's had a seizure. She . . . oh God, Im, it was awful. We're in Mount Pleasant Hospital. Ward 11. Will you come? Please?' The words collapsed, disintegrating into a sound, something between a wail and a groan.

'I'm on my way, Mar. I'll be right there.'

Imogen hung up the phone, stood for a moment in the darkness. Feeling the floor moving beneath her.

'What is it?' Dave's voice came out of the dark.

'Amy. Mara said she's had a seizure. I don't know, I just . . . I have to go.' She slipped into jeans, all fingers and thumbs now.

He lay for a second, absorbing. 'Well, did Mara—'

'She didn't say anything else. Just that they're there, that she needs me to go. I . . .' Imogen had the sudden thought that she should say something, that there should be more to say to your fiancé when the world had spun off its axis.

She heard him sit up, the movement of bed-springs. 'Do you need me to go with you?'

Imogen pulled a T-shirt on over her head, her voice muffled by the fabric. 'You have work. Get some sleep.'

Silence, then a song of creaking springs as he lay back down. 'All right. Let me know what they say.'

'I will.' Imogen tugged on a pair of jeans, balancing awkwardly on one foot, and then leaned in, kissed him quickly, an awkward kiss so that their teeth bumped.

Traffic was light, few cars out on the late-night Swansea streets. Imogen wove through the narrow Mumbles streets, all hills and terraces, out onto Mumbles Road. The sea ran parallel with the road, inky-black. Imogen pressed her foot onto the accelerator, pushing back the growing sense of nausea.

The car park was quiet, just a police car, its blue lights still swirling. Imogen slid the car into a space, running across the tarmac, past the police car, her flip-flops flapping against the ground. Up the stairs, past an elderly security guard, standing – arms folded, legs akimbo – against the door of the adjacent ward, a rapid knock that hurt her knuckles. Amy Elliott-Lewis. I'm her aunt. She threw the words at the intercom. A buzz, a click, and she tugged on the door handle, trying not to slip in her inconsequential footwear.

Her sister stood, a statue on grey linoleum.

Beyond her, a wall of white, the doctors buzzing around the bed, bees around honey. Their voices piano-wire tight, movements quick. Imogen could see the urgency, in their backs, the turn of their heads. And there, at the centre of them, Amy's tiny figure, smaller now than she had been just a few hours before, her body dancing to an awkward beat, arms flailing. A noise coming from her that Imogen had never heard before, an animalistic cacophony of grunts. The smell of urine.

Imogen grasped Mara's arm. Her twin didn't look at her, didn't once take her eyes off her child, as if the world had narrowed down for her now, vanishing into this one tiny figure. Mara's arms were wrapped tight around her stomach as if she were in pain. She was keening, a low moaning sound that tore at Imogen's heart.

Imogen pulled her sister into her, trying to keep the fear from her voice. 'It's okay, Mar. She's going to be okay.'

6

Charlie: Tuesday 26 August, 6.45 a.m.
Five days before the shooting

I plunge through the water, unnaturally blue. The sunlight cascades through it, sending a kaleidoscope of colour spiralling down to the tiled floor. Pull my arm back, over my head, angling my hand, slicing it back into the water. Stroke, stroke, breathe. A shoal of bubbles litters the water ahead of me. I can't make out Aden's feet, but I know he's there. I can feel the way his body changes the flow of the water, picking me up in its current. We take it in turns to lead, geese flying south for the winter, sharing out the drafting. Stroke, stroke, breathe. My arms ache, the muscles pull across my chest. The bubbles vanish, and I know that Aden has turned, is starting back, but I don't have time to look for him, because now I'm at the wall and it's my turn, so I flip, tumbling in a tight turn, press the soles of my feet against the tiles and then I'm off again, returning whence I came.

I didn't sleep much last night. Kept finding myself back on that embankment, peering over Del's shoulder down at the body lying prone on the eastbound carriageway of the

M4. Only this time, I can see her face. I know that I didn't, would never have known that it was Emily had Del not told me, but my memory doesn't seem to believe that. Now, when I think about it, I can see those tight curls splayed around her shoulders, dirty blonde, dirtier now than they should be. Rounded cheeks, nose just that little bit too large. So I can't sleep. Because every time I try, I see Emily lying dead.

I blow out a breath, turn my head to suck in more air. Stroke, stroke, breathe. Aden hits the opposite wall, a quick spin and he's gone again. Only this time he catches my eye through the chlorinated blue, gives me a waterlogged grin. I smile back, leaving my tumble a little late, so that I have to pull it in and it's clumsy, my foot hitting the wall at an off angle. I swear under my breath.

Fourteen years. For fourteen years, I told myself that Emily and I had grown apart. But in truth, the distance that separated us came from me running, as fast as I could, in the opposite direction. My gentle, kind, brilliant father, dead of a heart attack at the meagre age of forty-five, and me, sixteen years old and so angry I could barely breathe. It had seemed easier, at the time, to mourn all of it together, my old life, rather than to be reminded, every time I looked at remnants of it, about the hole that my father had left. Emily tried for a while, kept calling, but in the end the calls tailed off and the bifurcation of my world became complete. I assume that she moved on, found new friends, perhaps ones less fickle.

I can see Aden up ahead, his bare skin blue through the water. Can see that he has stopped, can tell from the position of his shoulders, the shape of his back, that he is looking upwards, checking the time. We'll have a two-minute rest. Then another set of thirty.

I reach my hand out ahead, allow my fingers to grasp at the lipped edge of the wall.

Aden smiles at me. Gives a nod down the increasingly crowded swim-lane. 'Busy today.'

'Yeah.' I shrug. 'You know what it's like. As soon as the weather turns, people will suddenly decide that the idea of getting soaking wet isn't such a great one.' I spare a quick glance at the clock. Thirty seconds in. 'So, how's work?'

He doesn't look at me. Keeps his gaze on the swimmers. 'It's . . . okay. You know how it is. Rhys and Tony are back on Firearms, did I tell you that?'

I shake my head. 'How are they finding it? It's been a while for them, right?'

'A year, just about. Tony's Tony. It's like water off a duck's back with him. Rhys, I think it's knocked his confidence. I get that. That kind of thing, it stays with you.' Aden glances at me. 'You saw how it was.'

I didn't know Aden then, not really. He was just some guy from the pool, both of us gluttons for punishment, crawling out of bed in the pre-dawn darkness and plunging into the frigid water. We didn't speak, not for a long time. I can be difficult to get to know. I would come and swim my lengths, and Aden would come and swim his, and then we would leave again. After a while – a couple of months maybe – we progressed to hello. I was fairly impressed with myself. He became, I suppose, a part of the scenery.

Then the night of the shooting.

I was working a late shift in the newsroom. I was bored. So bored that when the police scanner sparked to life with the flurry of words, each tilted with the inflection of stress, I grabbed my coat, poured out into the driving rain and ran for my car. I wove through the city traffic, heading away from the bright lights, wide streets, up the hills, so that the sea splays out behind you, and you inevitably think what a beautiful view this would be to wake up to. And then you turn around to face the club-footed council houses, the shells of cars hoisted onto breeze blocks, the general air of decay and despair, and you remember that the view isn't everything.

They were easy to find. The blue police lights shining out from the hill of Harddymaes like a beacon. I'd parked the car, just beyond the police line, had pulled an old black umbrella out from under the driver's seat, cursing at the exposed wire that worked its way free. Tucked my coat tighter around myself and walked quickly.

At first it was hard to make out what I was seeing. There was the ambulance, its blue light swirling, back doors flung open. A shadowy dance of figures down a narrow alley, all speaking low and urgent. And a dark shape, sitting on the kerb, a river of water running along the gutter beneath his legs, a guttering cigarette cupped in his hand.

I didn't realise that it was Aden. Not at first. Then he had looked up at me, and in spite of the dark uniform and the look of horror that he wore, I had realised who he was.

The rain was driving, a torrential downpour that would, in the days to come, lead to flooding in the lower grounds, a school closing when its assembly hall became steeped with rising waters. But on that night the rain had only just begun its deluge. Aden had stared at me. Not at my face at first, his gaze resting rather at chest height, on my press pass, and that look had crossed his face – the one that I am so accustomed to now, fear and anger combined. Then his gaze had tracked upwards, recognition slowly dawning.

I had stood there like that for long moments, before time unstuck. I stepped closer, allowing my feet to sink down into the river in the gutter. Had sat down beside him, repositioning my umbrella so that it covered him too.

I remember him looking at me, features twisted into a murky confusion. I know that he was waiting for me to start poking, trying to scratch out the story. And of course I had an in, didn't I? We swam together.

I never did ask. We just sat there, in the pouring-down rain, as the water rose above our ankles, sharing a companionable silence.

After that we became friends.

'A friend of mine died yesterday,' I say now in a conversational tone, then want to kick myself – the neediness of the words, the way they seem to caw for attention. 'I don't know if you heard about it?' I mumble. 'It was on the news. Emily. They found her on the M4.'

Aden looks at me, and I can see the interplay of emotions darting across his face, trying to select the right thing to say. 'I . . . I'm sorry. I heard on the news. I didn't know you knew her.'

I thought of my father's funeral, stuffy in spite of the cold outside. Walking back down the aisle, seeing the doors ahead open, orange and brown leaves mounding into piles just beyond. My mother's hand on my shoulder. Emily sitting at the back, watching me, face taut with sympathy. I still think about that, how much courage that takes, facing that much raw grief head-on. Never once looking away.

'A long time ago.' I said. 'I haven't seen her in . . . a long time.' I watch the swimmers and suppress a shiver, inactivity making me cold. 'She was a nurse. In Mount Pleasant, I think.' An old man swims awkwardly towards us, his gait uneven, stroke wild, and we both move slightly as he claws for the wall, stops to pull in a rasping breath and then, a look of determination to him, turns to set off again. 'Emily was a nice girl. It's . . . sad.' Such a small word, so inadequate, in the circumstances.

Aden doesn't say anything for long moments, is watching the old man as he swims, an awkward half-doggy paddle, and I feel briefly ridiculous, that my unsolicited confidence has landed awkwardly, has made the air chill. Then he looks at me, with a look that seems wary, fearful almost. 'She worked in Mount Pleasant Hospital?'

I frown. 'I . . . yeah, I think so.' Then it comes back to me, something that Del said on the side of the M4, lost in the ringing of a phone. 'Yes. She did. She worked on the ward with . . . with that boy.'

'Dylan Lowe?' He doesn't look at me when he says it, the words coming slow, like they are more than he can handle saying.

I nod. A heavy silence settles between us, broken only by the sound of lapping water.

'She called the police, the night before last. Did you know that?' Aden still isn't looking at me, is staring off into the distance.

'Emily did?'

He nods. 'She called to report a man trying to get into the ward. Said that she saw a gun.'

I stare at him, suddenly far, far colder.

7

Imogen: Tuesday 26 August, 7.15 a.m.
Five days before the shooting

It was the fall off a perilously high cliff that had woken her. Imogen sat up, the wooden-armed chair groaning with the movement. A spiking pain raced its way up the nape of her neck, the hangover of an awkward night in the dimly lit hospital room. Amy was asleep still, her elfin frame curled into a knot beneath the rough hospital blankets, fine red hair splayed out across the pillow. Imogen pushed herself up, squinting with murky eyes. Could see the soft rise, fall, of her niece's chest, rosebud lips lightly puckered. The ragged dog that she slept with lay curled in her baby-fat fists. Imogen's heartbeat slowed, just a little.

Imogen had stood, had felt as if she was sunken into the linoleum floor, watching as the doctors moved around Amy, her little body shaking, so that the bed clattered in a painful drumbeat. Mara crying silent tears, clutching at her stomach, as if the pain were a physical one. Imogen not breathing, holding her twin upright, just to keep her from crumbling to the floor. Seemed impossible that there could be any coming back from this. Then, with one final thud, a silence

2

had fallen. Amy's body sinking down against the bed and not rising again, and then, after hours, the sound of a deep, difficult breath. Imogen had watched as the white-coated shoulders sank, heads turning in shared glances of relief. Then waiting, long moments as the observers hung there, waiting to see if the peace would hold.

Finally, after centuries of silence, a doctor, middle-aged, jeans sticking out from beneath his white coat, turning to them. A brief nod, a tight smile. 'The seizure seems to have passed.'

Mara had let loose a noise, something between a yelp and a sob, had broken free of her sister and run the scant few yards that separated her from her daughter. Imogen had grasped the doctor's arm, in gratitude or to steady herself, she wasn't sure. 'Thank you. Thank you so much.'

'You're Amy's aunt?'

'Yes.'

The doctor had nodded, eyes on his patient, curled now inside her mother's arms. 'Has she ever had a seizure before? Any family history that you know of?'

Imogen shook her head. 'No, I—'

'Her father . . .' interrupted Mara, 'her father had some seizures, when he was little.'

'Will she be all right? Will this happen again?'

'We'll keep her in for a couple of days. Run some tests. See if we can't figure out why it happened.' He had glanced back at Mara, cradling her daughter tight. 'Try not to worry. We'll get to the bottom of it.'

There was daylight now, a line of it working its way through the crack in the thin curtains. Imogen shifted, thinking that she could smell food, wondering if it was possible that there were people here in this children's ward who could still eat. Mara was lying now, stretched out on her daughter's bed, had wrapped herself around Amy, one arm flung across her waist. Matryoshka dolls, nested one within the other. Her eyes wide open, staring across the top of the little girl's head.

'Mara?' said Imogen, softly. 'Did you sleep?'

Mara started, her eyes wide. 'No. I wanted to stay awake. In case . . .' She seemed to wince, turning her face into her daughter.

'She's going to be okay, Mar.'

Seemed like it had always been this way. Identical twins, born three minutes apart. Imogen was the older, in time, in everything really. Had come out lusty and screaming, a respectable six pounds. Mara had followed – by all tellings of it – limp and blue, barely touching the scales at four pounds one. There was, they had said, a heart condition, something they hadn't picked up during pregnancy, because scans then weren't what they were now, and so much of the foetus inside remained a mystery, something waiting to be unwrapped like a gift on Christmas morning. But not all gifts are equal. Mara had survived, grudgingly, each breath a struggle that it seemed inevitable she would lose. They had operated, once, twice, three times. So much so that the hospital had become a second home to the twins, the smell of detergent and death an integral part of their growing up. You must take care of your sister, their mother had said, she's so much smaller than you, and she's very, very poorly. She'll need you to look after her, Imogen.

Mara raised a hand, movement tremulous, wiped a tear away.

'I'm sorry,' said Imogen. 'I shouldn't have slept. Look, I'm awake now.' Leaned forward in her chair, a bright but plastic smile to demonstrate just how alert she was. 'I'll keep an eye on Amy, I promise. Why don't you just try and close your eyes?'

Mara nodded, obedient as a child, her eyelids drifting shut. It would, Imogen supposed, never end. It would never be the case that her first instinct would not be to take care of her sister. That was simply how they were made, two halves of a whole. Once the heart was mended, and Mara had gained her strength, they had never again left one another's side. Had gone through school, sitting side-by-side at the same desk. Had stayed on to do A-levels, applied for the same university, the same university halls. Because when you were a twin, what else did you do? Marriage, Imogen supposed, was what made the biggest difference, although even that was in name only. They lived around the corner from one another. Imogen in the small terrace that had been as much as she and Dave could afford in Mumbles, on the combined salaries of a small-time journalist and a psychologist. Mara in the larger house that sat on top of the hill – a perk of Jack's well-paid chief-inspector role. Imogen didn't mind that, the smaller house tucked into a quiet terrace. It was homely, they had a view of the sea. And it meant that she got to see Imogen and Amy every day.

There were voices outside the door, the low rumble of conversation, and Imogen glanced up, a quick look at the clock. Her parents would be here by nine. Her father quiet, stoic, keeping his jaw locked tight so that no one saw the pain when he looked at his granddaughter in her hospital bed. Her mother, face a storm of tension. Blaming the doctors, blaming everybody, because that way it felt like control. Imogen rubbed her eyes, needed a shower, a change of clothes. But her first client was due in at 8.30, and then she had back-to-back appointments for the rest of the day.

There was a sound that seemed to be coming from nowhere, a buzzing that for a moment Imogen thought was in her head, the result of exhaustion, a night on an awkward chair. Mara started, her eyes snapping open. She turned her head towards the bedside cabinet, where her mobile phone vibrated hard against the wood.

Amy shifted, sighing in her sleep.

'Is it Jack?' asked Imogen.

Mara didn't answer, studied the phone. Then, her fingers moving quickly, she turned the ringer off. 'No. It wasn't Jack.'

A long, loaded silence. Imogen stared at her sister, Mara's eyes downturned. Waiting. There was that feeling in the air, that stifling, oppressive feeling of a secret, sitting just out of view. Imogen's lips parted, the question waiting to be asked. But she closed them again. They were in a hospital room, and her two-year-old niece had brushed death last night. It seemed churlish, unfair even, to level accusations at her sister.

There were more voices outside the room now, the ward beginning to stir to life. The rough grumble of trolley wheels creaked along the corridor. Marriage was complicated, people were complicated, and you made sacrifices and you made mistakes. That was life, what growing up was all about, learning to balance all of these things out. She shouldn't judge her sister, because after all none of them were flawless – they all made bad decisions at one point or another.

The door swung inwards, the corner of it grazing against Imogen's chair.

'Morning.' The nurse – Natalie, a talkative girl with whom

Imogen had often passed the time of day, in the canteen, the overlarge hallway – kept her voice low, didn't meet Imogen's gaze, moved into the room towards her patient.

Maybe it was the light, the cast from the early-morning sunshine through the curtains, giving the room a pinkish tinge, maybe that was why Natalie's eyes looked red. Imogen studied the nurse as she moved, her jaw slack, swollen pouches beneath her eyes.

'Are you okay?' asked Imogen.

It seemed that, in the brief moments she had been in the room, the nurse had forgotten they were there, because her head snapped up, seemingly startled. There was no doubt now. The young woman had been crying. Imogen shifted, leaning forward in her seat. 'Is everything all right?'

Natalie nodded, an unconvincing dip of the head, her eyes filling with tears once again. 'I'm sorry, Imogen. How unprofessional.' She brushed at her cheeks with the back of her hand, attempted a smile. 'I'm awfully sorry. It's just that we've had a bit of a night of it, and now some really bad news.'

'Oh, I . . .' Imogen watched her, wondering how far to go. Natalie wasn't, after all, a client. Imogen was a worried aunt now, not a psychologist.

But often it seemed to her that all people are looking for is that opening – the signal that their worries are welcome – and they will unfurl them before you, faces suddenly lighter with relief. 'The thing is,' Natalie glanced over her shoulder, lowering her voice even though the door was closed, 'we've had some trouble. I – ah, I shouldn't say this probably, but there's been a man, coming to the hospital at night. They've seen him outside Ward 12, the one across the way. He's been hanging about, and there's talk that he has a gun.'

Imogen glanced at her sister, could see Mara push herself up in the bed, eyes wide.

Natalie reached down, stroked Amy's hair, unconsciously it seemed. 'We've had the firearms police here, and all sorts. They were here last night. I'm surprised you didn't see them when you came in.'

Imogen shook her head slightly, privately thinking that unless they had parked a tank across the entrance to the children's ward, it was unlikely she'd have noticed them anyway, so focused had she been on Amy, and only Amy.

'It's been stressful, people have been afraid. I mean, you hear such terrible stories these days. And then, this morning . . .' Natalie broke off, her voice uneven. 'Sorry. This morning we found out that one of our nurses has died.'

Imogen frowned, could see her sister's hand fly to her mouth. 'Oh, I'm so sorry.'

'It was an accident, they say. Said that Emily got hit by a car. But it's just – it's so awful.' Natalie brushed a tear from her cheek. 'She was a lovely girl. Lovely.' The nurse took a breath, pulled herself up and gave a small, brittle smile. She looked from Imogen to Mara, back again. 'The police are saying: just be aware if you go out of the ward. Keep your eyes open, and try not to go alone. Just in case. They say they've searched the hospital, the grounds, that he's gone. But just . . . be on your guard. Okay?'

Imogen nodded, a knot forming in her stomach.

Natalie shook her head. 'I don't know, you just think: what next? I mean, it comes in threes, doesn't it? Bad luck, I mean.' The nurse looked at Imogen. 'I just can't imagine how it could get any worse than that, though. Can you?'

8

Aden: Tuesday 26 August, 8.30 a.m.
Five days before the shooting

'I still hear the sirens. From us, the other ARV. Seems like I hear it everywhere. Especially when I'm falling asleep.' Aden looked up at the ceiling. Artex. Who the hell invented Artexing? Why would someone look at a perfectly smooth ceiling and think: I know what'll make that better – some crazy-ass swirls. 'And the rain. I dream about the rain. All the time. The way it thumped on the roof of the car. The steering was so light. I could barely keep the damn car on the road. Every time it rains now, every time, it reminds me of that night. Is that normal?'

'What's normal?' asked Imogen.

'You know,' said Aden. 'Is this what it's like for everyone else?'

Imogen smiled. Aden could tell she was smiling, even though he wasn't looking at her, still studying the whorls and swirls that littered the ceiling. They appeared to dance before him. But that was probably the exhaustion. He had finished the night shift an hour ago, was supposed to be at home sleeping by now, especially seeing as today was a training day, so they had to be back on the firearms range by 5 p.m. But he had needed to see Imogen today, had needed it more than he had needed sleep.

'You know, the interesting thing about "normal" is that pretty much no one is,' said Imogen.

Aden gave a quick bark of a laugh. 'Cynical, much, Doc?'

'Normal suggests there is a specific way of operating that is appropriate in any given situation.'

'Okay?'

'Well, the truth is that people respond in a huge range of ways. Many of those different ways of responding can be considered normal.'

Aden raised his head, looked at her. 'So you don't think I'm screwed up?'

This time he saw Imogen smile, saw her shift, the notepad balancing on her knee. 'Is that what you think?'

'I hear the sirens. All the time. The rain . . . I think about that night. I think about it all the time.'

The rain had lashed down, so that you could barely see your hand in front of your face. Just a grey curtain, thumping, thumping on the roof of the car. It had been one of those nights, so quiet that it seemed to last for ever. They were parked up, he and Rhys, watching the rain, the cars, driving too fast on the dual carriageway. The younger man had been on Firearms for just over a month, had been partnered with Aden, because, as the sergeant said, Aden would teach him a thing or two, about what it meant to be an AFO, about how you did it right. They had eaten chip-shop chips, sausage in batter, curry sauce. The wrappers were still balled up on the dashboard, the car reeking of grease.

'So, we just wait?' Rhys had asked.

'We just wait.' Aden confirmed.

Rhys had nodded, had brushed his dark hair out of his eyes. Aden had wondered if he knew it yet: that the other guys on the team called him Brad, the word pronounced with a slight hint of envy at the younger man's filmstar good looks.

'The sarge told me that I was lucky you'd volunteered to partner with me.'

Aden shrugged. 'No big deal.'

'He said you're the best.'

Aden hadn't answered, had shifted, a little uncomfortable. The rain thrummed, hitting the tarmac so hard that it rebounded, meeting itself coming down.

'He told me about the bravery award.'

Aden shook his head, stared out at the waterlogged headlights. 'That was years ago now, when I was back in uniform. Besides, I was only nominated. Didn't win or anything.' A plungingly cold January day, a call to the River Tawe, a knot of hysterical teenagers pointing at the bulbous banks, the river swollen after a week of solid rain. Staring down into the black water, for a moment not knowing what it was they were seeing. Then, the scene shifting and suddenly there were hands, arms, not waving but drowning, and before Aden even knew what he was doing, his helmet was off, his boots, and he was underwater. Thinking, if he was thinking anything, that it was just another day at the pool. Only this wasn't the pool. The current was strong, swelling against him, tugging him downriver faster than he would have thought possible. His arms, cutting against the current, pushing as hard as was humanly possible, because the girl – he could see now that was what she was – was sinking under. Swimming and swimming, every inch a fight just to stay alive, and then, just when it seemed like there was nothing left in him and that he had attempted an impossibility, questing fingers feeling sodden fabric, beyond that ice-cold skin. Wrapping his arms around her, her body inert, useless, shifting onto his back and fighting towards the opposite bank. Because he had come so far that there was nothing to do but fight onwards. And then, miraculously, his knee hitting something solid, sending a shooting pain arcing up his leg, into his spine. Land. And then Aden breathing, not for one but for two, into the girl's mouth, a sinking realisation as it distantly connected just how young she was, the teenagers screaming from across the river because it seemed inevitable that their friend was dead. But then a splutter and a heave of river water, and she was alive, shaken and shaking, but alive.

'So, have you ever shot anyone?' Rhys asked tentatively.

Aden shook his head. 'Nah. We've never had a shooting in the Southern Wales force.' Words that would replay for him, over and over again.

They had sat, listened to the rain.

'It's really quiet, isn't it?'

Aden had turned towards Rhys, stared at him. Had let his mouth drop open in disbelief. Rhys looking suddenly sheepish.

Then the radio had crackled to life.

Aden had stared at the radio, back at Rhys, had shook his head. 'You've got to be bloody kidding me.' Aden pulled the radio free. 'Whisky Tango Three Eight.'

'Shots fired at Harddymaes off-licence. Reports of a group of people running from the scene. Permission to arm.'

Aden shook his head, looked at Rhys. 'Dude! NEVER use the Q-word.' Pushed open the Armed Response Vehicle door, dived out into the pouring rain, iced fingers down his back. Kicking though puddles, water slopping up over his high-laced boots. He could just about make out Rhys, splish-splashing from the passenger side. Aden opened the boot, punched numbers into the lock-pad of the gun safe, pulling free the Glock, grabbing the magazine that he had pressed bullets into earlier. Another magazine. Just in case. But that was the thing, wasn't it? There had been so little chance that the just-in-case would happen. They trained for it. They trained and trained and trained. Just in case. But there had never been a shooting. Not in this force. So, odds-wise, they would get to the end of this shift, same as any other, and the guns would go back into the armoury, and the magazines would contain the same number of bullets as they did when the shift began.

Odds-wise, that would be what would happen.

'Sometimes, I wonder if it's because I wasn't prepared,' Aden said, studying the Artexing.

'What do you mean?' Imogen tucked a strand of red hair behind her ear.

'I didn't expect it. I mean, you know that it could happen. It's what you train for. But still . . .'

'You weren't anticipating it.'

'No. I wasn't anticipating it.'

Aden had put the sirens on, the blues-and-twos wailing. There weren't many cars on the road, with the weather, the late hour. But those that were there moved out of the way. Ploughing down Carmarthen Road, throwing standing water that must have been a foot deep up over the windscreen in a wave. A sharp left at the lights, climbing, the rain driving into the windscreen, road so slick it felt like the car couldn't possibly hold on. A second tone. Another

ARV coming up behind them. High up on the hill now, Harddymaes grim and grey, buffeted by the wind that was screaming across the bay.

Aden scanning, scanning. Had seen the off-licence, buried in between rough-faced council houses, spiderweb fractures spread across the wide glass. Looking. Looking.

Then he saw them.

'I was the first.'

'The first?' asked Imogen.

'To see them. The kids.' The word scratched at his throat, clawing on its way out. 'I saw them as we were coming up the hill. It was dark, really dark, and raining so heavily, and I saw these figures.' Aden wasn't looking at her now. Wasn't looking at anything. 'I didn't know they were kids. I mean, I could barely see. And they were tall . . .'

Aden had slammed on the brakes, so hard that it seemed inevitable there would be whiplash. Flung open the car door. And then he was running. Through puddles and rain. Could hear the squeal of brakes behind him, another ARV door slamming, Tony splashing, just behind them. Aden could barely see. Just rain, shadows. Figures up ahead, sounds of shouting, then like a shoal of fish they veered off, vanishing into the walls apparently. Aden running, looking, and then, out of nowhere, had loomed a pool of blackness, an alleyway that had not been there before. Aden had taken a sharp turn, plunging after the figures into the black conduit that fed through the rows of council houses, the smell of ammonia almost overwhelming. The walls reared up alongside him. No street lights, so that it was dark, pitch-black, it seemed. Rhys at his shoulder. Then hearing something, footsteps up ahead, and another sound – sounds like the figures' breathing – and later, in his dreams it would become breathing, but surely he couldn't have heard that, not with everything else.

'Armed police,' Aden bellowed. 'Stop. Stand still!'

Another set of footsteps, just behind them but gaining fast, and Aden threw a glance over his shoulder, adrenaline spiking. Tony, weapon out, squinting into the rain.

'He fell.'

'Who fell?' asked Imogen.

'The boy.' Aden gave an almost smile. 'I don't say his name. I should. I know I should. Dylan Lowe. Dylan fell. I heard him. I didn't know what it was I was hearing – you know, at the time. Just splashes. Shouting. I know now that it was him, Dylan, falling. His mates – I'm guessing they were his mates, the other kids or whatever – they left. We, I . . . I never saw them, not up close. Just figures, running. They left him there.'

There were shrieks, cutting through the darkness; it had seemed like they were bouncing off the alley walls, rebounding, coming from everywhere at once. Aden had drawn his gun, tracking the sound, heart pounding so loud it seemed that his eardrums would not be able to stand it.

Then a figure, large in front of him. Seemed to rise up out of nowhere. A jolt of electricity shot through Aden. 'Armed police. Don't move.'

Aden couldn't see; was trying, squinting through the rain. But no matter what he did, he just couldn't see, not really. And he hated that, his adrenaline spurting, higher, higher.

'Freeze! FREEZE,' Tony had screamed.

'He stopped running,' Aden said, voice soft.

'Dylan?' Imogen was watching him, her green eyes fixed on him like there was nowhere else she'd rather be, and no one else that she'd rather listen to. Even though she must have heard this story a hundred times before.

'Yeah.'

'He stopped?'

'Yeah. I thought . . . I thought he was giving himself up. At least, I think that was what I thought. But then maybe I'm just telling myself that.'

'Why would you do that?'

'Because of . . . you know. To make it better. If . . . if he was giving himself up, if that was what I thought, then it was okay that I didn't shoot.'

The figure had stopped, so they stopped, Aden and Rhys and Tony. There was shouting. They were shouting. Because sometimes people freeze and they can do stupid things, even without intending to, so you yell at them and tell them exactly what to do, loudly. Anything to break through the freeze.

'But then,' said Aden, 'he turned.'

They were standing, yelling at him to put the fucking gun down *now*. And then there's movement. A pause as the world draws a breath. Then sound, so much sound that it seems like the world will end in it. Later, he would try to remember the shots, but no matter how hard he tried, he would only ever remember the one – that first crack, the sound wave racing through the air, burning against his eardrums. It would later turn out that there were three shots. Two from Tony. One from Rhys. From himself, none.

And Aden, finger on the trigger, willing it to move, willing it, but it won't, and it's like the finger doesn't belong to him.

Then it is over.

'I keep playing it, over and over again. What's wrong with me? Why couldn't I pull the trigger?'

He was stuck there, gun still pointed, only now it was pointed at nothing because the boy had slumped to the ground, a motionless pile in a yawning puddle. The air thick, dense, like a sudden fog had descended, the smell of cordite burning his throat.

'Why do you assume that something is wrong with you?' asked Imogen, forehead wrinkled into a small frown.

'What the fuck is wrong with you?' Tony's voice had come from a long way away. Aden had felt Rhys, the new boy, his pupil, darting past him, felt the cold water splash from the puddles, saw him dropping to his knees beside the figure. If you looked hard enough, really squinted, you could see the blood beginning to pool. Had stood there and watched, useless, as Rhys began to give CPR.

'I just stood there, staring at the boy.' Aden had leaned back again, was staring up at the ceiling. 'At Dylan. I couldn't . . . I mean, it took me for ever to lower the gun. Seemed like my arms were stuck. I just couldn't move. Rhys, I mean, he's little more than a kid himself, and he was giving first aid. God, there was blood everywhere.'

Tony had moved forward, Glock still raised, kicking away the dark-grey gun that Aden could see now, because lights were flicking on in the surrounding houses, people awoken by the noise, so that now the gun was surrounded by a patch of light, almost like a spotlight on a stage. Aden forcing his arms down, Tony shouting at him, eyes glaringly large, flecks of white spittle flying from his mouth. Aden would not remember what it was Tony had said, just the thick rolling vowels, the accent so Welsh it had seemed that he was speaking a different language, the fury in him. Aden's hands were shaking, could barely force the gun into its holster. There were noises coming from the body on the ground, sounded like coughing, but like no coughing Aden had ever heard before. Rhys looking up at him, wild-eyed, blood dripping from his chin, in some macabre vampiric tableau. Sirens, sirens, coming from everywhere. Aden knew there were things he should be doing, a list of tasks to be completed, but for the moment he just couldn't think of them.

The boy had been shot in the torso, the bullets – three of them in all – landing exactly where they were supposed to land. It would later transpire that he hadn't been standing on the ground, that the darkness had concealed a low wall, that Dylan had stood on that, so when he was hit with the force of three bullets in his chest he was flung backwards, his head impacting the ground with bone-crushing force, the blow to his brain causing contusions, bleeding. The ambulance had arrived quickly, the speed of the medical intervention saving his life. Too late for his mental faculties, though, the damage there proving irreparable.

'I didn't do it, see.' Aden followed the thread of the Artexing, the peaks and troughs, knew in his conscious mind that it was white. Also knew why it appeared red to him. 'That's the thing that I just can't shake. I mean, I knew the job so well. I'd been doing it for five years. I was . . .'

'What?'

'I was one of the best. I know that sounds cocky, and I don't mean it like that. But I was supposed to be going for the Tactical Unit, the top team on the department. My sergeant was pushing me, saying that I was born for it. And so, you kind of think that if the shit ever does hit the fan, then of course you'll handle it, you'll do the job properly, cos everyone says that you're good at it. But that night . . .'

'Go on.'

'I don't know. I was waiting for something. Some sign that pulling the trigger was the right thing to do.'

'But you didn't get one?'

'No. But the others did. Rhys. Tony. And the thing is, if they hadn't done what they did, if they hadn't shot, I probably wouldn't be sitting here. If they had been like me, if they'd hesitated in pulling the trigger . . . Jesus!' Aden pushed himself up on the sofa again, looked at Imogen. She looked tired, he suddenly thought. Felt a flash of guilt that he was here, again, that she was listening to him, again. How many times had she done this, how many different versions of this same conversation had they had? Months-worth. Too many to count. 'The thing is, I know I made a mistake. I know I didn't do the job properly. But I keep twisting it around in my head and, whichever way I turn it, I just can't get to the point where I would have pulled that trigger.'

'So, isn't that your answer then?' asked Imogen.

'How do you mean?'

'You've blamed yourself for your actions – or, as you've phrased it, your inaction. But if you are saying that your perception of the scene, what you were seeing unfold in front of you, simply didn't support you pulling the trigger, then why would you have? How could you have? What you have to remember, Aden, is that there are a number of different perspectives on this event. At least four that we know of – yours, Rhys's, Tony's. Dylan Lowe's. No one person had a full view of everything that was unfolding. And I think it is dangerous to automatically assume that your reaction to the event is in some way faulty. The IPCC didn't think it was, the firearms commanders didn't think it was. You behaved in a way that, based on your information at the time, appeared most appropriate to you. The fact that others behaved differently means that they perceived something different.'

'So . . .'

'So, the world isn't a simple place. And sometimes, in order to understand what has gone on, we have to understand what those surrounding us were seeing.'

Aden nodded, thinking about the stationary figure lying in the bed, unseeing eyes studying the ceiling. Thinking about Dylan Lowe and the decisions he made a year ago that led him to be lying here. And then, inexorably, thinking about the ward, and the glass-panelled door, and, even though he wasn't there and even though he can only imagine, thinking about looking through it, from the inside out: a figure standing, waiting, gun in hand. And Dylan Lowe, in his deep and dreamless sleep.

9

Charlie: Tuesday 26 August, 8.30 a.m.
Five days before the shooting

I push the car door open, squeezing out of the space that is, in truth, too tight. My hair is still damp to the touch, swinging around my shoulders, but the heat of the day is beginning to build and soon it will dry. I leave my swimming bag on the passenger seat, push the door closed behind me.

I called the office, spoke to Dave. 'I'll be a bit late in, okay? I'm chasing a lead. Just let Lydia know, will you?'

She's going to be pissed off at me. I feel it in my gut. But then Lydia's default setting seems to be pissed off these days. I pull my handbag onto my shoulder and duck between the cars, can feel the sun reflecting off them, bouncing against my cream trousers. There are murmurs around the office. Talk that the paper isn't doing well, that redundancies are inevitably going to follow. I do my best to ignore it, just get on with the job. Because, in the end, that is all I can control.

The tarmac is starting to heat up, and even this early in the morning is becoming sticky. My slip-on shoes graze at the back of my heels as I hurry along it. I'm hoping that he'll be alone. That it's early enough for me to catch him on the tail of a night shift. I duck in through the doors of the hospital lobby, feeling the gasp of air conditioning, and the first thing that I see is a gun, staring me right in the face. I start, my heart racing for a moment. Then my gaze tracks up, and I see the firearms uniform: Tony, his face set into a heavy frown as he looks at me. I smile, even though I have a sneaking suspicion he doesn't like me. Rhys stands behind him and I give him a nod, my face flushing slightly, even though I am fully aware that this is ridiculous. He is terribly young, but God, the kid is good-looking.

'All right, guys?'

Rhys flushes as if I've just asked him to strip naked and dance a tango with me. Tony shrugs, a heavy movement that leads to the artillery shifting. 'Supposed to have finished an hour ago, but no. Bloody bosses want one more sweep. Got to be back in again by six this evening for training too, don't we?' He gives me a sharp look. 'Don't go putting that in your paper, mind.'

I suppress a sigh. If only the mundanities of people's lives were as interesting as the people themselves thought they were. 'Scout's honour, Tone. Well, hope you guys get to finish soon.'

Rhys mumbles something that I miss, and turns sharply away, heavy boots scuffing loudly against the linoleum floor. I suppress a smile, turning into a service stairwell. It is quiet down here, industrial and cool. But then I suppose it is an area few people have cause to visit. I pull open the door to the basement, slip inside the long narrow corridor. The security office is the third door on the right.

I know before I get there that I am right, that he is still here, hasn't gone home yet. Kenny Rogers croons, the music set low but inescapable. I rap smartly on the door, duck my head around without giving him time to answer, the fleeting and uncomfortable thought occurring to me that one day I'm going to catch someone naked if I keep doing that.

But Ernie is not naked, thank God. He is sitting in an office chair, one that looks like it is struggling to support his weight, is leaning back so that his head is almost lost behind the belly on him, and I wonder if I have woken him. He has that look about him, that vague sleepiness as his eyes struggle to focus on me. I grin, give him a small wave, trying not to let my face know my thoughts. That he looks old today, older than I have seen him before.

'Well, young Charlotte. Now this is a pleasure.' Ernie pushes himself up in his chair, the movement straining the fabric on his shirt so that it seems impossible the buttons will hold, and runs his fingers through his grey hair. I smile at the vanity of it. His fingers finish their work and the hair stands further up on end than ever it did before. 'Come in, good girl, come in.'

I move around the door, leaning to avoid the dachshund calendar. Ernie loves dachshunds. 'Do you ever go home, Ernie?'

He gives a rough bark of a laugh. 'Now then, you know how it is here. Thin blue line, that's me.' He glances down at the mound of his belly. 'Well, thick blue line.'

I fish in my bag. 'I brought you a present.'

He grins, catches with one hand the chocolate digestives I throw him. 'Aw, Charlie, love. How did you know?'

'I know everything, Ern. It's my job.'

He pushes a second chair towards me with his foot, the lion's share of his attention caught on unwrapping the biscuits, freeing the top one from its cover. He studies it for a moment, the way a wine connoisseur would study a fine vintage, and then eats it in two swift bites. 'Ah, tha's good. Yourself?'

I wave away the proffered packet. 'Got to watch my waistline. How am I going to catch myself a husband otherwise?'

He laughs, a shaking, silent kind of laugh, and swallows another digestive. 'You? You're a scrawny little thing.'

I glance around. 'I wasn't sure you'd still be here. Bit late after a night shift, isn't it?'

'Well, aye. I just wanted to have a final walk-through – you know, dot the i's, cross the t's.' He sighed. 'I suppose you know what's been happenin'? That fella with the gun?'

I nod. 'I heard.'

Ernie lets fly a laugh. 'Course you did. You hear everything.' Then his face settles, worry working its way through the creases. 'Missed him, didn't I? Was way over the other end of the hospital, and with my knee being what it is . . .' He shakes his head. 'I'm too old. That's the truth of it.'

'You're not old, Ern.'

'I'm sixty-eight. I'm old. Truth is, I should have retired before now. My wife's been on at me, says I need to take it easy.' He isn't looking at me, is staring past me at the bank of CCTV monitors. 'Thing is, if it had been a younger man on – a fitter man – they might have got him.'

I lean forward, pat Ernie on his thick arm. 'Come on, Ern. Give yourself a break.'

Ernie shrugs, crams another biscuit into his mouth. 'Anyway,' he pushes himself upright, an attempt at levity coming into his tone, 'you didn't come here to listen to an old man moan. What can I help you with, Charlie?'

I smile, brush a crumb from Ernie's sleeve. 'Well, it's about that, actually. The man with the gun. I was wondering: did you get it on CCTV?'

He frowns. 'Well, yeah. Kind of. It's not great. Police went through it yesterday. You can't see his face.'

'Um . . .' I bite my nail.

He fixes me with a look. 'You want to see it, don't you?'

I grin.

Ernie sighs heavily, pushing the digestives to one side. 'You know, you'll be the death of me. Close the door.' He works the monitors. 'You can't tell anyone, mind. Don't want to give the buggers an excuse to sack me, before I get the chance to quit.'

I pull my chair closer to the neat little screens. 'Ernie, you are an angel sent from heaven.'

He shakes his head. 'You want our boy's first visit or second?'

'Let's start with the first night.'

The left-hand screen fills with a hallway, brightly lit, empty.

'I'll forward through it a bit.'

The footage begins to crease, a nurse moving into view and out; a cleaner, then Ernie, coming towards the camera, moving at a faster lick than he could manage in life.

'Hold it there, Ern.'

Ernie's pace slows and, as he reaches the camera, he pauses and scratches his crotch. I look at him, can see his face flush, fight back a laugh. Camera Ernie vanishes and then, after long minutes, a figure moves into view, dark-clad, moving quickly.

'There he is,' murmurs Ernie.

I study the figure, looking for something – anything. But Ernie's right, the footage is rubbish. The figure never turns his head, his face hidden within the folds of his hood. I scan the surroundings. He looks to be tall, his head level with the top of the noticeboard on the wall, and has a narrow frame. I will him to turn, even though I know he won't. He moves quickly across the screen, then is picked up in the lobby, a dark figure cutting through the centre of it, out into the car park.

'What about the car park? Anything from there?'

'Nah, the boy was smart. Seemed like he knew where the cameras were positioned out there, kept to the sides, out of view. Guess he couldn't avoid them inside the hospital, but once he got out there, he managed to disappear. You want to see the next night?'

'Can we just forward this one a little?'

Ernie nods, speeds up the footage. And there they are, two figures, dark-clad, carrying guns. I try to ignore the little flutter in my stomach. Aden leads the way, gun visible, his head scanning the hallway. Behind him, a little taller, Tony. They walk steadily, towards the camera, then vanish beyond view.

I wait, thinking that Aden will reappear. Then want to slap myself for being such a teenager. The odd figure drifts by, but nothing of note. And then, finally, I see her. Emily Wilson, walking away from the camera, her dark-blonde curls pulled up into a high ponytail. She is walking quickly, her arms folded tight across her chest, her head darting, left to right. She looks afraid. I study her surroundings, the shadows, wonder if someone is waiting for her there, if this is when it happened – if he followed her, caught her. But she keeps walking, arms folded tight, vanishing from one camera into another: hallway, lobby, then out of the front doors.

'Can I see the car-park footage for this timeframe?'

Ernie looks at me. 'Yeah, but you can't see him, mind.'

'No, I know. But, if it's all right . . .'

He frowns slightly, fingers moving ponderously across the keyboard. The car park appears in the right-hand monitor. It is quiet, few cars there at that time of night. A police car, parked by the lobby doors. The floodlights pour puddles of orange light, somehow making the surrounding darkness darker. I wait. Emily appears into view. She is walking more quickly now, seems like she's almost running. My heart beats faster. I watch her, watch the shadows, the few cars there are, looking for a figure, a face, thinking that at any moment I will see him and my hunch will have played itself out. Emily hurries to her car, a little red Peugeot, slipping quickly inside. I scan the surroundings. Where are you? But there is nothing. Just darkness. The headlights of the Peugeot spring to life and the car slips steadily out of its space. I can't see Emily now. I try, looking for her face through the windscreen, but the angle is wrong and she is gone. The car drives carefully out of the car park. Now I'm waiting for someone to follow her, for a second car to spring to life, falling in behind her. But long minutes pass and there is nothing.

Emily is gone.

I lean back in my chair. 'Dammit!'

'What?'

I bite my lip. Unsure how to put it into words. That I

can't accept the Emily's-death-as-an-accident theory. That coincidences – like calling the police to report a gunman, and then showing up dead twenty-four hours later – give me heartburn. That I need there to be answers beyond the obvious: that sometimes life just sucks.

'Nothing. Just a hunch.'

10

The Shooter: Sunday 31 August, 9.15 a.m.
Day of the shooting

The Mumbles street is still, the world holding its breath. The sun has begun its ascent, the heat of the day beginning to climb, turning my car into a greenhouse. I could open the window, make myself more comfortable, but I don't. The road in front of me curls down the hill, and beyond that you can see the sea, sparkling blue today. But the sea is irrelevant. All that matters to me is Mara.

I study the house. It sits on a generous plot, an over-wide drive, the front porch supported by Doric columns. The white light of the early sun has bleached the front windows so that they are blind, and I stare at them, even though it hurts my eyes, watching for movement. I wonder if Mara knows that I am here, if she senses that her time has come. I look down at my phone, at the text message I sent. *Meet me at your house. It's urgent.*

Does she think about me, I wonder? When she lies asleep in her bed at night, do her eyelids flutter with dreams of me? Does she toss, turn, thinking of what she has done?

The gun is on my lap. I'm not looking at it, am not

taking my eyes off the house, but my thumb caresses it, rolling across the cool metal. It is loaded. Ready.

It seems that my heart is no longer beating, has stilled. I glance down, look at my hands, as steady as I have ever seen them. I have lived for this day, the relief of it, an ending at last. I know how it will go, it feels like I have done it a thousand times before. I will walk down the tarmac drive, keeping my steps light. Will jam my thumb onto the round of the doorbell, will hear the distant ringing. I will wait. As long as it takes. After one minute or five, there will be the creaking of footsteps. A murky silhouette through the warped glass of the front door. And there Mara will be. She will stand there for a moment, a flood of emotions will cross her face. Perhaps one of them – before she realises what is to come – will be pleasure at seeing me. Then she will look down, she will see the gun. And she will know that she is going to die.

Will she beg, I wonder? Will she apologise for what she has done?

I will lift up the gun, watch her beautiful, big green eyes go round with horror. I will pull the trigger.

My breathing is steady, easy.

A bird, a magpie, lands on the bonnet of my car. It stares at me through the windscreen. One for sorrow. I lift the gun. I'm ready.

But then I see something, a movement from the quiet house. I pause, stare. But there is nothing. My eyes playing tricks on me. I wait, though. Just in case. Then I see it again, a flutter of motion behind the glass. My heart beginning to beat a little faster.

I pull the door handle. Quiet. Careful. I push the car door open, slip out, keeping low behind the hedge, hugging the gun close to my side. I peer through the leaves, the world turned green. Can make out the front door, sunlight catching on the letter box.

There is a creak. The door beginning to open. I move, adjust, lift up the gun. Take aim through the leaves.

Then I see Mara. She is framed in the doorway, the sunlight catching on her red hair, dousing it in flames. It is pulled back, tied in a rough bun. She is wearing jeans, ones that I have never seen on her before, and the barest slick of make-up. She has something in her hands, although I can't see what it is; is looking at it, is shaking her head. She hasn't seen me.

I stare at her. The gun is shaking. She is more beautiful than I remembered.

I stand up, make the gun steady, step out from behind the hedge. I want her to see me before she dies.

She freezes. Stares at me. Her mouth falls open.

I pull the trigger.

11

Charlie: Tuesday 26 August, 10.32 a.m.
Five days before the shooting

'Stuart.'

'Hey, Charlie. God, it's been . . . what, an hour now?'

'Yeah, I know. I know. I was just wondering if you had anything new on Emily Wilson?'

'In the past hour?'

'Yes.'

'No.'

I'm flicking my pen against the surface of the desk, flick, flick, flick. Can feel Dave looking at me. I'm annoying him. Flick. Flick. Flick. The sound merges into the low hum of the newsroom's feeble air-conditioning unit, the distant click-clack of computer keys. 'Oh.' I don't know what I was expecting. Why I thought he would tell me something different. Perhaps I thought it would be the same for everyone else, that the snaking rivulets of their thoughts would all wind their way back to Emily. 'So, there's no sign of the—'

'I told you, Charlie. The PM will take time. They've got a backlog down there. You're looking at a couple of days at least.'

'And tox—'

'Toxicology will follow the post-mortem. Patience isn't one of your virtues, is it?'

I sigh. Cradle the handset of the phone between my shoulder and chin, rub my hand across my eyes. My other hand keeps flicking the damn pen. I'm starting to irritate myself now. My vision has begun to blur at the edges, a dull throbbing headache building from the base of my skull. The air in the office is thick, feels like you could reach up and grab a handful, and I wonder if it is this that is making my head ache. It isn't. I know that. It's the fact that I've had three hours' sleep in as many days, but I like to cover all my bases.

'Sorry, Stu. I know I'm being a pain.'

I can hear the force's press officer smile. He's a big guy, around six-foot-four maybe, with these huge round cheeks that put you unavoidably in mind of Santa. 'Charlie, my day would not be complete without you being a complete pain in my backside.'

I laugh, even though it sounds a little forced. 'You're a gem, Stu. I'll talk to you in an hour.'

'I know you will, Charlie. I know you will.'

I put the handset down, lean my head back against my chair and stare out of the window. The sky is still that painful blue, a colour that is beginning to seem unimaginative, predictable. Seems like there's not a breath of air in the whole newsroom. The room is quieter than normal. The morning meeting is over, the reporters spilling out, clattering down the stairs, taking with them a wave of sound. There are few of us left inside, just me, Dave, a couple of others. I glance up at Dave. He's staring at me, staring at the pen.

Flick, flick, flick.

I stop, smile in what I hope is an apologetic manner.

'Penny for them?' Dave leans back in his chair. He's chewing the end of a blue biro. The plastic cap has broken, has been twisted out of shape with teeth marks, his fingers stained navy. How much damn gel does he use on that hair? It's blond, veering towards brown, a wave to it, of which Dave is profoundly proud. You'll catch him sometimes, when he doesn't know you're looking, studying himself in the nearest reflection, twisting the waves back out of his face, placing them so that they're just so. He's a plain man. That sounds cruel, doesn't it, but there are few other words I can think of to describe him. His features are irregular, his nose overlarge, hooked at the end, lips vanishingly thin. I blow at a strand of my own hair, which has worked its way free from the rough topknot I threw my hair up into this morning. Wonder if perhaps I should take a leaf out of his book, spend a bit more time in front of the mirror. Probably not.

I've never been a girly girl. My mother is a girly girl. She has manicures and spike heels. I have clear lip-gloss, brown/black mascara and, if you're lucky, a hairbrush. She's mortified, which of course makes me feel like I have done my job. It occasionally occurs to me that, at thirty, I'm too old to play the rebellious teenager. Then I speak to my mother again. The resolution never lasts long.

'Just tired.' I reply. 'Didn't get much sleep.'

'Hot date?' Dave grins, and I fight back a grimace. He's been here – what, two years, I guess. Had come into the paper, full of his own capabilities. Had smiled at me that first day, a lingering, up-and-down kind of smile that made me shift in my chair. Oh, you're the crime reporter? That's what I want to do. Had looked at me, like he'd expected me to get up. Oh, you want my job? No worries, have a seat. It turned out, though, that his transition to the role of full-time reporter was not as easy as he had anticipated. He struggled; struggled to find the right stories, struggled to write them when they were handed to him, struggled to get people to open up to him. Just struggled.

He looks down, studies his phone – the one that never, ever seems to leave his fingers – and I turn back towards the computer, carefully placing the pen down. 'Nah. Too much coffee.'

I gave up on sleep, some time around four. Padded down the hall to the cupboard, the one that is packed so tight with junk that I avoid opening the door, afraid that if it were to escape I'd never get it back in again. The cardboard box was hidden behind the mop and the Hoover, providing an ad hoc bookshelf for those books that I've already read and know deep down I'll never read again. Written on the side in big red letters: *Charlotte: school.* My mother is one of the few people who ever calls me Charlotte. I have my suspicions that she only does it because she knows I hate it.

I pulled the box free, sinking down onto the carpeted hallway floor in my fleece pyjamas. It was a mishmash – sixteen years of education crammed into one cardboard box. My comprehensive school yearbook was at the bottom. Red faux-leather.

I flicked through. A travesty of Nineties hair, inexperienced make-up. Was looking for Emily, but couldn't avoid myself. Seemed like wherever she was, I was; Emily's tight fawn curls merging with mine, looser, the colour of cocoa, my narrow face reaching to her shoulder, awkward smiles. We hadn't moved in the same circles, not really. Her family were devout Christian, went to church three times a week. She sang in the choir, attended Bible studies. Me, not so much. She moved through the school, ignoring the catcalls, the whispers that inevitably seemed to follow. And yet somehow we had fitted together, two halves of strangely different coins. Until my father died and my life tumbled upside down.

'You're going to see the parents?' Dave leans forward, elbows on the desk. There is a small ochre stain on his collar, sitting just to the left of a pale-blue check. Looks like blood. There is something oddly unsettling about the image of Dave shaving. I somehow find myself picturing him standing at a bathroom mirror, fossil-ribs protruding above boxer shorts. I look away.

'Yeah.'

He's watching me, like he's waiting for me to ask him to come along. But I won't. I need them to talk to me, and there's just something about Dave, something that tends to make people clam up.

I had put the story – for that was what it would dissolve down to, when push came to shove – forward at the morning meeting. In amongst the jabber of county fayres and stolen cars, I offered Emily up. 'She was found dead on the M4. She was wearing going-out clothes, high heels, no coat. They're not sure how she got there.'

Lydia, my editor had frowned. 'Sounds like she was drunk.'

You could feel the interest ebbing away, people looking down at their own notepads, rehearsing their own pitches, while Emily vanished, just another casualty of a too-heavy night. My hand began to shake. I sat on my fingers to hide it. 'I knew her from school. She was a nice girl.

church-going.' There was a wobble in my voice, and I fought back a flush of irritation with myself and my own weakness. Because you can't do that; go into an editorial meeting and cry, and say you want to cover this story because, for a while at least, the victim was your friend and because you let her down, so now you owe her, and, even though you haven't seen her in years and years, you just need to make the pieces fit. You can't tell your editor that the reason it's this story, and not some other, is that you just can't live with the idea of the world believing that this is who she is. Some skank in heels who drank too much and meandered into motorway traffic. Just one more death put down to idiocy and booze. But you can't say any of that. Because it is, after all, about the story.

Lydia had shrugged, bulbed shoulders heaving. 'People change.' Her fingers were dancing on her notepad, long manicured nails that led into sausage-round fingers. Her toe tapping on the floor. Looking at me, but seemed like she was struggling to keep her attention there, her gaze pulling itself back towards her office. She's put weight on, was straining at her size twenty-four blouse, something that generally means she's worried about something. 'Sounds like she rebelled. Now, what about this whole "gunman at hospital" thing? What do you have for me on that?'

I had leaned forward, my notepad digging into my ribs. 'Well . . .' Injecting faux-enthusiasm, a little suspense, into my voice. 'Now I also have an interesting little link there. The night before Emily Wilson died, she called the police. She was the one who reported the man with the gun. So what I'm thinking is: I can cover both stories at once. You know, maybe just go and see her parents, dig a little. See if I can find an angle the other papers won't have.'

Lydia had studied me for a moment, teeth picking at her lower lip. And I know what she is thinking: that I am good at my job. That sounds arrogant, doesn't it? But I don't mean it that way. I just . . . I seem to know the words to say, what will draw the story out: from victims, from the police, sometimes from the perpetrators themselves. In my four years as crime reporter I have provided more front-page stories than any other reporter here. And I can see all this, running through her brain.

Then she sighed. Throwing me a bone. 'Fine. Look, go and see the parents. See if there's anything there with the gunman. If not, write up a little something on the tragedy, y'know: nice girl, so young, et cetera. Okay, what about this mugging on Queen Street? What have you got on that?'

I glance at my watch. I should make a move, go and see Emily's parents. I don't need to look them up – I know where they live. Four doors down from our old family home. I stop for a minute, scrunch my face up, thinking. I'd be terrible at poker. Should I ring them first? Wouldn't normally, but then this isn't normal, not really. I can feel Dave watching me, his eyes burning into the side of my face. 'So . . .' I'm not really interested in chatting, but quite frankly it's starting to get awkward, so I cast around for conversation. 'How's Imogen doing?'

He shrugs, fingers fumbling at his phone. ''kay. Busy in work.'

I don't bite – wonder if he knows, if Imogen has told him. But then surely she wouldn't? Psychologists aren't supposed to do things like that. Can feel my face flush, busy myself typing the Wilsons' address into the telephone directory, trying not to let my mind run away with me. Imogen wouldn't do that.

'Well, tell her I said Hi.' I'm studying the computer screen, still not looking at him.

'Yeah, sure. Oh Jesus!'

'What?' My heartbeat steps up a pace, because for a second I think he knows something. But when I look up he isn't even looking at me, has turned his chair towards the door, watching the figure in the doorway. I suppress a groan, look back down, hope like hell that Steve Lowe hasn't seen me.

'Your boyfriend's back.'

I can hear the glee in Dave's voice, kind of want to slap him. I keep studying the screen, willing Steve to keep walking right by my desk, on towards Lydia's office. Please God, let him not be my problem, not today. I hear his footsteps, a stalking, bouncing step, hear them slow as he reaches me.

I turn reluctantly.

Steve stands beside my desk, lean muscled arms folded across his chest, like he's already anticipating irritation. He's wearing a T-shirt, a faded Levi logo, jeans that are streaked with grease. Smells of garages and hard work, lips pressed tight together, diamond-glint beads of sweat sprinkled across his close-shaved head. Could be considered good-looking, in a certain light, if you were into that kind of thing – the whole macho, slightly dangerous look. I'm not. Not even a little bit.

'Mr Lowe. How are you?' I try to sound sincere, I honestly do; try to remind myself of all that he has had to deal with.

It's a monthly thing, these visits, has been ever since the night of the shooting. He keeps coming back, over and over again, and it's as if he thinks that somehow I have the power to change things.

I smile, and he shifts, pressing his thumbs hard against his biceps so that the colour bleaches out of them. Shrugs heavily, lips compressing tighter. 'About as well as you can expect, I suppose.'

I nod. Going for understanding. Hoping like hell that my face isn't letting me down. Because even though I have this man standing in front of me who has been through so much, all I'm thinking is: what will the traffic be like this time of day? How long will it take me to get out to Brynhyfryd and Emily's parents?

'Any change with Dylan?' I try to focus on him, ask like I'm expecting a different answer this time, even though I know there won't be. Persistent vegetative state. By its very nature, persistent.

Steve shakes his head, face grim. 'Nothing. I'm telling you, what they've done to my boy . . . it's criminal. Bloody criminal.'

My face flattens out, and I glance back towards my computer screen, because I don't want to do this with him. Not again. I think of Aden. Sitting on the kerb, his head in his hands, looking like his world had just ended. Me wanting to hug him, even though I barely knew him at all. But seeing it in him: that his world has just come crashing down around him and now a boy lies dying.

'You know that those bastards are back on Firearms again, don't you?'

I did.

'Really?'

'After what they did. Leaving my son in that state.'

Dave is peeking out at me from behind his computer screen. Grinning. I have a powerful urge to slap him.

'So, what can I do for you today, Mr Lowe?' I ask, trying to sound like I'm not trying to hurry him out, even though, in truth, that's exactly what I'm doing.

'We've filed.' He brings himself up to his full height – an impressive six-foot-four, give or take an inch – bouncing on the balls of his feet. Smirks a little.

I wonder briefly when it was that the man last had cause to actually smile. 'You've filed?'

'Civil suit. We're going after those bastards ourselves. The IPCC – well, they're all in each other's pockets, aren't they? We've filed a wrongful-death suit in a civil court, against the firearms officers. I thought you'd want to know. You know,' he gestures to the computer, 'write a piece on it.'

I wonder if Aden knows?

'Okay, Mr Lowe.' I give him a half-smile, trying hard to look like I mean it. 'Well, tell you what. You let us know the date, and I'll pop down to the court and cover it.' That's all he's getting from me.

His face hardens, hands balling into fists. 'Well, can you write something now?'

'As I've said, Mr Lowe, I'm not allowed to cover these kind of things until they're in front of the court. But the second it is, I'll be there.'

He's not looking at me now, is gazing down at the ground with a deadened stare. I glance at Dave, see his eyes open wide, a sideways nod to the phone, and I shake my head, even though my heart is in my throat. After all, he is still a man who has lost his son.

'You're not interested, are you?' Steve's voice is low, full of storm clouds.

'Mr Lowe . . .'

'No, I know how it is. You're in their pocket too, aren't you? You're all the fucking same, the lot of you.'

'That's enough now, mate.' Dave has pushed himself up, manoeuvring his thin frame around the desk, practically bumping chests with Steve Lowe. He has set his face, is trying to look stern, like he will brook no more trouble from this man who can snap him like a twig. But there's something else there too, flitting underneath: the thrill at being my defender. I reach up, touch his arm. 'It's okay, Dave. Mr Lowe . . .'

But I am invisible now. Steve Lowe has lowered his chin, his nostrils flared out flat, and for a moment I think that he is going to hit Dave. 'Think you're a tough guy, yeah? Come on then.'

People are looking, the few of us who are left in the newsroom are staring, waiting for it all to go bad, and I can see the day tumbling away from me, into police statements and recriminations.

'The lady has said her piece,' says Dave, his face pantomime-grim. 'Now out!'

The lady? I suppress a sigh, wish to God that Dave had some – I don't know – sense. Some idea how to talk to people.

'Okay.' I stand up, sliding myself in between them, bouncing on my toes, trying to make myself look bigger than I am. Wishing that one of them at least had thought to take a shower this morning. 'Look, boys, come on. There's no need to get wound up. Steve, I'll have a chat with my editor, see what I can do for you.' I am smiling up at Steve in what I hope is a winning way.

He isn't looking at me, hasn't taken his eyes off Dave. Bugger!

'Go on then,' Steve says, his teeth gritted. 'Do it now.'

I don't know which of us he's talking to, but I choose to believe it's me. 'The editor isn't in right now, she's had to run out to a meeting.' I pray as I lie, hope like hell Lydia doesn't choose this moment to come out of her office. 'But as soon as she gets back I'll have a sit-down with her.'

He's coming down – I can see the way his shoulders are beginning to sink, the way his gaze shifts, ever so briefly, from Dave to me – and I think: good, I've got him.

And then Dave says, 'Yeah, so fuck off out of here.'

Sometimes I just despair.

Steve's gaze has shifted now, is fully focused on Dave. I can see his fists balling, can tell by the shape of them that he's just dying to kill somebody, that this has been inside him for too long and needs to get out. He pulls back his arm and I reach out, clasp hold of his fingers. They feel rough, feel like they could land one hell of a punch. He looks at me, wasn't expecting me to touch him.

'Steve.' I speak quietly, my words just for him. 'This isn't going to help Carla and the kids. This isn't going to help me make a case to my editor. Just leave it now, eh?'

He studies me, and I can see the agony of indecision in his face; that he still really wants to thump Dave. I feel a modicum of sympathy for him on that point. Then he lowers his arm. Gives me a quick, awkward nod. 'Yeah.' He studies me, like he hasn't seen me before. 'You're all right.'

Dave stands there, has folded his arms across his chest,

and I pray that he'll be sensible enough to keep his mouth shut.

'But you . . .' Steve points at Dave, a thick, oil-stained finger. 'I'm going to fucking do you, mate.'

12

Imogen: Tuesday 26 August, 12.11 p.m.
Five days before the shooting

Imogen pulled her office door closed behind her, took a quick glance around the small waiting room. It was empty, as she had expected it to be, and yet still her heart beat a little faster. It was as if she had expected the gunman to be sitting there, waiting for her. But then, thought Imogen, wasn't that always the way of it. Even though this person could have nothing to do with her, could have no reason to make her a target, the hubris of humanity was such that our minds turn it into something seemingly inevitable. She pulled the handbag strap onto her shoulder, slipped into the corridor.

She could tell, instantly, who had heard about the gunman and who hadn't. Could see it in the way they walked, the movement of their heads, whether their eyes darted or remained fixed. Doctors, nurses, the ones who knew, walked more quickly than normal, their shoulders held higher – seemed for all the world like they were waiting for the other shoe to drop. Then there were the visitors, the ones who hadn't heard the story yet. They moved at a slower pace, unaware of danger. The perfect victims. Imogen nodded at a pair of uniformed police officers as they moved past her, heading in the opposite direction, their jaws tight.

Security had been increased – now a notable presence. They would, hospital officials had assured staff, catch this person before they could cause any harm. Imogen had wondered how they could be so sure. She glanced at her watch, picking up her pace. She had an hour until her next appointment, would grab a sandwich from the coffee shop, pick up something for Mara too, would head down to Ward 11 to see Amy before work started again.

Amy was doing well. That was what the doctor – still wearing the same jeans, same scuffed trainers – had said before Imogen had left this morning. We're going to keep her in, another couple of days, runs some tests. We have her scheduled for a CT later on today, an MRI. What about blood tests? Imogen had asked. Does she need those? Oh, said Mara, let's wait and see what the other tests say. We don't want to stick her with needles unless we absolutely have to.

Imogen picked up her pace, weaving past an elderly couple, their movements slow and painful. Could feel a band of pressure wrapping itself around her forehead: lack of sleep combined with a heavy morning. They had come in back-to-back today, her firearms guys – Aden and Tony and Rhys. Three men, all carrying the same burden, each handling it so differently. They wave it off, say they're fine. But you can see it there, that wellspring of pain resting just beneath the surface. Tony's marriage was crumbling. He didn't say it, was a master of talking around the problem, but you could see it in the snippets that he told her; words that his wife had said, his absence where there should be a presence. Imogen wondered if he was cheating – things he said, little wisps of words, seemed to suggest that it was likely. She had considered pushing it, trying to unfurl that particular secret, but in the end had backed away. Tony didn't want to be there anyway. He had made that much clear. So in the end Imogen had offered to refer them for marriage counselling. Tony had shaken his head. One shrink is bad enough, no offence, Doc.

It hadn't been a deliberate choice. There had never been a moment when she had made the decision that she would be a psychologist, that she would work with the people who had walked through fire, seen things that no one should see. She had stumbled into it, after a degree, a research PhD that had lasted about three years longer than she had wanted, had taught her little more than that an academic career wasn't for her. She was a year into her PhD, quietly wondering what the hell had inspired her to select the study of prosopagnosia for a subject, was in the student bar waiting for Mara, as she always seemed to be, when the news had flashed on. She had sat at the bar, her research papers forgotten on her lap, had watched as the second plane flew into the second tower, as a mushroom cloud of fire had spurted horizontally into the vivid blue Manhattan sky. Had watched as the helicopters flew overhead and the people spewed from the building, and the rows upon rows of firefighters, weighed down by impossibly heavy loads, the police, badges glinting in the sunshine. Faces upturned, studying the buildings with that thousand-yard stare that she would later come to know so well. Then looking down, forward, marching into the buildings, off to war. And then she had watched as the second tower shuddered, ever so slightly, then fell, tumbling to the earth in a tsunami of concrete. She had cried out. It hadn't mattered. Because there were dozens of them then, young people with their lives ahead of them lining the bar, staring at the television, tears pouring. Then the first tower following, and it seemed it was almost inevitable. The wave of dust that raced through the Manhattan streets. The silence that hung afterwards. Then the cameras returned to the firefighters and the police, the ones who were lucky enough to be outside, the ones who survived, and they were racing towards the downed buildings, looking steely with fear.

Imogen had sat, cradled the drink that was now flat, hand fluttering to the scar that cut through her eyebrow, wondered how they would go on – these people whose fingers were plunging into concrete and glass and body parts. Wondering what their world would look like tomorrow and the day after that and the day after that.

She'd completed her PhD. It was, after all, something that she had committed herself to. And it had an intrinsic worth, in and of itself, she had convinced herself, afterwards. And she had taught herself about trauma, the scars of psychological wounds. Had carved out a career that fitted.

Imogen slowed as a pair of porters guided a gurney out of a lift, the elderly man on it lying prone, blue blanket tucked up tight to his chin. Aden had come in before Tony, weighted down by a different kind of grief, the guilt of inaction, his confidence shuddering under the pressure of it all. And Rhys, her final client of the morning. So much younger than the other two, sometimes he seemed little more than a child. Always so correct, so precise, and yet you could see it in him: the price he had paid for what he had been forced to do.

They come in, the police officers, the paramedics, the firefighters. They bring with them their stories, darker than you have ever heard. About blood and death and tragedy. They cradle them to their chests like shields, so heavy that it stops them from sleeping at night, from eating, from wanting to be anywhere near the ones they love, but perhaps, if they hug it tight enough, the next tragedy won't get through. They are exhausted by the time they get here. Always so reluctant to give in. Will rarely look at Imogen for the first session, spend the hour studying the institutional beige carpet, as they slowly begin to unpack their secrets.

It's no big deal, really.

It's not really an issue, but . . .

My boss told me I had to come.

Then they hand her their stories. Some of them like they are sharing a tale over a beer at the pub, others like they are peeling off their own skin. They talk about the woman with the carving knife who stands in front of them, digging the blade into her own wrist, daring them to come closer. About the ceiling, weighted down by fire and heat, that tumbles down in front of them, missing them by inches, landing instead on the man in front, so that where he was now lies a pile of timbers, a smoking carcass. The child, dead by its father's hand, that they cradled in the ambulance, wouldn't put down even when they know it's too late and the doctors are begging them to let go. The gun pointed at them, the mouth of it so wide it seems to swallow the world.

Imogen turned into the lobby, suppressed a groan at the line in the coffee shop. She considered skipping it, just turning around and heading up to Amy and Mara, but she hadn't eaten since yesterday and her stomach felt hollow, her head beginning to swim. She ducked through the crowds, reaching into her bag for her phone, thinking to squeeze in a quick call to Dave. Tell him that she wouldn't be home late tonight, that she would pick up an Indian, maybe a bottle of wine. He'd like that.

Then came the sound of footsteps, running.

It was like a spark of electricity that rippled through the crowd, faces creasing with split-second anxiety, heads snapping towards the sound. Imogen's stomach lurched, the sudden thought shooting through her mind that she had been right, that the gunman did want her after all. She turned towards the footsteps, bracing.

'Imogen!'

It took her a moment to process the scene before her, to recalculate her fears. Mara's hair was flying loose, her face streaked with tears. She reached Imogen, threw herself into her sister's arms, shaking so badly it seemed that she would vibrate right into the floor.

'Mara. What is it? Is it Amy?' Scenarios shifting for Imogen, one horror replacing another.

'No.' Mara almost shouted it, seemed utterly unaware of the gathered crowd, that all eyes were turned towards her now, watching. 'It was him. He was out there.'

'Him – who?'

'The man. The one they said had a gun.'

It rippled through the crowd.

'She's seen him.'

'My God, I thought they said he'd gone.'

'Oh, that poor girl.'

'What? Mara, are you sure?' Imogen held on tight to her sister's hands, bitter cold in spite of the heat of the day. 'Where did you see him?'

'I . . . I went to the car.' Mara's voice shook, but came out loud, louder than Imogen had expected. The surrounding crowd seemed to press in, no one speaking, not a word, every breath bated to hear Mara's next. 'Amy wanted her dolly, so I just went to get it, that was all. I'd parked right over on the side, by the woods. And when I closed the car door, I saw him, standing in amongst the trees, watching me. He had a dark hoodie on, had the hood all pulled up tight so that I couldn't see him.' She gripped her sister's hand tighter. 'But I was scared, so I started to run and, Im, he followed me. He ran through the trees, chasing me, and I thought that at the door, that's where he would catch me and . . . oh, Im, I was so scared.'

Imogen sucked in a breath. Trying to keep calm. Trying to think. 'So you didn't recognise him? You didn't see his face at all?'

'No, nothing. He was too far away. But, I mean, he couldn't have been there for me, could he? I mean, why would he be after me?'

Imogen shook her head, studying her sister. Trying not to think about a day, perhaps six weeks ago. An early-morning visit to Mara's house, one that Mara wasn't expecting. Imogen had left her phone there the night before, had realised too late to call, had cursed herself, knowing that she would need it for work the following morning. It was fine. It was fine. She'd go there, would stop by on her way to work.

Imogen had arrived a little after 7 a.m. Could immediately tell that her sister and niece were still asleep, the whole house heavy with a soporific silence. She had slipped her key into the lock. The phone would be on the kitchen counter – that was where they had been

91

standing. She would just grab it and be on her way. That was when she had seen it. A pair of men's shoes. Boots, rather. Lace-ups that looked like their wearer was accustomed to hard work. On the kitchen table a bottle of wine, two glasses. A round burgundy stain scarring the marble worktop.

Jack had been working in Dubai for two weeks.

Imogen had bitten her lip, stared at the boots, the wine glasses. There would be an explanation. Her sister would have had a friend over, perhaps someone she had met in playgroup. The boots, they must be Jack's. They did look a little familiar, she thought. Then she had heard footsteps on the stairs, a light, bouncing gait.

Mara was wearing a T-shirt, boxer-style knickers, bare feet. Had looked up and seen Imogen, had pulled up sharp, her eyes darting towards the boots and then to the kitchen chair, a man's coat thrown across its back.

'Im . . .' Mara had stopped on the stairs, her hand over her mouth.

'I needed my phone. I left it here.'

'Oh.' Mara nodded, dropped down a step closer. 'Okay, I . . .' She glanced back up the stairs, fingers dancing nervously.

'I should go. I have early appointments.'

'Okay.' Mara's toes curled around the bottom step. 'Imogen?'

'Yes?' Imogen had slipped the phone into her pocket. Wasn't looking at her sister.

'Don't tell Jack. Okay?'

The crowd in the lobby had pushed closer now, the murmurs building until it felt like a roar.

'Someone call the police.'

'Poor love, something needs to be done.'

Imogen hugged her sister in to her. 'It's all right, Mar. It'll be okay.' Mara slumped into her, and Imogen tried not to think about the secrets her sister kept, the people she may have angered, and how it could all end.

13

Aden: Tuesday 26 August, 6.36 p.m.
Five days before the shooting

'Ready.'

Aden's hand moved to his waist, thumb flicked the catch on the holster. The metal of the Glock cold against his fingers. Palm to the grip. Index finger stretched along the barrel. Waiting.

'Aim.'

Pulling the Glock free from the holster, index finger against the trigger, feeling it taut. Pad of his fingertip against cold metal. Then that thought: ice-cold rain, plunging darkness and the sound of footsteps, running. Breathe. Aden focused along the sight – entire world narrowing down to little more than a pin prick. There, fifteen yards away, a cardboard torso, stomach lined with a series of concentric circles.

Breathe.

'Fire.'

He squeezed the trigger. Felt the Glock kick back against the palm of his hand, bucking like a frightened horse. Steady. Find the circles. Squeeze.

Aden hadn't slept much. Had managed four, five hours

at the most. He had come into the office early, well before training started. Had pulled up the records for Emily Wilson's three-9s call, late on the Sunday night. Emily had strained to keep her voice level and calm, but every so often there had been a little shake, a stumble over words, anxiety breaking through. There's a man, at the door of the ward. It's Ward 12. He has a gun. A long breath, and it seemed that Aden could see her, pulling herself together, reminding herself to be professional, stay calm. The man – he left when he saw me watching. No, I couldn't see his face. Then, when she had almost done, a crease in her resolve. Please, tell them to hurry.

Find the circle. Squeeze the trigger. Let the gun buck against you. Breathe.

Aden could not erase Emily's voice from his mind. It reverberated, over the boom of the gunshot. It felt, after listening to the call, that he knew her now. That were he to pass her in the street, he would recognise her instantly. Of course that would never happen now, because Emily Wilson was dead. Twenty-four hours after making that call.

Find the circle. Squeeze the trigger. Let the gun buck against you. Breathe.

Was it her then? Was that why the gunman had been there? Had he followed her, killed her? But no, that couldn't be right. Because on the second night, when he had returned, Emily was already dead. So why go back, why risk capture? It came back to Dylan Lowe, as all things did since the night of the shooting, everything revolving around that pivot point. Emily could not have been the target, the reason the gunman was there, because if she had been, he would have had no reason to return. Perhaps then her death was exactly what it appeared to be, what the investigation had

95

concluded – an accident. A tragic confluence of random events. And, if that was true, if Dylan was the draw, then the gunman would return.

Find the circle. Squeeze the trigger. Let the gun buck against you. Breathe.

Aden thought about that night a year ago and the sound of footsteps running through the pouring rain. There was much they did not know. They had never found the people with whom Dylan Lowe had been. And of course Dylan had been in no condition to turn them in. Aden had assumed they were kids, a group of juveniles pissing about, scared when things got so real so fast. But then, he thought, what did that prove? Dylan was a kid. But still he had turned on them, had pointed a gun at them, had planned to kill them and would have done, had it not been for Tony, for Rhys.

Aden felt his arm tremble under the pressure of the thought, his last shot going wide. Corrected his stance, his grip, reminded himself to breathe. Was that it then? Was it one of the accomplices, spooked suddenly after Dylan's long sleep, deciding that they could not risk him waking, telling his story? Was Emily's death nothing more than a tragic coincidence?

Charlie wouldn't like the theory. Aden knew her well enough to know that. He had seen her face, as he talked about Emily's 999 call, had seen the thoughts whirring into place. Felt himself smile a little as he thought of her – another shot dropping low from the distraction of it.

Aden had seen Charlie coming towards him on the night of the shooting, in the tumbling-down rain. Had wanted to swear, because the last thing he had needed then was some hack badgering him for details of the bloodbath in the alley. Hadn't recognised her for a moment. Then he had, and hadn't felt any better, because now she had an 'in', a direct line to his story. Had been summoning up all of his seeping reserves, ready to be polite but rejecting, when she had sat down, dumping herself into the puddle in which he already sat. She hadn't said anything. Hadn't even looked at him. He had been dimly aware of the rain drying up, had glanced up to see the umbrella that she held over his head. Had felt so pathetically grateful that he had wanted to cry.

She had never asked him, then or after. He was fairly confident that she would have picked up the gist of it: the firearms hotshot who failed to shoot. After all, Charlie knew everybody in the force, was friends with everyone. Someone would have told her. But she had never asked him.

The trigger pulled, clicked, top-slide zinging backwards. Ammunition gone. Aden lowered the gun, muzzle towards the floor. The air was thick, the silence beyond the sound.

'All clear. Holster your weapons. Ear-defenders off.'

He tugged the bulbous ear-muffs free, sound flooding back into the muffled silence, laughter. Rhys was standing beside him, shaking his head.

'You all right?' asked Aden.

'That was shit. Look!' Rhys pointed down-range towards his target, the shots riding low and to the left.

Aden nodded. 'You're anticipating the recoil. Just take your time. Keep each shot nice and slow. And keep that focus on the front sight – that'll tell you how you're performing.' He grinned. 'That'll teach you to be late. Again.'

Rhys smiled, a guilty laugh. 'I know. Traffic was terrible. I'm too stressed to concentrate then.'

'Don't worry about it.' Aden caught his eye. 'You're doing well, mate.'

'Nice shooting, Ade.' Iestyn, the training sergeant, had appeared next to him, six foot and lathe-lean, white-blond hair in a crew cut. Folded his arms across his chest. 'Couple of dropped shots, but other than that very nice.'

'Thanks, Sarge.'

'You, ah,' Iestyn kept his voice down, watching as Rhys ducked his head, following the others down-range, 'you thought any more about the Tactical Unit?' He glanced at Aden, studying. 'You know they're recruiting again, right?'

Aden shrugged. 'Yeah. I mean, I heard. But I thought that what with—'

'Ade, I'm not being funny, mate.' The sergeant clapped a lion's-paw hand on his shoulder. 'Bloody go for it. You've always said it's what you want, yeah? Well, go on then. You'll walk the assessment.'

Aden looked down. 'Yeah, thing is . . .' The sentence petered out, because it was impossible to say what the thing actually was. That he couldn't forget the fact that he had failed. That he was terrified of doing it again. That now every day it felt like he was holding on by his fingertips.

The sergeant was looking at him, appraising. 'Look. Okay. Have a think. But I'm telling you, that job is yours for the taking.'

Aden nodded, could feel the eyes burning into the back of his head. 'Thanks. Ah, Sarge?'

'Yeah?'

'About the Mount Pleasant Hospital call? You know the one?'

'The gunman having a wander about?'

'Yeah. You know that the ward – Ward 12 – you know that's Dylan Lowe's ward, right?'

The sergeant frowned. 'Okay?'

'No, well, I was just thinking . . .' Aden lowered his voice. 'I was wondering if it was a connection that we should be looking at. You know, the others who were with him. We never did find them.'

'So you think one of them is planning on finishing him off?'

Aden shrugged, trying to look nonchalant. 'Just a thought.'

Iestyn studied him for a moment. 'All right, I'll pass it on. But I got to be honest, mate, I don't think it's going to make too much difference. The powers that be have already ordered extra patrols. Besides,' his voice dropped lower, 'when you think about it, what would be the point of shooting him? Kid isn't likely to be talking any time soon.'

Aden nodded, caught Rhys's eye. Moved closer as the sergeant passed on to the next AFO on the line. 'What do you think?'

Rhys shook his head. 'I don't know, Ade. I get what you're saying. I really do. But that kid . . . As the sarge said, what would be the point? He's not going to tell anyone, is he?' His colour had slipped, a greyish tinge now to his pallor. 'You know, I have nightmares sometimes, about him lying in that hospital bed. It gets to the point sometimes where I'm afraid to go to sleep.' Then he caught himself, glancing around in case anyone else had heard. 'Shit! Don't, I mean, don't say anything to anyone, will you? I don't want them thinking I shouldn't be back on Firearms. That I can't handle it.'

Aden studied him, a wave of guilt threatening to drown

him. 'No. Of course not. If it helps, I have those dreams too.'

'Yeah?' Rhys watched him, face hopeful almost.

'Yeah. Especially in the beginning. Sorry, mate. I didn't mean to make things worse for you.'

Rhys shrugged. 'It is what it is. But, the thing is, I just don't get why anyone would be going after him. I mean, there are a ton of people on that ward. Ward 11 is right next door, so we don't know that it wasn't that ward the gunman was looking for. I sometimes wonder if we are just assuming it's got something to do with Dylan because, you know, it's personal for us.'

'Yeah. I guess you're right.' Aden broke off as a figure moved closer. 'All right, Tony?'

Tony stood just behind them, his arms folded, legs akimbo. Had tucked his Glock back into his holster, but it didn't seem like he needed it. Just the general impression he gave: that unarmed he could do as much damage as a firearm. The others billowed around him, walking in groups, conversation low. But they gave Tony a wide berth, a couple shooting him sideways glances. He was, he would tell you with dizzying frequency, a military man at heart. The Marines. Had joined right out of school. Still wore the tattoo, insignia wrapped around the girth of his upper arm. Had left, in the end, to marry the woman of his dreams. Had joined the police because it had seemed, at the time, to be the next best thing.

Life, however, had seemed determined to disappoint Tony. The marriage was in trouble, everyone knew that. And there was the shooting. Tony had done what Aden could not; had delivered two shots. He'd been off Firearms for nine months, bitter and piqued.

Tony indicated towards Aden's target, a rough gesture. 'Not bad.' Pursed his lips together, suggesting that there was more he wanted to say, but that he was forbearing, for the moment.

'Thanks.'

Aden studied Tony. We have to understand what those surrounding us are seeing.

'Can I ask you something, Tone?'

'What's that?' Tony wasn't looking at him, was still staring down-range towards his own target. Frowning.

'I was, ah . . . I was talking to Imogen – you're still seeing her, right?'

Tony's head snapped around then, a quick scan to see that no one was listening. 'Yeah.' His voice dropped. 'Like the good little boy that I am.' Shrugged. 'One of my conditions of return to Firearms, wasn't it?'

'Well, the thing is, she said something that made me think. That night.' No need to name it, they all knew which night 'that night' was. 'What did you see?'

Tony had pulled back now, was staring at him. 'What do you mean?'

'Well, we were talking about perspectives, you know? How we all see things differently.'

'You mean, like how you somehow missed the fact that the kid was pointing a gun at your head?'

So much blackness it seems impossible that Aden will ever see again, an explosion of sound that comes from everywhere, all at once. His finger, the trigger, just not moving.

'Mate,' Tony said it so that it sounded like a curse, was shaking his head slowly. 'I'm not gonna hold your dick while you piss. Kid had a gun. Would have killed you, if it weren't for me and Brad over there. Would have shot you through with that nice little Browning HP, just like the one my old granddad brought back from Normandy.' He turned away from Aden, his shoulder hefting like the movement of mountains. 'You missed it. That's on you. And I'll tell you something else.' Tony gestured towards the training sergeant, his voice dropping further still. 'The sarge may think your shit is chocolate. Me, not so much.'

He gave Aden a look, one that scrolled up and down him. A little shrug. Turned on his heel.

Aden could feel a swell of anger, wanted to reach out, grab hold of Tony's throat. But didn't. Stood there, his hands flexing uselessly at his sides. Because, after all, wasn't he right?

'You okay?' Rhys's voice was quiet, softer even than it usually was.

Aden shrugged. 'What can I say? He's not wrong.'

'That Tony – he's all wrong. Don't listen to him, Ade. He's a prick.'

They began walking towards the targets, where the others were clustered, Iestyn waiting for them, look expectant. 'All right, boys and girls. Nice work, some nice groupings. Colm, think you took out a light fitting. Try not to do that again, 'kay, butt?' A smattering of laughter. 'And our winner, with the highest score, is Mr Aden McCarthy. Nice job. Right, up to the armoury, lock up your weapons and then grab yourselves a cuppa. Thirty minutes and we'll have you back down into the tactics house, if you don't mind. Thank you.' The sergeant turned, catching sight of Aden and Rhys. 'Guys, hang back for me a sec. Tone? You too.' He didn't say anything for a moment, watching as the others filtered out, curious glances thrown back over their shoulders. Tony had folded his arms, a brick wall across his thick chest, his face locked down. Rhys stood beside Aden, seemed to have shrunk, head tucked back into his shoulder blades. Aden's heart beat a little faster.

'Right, guys. Quick word. I have some news. I've spoken to the inspector and he's asked me to have a chat with you. We've heard from Dylan Lowe's family.'

The name sent a ripple through the group. Aden's stomach flipped.

'Now, obviously they weren't pleased with the IPCC ruling – no surprises there. I'm sorry, guys. But they have filed a civil suit against the force, and against you two,' he gestured to Rhys and Tony, 'as the primary shooters.'

Rhys's head sank further. His eyes closed. Tony was staring at the sergeant.

'Ade, obviously you have not been named in the suit. You will be pulled in as a witness, though, so I just wanted to give you a heads-up.'

'This is bullshit,' said Tony.

'Tone.'

'No. No. This is bullshit. We've been cleared. The IPCC. We've been fucking cleared. And this wanker,' Tony waved at Aden, lip curled, 'of course he's all right: too chicken-shit to pull the trigger. That's the way to do it, isn't it? Hide behind the big boys.'

'Come on, Tony. No call for that,' Iestyn said.

Tony was bouncing on the balls of his feet, thick fingers flexing into fists. Iestyn turned, gave Aden a look, a quick eye-roll. 'Ade, another thing. Just, ah, obviously this is going to be quite a sensitive time. So watch yourself around that reporter friend of yours. That Charlie one? You know: loose lips sink ships, and all that.'

'Charlie's not like that, Sarge. She's . . . she's okay,' said Aden.

Iestyn shook his head. 'Yeah, fit isn't the same as okay. Just watch yourself, okay?'

'Yeah.' Aden wasn't looking at him, but down at the floor, gave a quick nod.

'This,' said Tony, voice rumbling across the cavernous space, 'is fucking bullshit.'

14

The Shooter: Sunday 31 August, 9.38 a.m.
Day of the shooting

I pull open the car boot, easing the lock. The click seems
to be startlingly loud in the quiet street, and I glance around,
can't help myself. But there is no one here. Harddymaes
enjoying a rare kind of peace. The sun is still low, but still
there is a warmth to the air, a potency, as if the world
knows what is about to come. I realise that my hands are
shaking, lift them up and stare at them like they don't belong
to me.

It seems unreal that people can still sleep. They don't
seem to realise that this is it. The last day. That after this
day I will be free.

I pull the duffel bag towards me, ease the zip down. It
screams, louder than any zip ever should, and again I look.
But still there is no one. I am all alone, and that should
come as no surprise to me. When have I ever been anything
else?

I ease the gun free. I know that it is loaded. I remember
loading it. But now, at the eleventh hour, the urge to check
is overwhelming. But there they are, the round bullets. Just

waiting. I pull a box of ammunition free, slip it into my pocket. I know that will be enough. I'm a good shot.

I reach up and tug at the boot. Can hear my heart thumping.

Stick to the plan. Just stick to the plan.

Ease the boot down slowly, wincing as it squeals. There is a smell hanging in the air, one that I have come to associate with this house, the scent of rotting food, dirty nappies, the filth that spills from the overstuffed bins. The council don't collect them like they should. The bins have stood out for too long in the heat, are poisoning the air. I'm not surprised. This place is already hell, what difference does a few more shitty nappies make? I turn, lift the gun and begin to walk softly along the garden path.

I look up at the house. Most of the curtains are closed, thin cotton affairs that barely cover the fingerprint-smudged windows. But there is one window that remains uncovered. Dylan's room. What would be the point of closing the curtains? He doesn't sleep there any more. A bike lies on the front step. One of the children too tired from play to bother putting it away, Carla too caught up in her nearly dead son, the hanging fragments of her disappointing life. An empty paddling pool lying slack-jawed on the meagre front lawn.

I suck in a breath. Heft the gun.

Stick to the plan.

The front door is closed, locked, but that won't present a challenge to me. I see it like it has already happened, slipping in through the door, up the stairs to where they are all asleep. Raising the gun, resting my index finger on the trigger. Bam. Bam. Bam. There will be blood, but, when you get right down to it, it will be a mercy for them. I glance back over my shoulder at the glory that is Harddymaes. Life should be more than this. So I will pull the trigger, again and again, and then, eventually, it will be over and we will all be on the road to peace. I suddenly realise how very tired I am, how badly I want this day – all days – to be done.

'Wha's dat?'

My heart screams, makes to leap out of my chest, and I spin, almost shoot blindly at the sound. It is a child, little more than three, standing on the doorstep of the house next door. Behind him there is the sound of voices, television English. He looks at me, studying, naked but for a nappy that hangs down to his fat knees. There is chocolate ringing his mouth, a slick of jam that has been wiped through his blond hair, leaving it standing erect.

I am frozen. My mouth moves uselessly.

'Dat. Wha's dat?'

I look at him, look down to where he is pointing at the gun, now held limp in my fingers. My heart thumping.

'A walking stick.'

There is a plan. Stick to the plan. He stares at me, considering, and I find myself praying that this little wisp of a person will accept my explanation and leave me the fuck alone.

'Why?'

I frown, pull my face into an expression that I think should be menacing to a toddler. 'You should go inside.'

The kid stares at me, chews his thumbnail. Unimpressed. 'Mammy's in da shower.'

'Go inside,' I snap, shout at him, pulling myself up to my full height. Expect his face to crumple, lip to shake. But he just keeps staring at me. A child used to being shouted at.

'Want to play?' he asks, hopeful.

I stand there. Gun in my hands. There is a plan and I want to stick to the plan, but now my heart is thumping and my hands are shaking, and the absurdity of this is just beginning to settle on me.

I stare at him. Watch the bubble of snot that hangs from his left nostril.

I just want it to end.

I turn, walk away.

15

Charlie: Tuesday 26 August, 6.36 p.m.
Five days before the shooting

'The thing is, I just . . . I don't understand. That's the thing, isn't it, Jeff?' Emily's mother turns, looking vaguely at her husband, like she has forgotten where this sentence is going, is looking for him to guide her. 'We don't understand what she was doing there. I mean, walking on the M4. Why would she?' She gives a little nod, proud that she figured it out after all – made it to the end of her thought on her own. Then you see it, the silence bringing with it the recollection of where she is, what has come to pass, and two tears, thick and fat, begin to glide down her concave cheeks.

I've never been good with tears. Not mine. Not anybody else's. It's the wrenching, raw honesty of them that throws me. The courage to allow your pain to get out, it unnerves me, I suppose. I never quite know what to do, if there is some magic word that I can say that will make things better, or if I should be all British and discreetly look away, affording the crier a privacy they never asked for, and, quite possibly, never wanted.

It's the coward's way out.

Seems that Emily's mother knows this, can somehow sense that all I want to do is run like hell. She is squeezing my fingers, so tight that it hurts. I pat her hand with my free one – a feeble attempt – and manage to hold back the 'There, there' that's just waiting to slip out. Mrs Wilson is dressed, but just barely: a skirt that comes down to her ankles, a sweatshirt stained at the cuff. Looks like she has pulled on the first thing that came to hand. A small gold cross hanging at her neck, catching the light. I study it, so that I don't have to look at her face: slack, the grief washing away all of the muscle tone. Alexandra Wilson has aged in the years since I saw her last, a whooshing slump into seniority. The hair that was blonde is now pure white, laughter lines all but vanished into the deeper crevasses of premature old age.

'It's good that you came.' Alexandra squeezes my hand. A little nod to herself. 'It's good.'

Guilt rolls across my stomach. 'It's been a long time, since I've seen Emily.' I hold it out to her, as if it's an apology.

Alexandra nods. Gives a heavy, wintery sigh. 'That's how life is. People drift apart.' Squeezes my hand again. 'I'm glad that you came, Charlotte dear. It's so very good of you.'

It took me for ever to open the car door when I arrived in the Wilsons' road. I sat, my knees pulled up so that they almost touched my chin, and stared out into the street where I grew up. You couldn't see the sea, not today, the trees a dense curtain of leaves. I parked at the top of the road. Could see the Wilson house, its whitewashed walls, its hanging baskets, pink and orange and yellow. The curtains had been pulled across the front windows as if the entire house had its eyes closed, signalling the presence of death. I tried to focus on the hanging baskets, on the colours. Tried not to look beyond it. It lies four doors down, the house where I grew up. I haven't been here since we moved, fourteen years ago. It looks different than I remembered. Someone has built a porch on the outside, changed the windows. I try not to think about the family that must live there now, try not to wonder if they are happy.

'It's just . . . I wish I could understand, you know? What on earth she was doing there. I mean, she wasn't driving – not that night. Her car was in the garage, wasn't it, Jeff?'

Emily's father nods, a slow, vacant movement; isn't looking at his wife, but is staring into space, his hands moving, like in his mind he is washing them, as if the motion itself can cleanse him of what has happened. He sits in an armchair. It's his chair, you can see that. The way it moulds itself around him, the remote controls lined up along the arm, a newspaper folded, tucked down the side. Then he takes a deep breath, steeling himself, and glances up at his wife, a fresh spasm of pain blossoming across his face, looks back down, and it's like he has got smaller suddenly, as if he has folded inwards. I can't help wondering what will happen to them. How their respective wounds will fit together. Will the scabs form across them both, pulling them tighter? Or will they grow jagged, their scars not matching, so that they no longer seem to fit?

'That's right, wasn't it, Jeff? She'd been having problems, see, with her – you know – the watchamacallit.'

'Power steering.' Jeff's voice is low, gruff.

'The power steering. Jeff said he'd run her, if she wanted to go anywhere. She promised she'd call. But she never did,

did she, Jeff?' Alexandra looks down, her fingers plucking at mine. Shakes her head. 'Never did call.'

I saw Emily this morning, loading a toddler into a Citroën Picasso. I saw her last night, waiting in a queue in front of me at the Chinese, picking up an order of chicken chow mein. I saw her on my way out of my flat, when I stopped to glance in the mirror, and saw hair wild with teenage frizz, teeth misshapen with braces. Drew in a sharp breath. Glanced across my shoulder. But, of course, she wasn't there. It shouldn't have surprised me – that now it seemed that Emily was all I could see. Although, in truth, I couldn't say that I had thought of her more than once, twice, in the years that had intervened. It was, I suppose, a deliberate forgetting. But then I suppose that is what death does. It makes the forgotten unforgettable.

'So, the thing is, that's what I just don't understand. I mean, where she was . . .' Alexandra looks down, her voice failing. 'She had no car. And it's such a long way from her house. It just . . . it doesn't make sense to me.'

'Did you see her that day?'

Alexandra nods slowly, a hesitation to the movement. 'Yes. We were . . . it was the church, you see, we were having a fete, a fundraiser – she came there, to the church, to see me. Said that she would help. But she was, I don't know, quiet, almost like she wasn't really there, you know?'

'Did you ask her why?' I ask.

Alexandra looks down, biting her lip, and when her voice comes it is rough-edged and worn. 'I was going to. I could see that she wasn't right, that something was just off. You see, Emily and me, we're very close, and she tells me every-thing, so of course I was going to ask her about it. But then . . .' Her voice shakes, 'I was busy. It's not much of an excuse, is it? For a mother not to talk to her daughter? But that was all it was – I was too busy to pay attention. I made myself feel better by saying that she was okay really, just a bit quiet, and everyone gets days like that, don't they? And Emily, she's such a one for putting a brave face on things, always managing to muster a smile. I told myself that she was tired, it was just that. She didn't stay too long. She told me that she was going out, was meeting a friend in town. She didn't say who, though, and I . . .' her voice shrinks until it is barely there, 'I didn't ask.'

'Probably someone from work.' Jeff's voice is so quiet, it would be easy to miss it. Looks up at me. 'She's very popular at work.'

'She's a nurse.' Alexandra raises her chin. 'Did you know? In Mount Pleasant Hospital. She's very good. Very, very popular.'

I glance across at the mantelpiece, at the pictures of Emily. A pudgy baby. A teenager, blonde curls sitting on her shoulders. A woman in her nurse's uniform, a gold cross just visible at her neck. 'You must be very proud of her.'

'Very proud.' Alexandra isn't looking at me, is talking over my shoulder to her daughter on the mantelpiece.

I had sat in the car, in the street where I used to live. Had watched as seagulls swirled overhead. Had called Aden.

'Hey. It's Charlie.' In case he didn't know. Which, in fairness, was reasonable. I mean, we rarely talked on the phone.

'Hey.' Aden had sounded surprised. Pleased. 'How are you?'

'I'm okay. Look, I wanted to give you a heads-up. Steve Lowe came by the office today.' There was silence on the line, seemed like I could hear his head sinking into his hands. 'Steve Lowe, he's . . . he's not happy, with the IPCC findings. He's . . . they're filing a civil suit.'

I wondered if he was holding his breath.

Then a soft sigh. 'Yeah, the training sergeant told me. Just when you think it's over, eh?'

My stomach writhed. I could see Aden sitting on the kerb, head in his hands, in the pouring rain. The darkness cut with blue lights. Wanted to reach down, hold his hands, but I knew that wasn't appropriate, so I didn't. Just held the umbrella above him. A paltry offering. 'It won't be you. They won't be coming after you, Ade.'

'No. I know you're right. I'm lucky, I guess.' A little laugh that he didn't mean. 'Look, thanks for calling, Charlie. I really appreciate you wanting to let me know.'

'You know people are saying she must have been drunk?' Alexandra isn't looking at me. Still staring at Emily in the silver frame, the nurse's uniform, Emily's face twisted into an awkward smile, like the last thing she wants is a camera pointed at her. 'They don't say it to my face – not when they think I can hear them – but I hear them talking. They say that she must have got drunk, wandered onto the motorway.' She looks back at me, pleading. 'It's not true. It can't be.'

'Did Emily ever drink?'

'Not a fan of the stuff,' offered Jeff.

'I mean, she wasn't teetotal or anything,' added Alexandra, 'and I'm sure she did occasionally have a drink, but she wouldn't have got drunk. She's just not that kind of girl.'

'I see.' I find myself thinking that parents so rarely know all there is to know about their children.

'She was a Christian. We all are.' Alexandra Wilson releases her grip on my hand, turning the cross over in her fingers, her movements distant, unconscious. 'Our faith, it's very important to us. And there was another thing.' She sits up a little, the thought bringing her to life again. 'Her necklace. They never found it.'

'Her . . .'

'Her necklace. She had a gold chain with the word "Emily" on it. We bought it for her when she turned twenty-one. But when . . . when they found her, she wasn't wearing it.' Alexandra leans closer to me, voice confidential. 'She always wore that necklace. I don't understand where it went.'

I frown. 'It wasn't in her house?'

She shakes her head. 'We looked, didn't we, Jeff? We searched everywhere. I just don't understand where it went.'

I hesitate for a moment, making a mental note, then take a breath. Steeling myself. 'Can I ask . . . ? There was an incident at the hospital. The night before Emily's accident.'

Alexandra nods. 'Yes. She said something, didn't go into details. Just said they'd had a couple of problems with a visitor, that she'd had to call the police.' She looks away, thinks for a minute. 'It's odd, though.'

'What is?'

'Well, it really upset her. Said she couldn't sleep at all that night. I thought that was strange because Emily . . . she's, well, unflappable. Very calm. I was surprised that it bothered her the way it did.' She isn't looking at me now, is looking over my shoulder at the picture of her daughter. 'I gave her some of my sleeping tablets. Told her to try those – you know, just so she could get a good night in, before she went back to work.'

I nod, trying not to let my face give me away. Because now all I can think is: was that it? Was that what killed her? Did she take more pills than she should have? Did she have a bad reaction? Find herself confused, disoriented, and begin walking, ending up on the M4? Could it really just have been a coincidence? The gunman, her death. And then the piece that I just can't make fit: if the gunman had been there for Emily, why did he go back? What was the point of returning on that second night, when Emily was already dead?

'I think that's the worst thing, though,' said Mrs Wilson. 'These things people are saying about her – about her being drunk. Her patients are hearing that, her friends, people at our church. They're hearing all these things about her. All she is, all the wonderful things she's done, it will all be washed away, and all people will remember is this. That she died because she was drunk.' She grips my hands again, nails digging into the flesh on my palms. 'This wasn't her. It wasn't her. She wouldn't have done that. Something else happened that day.'

16

Aden: Wednesday 27 August, 7.45 a.m.
Four days before the shooting

Aden swung the Armed Response Vehicle to the left, pulling
into the hospital car park, and joined the queue of cars
waiting at the barrier. It was rarely used, this barrier,
normally unmanned, cars simply coming and going. But it
was all change now. A security guard, young with rippling
muscles under a too-snug shirt, waiting with a flat face, a
steady stare, like he could dissuade a gunman by his expression
alone.

'Here we go again,' murmured Rhys.

'Yup.' Aden eased the car forward, suppressing a sigh as
the silver Picasso in front stalled, the driver fumbling to
restart. 'Starting to feel like I live here.'

It was early, the sun still low across the bay, but it was
warm. They had predicted storms on the news, had said
that the sky would split apart, bringing with it torrential
rain and sheet lightning. It had felt like a reprieve – the
thought of rain, a break from the heat. But it hadn't come,
there had been no reprieve, but instead a constant, relentless march of heat. Aden drummed his fingers against the

outside of the car door, feeling the pads of his fingertips burn. He and Rhys had worked the night shift. A quiet night, lots of time to sit around, to think. He rubbed his hands across his eyes, feeling them prickle and burn. Another couple of hours, then they would be done. Aden tried not to think about his bed waiting for him. The Picasso driver had managed to start its engine, was creeping forward towards the security booth and its grim-faced guard. Aden glanced up at the hospital itself, his eyes finding the second floor, counting the windows. One, two, three, his gaze snagging there.

'Still no sign,' said Rhys.

'Huh?'

'The bloke. The gunman.'

'Yeah, well, you heard about yesterday, yeah?'

'Yesterday?'

'Some woman reported seeing him in the hospital car park. Said that he chased her. The team onsite did a search for him, but nothing.' Aden shrugged. 'Think they thought she was imagining it. You know how it is: people hear the stories, get all excited about them, and suddenly everyone they see has a gun. Whoever he is, he vanishes like Lord Lucan.' The Picasso was waved forward, moving into the car park with an awkward, jolting motion, and Aden slid the ARV up to the barrier, looking up at the security guard. 'All right, mate?'

The man was younger than he looked from a distance, couldn't have been older than nineteen, twenty at most, his head shaved close, the creeping darkness of a tattoo snaking its way from beneath the arm of his short-sleeved shirt. He leaned in, a sudden smile breaking across his face, eyeing the marked car, their uniforms hungrily. 'All right, boys.

''ow's it goin'? God, there's bloody tons of you lot about the place. More coppers than doctors now.'

Aden smiled. 'It's the canteen, mate. We can't get enough of it.'

'Well, look now, lads. I don't want you to worry, okay? The bosses, now, they've had a good look at security. Between you and me, the old ones, like that Ernie, they're on their uppers, they won't be long for the job. I mean, they just can't be, can they? Too old and slow. The bosses 'ave made a bunch of us fitter ones up to full-time, so we can catch this bastard.' The security guard pushed himself up, folding his arms across his chest, and Aden suddenly thought how young he looked, how hopelessly clueless. 'We'll get him now, for sure.' He gave a firm nod, the muscles in his arms flexing.

'That's great.' Aden nodded, deliberately not looking at Rhys. 'Good news. Well, we'd better get going.'

'Oh yeah, boys, on your way.' The barrier swung up and the security guard leaned back in, a sudden overpowering smell of Lynx filling the car. 'And don't forget, right – give me a call if you need anything.'

'Will do, mate. Thanks.' Aden pulled the car forward with a wave. He could feel Rhys grinning.

'Wannabe firearms officer, by any chance?'

Aden glanced in the mirror, could see the security guard standing, legs akimbo, watching them drive away, oblivious to the line of cars behind him. 'I'd say so.'

Rhys shook his head, voice quiet. 'Should try doing the damn job. Might figure out then it's not all guns and women and fast cars.'

Aden glanced at Rhys, his gaze far-off. Thought of the night of the shooting, after it was over and they were safe, back in the debriefing room, sitting around on hard plastic chairs, sipping water-weak coffee, the air thick with suspended belief. You talked about this. You trained for this. They told you what would happen when it happened. *If* it happened. Then, just like that, you were sitting there, on those ridiculous chairs, and it had happened, and now everything was different. Aden would remember the smell afterwards, cigarette smoke drifting in as the door opened, closed, trapping it inside. Would remember Tony, his voice clambering back into the room along with his cigarette smoke, reliving the shooting, Welsh and loud; seemed like he couldn't stop talking about it, his words repeating themselves, over and over. Rhys sitting beside him, his head in his hands, looking so much younger all of a sudden, as if he has shot backwards in time, now a schoolboy playing dress-up in an overlarge police uniform. Aden would remember his own fingers shaking so that the coffee slopped against the rim of the cup, pulled by an invisible tide.

He should have said something. He had thought that a lot, afterwards. He should have patted Rhys on the arm, should have said something. Aden was his teacher. Had been partnered with Rhys because he was young and new, and Aden really should have said something, should have done the job he'd been given to do. But, on that night, his mouth – like his trigger finger – simply wouldn't move. He had failed. Had known that, before the muzzle-flash had died away, before the ringing in his ears from the cacophony of sound had finally stopped. He had failed and was now no longer entitled to say anything.

Funny how so much can change, in the space of an hour, a minute. How your whole world can be upended by one simple inaction, so that afterwards it seems like there has been a death and that it is you, or who you thought you were, who has died.

'You doing okay?' Aden tried to keep the words light, as if they weren't really asking what they were asking. Didn't look at Rhys, just concentrated on steering the car, slipping it into the area that had become the hospital's unofficial police parking site. So he sensed rather than saw the shrug.

'This doesn't help,' said Rhys, quietly. 'Being here. I mean, it's with me a lot anyway, but with this . . .' He shook his head. 'It's all I can damned well think about.'

'Yeah,' Aden murmured. 'Me too.' A stealthy silence crept over the car, words sucked away by the torpid air. Aden's gaze tugging upwards to the second floor, third window across, to Dylan Lowe's room. 'You ever wonder why?'

'Why . . . ?'

'Why he did it. The kid, I mean.' Easier somehow to refer to him that way. 'The kid' – like he wasn't a real person, like it wouldn't sting so much then. 'I mean, it doesn't seem to fit in with the kind of person he was. I looked up his police record, after it happened. Clean as a whistle, nothing. The newspapers, they make him sound like he was some kind of choir boy.'

Aden had slept late, the morning following the shooting. Or rather had lain awake, had finally slipped into some kind of uneasy rest somewhere around dawn. When he awoke, the paper – a national that he had long since stopped subscribing to – had been waiting for him on the mat. The dead boy's face staring up at him. Aden had stopped, there in the front porch, with his bare feet and his head spinning like he had been on a two-day bender. Had stared at it. Seemed like it must be some kind of sick joke. But there was no one there, and it was certainly not funny. Aden had sunk to the floor, sitting in his underpants in the cold, tiled hallway. Had pulled the paper towards him.

That was how he had learned that the boy wasn't dead. Was in some kind of coma. The details were foggy on that point. But he was in Mount Pleasant Hospital. In intensive care. Aden had sat for a long time, staring at Dylan Lowe – long, lean, the gawky angles of puberty, bone pushing against skin that hadn't yielded yet. Dark eyes, hair shaved down to the scalp around the sides, the top spiked. His face round, soft curves, still that of a child.

The face of an angel, the papers had said. The tragedy of a child.

Aden had scanned the story, knowing that he shouldn't, that this would not help. Dylan was a good boy, said friends and teachers, had no history of violence, nothing that you could point to and say 'There, right there, that's where the trouble began.' The boy's parents were pictured in front of their council house, standing arm-in-arm, faces set into a made-for-papers grief. The mother thin, hair pulled back flat against her head. Father, his eyes blistering with anger. *We've lost our child. The police have destroyed our family.*

Rhys looked at him then, his gaze steadier than Aden would have expected. 'To be honest, I never read the newspapers. Or watched the news. I just . . . couldn't.'

Aden nodded, watching as a young couple trooped slowly past the ARV, the woman's belly swollen and ripe, her steps unsteady. 'That's probably sensible. I kept the paper, the one from the shooting. Just couldn't seem to get rid of it. I don't know, sometimes I think I'm almost obsessed with the whole thing.'

Rhys frowned. 'I'm guessing you haven't told Imogen that? Or the sarge?'

Aden let out a laugh that felt forced. 'Nah. I mean, it's not like I'm stalking the kid or anything.'

'You sure you're not the gunman then?' Rhys's voice had taken on a faux-serious edge, his eyes sparkling.

Aden grinned. 'Not this time.' The couple were crossing the road now, heading to the maternity unit, the woman's steps getting slower and slower, the man's face creasing up in worry. 'It just . . . it makes you think, doesn't it?'

'What does?'

'The gun. The one Dylan used.'

'What about it?'

They had been waiting for the debrief, Tony standing, looking out of the window as he bounced on the balls of his feet, like he just couldn't bear to sit down. 'Thing is, these Browning HPs, Second World War guns,' Tony had said, 'they're all over the place. You know how it is. Granddad brings it back from the war, shoves it in a box in the attic. No one ever knows it's there, until some little fucker uses it to shoot someone. That's what will have happened.' Tony had nodded, confident. 'You mark my words.'

'Steve Lowe, the kid's father – he said Dylan had no way of getting hold of a Browning, that there wasn't one in the family.'

'Yeah, but it could have come from one of the other kids, the ones we never caught.'

'I guess. But I just wonder . . . the Lowes are a farming family. Got a decent spread up in Rhydypandy. I've dealt with them a few times over the years and they're a solid lot.'

Rhys snorted. 'Steve Lowe's fallen a long way from the family tree then.'

Aden nodded. 'You're not wrong. They've got another son. Decent bloke, helps his father on the farm. But Steve . . .'

Aden had been called to the Lowe family farm once, years ago when he was still in uniform, the mother crying as Steve bellowed into the face of his smaller, thinner father. He was just, he was so angry. He just erupted. You never saw it coming. Had arrested Steve for breach of the peace, listened as he threw himself against the cell door, spitting a venomous tirade. Steve was a mechanic now, or something like that. Had settled in a council house in Harddymaes with his narrow-faced, downtrodden wife.

'The thing is,' Aden said, 'the kid would have had access to shotguns. The Lowe family has a licence. If he wanted a gun, why not take one of those?'

Rhys shrugged. 'Maybe Grandma and Gramps are a bit more careful than whichever family let their kid play with the family's Second World War weaponry. Who knows.' He pushed himself upright, hand on the car door. 'Shall we?'

Aden, still seeing the boy lying in the puddled rain, the iron-grey gun fallen beside him, nodded. 'Yeah, let's get on with it.'

They were just climbing out of the car when they saw Charlie, a mid-length summer dress swirling around her knees, her hair pulled up into a loose bun. Aden felt his stomach flutter.

'Hey.'

Charlie looked up, startled. 'Hi. I didn't expect to see you guys here. Hey, Rhys. How's it going?'

Rhys nodded, his gaze captured on something fascinating somewhere around the level of her knees. 'Good. Thanks.'

Aden grinned. 'What are you doing here?'

She was wearing lipstick, something that struck him as

odd. After all, when he saw her swimming she wore no make-up, her hair tugged back into a ponytail. But now she looked different, softer.

'I, ah . . . I have an appointment.' Her gaze fixed on Aden's, the look meaningful. Imogen. 'There was no point in me going home after swimming, so I'm going to pop and visit Ernie before he finishes. Grab a cuppa.'

'Right.'

It was getting awkward, Rhys shuffling uncomfortably from side to side.

Charlie smiled brightly. 'Okay, so I'll see you guys anyway.'

'See you, Charlie.' Aden watched as she turned, the low sun catching on her chocolate-brown hair, and vanished through the hospital doors.

17

Imogen: Wednesday 27 August, 7.45 a.m.
Four days before the shooting

Imogen slid bread into the toaster, pushing on the lever. She had spoken to her sister early, had called, just to check in. 'Amy's doing fine.' It had seemed that Mara's voice was lighter than it had been in days. 'There have been no more seizures. The doctors are really happy with her progress. Let's just hope the gunman doesn't come back – that's the only thing I worry about now.'

The kitchen smelled of coffee, the percolator bubbling quietly in the corner. Imogen glanced up, her gaze drawn by Dave's footsteps on the stairs. He wasn't looking at her, hair still wet from the shower, his attention focused on the phone in his hand. Frowning.

'You okay?'

'Huh . . . oh, yeah.'

'You trying to call someone?' Imogen pulled plates out of the cupboard, glanced around for the butter knife.

'No. Just checking my emails, that's all.'

Imogen nodded, tried not to sigh. It was an obsession with Dave, that phone of his; rare that he ever let it out of his fingers, let alone his sight. It was a guy-thing, that was what she told herself. 'Coffee?'

'Yeah.' He snapped the television on, pulling the dining chair free from beneath the kitchen table. 'Do we have cream?'

'Um . . . no. I can try and get some later.'

He pulled two cups from the mug stand, poured the thick black liquid in a steady stream. 'It's okay. Milk will do.'

'I—' Imogen's sentence began and finished, her attention caught by the television screen, the block form of Mount Pleasant Hospital. Her stomach somersaulting suddenly, the instant thought that something had happened since she had spoken to Mara, that there was more bad news.

The reporter stood in front of the lobby doors, seemed oblivious to the smokers behind her watching the cameras curiously. 'Police are no closer to finding the gunman that they say has been stalking the halls of Mount Pleasant Hospital. Despite three sightings, it seems there are no signs of an arrest.'

The scene changed, a cut-away to a hospital corridor. Imogen recognised it instantly. Could see the sign for Ward 12 in the background. It was ironic that it took her longer to recognise herself.

'Yesterday the gunman pursued this lady, Mara Elliott-Lewis, through the car park. "Mara, how did you feel when that happened?"'

It coalesced then, the image that she was seeing. Her sister standing in front of the ward door, a tentative smile, her hair tucked back behind her ears, a hint of make up. 'It was terrifying. It really was. I mean, we had heard the stories that he had been seen, but of course you never think someone like that could target you.'

'So what did you do?' The reporter's voice was breathless.

Mara shrugged, a quick glance to the camera. 'I ran. Fortunately he didn't follow me into the hospital itself, but . . .' She left it there, the implications of what could have happened hanging heavily. 'I mean, you bring your children here, thinking they will be taken care of, that it is a place where you can be safe. You never think that something like this could happen.'

The footage snapped away then, returning to the reporter, her face impassive as she stood before the lobby doors. 'Police say they are deploying substantial resources towards finding this individual and that, at the moment, there is no need for alarm. Mount Pleasant Hospital, Sharon Elderwood.'

Imogen stood, staring at the screen.

'Bloody hell!' said Dave.

'Yes.'

'Did you know? Did Mara tell you?'

'That she was on TV? No.'

The toaster popped loudly, a slice of overdone bread leaping onto the counter. Imogen grabbed for it, without thinking.

Dave shook his head. 'It's mad, mind. All this. I mean, it must have scared the crap out of Mara.'

Imogen thought of that moment in the lobby, her sister flying into her arms, that feeling of her heart pounding against Imogen's own. 'Yes. She . . . It was awful.'

'Wonder who the hell it is, then?'

Imogen pulled the butter closer, began to smear it over the toast. Tried to push away the crowding thoughts. So what if Mara had an affair. People did. It wasn't good, but it happened. That didn't necessarily mean it had anything to do with her sister flying into the hospital lobby, terrified, with this unknown man chasing her. Imogen swept the golden butter so that it lined up against the ends, so there were no dry cracks. And yes, it wasn't the first time Mara had done it. There had been that fling when Amy was six months old, ex-army guy – the one Mara had said had been a dreadful mistake, that she had ended unceremoniously. That couldn't have anything to do with this. Why wait so long, if you were angry? Imogen slid the toast onto a plate, handed it to Dave, reached for another slice. Felt the guilt nestling inside her. She kept her sister's secrets. She was her twin. That was her job. Did that make her just as guilty? And if it worked out that the cost of those secrets was higher than either of them had ever imagined, would that mean Imogen was culpable as well?

Imogen made excuses for her sister. She knew that she did, and that to some extent she always had. But she was Mara's sister, her twin, older, healthier. It was, after all, her job to protect her. And Mara was – always had been – the kind of person who needed someone there, needed to be reassured that she was loved, had not been forgotten. A fact that Jack had overlooked when he took the job in Dubai. An awesome opportunity, the chance to experience how another police force ran. It would look good for promotion, could lead to more money. 'Thing is, Im, I just can't pass up a chance like this.' Imogen remembered Mara's face, pulled up into a faux-smile that got nowhere near her eyes, could see the diamond sparkles of tears, could have told Jack then that he was heading for trouble. But she didn't, because Mara was her sister, and Imogen would protect her, whatever the cost.

'So, is Jack actually going to come home now?' asked Dave.

'You need to call Jack.' It was after the police had taken

their statements, after the curious crowd in the hospital lobby had spilled back into their lives. Imogen had tucked her sister's arm into hers, guided her back towards the ward, where Amy waited. 'You need to tell him what's been going on. He is Amy's father, Mara, he deserves to know.'

Mara hadn't spoken at first. Had clutched Imogen's arm, like a child on her first day of school. 'I can't, Im. Not right now.'

Imogen had stopped then, pulling away, a sudden un-familiar feeling shaking her – anger. 'Why, Mara? What aren't you telling me? It's about him, isn't it? Your boy-friend.' The word felt like a glass shard in her mouth, piercing her tongue.

Mara hadn't looked at her, had folded her arms around herself, seemed to wince almost, and turned away. 'You don't understand anything. I just . . . I don't want to talk about it.'

Imogen took a bite of cold toast now. Chewed slowly. 'Dave?'

'Yeah?' He was sitting at the table, playing with his phone.

'I . . . I've been thinking.' A deep breath, courage. 'About the wedding.'

Dave looked up at her, studying her, and Imogen felt her breath catching in her throat. 'I was just wondering if maybe you wanted to, I don't know, set a date?'

It felt like such uneven ground, the words that had been trapped within her head finally eking out. He didn't say anything; seemed like a lifetime within which there was only the drip of the percolator, the chatter of the television, and Imogen reached out to hold onto the kitchen counter, wondering if this was it, if her words had precipitated the fracture she had feared.

Then he smiled. 'Yeah, let's do it. Why don't you bring your diary home tonight and we'll have a sit-down, see what we can work out?'

Imogen felt herself flush, relief making her dizzy. 'Oh, okay – well, I have it here. I mean, not here. It's online. Let me just . . .' She flipped open the lid of the laptop, keeping her eyes averted from him. Because if she looked at him now, then he might see the fear, the way it had rushed into her from nowhere that she could define. Her fingers fumbled against the keyboard.

The computer screen filled up with a picture of Amy. And a narrow box.

'Dave? What's this?'

'What?'

'The computer. It won't let me in.'

A long silence, and Imogen glanced at Dave, thinking that he hadn't heard her. There was a look on his face: a boy caught throwing stones, a brief flit of an expression, gone as quickly as it came. Then, 'I set up password protection. I did it for you too. Your usual password. AmyMara1. Hardly hacker central. Just change the username at the top.'

There was an uneasy feeling in Imogen's stomach, a premonition of things to come. 'Can't I just use yours? What's your password?' She said it, her voice a little breathless, like she was walking along a narrow ridge, could slip at any time.

Something flew across his face, a flash of irritation. 'Imogen, it's not rocket science.' His voice was hard-edged now. 'Just change the username.'

Imogen sat, her fingers frozen above the keys. The feeling nestling in her that something had been confirmed, that she just didn't know what.

Silence settled between them then. The quiet after a storm. Imogen pressed the keys slowly, movements stilted. She wanted to cry. It wasn't meant to be like this. When you were engaged, and supposed to be getting married and planning on starting a family. It wasn't supposed to look like this.

It was Dave who punctured the silence first. 'You know,' he said, 'I'm not being funny, but Jack's a prick.'

Imogen paused, her fingers hanging above the keys, thoughts dislocating with the speed of the conversation change. 'What?'

'Well, I'm saying. If Mara was my wife, no way would I be in bloody Dubai.'

Imogen stared as the Google image filled the screen. *If Mara was my wife.*

18

Charlie: Wednesday 27 August, 9.05 a.m.
Four days before the shooting

'You came back.'

'I did.' I smooth my dress down, the purple thread of it curling back on itself.

'I wasn't sure that you would.'

I give a laugh, shift in my seat, studying the hem. It's beginning to unravel, a single thread breaking free from the mass of it. 'I'm still hoping you'll give me those sleeping tablets.'

Imogen smiles. Not a professional smile: the kind that sits just at the lips, lasting that little bit longer than it should. A proper smile. 'You know that I can't prescribe.'

I nod. A little laugh. 'I know.' I look down at the hem again, rolling back in on itself. I don't know why I came. Don't know why I came the first time, or the second time, or why I kept coming. I just wanted sleeping tablets, something to take the edge off the endless hours watching the clock tick around. One o'clock, two. Studying the patchwork of digital lines, the realisation – after hours of watching – that a line is missing, so that an 8 becomes a 6. Then thinking how ridiculous it was that this was how I spent the night hours of my life. Falling into an uneasy sleep, somewhere around three. Then the dreams. Always the same. The casket the colour of polished chocolate. The weeping strangers that crowd around it.

'I'm glad you did.' Imogen smiles again, balancing a notepad on her knee, pen poised, waiting to capture the brilliance that will surely spill from my mouth. She's a thin woman, the kind of skinny that comes with nervous energy, flame-red hair tied neatly at the nape of her neck.

I went to the doctor, got a last-minute appointment with a locum GP in my surgery, a narrow woman with a long swishy skirt, thick-soled shoes. Can I have some sleeping tablets? She gave me a long look over narrow glasses. Why do you need sleeping tablets? I bit back the sarcasm that sat on my tongue. Managed a sweet smile, in case it would help. I'm having trouble sleeping. She gave me a long look, canted her head to one side. What I'm reluctant to do, Charlotte, is treat the symptoms rather than the underlying problem.

I really wanted to roll my eyes.

We have a wonderful counsellor here. She rolled the word 'counsellor', adding in another syllable where there shouldn't be one. She leaned forward, lowered her voice conspiratorially. She's a good friend of mine.

Yeah. Not a chance.

I had mentioned it to Aden, one day in the pool as we were resting between swim sets. Had presented it as an anecdote: insomnia, the twenty-first century disease. But he hadn't laughed, had watched me as I talked, his eyes red-rimmed from the chlorine. I know someone who can help. She's a psychologist. She's good. He'd looked away then, down the swim lane, like he was giving me a chance to think about it without his presence. She won't be able to prescribe anything, but she may be able to help, if you . . . you know. Had turned, looked back at me, a bead of chlorinated water rolling down his forehead. She's my psychologist. Because of the shooting.

'So,' says Imogen, 'how have you been sleeping?'

I shrug, pull a face. 'About the same.'

'The nightmares?'

I nod, go back to rolling up the hem of my dress.

It took me longer than it should to make the connection. After all, Imogen isn't a common name. It wasn't until I was in her waiting room with its lavender-coloured walls, neatly lined wood-backed chairs, its crisp green ficus, that I really made the connection with Dave. I had almost run then. The thought of Dave knowing your deepest and darkest secrets is enough to make anyone run like hell. But, for reasons that I still can't explain, I didn't run. I stayed. Maybe it was because there is simply something about her, this narrow woman with the overlarge eyes that seem to lock onto yours, listening to you in a way you have never really been listened to before. Maybe it was the relief of finally allowing my thoughts out. And besides, once I had met her it became unconscionable to me that she would repeat my words to anyone, least of all Dave.

She's watching me. 'You said it was the anniversary of your father's death this week?'

'Monday.'

'Monday.' Imogen nods. A quick note on her pad, fingers pressed white-tight against the biro. Looks back up at me. 'How are you doing with that?'

My thumbnail has cracked again, the result of so much

time in chlorinated water, has split right below the line of skin. I pluck at it, a stinging pain zinging along my thumb. 'Okay, I guess.' Am planning on sitting here, enjoying the companionable silence. But without me meaning to, my mouth spills open. 'I try not to think about it.'

I think instead about yesterday afternoon, what happened before I left the newsroom. I had heard the newsroom door open, my gaze pulled by some kind of sixth sense. Had felt my stomach drop when I saw the narrow outline of Steve Lowe, had braced myself, thinking, 'Here we go again.' But he wasn't looking for me this time. Steve came into the office with a bouncing stride, chin up, so that his lip was curled into an almost sneer. He wasn't looking at me. Was looking at Dave. Dave glanced around from his computer, attention drawn by the sense of being stared at, all colour draining from his face. For a moment I wondered if he was about to cry. Steve stared at him, a hunter looking through a scope. Then he passed us, and although it seemed there should have been relief, I could see Dave's face – the know-ledge that there was worse to come. Steve Lowe walked straight into Lydia's office, closed the door behind him. Then it seemed that everyone was watching Dave, because whether they saw it or heard about it – a newsroom is a fermenting pot for gossip – it seemed that everyone knew about Dave going toe-to-toe with Steve Lowe. Trying to work, but in reality watching the clock and watching Dave, who was sinking lower and lower in his chair. Then, after twenty-seven minutes, the door swung open and Steve emerged with that bouncing stride. Smiling.

He had slowed as he reached us. Had looked at Dave, fingers forming the shape of a gun that he pointed at Dave's head. A soft, whispered 'Pow!'

'Do you think that helps?' Imogen's voice startles me.
'What?'

'You know, not thinking about it. Do you think it helps?'

I pluck at the nail. It's going to catch on everything now, tugging at threads so that it pulls everything apart. 'I guess. I mean, it was a long time ago. You can't spend every day crying over it, can you? You have to just get on with things.' Then, apropos of nothing, 'My mother, she says I put my father on a pedestal. That no one is perfect.'

'Do you think that's true?'

'I guess. I mean, you never really know anyone, do you? People – they don't show you who they really are. They show you what they think you want to see.'

Imogen smiles a little. Another quick note. 'That's rather cynical, Charlie.'

I shrug. 'It's true, though, isn't it?' I nibble at the nail, a sharp pain as it rips, tearing at my skin. 'I mean, like this girl who was in school with me. Did you hear about it? The woman who died on the M4?'

Imogen nods.

'Well, we were friends. In school, you know. I knew her well. I mean, it had been a few years, we grew apart – you know how it is. But still, I thought I knew her; the kind of person she was, I mean. But what happened to her, the way she died . . . It doesn't make sense, just wandering onto the M4 like that. There's talk that she was drunk, but . . . I don't know, I just don't want to think that of her, you know?'

Imogen allows the silence to spool out, puddling around our feet. I can hear the clock ticking, the distant sound of voices. I cup the remnant of my thumbnail in the palm of my hand, feeling it scratch against my skin.

Then Imogen shifts. 'I think that, to a certain extent, what you said is true. I mean, we all put our best face forward, show others what we want them to see.'

I nod.

'But, that said, I also think that when you are very close to someone, you can often know precisely who they are.'

I must be looking doubtful. Like I said, I'd be a rubbish poker-player.

'Don't you think that's true? That this is the very nature of close relationships? That we learn who others are – who they really are – and we allow them to see who we are too.'

'I guess.' My thoughts flutter, struggling to settle anywhere, a butterfly in a strong breeze. Words form, a sentence that I know I'm not going to say. How the hell would I ever know this? I've never been in a relationship long enough for it to happen. I've never allowed myself to be in a relationship long enough.

My hand goes to my necklace, a cheap silver thing that I picked up somewhere for a tenner. And I think of Emily's necklace. Where did it go? How is it that she ended up dead on the side of the road without it? I think of the covered body, the blue flashing lights, the figure of the gunman on CCTV. And it strikes me that I am not working with facts. I am searching for that which I want to find. Because, if I am honest, I want to think that she was murdered. I want to think there is a connection between her death and the gunman at her door. I don't want to believe that Emily died because she was drunk and stupid, that life can be so wasteful. I don't want to think good people can be so foolish. Even though I know they can be. That anyone can, given the right set of circumstances.

19

The Shooter: Saturday 30 August, 1.05 p.m.
Day before the shooting

It is raining. The weather has finally broken, great sheets of rain driving into my windscreen. I'm going home. I'm going home because it is my mother's birthday and it is expected and that is what you do.

I pull up at a red light, the rain washing it out so that it appears to run, bleeding. The *Swansea Times* offices are beside me, lights breaking through the gathering darkness. I look, then look away. I don't want to see them. Allow my gaze to trickle down to the road, and my eyes arrest on a figure in the doorway. Charlie stands on the front steps. She is squinting through the rain, watching something that I can't see. Then suddenly she is running, down the front steps, out into the roadway, seems almost like she hasn't noticed the pouring rain. She runs, and she is heading for something, although I cannot see what it is.

The light turns to green. I pull away.

I ease the car through the built-up streets, filled with quiet houses, families at peace. I know these streets. Grew up in them. Built a den from fallen branches, some discarded plastic sheeting, a cardboard box buckled and warped with the weather, in the park just there. Fell from my bike, a tumble turning over the red-wrapped handlebars, sparking pain down my cheek, my knee ice-cold, blood seeping through the denim, on that road right there.

I pull up outside the house, climb slowly from the car. They are all there, I can see them through the windows, and it seems to me that this is how it has always been: me on the outside, looking in. I see my sisters, Courtney and Leila and Beth. My brother, William, still in his suit, looks like he is fresh from work. Courtney's kids, all three of them, so loud that the roar of them echoes in the street. Seems impossible that they ever draw breath. I stand there, for long moments, and I ponder changing my mind, just turning and walking away. But they have seen me, are looking my way. So I walk down the drive, let myself in through the front door.

My mother has roasted a joint of beef, the house thunders with the smell of garlic and rosemary. She looks up as I walk in, gives me a smile that lifts me. She is beautiful, my mother. Larger than she should be, rolls of fat where there should be flat skin, but such softness. Her smile can fracture the chaos, feels like a sunbeam in the middle of a storm. And maybe that's why I came here today. Because there is so much darkness that I desperately need to see the sun.

'How are you, my love?' my mother asks.

I open my mouth. I'm not sure what it is that I will say, here in the living room full of sound, but then the moment has passed and someone has pulled my mother away, and I am left standing. The sun vanished behind a cloud.

The table is set with my mother's good china. There is

dinner, roast beef, mashed potatoes, home-made Yorkshire pudding. A glass of rosé to toast the day. My mother raising a glass, a brief moment of silence at the overcrowded table. 'To your dad. Always with us.'

Leila wiping a tear from her eye, and I feel an urge to roll my eyes, because all I can think of are the screaming rows she had with my father, when he looked at her with her short skirts and low-cut tops, his lip curled in disgust. William purses his lips, and the children look to one another as if they are unsure what comes next. I stare at my plate, the cooling gravy forming patterns of grease. Think of my father with his large frame, larger anger. There are no tears.

Then the moment passes, and is forgot, and there are birthday presents to be opened, the children leaping from sofa to sofa while Courtney texts. Beth has bought my mother a scarf, bright with flowers, lays it around her neck like a lei. I watch as my mother pulls Beth close, kissing her cheek, think how alike they are. The same aquiline nose, same wide hips. It is in William too; he has my mother's eyes, my father's frame.

I move mashed potato around my plate, study it like I will find meaning in its patterns. Glance up at Courtney. She and Leila are a matching pair almost. Separated by two years, dense black hair, the same eyes, same lily-white skin. It has always been the same in this house, that there are sets, people who belong together. And then me.

My mother looks around the table, smiles. 'Well, this is lovely, isn't it?'

20

Charlie: Wednesday 27 August, 12.15 p.m.
Four days before the shooting

The police station is quiet, the air thick and heavy. I walk past open doors, offices with empty chairs, computers left humming quietly. It's lunchtime, and those who can have flocked their way out into the thundering sunshine. I check my visitor pass, adjust the cord so that it sits mid-navel.

Del is seated in the sergeant's office, little more than a cupboard. The window pushed open, an inch if that – hinges taut, won't give any further. He has rolled the sleeves of his uniform shirt up, beads of sweat standing proud across his forehead, and for a moment he doesn't see me, is typing on his keyboard, tongue protruding from between his teeth, fingers moving ponderously, awkward.

'Del.'

He glances up at me, squinting. 'Oh God!'

I fold my arms, lean against the doorframe. 'Now, Del. Be nice.'

'You're stalking me. Aren't you? I'm telling you, my missus is going to be pissed.' He pushes his chair away from the computer, grinning.

'Your missus is going to be friggin' astonished.'

Del laughs. 'You know, you . . . you're a real charmer.'

I shrug. 'That's what all the teachers at my finishing school said. How are you? How's Mrs Del? Any sign of her popping?'

Del groaned. 'Oh, she's a nightmare. She's huge, seriously pissed off. I'm telling you, I'm in hell.'

I pull a face. 'Poor you. You really are the unseen victim.'

'Right.' Del shakes his head, then frowns, glances behind me. 'How the hell did you get in here anyway? Do you actually work here now?'

I grin. 'What can I say? People like me.'

Del scoffs. 'No, they don't. Anyway,' he gestures to the chair tucked into the corner of the small office, 'what do you want this time?'

I slip into the chair, crossing my legs in front of me. Suddenly aware that my stomach is churning. 'Emily.'

Del sighs, leaning forward on his desk. 'Yeah, that's shit. Did you hear? Funeral's a week Friday.'

I nod. 'I heard. Del, there was something I wanted to ask.'

'Go on.'

'There are rumours. People saying that she was drunk.'

Del sighs again. 'I have no idea how this stuff gets out. I really don't. Look, there were a few witnesses. The couple in the car that hit her. The other car on the scene. They said she was staggering.' He shrugs, like it's just another day's tragedy. One more person who isn't who you think they are. Del moves the mouse across the desk, computer screen lighting up. 'I mean, I've got the police report here. It's tragic. The couple in the car, the one that hit her, they're just devastated. Say she wandered right out in front of them. They were overtaking another car, so the husband estimates they were doing maybe seventy miles per hour. Poor sod didn't stand a chance.'

I look at him. 'What lane were they in?'

He glances up at me, a brief frown, then looks back at the screen. 'Ah, I don't know if they . . . no, hang on. Here it is. Centre lane. They were overtaking a car on the inside lane.'

'So . . . Emily came from the central reservation?'

He looks at me blankly.

'No, I'm just saying – I thought she was walking along the hard shoulder. But if she had been, she'd have staggered out in front of the car on the inside lane. The one they were overtaking.'

Del looks back at the screen, stares. 'I guess.'

'So how did she get there? You know, if she had just wandered onto the M4, then surely she would have been walking along the inside lane. Wouldn't she?' I suddenly become aware that I am biting my nails. 'Unless she came from a car. Unless someone dropped her in the centre of the carriageway.'

Del shakes his head. 'Charlie, look . . .' A pause as he considers, then another sigh. 'Okay, I'm not supposed to show you this. So this is just between you and me. Okay?'

'Okay.'

'Toxicology is back.'

'Already? You're kidding?'

'Someone put a rush on it. I couldn't believe it myself.'

I take a breath. 'Was it sleeping tablets?'

'What? No.' Del sighs. 'Look, Charlie. Her blood alcohol levels – they were pretty high. One hundred and ten milli-grams of alcohol per hundred millilitres of blood. Bear in mind that the drink-drive limit is eighty milligrams. She was drunk. If she wasn't much of a drinker . . .'

'Her family says she isn't.'

'Well, in that case the amount of alcohol in her blood-stream would have been enough to make her pretty loaded. Maybe enough that she wouldn't have realised what she was doing, where she was walking.' Del studies me. 'I spoke to some of the boys in Traffic, the ones who did the follow-up investigation. She spent the night in some bar, looked to be drunk when she left. Look, I know this isn't what you want to hear and, believe me, I'm as surprised as you are. I mean, I wasn't friends with her in school or anything, but she seemed a nice girl. But then, Charlie, you just never know. Lots of people aren't who you first think they are. If you're asking me for my professional opinion, it looks like she was out partying, that she decides to make her way home, takes a wrong turn and ends up on the motorway. She's disoriented, ends up in the centre of the carriageway. She could have come from the hard shoulder. We don't have the CCTV, no one saw her. We just can't say for sure.' Shakes his head. 'I'm sorry, Charlie. I know this isn't what you want to hear.'

'What about her necklace?'

'Huh?'

'She always wore a necklace: gold with the word "Emily" on it. Her parents say it's missing. Did you ever find it?'

Del shakes his head. 'Sorry!'

I sit there for long moments. 'You know about the police report she made on the Sunday night, right? The night before she died? You know she was the first one to report the man with the gun at Mount Pleasant Hospital?'

'I know, Charlie. But there's no connection. There's

nothing to suggest that her death was anything but an accident. Or . . .'

'Or what?'

'Nah – nothing.'

'What?'

He isn't looking at me, is examining his desk, his fingers, anything but me. 'Or she could have done it on purpose.'

I stare at him. 'You mean, suicide?'

He shrugs. 'It's possible.' Then, finally, he looks at me. 'I'm sorry, Charlie.'

It takes me a moment, time to gather myself, think of what Alexandra Wilson had said: that Emily had been quiet, not herself. Could she have been suicidal? And if she had been, was that really the way she would have done it? Then, with Herculean effort, I nod slowly, force a smile, like it really doesn't matter to me. 'No worries.' I push myself up from the seat, limbs loose. 'You going to the funeral?'

Del nods. 'See you there?'

I don't know what I was expecting, coming here today. I'm not sure what it was I wanted to hear. After all, Emily was a grown woman. So she wasn't the girl I remember from school. I'm fairly sure that she'd have said the same about me. And maybe it was all just a coincidence: that she had seen the gunman, that she had called the police and twenty-four hours later was dead.

I'm not looking where I'm going, have walked along the corridor, reached the key-padded door before I even remember where I am. Am just about to turn around, ask Del to let me out, when the door buzzes, is pulled outwards.

Aden is wearing jeans, a loose-fitting shirt. Pulls up when

he sees me, a sudden moment of confusion. 'Hey. What are you doing here?'

'I . . . um.' For a moment I am thrown, can't seem to get my words to line up in the proper order. Then I grin, shrug. 'Had to see a man about a dog.'

He smiles, comforted by the fact that this is the way we're going to play it, easy and loose. 'Don't trust any of the buggers here. They'll sell you a shih-tzu and tell you it's a greyhound.'

His sunglasses are tucked at the collar of his shirt, weighting it down. Sprouts of chest-hair work their way free, like spring shoots reaching for the sun, and it occurs to me how rarely I see him with his clothes on, and this one thought makes me flush. I duck my head, pretend to be glancing at my watch, and curse myself for being such a girl. 'I thought you were on nights last night? Did you sleep?'

Aden shrugs. 'I had a couple of hours, then . . . you know how it is. I'm not great at sleeping in the day. Anyway I'm not stopping.' He nods to himself, like he's answering a question that I haven't asked. 'I left my wallet in my locker this morning.'

'Oh.' I glance over my shoulder. The corridor is still silent, empty but for us and our inane twittering. 'I was going to ask – you seemed a little . . . ah . . . off this morning. Is everything okay? I mean, I know it's tough, what with the civil case and all, but I just thought . . .'

Aden stands there for a moment, not looking at me, and I can see in his eyes that's he's calculating, weighing up the cost/benefit of confiding in me. Then he looks up. 'I just . . . There's something that's been bothering me, and I don't really know what to do with it.'

'Okay.' I widen my stance, nod, waiting.

Aden glances over his shoulder. 'Look, are you . . . I mean, do you have a couple of minutes?'

I don't even look at my watch, know for a fact that I have fifteen minutes to make it to the council meeting, that I'm cutting it fine already. 'Of course.'

21

Aden: Wednesday 27 August, 12.40 p.m.
Four days before the shooting

The heat shimmered above the tarmac on the hill, spilling across the road in front of them. The houses huddled together, seemed to push away the gaze of passing cars, paintwork cracking like too much make-up on an elderly woman. Every now and again, through a gap in the houses, was the sea, a dim and distant shimmer on the horizon. Aden leaned his arm through the open passenger window, heat from above and below, searing. There was a smell, stockpiled rubbish. Bins lined the pavement, spilling nappies and takeaway cartons onto the street. Someone had dragged a television outside, had left it balanced precariously on top of the wall, its glass punched out, a hollow shell left behind. Aden watched as it slipped past, his gaze trickling from the broken-down television to Charlie, one hand loose on the steering wheel, her hair whipping in the breeze.

'I'm sorry about the air conditioning.' She glanced at him, pulled a face. 'I've been meaning to get it fixed.'

Aden smiled. 'It doesn't matter. I like the breeze.'

They had walked in silence out of the still, hot police

station. Aden had smelled her perfume, thought that she smelled of lemon. Had slipped into the lobby, pushed through the people thronging reception, sweat mixing with the sweet tang of alcohol. Through the sticky bodies, out into the street.

Charlie had glanced around. 'So, what's up?'

But then Aden didn't know where to begin. 'I, ah . . .' Wasn't looking at her, was watching the crowd inside the lobby; a perilously thin man, alight with tattoos, gesturing wildly at the receptionist. 'You know the Lowe family, don't you?'

She had looked at him then, curiosity and caution combined. 'I, well – kind of. Why?'

How did he begin to explain? The boy's face, haunting him, filling up his dreams. The muzzle-flash in the darkness, the sound of a body crumpling to the ground. How did he begin to explain that it is all he could think of, that his brain was twisting it, turning it constantly round and round, trying to make it fit. What would make the boy – a good boy, a steady boy – turn, levelling a gun at firearms officers. And now, this patrolling the hospital, the same hospital where Dylan Lowe lay, night after night, waiting for a man with a gun, for the other shoe to drop. And all the while Aden's brain trying to make sense of the fact that his trigger finger had stayed resolutely still, while the night lit up around him. That he had failed.

Charlie had watched him.

Aden had shrugged. 'I need to know why.'

And that was it – all she had needed. Charlie had nodded. 'Okay. What can I do?'

Aden had run his hand through his hair. The man behind the glass had settled down now, had slumped into a plastic chair, spindly arms crossed across his vest. 'I don't know. I'm just trying to understand everything that happened. There are so many bits that I can't remember about that night. I just can't seem to piece it all together. And it's like it's all I can think about. I don't know what to do.' He had looked back at her, shrugged. 'Stupid, I know.'

Charlie had frowned. 'You been back there?'

'You mean, Harddymaes?'

'I was just thinking, maybe it would help. You know, help you remember?'

Aden had hesitated. Then, a nod. 'Yeah, perhaps you're right.'

Charlie had pulled her keys free. 'I'll drive.'

There was the off-licence, where it had all begun, the metal shutter pulled half down even in full daylight, a heavy steel door propped open, in unwilling welcome. Looked like it was waiting for nuclear war. Aden stared at it. There were posters in the window, radioactive-green bottles of Sourz. No sign of the cracks that there had been, radiating out across the glass. But then of course it would have been replaced by now, would not have lasted almost a year, not in this neighbourhood.

Aden's hand danced on the burning metal.

He hadn't been here, not since that night, with the rain and the sirens and the finger that just wouldn't move. But what had avoidance got him? Nightmares and flashbacks, and the perpetual feeling of failure. And he couldn't run for the rest of his life. He glanced at Charlie. Her hair was plaited today, something low and rough. Her lips pursed, like she was about to say something that she never does say.

He stared too long. Because she felt it, her eyes darting from the road to him, back again.

'You okay?'

'Yeah.' He looked away quickly.

There were children playing on the heaped scrubland that lined the roadway. It had once been a village green, laid in more optimistic times. Now, though, it had been abandoned, its green grass giving in to the rough dirt and the car tyres and used condoms. The children played, like children played anywhere. Only it seemed that the laughter was rougher, bitter-tinged, the shrieks stuffed with barely contained fury. But then that should have come as no surprise. Seemed like the anger was everywhere here, in the overflowing bins, the bottles smashed across the pavement, the tumbledown sofas abandoned in gardens, even in its children. A barely suppressed hatred that this is what their lives looked like, this is what their lot had become.

Was this where the gunman came? When he left Mount Pleasant Hospital, when he vanished through the trees, was this where he came? They had never found Dylan Lowe's accomplices; had tried, for days and weeks after the shooting. Teams had gone door-to-door as they had searched for the owners of the running footsteps. But there had been nothing, no information. This wasn't a neighbourhood in which people believed in talking to the police.

Aden tucked his arm back inside the car.

Then there was a motion, a flash of dark through the bright sunlight, and Charlie slammed on the brakes.

Aden's heart roared, and instead of a full sunlit day, it was a year ago, and the rain was pouring and the figure was carrying a gun.

The figure stopped dead in front of the car, studying them. A little girl, six, seven at the most, with long dark hair, legs black with dirt. She watched them, frowning, as if they were a puzzle she had to solve, then shrugged and stuck two fingers up at them.

Charlie watched as the girl turned and trotted across the road. 'Well, that was charming.'

'Yeah.' It was all Aden could manage. His heart was pounding, his vision narrowed down to nothing more than a tube. This was a mistake. This was a terrible mistake. He should never have done this. What the hell had he been thinking? He could get fired for this. And coming here: why? Why would he ever want to come here, so that he could relive his moment of greatest failure – and with Charlie of all people?

'So,' Charlie's tone was faux-chatty, 'any news on the hospital? You know, the gunman?'

'Um . . .' Aden breathed out slowly, a long count of four. 'Nothing. We're patrolling, seems like we're there all the time. But no sign.'

'I heard about that woman being chased in the car park. She okay?'

Aden glanced across at her and shrugged. 'I think so. I mean, we had a team right there, so they got out into the woods pretty quickly, but they found no sign of him.'

Charlie nodded, her forehead contracting into a frown. 'You think she was making it up?'

Aden looked at her, pulled a face. 'It was lunchtime. There should have been plenty of witnesses. No one saw a thing. No one but her.' He shrugged again. 'Don't know. I just think it's weird.'

They were passing a pub now, the kind of place that opened in the early-morning hours, pumping customers full of lager until day turned to night and then day again. A man was standing outside, leaning against the pub door, sucking on a cigarette, his gaze sputtering, hands unsteady.

Charlie gave a brief grimace.

They were coming to the bottom of the hill, a small clutch of houses huddled together at its base. Charlie pursed her lips, flipped on the indicator, easing the car into an empty lay-by. Turned the key, the engine falling silent. 'That's the Lowe house,' Charlie gestured across the road. 'The one on the far left.'

Aden nodded. Had seen it on the TV, Dylan Lowe's parents standing on the doorstep, tucked together, faces slick with grief. Beyond the knot of houses, visible now in full daylight, was the alley, a torn poster hanging listlessly from its frame, advertising something that he couldn't make out.

A few yards ahead: that was where he had stopped the car; that was where Tony threw himself out into the rain.

'Did you want to get out of the car? Or . . .'

'Yeah,' said Aden. 'Let's . . . yeah.'

He gripped the door handle, stepped out into the pulsing heat, his trainers sticky on the softening tarmac. Waited as Charlie climbed out, locking the door behind her. She dropped into step beside him. The world's least-ambitious date.

'Now that's nice.' Charlie shook her head.

The graffiti splayed across the red-brick wall, unsteady letters in an angry black: FUCK THE POLICE. Someone had left flowers, cream carnations wilting in the heat; had tied them to the lamp-post with blue parcel string. Aden's stomach turned.

They stood, stared at the house across the street. The windows were hanging open, music billowing. It didn't look like a house that tragedy had visited. A child's bike lay abandoned on the front step. Someone had filled a paddling pool, set it on what sufficed as a front lawn, but no children played in it. Aden wondered where they were, the other children: an eight-year-old boy, ten-year-old girl. Wondered what their lives looked like now – a childhood blown apart by gunshots, a brother turned inert with a bullet through the brain.

He felt a flood of nausea.

Then there was a sound, a creaking breaking through the still air, the front door of the Lowe house swinging open. Aden recognised Dylan's mother from the news. Carla Lowe's hair was pulled up into a tight topknot. She wore cut-off jeans, an off-white top with spaghetti straps. Stood on the doorstep, hands digging into the pockets of her shorts, gaze fixed on the sky, perhaps looking for clouds, some sign of a break in the heat. She pulled her hands free, lighting a cigarette, pulling in a deep, long draught.

'We should go.' Aden kept his voice low.

Then Carla Lowe lowered her gaze from the clear blue sky. Looked directly at them.

22

Imogen: Wednesday 27 August, 12.40 p.m.
Four days before the shooting

The smell of sausages hung in the still, hot air, the plate of food standing, largely uneaten, mashed potato congealing into soupy baked beans, turning the orange sauce peach.

'I wish she'd eat a little.' Mara watched as Amy turned the pages of the board book like she was examining jewels.

'She will. When she's ready.' Imogen flicked through a magazine, sticky with sweat. She could not have said what was on those pages already past, or even the ones that lay open in front of her. This, she supposed, was why people smoked, to give them something to do with their fingers. 'She's taking in plenty of fluids. She'll be okay.'

'They're saying her temperature is still higher than they'd like.'

Imogen watched as her niece fidgeted on Mara's lap. Did her breathing sound strange or was that the hospital effect, the innocent turned deadly within these whitewashed walls?

'Baaaaa. Mooooo.'

'That's right, sweetheart.' Mara smiled, kissed her daughter's head. 'Clever girl.'

'Look, A'tie Im. A do'key.'

'A donkey? Wow! They've done blood tests on her, right, Mar?'

Mara shook her head. 'No . . . said they'll wait for now. She's on antibiotics, though, so hopefully . . .'

They sat in straight-backed chairs, Amy snug on her mother's lap. A change of scene, Mara had said. Rather the same scene, just seen from a different height. There were voices outside, children laughing. Seemed out of place here. But then it was a children's ward, and children would be children. Even here.

'I wish we could take her outside,' murmured Imogen. 'It's such a beautiful day.'

'We can't risk it,' said Mara, turning the pages of the book. 'Look, Amy. A monkey.'

'I 'ike mo'key.'

'I know you do.'

Dave hadn't come to bed last night. Imogen had awoken with a start, the clock on the night stand flashing 2.08 a.m. Had lain there for a moment, alone, listening. There were sounds coming through the floorboards. She had pushed herself up, padding on the carpet with bare feet, a smell catching in her throat. It had taken her a moment to realise what it was. Cigarette smoke.

He was lying on the sofa, a burnt-out cigarette resting in an ashtray that she had never seen before. The television crashing and loud. Three cans of Stella lined the table, a miniature shooting gallery, a fourth open and sweating in his hand.

'Dave?' Imogen had said it quietly, like maybe she didn't want to be heard.

But he had heard her anyway, turned ponderous and

awkward. Looked at her like she was dancing, his gaze struggling to find her.

'Are you okay?'

He had shrugged. 'I'm watching a film.'

'I . . . well, it's late. Are you okay?' Imogen had studied him, the damn mobile phone still clutched in his fingers, and had felt a flush of irritation. She could just go back to bed. There would be no shame in that. She was tired, more than tired – the kind of exhaustion that seeps into your bones. 'Dave? What's going on?'

He hadn't looked at her, had stared at the television, but had let out a low laugh that didn't sound like a laugh at all. 'Nothing. Nothing at all. The father of the bloody vegetable is trying to get me fired, but apart from that, everything's sound.'

'I . . . what?'

'That Steve Lowe. The bloke from the papers. The one whose kid got shot by the police. He's filed a formal complaint about me. He went to see Lydia today. He's spoken to the paper's owners, saying I got aggressive with him. It's all bullshit, the whole thing. But they've just been waiting for this, for me to screw up. Lydia's had it in for me from the start.'

'I'm sure—'

'That bastard is determined. He's not going to be happy till he's destroyed me.'

'So has Lydia said anything?'

'She said they're investigating. That it's not great. She'll "keep me informed". Fucking awesome, yeah? You know the bloke I mean, don't you? I bet you see him at the hospital all the time. Probably bloody lives there.'

Imogen had looked down, could see her fingers shaking.

Was thinking of Steve Lowe sitting in her office, his head in his hands talking about his son. Stuck now, in a world of limbo. But she couldn't say that, of course she couldn't. Client confidentiality.

Dave had shaken his head, taken a long pull of the can. 'I'm telling you something now: I'd better not run into him any time soon. I'm not going to be held accountable for my actions.'

'A s'eep.'

'That's right, Amy. And what does a sheep say?'

'Baaaaaa.'

A spark of sound jolted Imogen out of her reverie. Her sister pushed herself up in her seat, made a grab for her mobile phone. Imogen watched her, waiting, could feel an irritation writhing in her stomach. Then, without looking at Imogen, Mara switched the phone to silent.

'That was him, wasn't it?' Imogen kept her voice low, light.

'Who?'

'You know who, Mara.'

Mara shrugged. 'Don't, Im. Look, Amy, a dog.'

'What do you mean: "Don't"? Was that him?' It felt like a pan, boiling over, too many secrets, too much acceptance.

Mara looked up, her gaze level. 'I know what you think of me.'

'I don't think anything,' Imogen replied, straining to keep her voice calm. 'I just think, with the situation being what it is, that your focus should be on Amy.'

'It is, Imogen. Besides, it's over. I've finished it. Are you happy now?' Mara's voice was climbing, becoming shrill. Amy glanced up at her mother, her forehead wrinkling into a frown.

Imogen started, stared. 'When?'

'When what?'

'When did you finish it?'

Mara sighed loudly, shifting Amy on her lap. 'What difference does that make?'

'It makes a difference if he's angry. It makes a difference if it's him who's been coming into the hospital, who followed you. Could he be someone who has access to, you know . . . ?' Imogen didn't want to say the word 'gun', barely wanted to think about it.

Mara frowned. 'I don't know. Lots of people do. I mean, Dave is in a gun club, isn't he?' There was a little something in her tone, a slyness almost, a barb stuck where it will sting.

Imogen stared at her, her mind swimming. She opened her mouth, thinking to reply, yet with little idea what it was she would say, when the door swung open, the nurse entering.

'Well then.' Natalie smiled. 'How are we doing in here? Ooh, Amy. What do you have there?'

'My A'tie Im got me book.'

'She did? Well, isn't that fab?' The nurse looked at the tray. 'Mara, why don't you take a little break? You haven't left the hospital since Amy came in.' Natalie glanced at Imogen for support. 'I'm sure Imogen would cover for you for a bit, just so you can pop home, get yourself a shower.'

Mara ran her fingers through Amy's fine hair and gave a quick shake of her head.

Imogen closed the magazine. 'She's right. You should take a break. It would do you good.'

'No, thanks. Look, Amy. There's a snake. What colour is the snake?'

The nurse stood, watched Mara, then let loose a low sigh. 'Okay, well, I'll be back in a bit. We're going to see about setting up a heart-trace on this little madame, just to see what her ticker is up to.'

Imogen started. 'Is there a reason to think there's a cardiac problem?'

Natalie hefted the tray, gave Imogen a half-smile. 'Oh, just being thorough. You know how it is with the little ones. We like to check everything we can. I'll see you in a bit. Call if you need me.'

An uneasy silence filtered in, the two sisters sitting, each waiting for the other to speak.

Then: 'I called Jack.' Mara wasn't looking at Imogen, was still studying her daughter's book, her voice defensive.

Imogen started. 'You did? That's good.'

'He's going to talk to the superintendent, see if he can get a couple of weeks off. Like some compassionate leave, or something. So you see, there is nothing to worry about, is there? Because once Jack is home, he'll be able to protect us.'

23

The Shooter: Saturday 30 August, 2.25 p.m.
Day before the shooting

I slip up the stairs, leaving behind the chaos and the voices. Leila has brought out a karaoke machine, has let loose on it the gaggle of squawking kids, so that now my mother's house is filled with screaming voices. I suppose you could call it singing, if you were feeling generous.

I glance across my shoulder, make sure that I'm not being followed, then quietly let myself into my mother's bedroom. I close the door softly behind me, walk carefully to the wardrobe and pull open the doors.

It is there, still buried at the back, where I knew it would be. It is half-covered by an aged throw. It looks like my mother is still trying to hide it, even though I have no idea why. I mean, what would be the point now? I pull the box free, setting it on the bed next to me.

I knew that I was adopted, right from the beginning. The beginning? Well, let me say this, it was something that I had always known. We were what my mother referred to as a 'modern family'. The two natural-borns, my eldest sister Beth, my brother William. Both blond, blue eyes, so much like my mother that it hurt. Then there were the rest of us, the waifs and the strays. Courtney and Leila, plucked from their natural mother when social services found her wandering high as a kite, the two little girls trailing her like vapour trails after a plane. She visited occasionally, her hair slicked back and greasy, ribs standing out proud beneath stained clothes, always smelling of urine. And then there was me. A last-minute addition.

No one ever came to visit me. No one sent me cards or presents. It was as if I had simply appeared, materialising one day amongst the daffodils and the long grass.

I asked. I would watch Courtney and Leila hanging off this awkward, smelly woman, would wonder where mine was, if there was anyone out there who knew that I existed. My mother would smile – the kind of smile that you can tell she doesn't mean, and that just by asking you have made her sad – and would murmur something about she herself being my mother, and how nothing else mattered.

But none of it made sense. I came from somewhere else. I knew that. They had told me. But it seemed that no one knew where. So I was left, a child adrift in a world of strangers.

Then I found out. Then I wished I could go back to the time before, the time when I didn't know.

I learned who I was from newspaper clippings. The boxed-up collection neatly tucked into the back of my parents' wardrobe. It was for me, my mother said, for when I was older. When I could handle it. But I didn't find them when I was older. I found them when I was eight and playing hide-and-seek with my sisters. I was always good at disappearing. I crept into the cupboard, nested inside the fur coats and the winter boots and the clothes that

Mum kept because, next year, she'd squeeze into them. And I found it.

I pulled the lid off the box, something to do while I waited for Courtney to figure out how to count to one hundred. Had smelled old newspaper, faded print. Pulled the cuttings into the dim light, rested them on the palm of my hand like one would a butterfly:

Toddler found abandoned at Mount Pleasant Hospital

A three-year-old boy has been found wandering through the grounds of Mount Pleasant Hospital. Staff say the child appeared to be malnourished and unkempt. Enquiries are being made by police as to the whereabouts of the child's mother, but so far no information has been forthcoming. The child has fair hair and brown eyes. Those with information please contact Swansea Police Station.

I read the piece, once, twice, a thousand times, but could make no more sense of it. I didn't know the hospital, had never been there. Not then, at least.

The next clipping:

Woman found dead in Swansea City Centre

A woman has been found dead outside a multi-storey car park in Swansea city centre. Early reports suggest that she was last seen on the upper floors of the car park. The woman is said to have been in her early twenties. Police are not looking for anyone else in connection with the death.

Such a small slip of paper to contain such a thing. I knew then what it was, with the surety that only a child can possess. Cannot now say how. I was only eight. But it felt somehow that someone was telling me something I already knew. I remember sitting, in that cupboard surrounded by the smell of my mother, and suddenly the smell felt alien, strange. I pushed myself up from the nest of coats, blankets, the box tight in my hands. Shoved past my sister, still only on 'sixty-three', ignored the loud tearless sobs that burst from her.

My mother was in the kitchen. Seems now that she was always there, that my entire childhood – at least that which can be accounted for – revolved around my mother in the kitchen. She looked up when I entered, the start of a smile, then down at the box, the smile vanishing.

'You shouldn't—'

'This was me?'

She stared at me, for long seconds, and I could see her choosing, which way she would go. Then she let loose a long, low sigh, wiped her hands on a teacloth. Turned, wrapped her arms around my shoulders. 'Yes. That was you.'

'This lady. The one they say is dead. That was my mother, wasn't it? My real mother.'

I could see her wince at my choice of words and felt a small sliver of satisfaction. But she pulled me tighter, nonetheless. 'The people at the hospital, they found you. You were only a very little boy. They took you in and called social services. And social services – they knew we wanted someone to love, so they brought you to us.'

I stood, staring. The kitchen, which I knew so well that it felt like a part of me, now the house of a stranger. And new memories – or rather old memories that I had mistaken for dreams – flooding in. An old man who liked to play the piano. A house with a lot of dogs. A big, big house stuffed with children who seem to be coming out of the walls.

'Did I live somewhere else?'

She studied me, her face more creased now than it was before. 'They . . . it takes a while, these kind of things. You went to stay with some other people first. Foster families. They were very nice people who looked after you while . . . while social services sorted everything out.'

'And then I came to you?'

'Then you came to us.'

'And my real mum?'

Again that wince, a small nod, an even smaller sigh. 'The lady in the newspaper article. We found out, after a while, that she was your mum. She was very young when she had you, and she didn't have any family, and things were . . . difficult.' Such an insubstantial word. 'What we think is, she just didn't know how to look after you, and one day it just all became too much.'

'She killed herself?'

A long look, biting her lip. Then, finally, 'That's what it looks like. We don't really know what happened. Just that it was very sad, and she must have been very unhappy and terribly desperate to have done such a thing.'

I stood, in the kitchen, could hear the others laughing, shouting, and wondered what kind of a monster I was that I could make my mother do such a thing.

I sit on the bed. Can hear the voices from downstairs, reaching a crescendo, then descending into shrieks – laughter or tears, I cannot tell. I run my fingers through the papers, look at them like I haven't looked at them a thousand times before, and wonder if this is all a part of saying goodbye. That when you get to the end you revisit the beginning, so that all may be in order. Then I close the lid, returning the box to its hiding place.

24

Charlie: Wednesday 27 August, 12.57 p.m.
Four days before the shooting

Aden and I stand in the street as if our feet have sunk into the melted tarmac. I shouldn't have brought him here. I should never have brought him here. What the hell was I thinking? Why didn't I just go to the damn council meeting, like I was supposed to? I look at Aden looking at Carla Lowe. Carla has pushed herself up from the doorjamb, has raised her hand to her eyes, protecting them from the sun. She is looking at us. Aden's face is pancake-flat, eyes hidden behind dark glasses, but still I can see it, in the clenching, unclenching of his fingers, the short, sharp breaths that make his chest rise and fall like a stop-motion tide. The guilt. I move, a little step; desperately want to reach out and take his hand, but of course I don't. So I just stand there, as useful as a unicycle to a goldfish, and watch him suffer.

Carla is staring at us with the open simplicity of a child. Or, rather, she is staring at me. I see her features change, the flood of recognition in the tilt of her head, and know that it's too late to run now. We're screwed.

'You're Dave, okay? You're a reporter and you work with me,' I mutter to Aden, not looking at him, and lift my hand into a wave.

Carla returns the wave tentatively, half-turns and presses the butt of her cigarette against the brickwork on the porch. Her skin is snow-white, blue almost, her arms thinner, her face more sunken than it was before. I wonder if this is the first time she has left the house since the heatwave has hit. She wraps her arms around herself, cradling her waist as if she's cold, although it is almost thirty degrees, and I put on a smile, like there is nowhere else in the world I would rather be. I try not to look at Aden. He'll be fine. It's fine. The names of the officers were never released to the media. I think this like I'm not one of the media, like I am somehow removed from that melee. And yet, in a way, I suppose I am. Because I knew. I never told Lydia, though. Never told anyone their names, or where the reporters with their cameras and their microphones could find them. That's why they trust me, because they know I've got their backs.

Carla is walking towards us now, her flip-flops schlopping against the slowly melting tarmac. My hand drops, brushing Aden's, his skin cold in spite of the heat, and I feel him start. He reaches out, seems like a reflex, and grips my small hand within his larger one, encasing it, and for a moment I am flung backwards in time, am a child again – my father's hand holding mine – and the world is smaller, easier. Aden rubs his thumb along the curve of my palm. Seems like it's an unconscious move, and I look at him, but I'm not convinced that he knows I am there, that the move isn't merely a form of self-comfort. I should say something. And then a car passes and the spell is broken.

Aden looks at me, then down at our hands, and I can see a flush that starts at his neck, racing up his cheeks.

'Sorry.' He lets go of my hand.

I nod, my cheeks warm, hand tingling.

Carla looks years older than the last time I saw her, scant days after her eldest son was shot. I didn't want to go, my God, I really didn't want to go. Of all the death-walks, this would be the worst, the death that wasn't a death. I had begged my editor to let Dave do it, had mumbled something about being too close, had received a look in return. If you're that close, get us a better bloody story. So I had gone to the Lowes' house, notepad in hand. A bargain to keep the firearms officers – to keep Aden – in the shadows. Steve Lowe had opened the door, had all but pulled me into the house, so desperate was he to spill his story. I had sat on the Lowes' sofa, the springs so worn that my knees seemed to reach up to my shoulders, my notepad resting on its arms, watching them on a sofa of their own. Carla hadn't been crying, her eyes perfectly dry, but her skin was grey. I had kept reminding myself that their son wasn't dead, so that I would curb my tongue, would not accidentally say 'he was'. Carla had sat about as far as it was possible to sit from her husband, wincing as the words tumbled from him, a relentless swarming cascade, so that it was impossible to separate one from the other. Steve, a lumbering, overwhelming presence, all chopping hands, curling lips; Carla trying to vanish into the upholstery, her fingers clinging to the cushion edge so tight it seemed that she would draw blood.

'Mrs Lowe. Carla. Hi.' I squint in the harsh sunlight, smiling brightly, like I'm supposed to be here. Can feel Aden shifting beside me.

She stares at me, and I feel the overwhelming urge to do something – dance or wave my hands – so that she'll keep looking at me, won't look at Aden, won't see that he really doesn't belong.

'You're that reporter.' Carla states it as a fact.

I can smell the cigarette that she has just extinguished. 'Charlotte Solomon. I'm terribly sorry to bother you.'

Carla folds her arms across her chest, pulls herself up to her full height. It's not impressive, five-foot-five at the most. But then she's still taller than me, so who am I to talk? 'Yeah, Steve said. He's been to see you, yeah?' Carla shakes her head, her ponytail slapping against the nape of her neck. A throaty sigh. 'You here about my boy?' She leans against the garden wall.

'Your husband,' I smile, but not too much, 'he told me about the civil suit. I thought I'd pop along, have a quick chat with you.' I'm thinking on my feet. 'Your husband was . . . um, keen for me to follow this up.' The lines seem to have run amok on her face. I realise with a start that we are the same age. Or, rather, that we have lived the same amount of chronological time. She, however, has packed far more life into her thirty years than I have into mine.

Carla studies me, and for a moment I think I am busted. There is something in those eyes, a sharpness that I had forgotten, and I have a fleeting vision of her, in a different life, perhaps one where she didn't have a baby at fourteen, her hair twisted into a chignon, pale legs sheathed in dark tights, a suit from an expensive store.

'I don't know how he thinks we're going to pay for it. Didn't happen to mention that, did he? Where we're going to get the piggin' money from? No. Good at forgettin' that kind of thing, is Steve. Did he tell you that no one's interested? None of the solicitors he's been to see will touch it.' Carla shook her head. 'I don't friggin' know.'

'No,' I offer lamely. 'He didn't mention it.'

Carla lets loose a tching sound, then inclines her head towards the house. 'You'd better come in.' She stops then, her gaze shifting from me to Aden. My stomach flips.

'Oh, this is my colleague. Dave.' I try to say it casually, so that it will slip through this woman's bullshit net.

Carla looks at Aden, then back at me, and for a moment I think that we are done, that somehow she has ferreted it out, she knows who he is, and at any minute holy hell is going to rain down on us. I glance across, can hear the sound of running water – her neighbour out watering an optimistic hanging basket, in blatant disregard of the hosepipe ban. He's holding the hose casually. Watching us. My stomach begins the long, slow climb up to my mouth.

'Well, come on then.' Carla turns on her heel, her pony-tail flying out in an arc behind her, and I glance at Aden, can see him pale beneath his glasses.

How could I have brought him here? What the hell is wrong with me? I walk, keep my head up, like it's all fine, all in a day's work, and I feel a little like crying.

A kid's bike lies sprawled across the front step, its handle-bars shimmering in the sunlight. The grass is high, brushes against my ankles as I walk, looks like it hasn't been cut in a long time. But then I suppose this family has more important things to worry about. The door is hanging open, the red paint beginning to flake away, leaving a dull brown behind, and we follow as Carla navigates her way around the bike, without breaking stride. A faint breeze has found its way into the dim house, sweeping around our feet, streaking through the hallway, into the narrow living room, darting out of the open window, like it too is desperate to escape. It smells of burnt toast and cigarettes.

''scuse the mess. Kids. You know.'

I nod, smile, feel something crunching underfoot and wince, thinking that I have crushed some kind of pet. Glance down. An assault course of Cheerios laces the thin pile carpet. Crunch. Crunch. Aden is close behind me. Not faring much better with the cereal alarm system, apparently.

Carla sweeps a stack of folded laundry from the sofa, the same one I sat on last time, setting it on the dining table, where it leans precariously. 'Sit.' It is an order, the kind she is used to giving to kids. 'You want, like, a squash or something?'

Aden shakes his head, is still wearing his sunglasses. I smile. 'No. We're fine, thanks.'

She mumbles something. I catch the words 'kids', 'play', but I confess that I'm not really paying attention. Because I'm watching Aden, and even though he has his glasses on, I can see his gaze trickle across to a coffee table that is set in the corner of the room, an oasis of calm amongst the toys and the laundry and the cereal. It has been dusted recently, probably this morning, the glass top gleaming, although the cupboard beside it is greying with an accumulation of dust. At its centre, a large framed photograph of a boy, a round face, all acute angles and teenage acne. I try not to stare. Three more photographs ring the larger one, a Stonehenge of memories: Dylan as a baby, as a toddler, at six or seven. His entire life laid out there on one coffee table, climbing from infancy to puberty and then – nothing. It is, in fact, a shrine. I look away.

Carla has sat, is perched on the edge of the opposite

sofa, within a hair's breadth of the coffee table, her son's memorial. But she doesn't look at it. In fact there is a lean to her, faint but there, as if it is an invisible forcefield pushing her away. She bites her lip, looks down at her fingernails, studying the yellowing edges. 'Steve. He can't . . . He won't let it go. That's why he keeps bugging you.'

'Oh, it's not . . .' I begin, lamely.

'I know he's bugging you. He can be a pain in the arse. Says we deserve justice. For Dylan.'

'But you don't . . . ?' I frame the words, twisting them to check that they fit. 'The civil suit. It's not what you want?'

She shrugs. Her eyes are full. 'What good would it do? It won't help Dylan. Thing is, it's different for Steve. Me, I've got three other kids.' She gestures at the toys splayed across the floor. 'I'm at the hospital every day with Dylan. He was in a residential care home, see, but they said he had a chest infection, that he needed IV antibiotics, so we're back to the hospital again. Every day.' Her voice has become murky, dense. 'I wash him, change him. I cut his hair. I read to him too. He likes to read. He gets that from me.'

I'm watching her, the splay of her features. 'His dad? Steve. Not a reader?'

Carla lets loose a squawk. 'No. He says it's a waste of time. He used to go on and on about it. Used to call Dylan a nerd.'

I nod, like that's a perfectly normal thing to say to your child. A quick side-glance at Aden. Can see, in the frown lines that have formed on his forehead, he's thinking the same thing as me: that a boy will do a lot to be respected by his father. Maybe even carry a gun, so that he can be a man. Just like Daddy. 'So, you said things are different for Steve? How do you mean?'

She looks up, spears me with a spotlight glare, flecks of doubt in her eyes. I can see her working it out, how much she is safe to say. 'He . . . he doesn't often come to the hospital.' Words careful, a step on unsteady ground.

I nod slowly. 'It's tough, I guess. Especially for men. I don't think they handle things the same way we do.'

A lightness creeps over her features, the relief of speaking English in the centre of Beijing and hearing familiar words, the knowledge that you are understood. 'That's the thing – he can't cope with it. Doesn't like to see Dylan like that. So he's got nothing else to do but get into all of this legal stuff. He thinks it will help.' Shakes her head. 'I don't know. I just . . . how? That's what I want to know. We've been through it once, with the IPCC, all that. How is this going to be any different? And if it is, so what? I don't know if he's thinking we'll get some money – you know, make things a bit easier.' She waves her hand around the living room. 'I mean, we're not exactly living in the lap of luxury here. But, thing is, I just don't care. All I mind about is taking care of my kids. And that's the thing – that's what Steve doesn't seem to get. We've still got four kids. Four. Not three. Our boy is still here, still in that hospital bed. Even if his own father won't admit it.' She is crying now, tears spilling down her pale cheeks. 'Do you know what he said to me? He said it would be better if he'd died. That Dylan would be better off dead.'

25

Aden: Wednesday 27 August, 1.23 p.m.
Four days before the shooting

The words seemed to bounce off the walls, hanging in the air. They settled on Aden, their implications digging roots under his skin, sparking with electricity. He could feel Charlie's glance at him, and from the corner of his eye could see her eyebrows shooting towards her hairline. Then Charlie leaned closer to Carla Lowe, looked like she wanted to reach out, take her hand, but couldn't quite make herself do it, so her fingers danced an uncomfortable beat on the tops of her knees.

'I'm so sorry,' Charlie offered.

Aden watched Carla Lowe, feeling as if his entire body was tingling. Studied the woman, a mother who had lost her child and yet not lost him. So she cared for him and tended him like it would make some kind of a difference. He studied her, thinking about her husband and his history, a rage that always seemed to sit just beneath the surface, barely contained. Thought of the man walking the corridors of Mount Pleasant Hospital, gun in hand. Again and again and again. Almost like he was building himself up to something, steeling himself for something that he had to do, but couldn't quite face. Not yet.

Carla Lowe nodded, swiped at her nose with the back of her hand. 'Ta. I think, the thing is, with Steve, it's guilt, I suppose.'

'Guilt?' asked Charlie.

'Steve and Dylan – I mean, they weren't close. Dylan, he's a quiet boy. Serious. Steve used to call him a mamma's boy. And he is. He is my boy.' Carla wiped roughly at the tears, pulling herself upright, used to dealing with the hardest knocks that life could throw at a person and then pulling herself back up again. 'Steve, see, he wasn't around much. We'd split, were apart for about a year. Just weren't gettin' on. So the kids, they didn't see that much of him.' She lowered her voice. 'Steve won't talk about it, but I think he was seeing someone else, while we were split. Spent all his time with her. The kids were gutted. And Dylan wanted so badly to impress him. Well, that's what kids are, innit? Always want their mam and dad to be proud of them.'

Was that it? Was that what led a good kid to pick up a gun, run amok? The promise of being just a little bit more like his father, with his criminal history, his fuck-society anger? Only for this kid, it had gone wrong.

'So . . .' Aden had interrupted something – some conversation that he hadn't caught – he could tell by the surprise in the women's faces. He pushed on. 'Your husband. Do you think . . . I mean, have you ever worried that he might hurt Dylan?'

It was like a sudden freeze, the change in the room. Carla Lowe sat up, leaning away from him, frowning heavily. 'No. Why?' There was an edge to her voice, a warning to tread no further.

Aden ignored it. 'Am I right in thinking that your husband has access to guns?'

'What the hell has that got to do with anything?' Carla was looking at him differently now, a full-on stare, and he could see the wheels turning behind her eyes, the suspicion that she might not have been told the truth. 'Why are you asking this?'

'Oh, it's nothing, Carla . . .' Charlie glared at Aden, turning back to Carla Lowe with a smile.

'But I'm correct in thinking that Steve has been reported as saying he could get access to his parents' weapons?'

Carla had folded in on herself now, her arms tight across her chest, face folded into a heavy frown. 'Steve hardly ever sees his parents. And, anyway, I don't understand why . . .'

Charlie was talking, was saying something to him, in that brittle, bright voice that she did when she was trying to be soothing. Aden stared at her blankly, wondering who the fuck Dave was. Then pushed himself to his feet.

'We'd better be going.'

They looked at him, startled, like he had lost his mind: Charlie; Carla, still scowling; the boy in the photographs, with his entire life ahead of him.

'He's right.' Charlie stood up, smiling, like it was no big deal. Everything fine here, nothing to see. 'I'm so sorry, Carla, but we have a meeting this afternoon. Thank you so much for sitting down with us.' She sounded sincere.

Carla looked at Aden, studying the arms that had somehow crossed themselves around his waist, the sunglasses that must have made him look like a prick. And he found himself wishing that the ground would open up beneath him.

She pushed herself up from the sofa, an awkward

movement, her spaghetti-strap top shifting, riding up across her waist to reveal protruding ribs. Behind him, Aden heard Charlie gasp. He looked at her, sharply, thinking they were busted, but she wasn't looking at him; was looking at Carla, her gaze shifting from her side to her face, and back again. Carla flushed, a darker red than you would have thought it possible for her pale skin to go, tugged quickly on her top.

And then they stood there, in an unsteady limbo in which it seemed to Aden a world of conversation was being conducted that he just couldn't hear. Charlie still wasn't looking at him, was still staring at Carla, who was staring back. Her eyes pleading.

'I . . .'

He didn't know what Charlie was going to say, but she never got a chance, because Carla was stepping forward and his guard was up, his heart racing as Carla's hands snaked out towards Charlie. Aden was about to move, about to do something stupid, when he saw Carla take hold of Charlie's hand, gripping it tight. They still weren't speaking, Carla clutching onto Charlie like she would fall, with a slight shaking of her head.

Then Carla said, 'Please.'

Charlie's face was shifting, a storm of emotions. 'Carla, I . . .'

'You can't. Please. Don't say anything. He's gone. I kicked him out after it. But if you write about it, and Steve sees it . . . he'll kill me.' Then the colour drained from Carla's face, the sudden sinking realisation of what it was she had done. 'Oh my God, I shouldn't have said . . . The things I told you, I didn't think . . . He's going to kill me.'

A long silence, broken only by the shriek of children playing.

'Look. It's okay,' Charlie said, eventually. 'It's going to be okay. I promise.'

They didn't say anything else, not as they stepped across the bike on the front step, or as they heard the door closing behind them and the muffled sound of crying. They didn't say a word until they slid into the car, the air full of a breathless heat.

'Did you see it?' Charlie had turned to him, her eyebrows pulled up tight together.

'What?'

She gestured to her stomach. 'The bruise.' Formed her small hand up into a fist. 'It was . . . bad. Someone had punched Carla in the stomach.'

Aden sat, could feel the seat fabric burning through his shirt back, a ring of sweat beginning to build around the nape of his neck. The pressure of it all sitting in his belly. This woman, this house, this boy – and he wanted to feel guilty, but even that was more than was allowed to him, because they weren't his gunshots. And he'd come here, trying to piece it together, trying to understand this boy who had shifted the axis of his world, trying to round out the bitty recollections, the newspaper stories, all of the bits that added up together to mean nothing. And what he had got was a shrine to an angel child; his bedraggled mother her husband's punching bag; and no answers, no cipher that could unravel the pieces of that night. Just more heaviness, more grief, when there was already so much sitting on his chest that it seemed sometimes like it was hard to breathe.

'Do you think it was him? Steve Lowe. In the hospital,' Aden asked Charlie.

'Well, you clearly do. Undercover much?' Charlie grinned.

'Yeah, I . . . Sorry. But it would make sense, wouldn't it? What with everything?'

Charlie sighed, started the engine. 'I don't know, Ade. They're a family in a lot of pain. I mean, to have your son in a persistent vegetative state for almost a year . . .'

Then it came, a sudden spurt of anger. 'Yeah. Well, perhaps they should have been more careful not to raise a kid who'll try to kill police officers.'

Charlie had leaned back in the driver's seat, pulled so far away that her head was resting against the driver's side-window, and he could see it – that change in her face as she vanished behind a locked door. 'I need to get back.'

26

Imogen: Wednesday 27 August, 8.23 p.m.
Four days before the shooting

The restaurant was full, thrumming with voices. Faux-grapevines gathered dust on the walls, plump plastic grapes peeking from between the green. A party had set up at a table, a ten-seater that lined the opposite wall, a birthday banner strung on the wall behind them, all raucous laughs, roaring voices. Imogen watched them; she was trying to be subtle, but they were loud, seemed like they were expecting an audience. The birthday girl sat at the centre of the crowd, marked out by a sash, a pink crown. She was laughing, her face flushed with the heat and the alcohol.

And then there was their table. They had been seated by the window – ostensibly the best table in the house, but today the sunlight had been pouring in, superheating the cutlery, the leather-backed chairs. The window gave way to a flawless blue bay, tumbling cliffs slowly being eaten away by ravenous waves.

Imogen's mother stared at the party, drumming her finger-nails against the white linen tablecloth. Her lips had pursed up, the crimson pout impatient.

'Just ignore them.' Her father wasn't looking at his wife, was focusing instead on his plate, where a deep-red blood had begun to seep from his ribeye. He handled the steak knife like a surgeon – three careful, neat cuts – skewering the square of meat with his fork, gave a little nod of satisfaction and took a wide bite.

Imogen looked down. Studied her plate.

It was her parents' anniversary. The table had been booked weeks ago. But in spite of this, Imogen hadn't wanted to come. An anniversary party, modest though this one was, didn't seem appropriate, what with Amy in hospital, and Mara not here. She had tried to say it, had suggested to her mother – careful, like trying to stroke a tiger – that they put it off for a week or so, just until Amy was out. That way it would be a double celebration. Her mother had waved her away. Nonsense! Amy's going to be fine. She'll be out soon. So, then, we could wait . . . ? Her mother had blown out a sigh, her face falling, the universal sign of a sulk on the horizon. I've booked the table, Imogen. It's all arranged. And so Imogen had capitulated, as she so often did.

The birthday girl let out a shriek of laughter, raising her glass high into the air.

'But I mean,' her mother sighed deeply. 'Really. Is there any need to be so loud?' She shook her head, earrings clattering, took a delicate bite of her salad.

A bulbous silence had settled over the table, punctured only by the sounds of cutlery scraping against china, the squawks of laughter from the birthday party. Imogen glanced at Dave. He was wearing a far-off gaze, his shoulders drawn up, tie twisted tight at his neck like a noose.

He didn't look at her.

She had been getting ready, had been trying not to think about hospitals and Amy and gunmen. She would wear her black jacket tonight. It was a little workish, but in truth nothing else was clean, and she was tired and just wanted to get dinner over with. Had run down the stairs barefoot, and had clearly been quieter than she had expected. Pushed open the door of her study. For a moment, when she had seen Dave standing there, she had thought they were being burgled. That he was an intruder about to murder her. Would later wonder at her vivid imagination, would put it down to work, the stories that she heard. She had caught herself at the doorway, her heart thudding. 'Dave. I didn't . . .' Only then had she thought to wonder what he was doing there. It was her study. It was out of bounds. They had come to the agreement early on. After all, her client work was confidential – there had to be some limits. She had looked at him, looked at his hands, the sheaf of papers gripped tight enough to tear.

'What are you doing?'

'You lied.'

Imogen had frozen, pierced to the spot. 'I . . . what?'

'You're seeing him.'

'Who?' For one ludicrous moment it seemed that he was accusing her of an affair. Imogen could feel an inappropriate laugh welling up. Did he not know how ridiculously unlikely that was?

'Steve bloody Lowe.'

Imogen looked back at the papers in his hand, the almost-laugh giving way to something else. Anger. 'Dave, you cannot look at those. This is . . . you know, they're confidential. I could lose my job.'

He had thrown back his head, laughed, looking now like

the stranger she had first thought he was. 'Well, how bloody ironic! Especially given that your boyfriend is trying to get me fired.'

'He's not my . . . he's a client, Dave. It's my job.' The anger swelling, turning her voice into something that she didn't recognise.

Then he had walked towards her, quick strides, a flat, furious stare. Had thrust the papers at her, releasing them so that they sprinkled the ground, confetti at a wedding. 'Here, have your fucking client! If you're not careful, that'll be all you do have.'

'So . . .' Imogen's mother set down her cutlery, forehead wrinkled in a frown. 'Any thoughts about wedding dates, finally?'

Dave had turned the fork, was shovelling the curry into his mouth. Sweat had begun to build up on his forehead.

'You'll want a summer wedding. A summer wedding is always best. And our church. Of course. You'll want our church.' She leaned in, patted Dave's arm. 'Imogen went to Sunday school there. I'll talk to our vicar. He'll be thrilled. Thrilled.'

Dave nodded, and Imogen could see the muscles tight in his jaw.

A knot settled into her stomach, a gnawing, biting fear. She chewed slowly on her chicken, tried not to wince as her stomach ached. Looked out of the window. She could see the sea, the waves building, thumping into the rocks.

'It's such a pity Mara couldn't come.' Her mother picked up her fork again, moving her salad around the plate. 'It's not the same without her.'

Imogen had invited Mara. Had known that it was a long shot. But she wanted her there, for moral support. And it would do her good to have a break, get out from the hospital, if only for an hour or so. And Amy was doing so well. The doctors would release her tomorrow, all being well. They had been standing at the foot of Amy's bed, watching as Natalie examined the little girl. Amy had been singing, 'Old Macdonald had a farm'.

'What do you think? It would just be for a couple of hours.' Imogen had smiled as Amy hit a high note, fell off the top of it. 'I tried to put Mum off, but you know how she is. So, will you come?'

Mara hadn't looked at her, had been studying Natalie, never taking her eyes off the nurse as she examined her daughter. 'I can't come, Im. You know that.'

Natalie was singing along with Amy, her face creased into a smile. 'Oh my, that's a lovely song, Amy.' Then she had glanced over her shoulder. 'Oh, go on, Mara. You go. It would do you good. Amy'll be fine.' Had stroked Amy's cheek. 'I'll be here.'

Imogen had felt her twin stiffen beside her, could see her face sliding into that smile – the one that she didn't mean.

'No, no.' Mara had said, tight-lipped. 'I'm fine.'

Imogen had watched her sister watching the nurse.

Natalie had glanced around, was waiting expectantly. 'You sure?' A smile, a shrug. Looked back down at Amy and ruffled her hair. 'Okay. Well, if you change your mind . . .'

Mara had watched the nurse as she adjusted Amy's pyjamas, had watched her as she gathered up her papers, as she turned, tugging the door open, closing it softly behind her.

'I don't like that woman,' said Mara.

A shriek of laughter broke from the party now, rolling across the restaurant. Imogen's mother tutted, Dave sinking further down into his seat. Imogen's father had divided up his chips, sectioning them off, ensuring that there was sufficient to be shared equally between mouthfuls of meat.

'I went to see the doctor yesterday.' Imogen's mother leaned forward, shifting to catch her eye.

'Oh?' Imogen worked to muster concern, but found only an empty space. So many of their conversations began this way.

'Terrible stomach pains.' Her mother rubbed her hand against her belly. Winced. 'Just terrible. He's sending me for tests.' She sat upright, a fleeting look of something that looked like triumph. 'Between you and me, I think he's quite concerned.' She shook her head. 'I just hope I'll be okay for your wedding.'

Dave took a long pull of his lager.

Her mother gave a little laugh. 'I don't know. We don't have much luck, do we? Seems that our entire lives begin and end in the hospital. But then,' another laugh, 'that's true of everyone, I suppose.' She leaned in, nudged Dave. 'I hope you know what you're letting yourself in for.' Shook her head. 'What with my health problems, Mara's heart and Imogen's "incident" . . . no, we're not lucky at all.'

It had been a tumbledown autumn day, the lawn thickly buried in crisp leaves, reds and browns, Imogen and Mara seven years old. Their father had been burning rubbish, a bonfire piled up high, a thick pall of smoke hanging in the air that caught in your throat, clambering its way into your lungs. They were playing, tromping across the bed of leaves, loud shrieks that grated on their mother's nerves. But they were being careful. You had to be, in this garden. Their home was built on the side of a hill, a not-quite-mountain that climbed up into the sky, then gave up for want of will.

187

You could see it from all around the city, could point to it and say, 'You see that castle? Right there at the top of the hill? That's where I live.' It wasn't a castle, not really. Merely a ruin of coal-stained days, a relic of the mining industry that sat precipitously above their childhood home, dominating the area. But when you were a child, it was a castle. The house clung to the side of the hill, an ungainly affair with a front door where the roof should be, a bedroom where there should be a basement. And the garden, steeply tiered, layers of lawns that gave way to cavernous drops. You had to be careful playing in the garden, had to stay away from the edges, not run too fast, just in case you couldn't stop in time. And Imogen was being careful. She was, after all, the good girl.

When she thought back to that night afterwards, it was that smell she would remember. The smoke, the burning pine, the spit, the crackle. Her mother's voice. *Be careful there*. The prickle of rain in the air, misting against her skin. Studying her feet, watching as the red patent shoes melted into the umber autumn leaves. Then falling. It seemed to last for ever, a limitless breadth of time in a child's mind, that tumbling, breathless, flashing by the brick wall, creeping weeds, falling and falling, thinking of Alice, wondering if there would be a rabbit with a pocket watch waiting for her when she reached the bottom of this rabbit hole. Then nothing. Later on, things would creep in. A scream. A squalling siren. The feel of hands. The smell of antiseptic, and knowing that she was in a hospital. She knew the smell well.

Her mother had never left her side.

She was, the doctors had said, lucky. A broken arm, concussion from the impact of her head against the brick wall. It was a miracle, really. She could easily have died.

Imogen reached up, ran her fingers across the ridged scar that cut across her forehead, feeling its contours, a disaster that stood proud above the plane of her life. A roar of laughter broke free from the opposite table, the birthday girl dry-humping a blow-up naked doll. Imogen's mother huffed, and Imogen shook herself, shifting her fringe back into position. Covering up the scar.

27

The Shooter: Saturday 30 August, 9.22 p.m.
Day before the shooting

It is late by the time I leave my mother's house, the rain coming down in torrential swathes. The others remain behind. They will stay until the food has run out, until the television is blaring with late-night infomercials, my mother falling asleep in her chair. They never have been very good at making a timely exit, not like me.

I steer the car along quiet streets, driving a bow-wave of water before me. I feel like I am all alone in the world. I don't go home, because what would be the point? Instead I follow the coast, watch as the waves lap against the shoreline, the bright lights of the pier up ahead. Imagine myself in that life, where a Saturday night is spent in a bar, a penny arcade, instead of in a car, contemplating your own death. I turn right without indicating, take the hill at speed. I can see Mara's house ahead of me, the whole thing swathed in darkness. I stop a few doors away. Turn off the engine, and listen to the rain thunder on the roof. I watch the house. Because what else do I have to do?

I had decided to kill myself once before. I don't remember

why, just that it had been a something and a nothing; there had been a straw, something that snapped the camel's back in two, and it had forced my hand. I would die that day. It had been decided.

The thought had come with a flush of something warm, a feeling so alien that it took me a while to recognise it. Relief. It would be over soon. I was almost there. People talk about the human urge to cling to life. Those people have not lived my life. They talk of life as a gift, a boon. But I was alone, no matter how surrounded by people I was, encased in this bulletproof bubble that nothing seemed to penetrate. I had tried to break through, had tried to reach the people on the other side, but no matter how hard I pushed, the world pushed me back. And so, to me, life had become the cross upon which I had been hung. And I just wanted it to end.

Then came Mara.

I was sitting in an empty waiting room, lavender walls, a line of wood-backed chairs, a fledgling ficus in a yellow-painted pot. Waiting for Imogen. The thrum of rain on the roof, a musty, damp day. Afterwards I would wonder what had kept me there, waiting. After all, I had already decided to die. Why had I not just left, got it over and done with? So Imogen would be disappointed when she opened her door, realised I was gone, maybe even angry. So what? It was my time, and nothing else should matter. And for a while I would cling to this – the fact that I had stayed – and would see it as fate, that life had repealed itself, placing something good in my way, something to make me want to stay. Now, I see it as proof that the world is never done fucking you.

Mara came into the waiting room, a hurricane of umbrella

and raincoat, dripping rain onto the grey carpet. The familiarity of a face that I have seen a thousand times. I looked up at her, couldn't not, because that's her – the kind of person who draws your eye in, forces you to look, whether you want to or not.

Mara looked at me. Smiled. Her always perfect smile.

'It's a terrible day.' She was looking at me, expectantly, and my voice had gone, hurried to death before me.

So I nodded instead. A bare dip of the head. And waited for her to leave, to see that quick, familiar frown fly across her face, the sudden awareness that I am nothing, the shutters sliding down. I held my breath.

But Mara didn't do any of that. Instead, she pulled off her raincoat, flinging it so that it hung across a chair, gave her umbrella a half-hearted shake, sinking into the chair adjacent to mine. Even though the waiting room was empty. Even though there were many other chairs. I didn't breathe, couldn't look at her. I could smell the rain on her, the way it mixed with her perfume, and part of me wanted to get up, walk away. I looked at Imogen's door, still resolutely closed, and I wondered if she could see through it somehow, if in some way she knew. I felt a splurge of something I couldn't put my finger on. Guilt, perhaps?

Mara sighed, a showcase sigh, and I looked at her. Couldn't help myself.

'So . . . how late is Im running?' She looked at me, her gaze locked with mine. Like she was waiting for an answer to a question she hadn't asked.

'I, ah . . . think you should settle in for a wait.' I was lying. I was there early.

She laughed, a full-throated laugh, and I wondered just what it was that I had said, and how it could have possibly been so funny. She was looking at me, was studying me with a smile, and I felt something shift in me, an unfurling. The sense of being seen.

And I resolved that I wouldn't kill myself. Not that day.

A car passes me, its waterlogged headlights flooding through my car, and I hunker down lower in the driver's seat. I watch as the silver Mercedes pulls into an adjacent drive. Then transfer my attention back to Mara's house. There is not a splotch of light, no sign of movement. But somehow it doesn't matter to me that she isn't there. Just being here is enough.

28

Charlie: Thursday 28 August, 9.25 a.m.
Three days before the shooting

I wave my key card across the sensor, listen for the low beep, tug the door towards me. The stairwell is bleached with light, heat like I'm standing on the face of the sun. I take the stairs, two at a time, trying to ignore the sweat that breaks out on my forehead, my shoes click-clacking, echoing against the whitewashed walls. Can feel my hair plastered to the nape of my neck, wish that I'd had the wherewithal to bring a hairband, know that there are rings of sweat beneath my arms.

God, I wish I had swum this morning.

I didn't. I stayed in bed. My body feels strange, aching for the lack of ache, naked without the smell of chlorine. I woke at my usual time, 5.58 a.m., a start as if my alarm clock had gone off, even though it hadn't. My stomach turning, for reasons that at the time I couldn't identify. I lay there, with the quilt thrown back, a star shape on an unmade bed, listening to the sounds that filtered through the open window – a passing car, a bird that would not shut up. I should have been pulling into the pool car park now, easing my way through the automatic barrier, my eyes skittering across the car park, the way they always do, searching for Aden's car. I had forced my eyes closed again, thought that I could get another hour of sleep. Should have been in the changing room now, tugging off the clothes I had hastily thrown on, dragging my hair back into a low bun. Now, slipping into the chill water. With Aden.

I had stayed in bed. Watched as the clock ticked around. Then, after a century or so, had dragged myself from sticky sheets, stood under a lukewarm shower, dressed without paying any attention to what I was wearing. Got to the newsroom early, empty desks, low morning heat.

I had thought I'd be alone. Had hoped it. But there was the low thrum of a listless fan, the soft click-click of fingers on a keyboard.

'Hi, Lydia.'

Lydia was hunched over her desk, shoulders curled in like she'd taken a body blow. She looked up at me. Frowned. 'What are you doing here?'

'Thought I'd get a head start.'

'Okay,' Lydia leaned back, arms folded across the rolling spare tyre where her waist should be, and I had felt a prickle of anticipation, 'making up for yesterday?'

Shit!

'Yesterday?' I had tried to look nonchalant, tried to train my face, suddenly wishing that I was a better liar.

'The council meeting. Yesterday afternoon. Why weren't you there?'

Shit. Shit. Shit! 'I . . .'

'Charlie, don't even bother trying to lie to me. We both know you're useless at it. Look,' Lydia had leaned forward, face hard, looking like she hadn't slept in a month, 'you need to understand the position I'm in. There are going to be cuts.' She had waved towards the empty newsroom. 'We're going to be letting people go. I really don't want that to be you, okay? You're good at what you do. People trust you, people talk to you. But I cannot have a member of my staff pissing about. Not at a time like this. And you know what it's like out there, Charlie. Newspapers are shutting down all over. There are no other jobs. So, I'm asking you: keep your nose clean. Go where you're supposed to go, when you're supposed to go. Turn in your work on time. Okay?'

I had stood there, in the doorway to the newsroom. Had felt like I was standing on a cliff edge. Watched her as she sank back in the chair, hands rubbed across her face. 'Okay.' I looked down, with a flush of guilt. 'I'm sorry.'

Lydia nodded slowly.

'Is it . . . it's that bad?' I asked.

'It's that bad,' said Lydia.

'Do you know, I mean, who . . .'

She had looked up at me, smiled. 'Not you, you pain in the arse. At least, not unless you give me no choice. I, ah . . . a couple of names.' Her gaze sputtered from me, hung on Dave's desk. Then she looked down. 'Nothing certain yet.'

I had hung there, in the doorway, watching as the fates shifted, pointing first this way, then that. Glanced across at my desk, the notes scattered where I had left them yesterday. Then across at Dave's desk. Felt a knot in my stomach. 'I'll be a good girl, Lydia. I promise.'

'Hmm . . . Anything new on that gunman at Mount Pleasant Hospital?'

I shook my head. 'A possible sighting on Tuesday, but

nothing since. Hardly surprising. The place is crawling with police.'

Lydia nodded, but I'd already lost her, her focus back on the computer screen. She dismissed me with a wave of her hand.

I walked slowly to my desk, dumped my satchel on the floor. Looked at the array of chaos that littered the faux-wood. I couldn't lose this job. If I lost this job, what else was left? I should never have done it, should never have taken Aden to Harddymaes. It was stupid, impulsive, born of a desire to fix his hurt. Why do I do that all the time? Think I can fix everything. I shuffled through my paperwork without seeing it. It was out of my control. All of it. I took him there to try and make things better, ended up making things worse. I thought of his face, the muscles in his jaw, the burst of anger. Felt myself shrinking back into myself, all over again.

I pushed the power button on my computer, waited as the screen slowly began to crawl to life. It was none of my business. The shooting. Emily. Del said that Emily's death was an accident, and in truth I had nothing. Just a gut feeling that something was off. Perhaps it was an accident, the call to the police just a coincidence. Perhaps she did get drunk. Perhaps she was down and had some drinks and then stopped caring about where she was, whether she was safe. And sometimes things just feel wrong. That doesn't mean some big conspiracy is in play, it just means that they feel wrong. And you can't fix everything, you can't dig and dig and pester until finally somebody gives you the answers you are looking for and you can say 'Aha' and suddenly everything's okay again.

Suddenly I was fifteen years old again, just brushing my

head against sixteen, and waiting. Because soon the whole world would open up before me. It was a day, just like any other, when I came home from school, pushed open the door and knew instantly that something was wrong, that something had changed beyond all recognition. My mother sitting at the kitchen table, crying. I should have reached out, touched her, but it's never been easy between my mother and I, so I didn't. I just stood there, wondered what catastrophe had befallen us. I looked around for my father, not piecing it together. Because why would you think the unthinkable? Then she had said it. Didn't look up; it was like she couldn't face me as she delivered the news. Your father's gone. He's left. I'm looking at her like she's demented, because I know she's lying. He wouldn't leave. Her, maybe. Me, never. We're a team. Daddy and daughter. He would never leave me. I ran up the stairs, pulling open their bedroom door, his wardrobe, the empty carcass of it hitting me like a punch to the gut. Back downstairs, because somehow, in some way that I couldn't possibly define, I knew that she was to blame. Where is he? Where has he gone? My mother shaking her head, crying, holding out a hand to me, but it's empty and I don't want it. He hadn't left a number. An address. He had simply vanished.

I waited a week. A colossal amount of time for a teenage girl. Every day more sure that today would be the day he would return. But at the end of a week my patience ran dry. I skipped school that day, caught the bus into town. I would wait outside his office. He had to come out at some point. Never mind that it was raining, that I had no umbrella. I sat on a low-slung wall. Waited. My father came out, hours later. Pushing open the glass door. Whistling. He stopped when he saw me. A look fleeting

across his face. Sometimes now when I think of it, I think
it was panic. Then a smile, eerily bright. He crossed the
car park towards me, pulled me into a bear hug. I'm so
glad that you're here.

Why did you leave, Dad? I tried to find you, but I didn't
know where you were. Why haven't you called me? Why
haven't you come back?

He lowered his head, a slow shake. I'm sorry, my love.
Your mother, she won't let me. She wants me to stay away
from you. A small smile, brushing my hair from my eyes
like he always did. It's only for a little while. You'll be
sixteen soon. Old enough to make your own decisions.
Hugged me again. Never forget how much I love you.
Kissed me on the forehead, made some noises about how
he had to go, a meeting – I understood, didn't I? Then he
left. I never saw him again.

I hang now in the breathtakingly hot stairwell. Suck in
a breath of stale air. I can hear the voices through the flimsy
wooden door, the chatter of the newsroom, and I pull at the
door. They are working hard, solid rows of reporters, their
heads down, fingers thudding against keys. Every now and
again one of them will look up, stare at Lydia's office.
I glance across, the door is shut, blinds pulled down. If I
didn't already know, I would have known now. It is hanging
in the air, the ghost of a conversation, and you can see it in
the reporters' eyes, the steadfast rhythm of their fingers. They
know it too.

I drop my satchel down onto my chair. Look at Dave. He
is leaning over his computer, his fingers poised, like he is
about to pounce, but unmoving, seems frozen in place.

'Dave? Dave?'

He doesn't answer for a moment, still staring at his

screen. Then seems to hear my words all at once, looks up at me with a start. 'Hi. How was the magistrates' court?'

I shrug. 'Hot.' Hot, and stuffed with neighbour disputes and car prangs, and drunk-and-disorderlies. Sitting there, and wondering what the hell I was doing with my life. 'You okay?' I say it casually, like it doesn't mean anything.

Dave grimaces, gaze rolling towards Lydia's door, back to me. 'Fucking awesome!' Drops his voice to a whisper. 'Something's going on.' Nods towards the closed door.

I try not to catch his eye. 'Well, let's not get carried away.' I sink into the chair, pull my mobile phone free from my bag. There is a text message waiting, one I hadn't heard coming in. Aden. I click it open, try to pretend that my heart isn't thudding. *Missed you this morning. Sorry about yesterday. I was a prick.* I stare at it, feel a heat rush through me.

'You got messages.'

'Huh?' It takes me a minute to realise that Dave isn't talking about the text. I look at him, but he's gesturing to the desk phone. I glance down. The red light is blinking.

'You got a call earlier.' Looks at me with a flat look. 'Steve Lowe.'

I stare at the blinking light. Sigh. 'Great.' I shake my head, pick up the receiver and punch the voicemail button. There is a tumbling static on the line, then his voice, hard. 'Miss Solomon, Steve Lowe. I need you to call me back. My wife, she says you came to see her, so thanks for that. I know you'll want to hear from me too, so ring me back, okay?'

I close my eyes, fight back a groan. Listen as he fumbles to disconnect, thinking about the livid bruise on his wife's abdomen, a perfect indentation of her husband's fist. And now, God, now I've let him think I'm writing his story, or at least she has let him think that. And when he finds out I'm not, it's Carla he's going to go after. Dammit. I pull the phone away from my ear, cradle the receiver against my forehead and want to scream. What the hell is wrong with me? When will I ever learn? Dammit!

I stay like that for longer than you'd think you could in a crowded office. But no one is looking at me; they are all too freaked out about the thought of losing their jobs to care about the possibility that I've lost my mind.

I'll have to speak to him. Will have to call Steve up, tell him I was trying to pursue the story, that Carla was right, but that we haven't got the budget for it, or I've been fired. Or I've emigrated.

There is a bang, the sound of a receiver crashing into its cradle, and I open my eyes. Stare at Dave. Can feel the others turning, momentarily pulled away from their fiscal woes by the sound. But that doesn't last. Within moments they have turned away again, click-clacking like their lives depend upon it.

'You okay?'

Dave isn't looking at me, is staring at the phone, and for a moment I wonder if I need to duck, if he's about to throw the thing across the room. 'Yeah, just . . . It's nothing. I was just trying to call someone, that's all.' His face is clouded, a sky full of storms.

I open my mouth to ask a question, then close it again. I need to learn when to mind my own business.

Then my desk phone rings, and my heart sinks and I brace, waiting to hear Steve's rough tones. 'Hello, *Swansea Times*. Charlotte Solomon speaking.'

There is a long silence and I figure that it's a wrong number, am about to hang up, when she speaks. 'Charlotte?'

'Yes. Who's this?'

'It's . . . I'm terribly sorry to bother you. It's Alexandra Wilson. Emily's mum.' A shuddering breath in. 'I'm so sorry to be a nuisance.'

'No, Mrs Wilson, no, of course. What can I do for you?'

'Oh, it's nothing really. I just . . . I was wondering if you were going to write that article. I mean, I know you have a lot of other stories – it's just that I've been keeping an eye on the paper, you see, and I hadn't seen it, and I wondered if I'd missed it or . . .'

'Oh, okay. Well, the thing is . . .'

'See, they're talking in church. People – you know how people can be. And they are saying things when they think I'm not listening, about how she must have been drunk . . .' Her voice fractures, breaks. A moment when she's not saying much of anything, and I can tell that she's fighting, trying to control the tears. 'And you knew Emily. That wasn't her. And that . . . it's just not right. So I was thinking that the story, if you were writing it, that the story would help, you know, put people straight.'

I listen as Alexandra cries. I have to tell her that I can't. I have to tell her that I'm not allowed to, that my job is on the line. I glance over my shoulder at Lydia's door, listening as this mother's heart breaks.

'Give me a little time.' I say. 'Okay?'

29

Aden: Thursday 28 August, 9.25 a.m.
Three days before the shooting

'I didn't say nothin'.'

The man stood at the centre of the small office, spindly legs akimbo, his fingers knotted across the top of his shaven head. He was looking at Aden, was trying not to, but couldn't seem to help it, his eyes pulled inexorably towards him, down towards the gun. Aden shifted, resting his hand on the Glock that sat at his hip, the man jumping, like he had been shot through with an electrical current. Aden suppressed a grin.

'Right, look, maybe I did say it, but I was jokin'. Can't take a fuckin' joke, that's the problem, innit?' Beads of sweat had begun to form across the man's brow line, creeping silently down his temples.

'So, you told the doctor that you were going to stab her, and everyone else on the ward, as a joke?' Del ran his hands across the back of the man's greased T-shirt, the underarms ringed in sweat, his face pulled up into a curl of distaste.

'I was just messin' around, like.'

'Oh, right. Arms up higher.' Del patted at his waist. 'So, have you got a knife then?'

203

'No, butt. Like, it was a joke.' The man shook his head vehemently, like a child caught in a lie.

'Oh, right. Ha-ha. Funny.'

Rhys glanced at Aden, rolled his eyes. Was standing, half-blocking the door. Didn't seem to notice the doctor, the one who had met them as they arrived at the hospital, dark-blonde hair tugged up into a high ponytail, pretty, unfeasibly young. He's been kicking off, she had said with a puff of impatience, has been threatening the nurses, saying that he's going to go all Dunblane on us. Her gaze had lingered on Rhys as she spoke. They've got him in the security office. Had walked with quick steps, keeping up with their longer strides with apparent ease. I don't know – the crap we have to put up with. Had glanced at Rhys, a quick smile. Thank you for coming. Aden had looked away, had suppressed a grin. She was sitting now, behind the desk in the office, her arms folded across her chest, ostensibly watching as Del completed his search, but her gaze wouldn't stick, kept trickling back to Rhys.

'Right.' Del pulled the man's arms behind his back. 'Let's get you down to the station.'

'Aw, come on. It's her, it is. Fuckin' got it in for me.'

'That's right.' Del put the handcuffs on, patting him on the shoulder. 'Everyone's whipping boy, aren't you?'

Aden watched, kept his hand on the gun. He hadn't slept much last night, had got a couple of hours at the most. Had been kept awake by the memory of Carla Lowe, of a boy/man's face. He shouldn't have gone to Harddymaes yesterday. Knew he shouldn't have gone, had known it then and yet had gone anyway, willingly hurrying towards his own demise. Had stumbled into sleep, once, twice, a fall into a blackened lake, and then the dreams had come. Not just the usual dreams. New ones now, all shrouded in the pall of cigarette smoke. The thumping of feet, the rain tearing at his skin, hardly running, more falling forward in a careless perpetual motion, feet barely connecting with the slick pavement. Then the alleyway, yawning in front of him. Had woken with a start then, slick with sweat.

Aden had lain on his bed, had stared at the ceiling, disoriented as the pieces of his memory moved. A collage of sights and sounds, shifting, so that now they make a vase, now two faces looking inwards. A boy's face, awkward in adolescence. The dark alleyway, lit with muzzle-flash.

Then something new, which hadn't been there before. A poster, flicking in the wind. Had seen it on his visit to Harddymaes, now inextricably wound up with Charlie's perfume. Now seeing it again, punching through the dark- ness as the car headlights fall across it. The boy, a thin, long figure running by it, so that the poster dances in his wake. A voice, a high childish lilt, from out of the darkness. Come on, Dylan. The boy stumbling through a puddle of waterlogged light. His hands in line with his waist, elbows pumping, back and forth, back and forth. Fingers splayed wide. Startlingly empty.

Aden had sat upright, had felt a rush of nausea. Put it down to the sudden movement, the rush of blood to the head.

He hadn't remembered it before. The poster. The boy running through the patch of light. The empty hands. It was . . . it was his mind, playing tricks on him. That was what it would be. Building a memory based on the foundation of a mother's grief. There was no truth in it. And besides, even if there was, it didn't mean anything. The kid could have had the gun in his waistband. Just because he wasn't carrying it, that didn't mean anything. Not really.

He had sat there, sitting amongst the detritus of his life. Trying to shift the shiny new memory of the boy's empty fingers.

'Aw, c'mon. You don't 'ave to arrest me. It's a joke, that's all.'

Del had angled the man towards the door. 'I know, mate. Friggin' hilarious. Come on.'

'You want a hand with him?' asked Aden.

'Nah. We got him.' Del nodded towards his partner. 'Come on, wide boy. We've got a custody sergeant who'll love your sense of humour.'

Aden stood aside, held the door open for the convoy, glanced back at Rhys. He was still standing, his arms crossed over his chest. Still hadn't noticed the doctor, that she was watching him. Aden shook his head, smiling, slipped through the door, thinking to get out of the way, giving a chance for love's young dream. But as the door swung shut, Rhys was there, on his elbow.

'What are you . . . ?' Aden caught himself, watched as the doctor slipped by, a quick nod and a smile and then she was gone. Aden flipped Rhys with the back of his hand. 'What the hell, dude?'

'What?' Rhys started.

'Mate, she was into you.'

Rhys frowned, looked over his shoulder. 'Huh?'

'Aw, Rhys. You are bloody hopeless.' Aden shook his head, laughed. 'Come on. Let's do this damn patrol.'

The hospital corridor was quiet, their tread unconscionably loud against the laminate floors. Few other people, the heat stultifying. There would be no respite. The heatwave was forecast to continue for the foreseeable future. You could see it in people's movements, like their limbs had been weighted, eyes heavy from the sleepless hot nights. They had come to an intersection, the place where four corridors met. Right ahead, up there on the left, that was where Imogen's office was. Felt like his feet wanted to walk that way, knock on the door, tell Imogen about the new memory, or his brain's fiction, whichever it was. She would understand it. Would know what to do.

He had almost called Charlie, last night. Had sat on the edge of the bed, had cradled the phone in his hands, had come so close to dialling that it seemed to him he could hear her voice. He wanted to speak to her, not because he thought she could fix anything, provide any answers. He wanted to speak to her just because he wanted to speak to her. Needed to hear her voice so badly that he could taste it. But he couldn't shake the moment, his temper jarred by Carla Lowe's grief, his quick flash of useless anger, and Charlie's recoil – the way she folded back in on herself, vanishing right in front of him. He had set down the phone. Waiting till dawn.

They had reached the crossroads, stood there as if they were lost, even though that could not possibly be true. They had both been here far too many times before. Up ahead, there was Imogen's office. To the right and up the stairs, Ward 12. Aden stared at the sign. Seemed to be larger than all of the others that surrounded it. Dylan Lowe was up there. Separated from them by little more than a narrow ceiling.

Rhys had folded his arms, the movement stirring Aden. He looked tired, dark circles ringing his eyes.

'You sleep?' asked Aden.

Rhys looked at him, let out a little laugh. 'Nah. Couple of hours here and there.'

Aden nodded. 'Me too.'

They were moving now, had begun to walk again without really meaning to, their feet doing what their minds seemed incapable of, sending them in the direction of Imogen's office.

'Do you . . .' Aden began. 'Do you ever wonder?'

'Wonder what?'

Aden didn't answer, listened to the tread of their shoes, had slipped into a harmony of his own. Then, 'Do you ever wonder if things really happened the way we thought they did?'

Rhys pulled up sharp. 'What do you mean?'

Aden shrugged. 'I never saw a gun.' He said it quietly, like it was a confession.

Rhys stared at him. 'But . . . I mean, the gun, you saw it. You must have.'

The Browning HP lying, abandoned in a puddle.

'Well, yes,' Aden allowed. 'I mean, I saw it after.' Tried to find the words, but then was floundering, swamped with the sudden realisation of what it was he had done. That whatever load he had carried was nothing compared to that laid on top of those who had pulled the trigger.

Rhys looked at him, like he was pleading with him to take it back, not make things any worse than they already were.

'It's nothing. I'm just trying to make sense of it all, that's all.' Aden shrugged, trying to wash clean the words he couldn't pull back. 'Your mind starts playing tricks on you, I guess.'

Rhys studied him for a moment, his lips forming into a shape, and Aden waited for the words to come. But they didn't, because instead Rhys glanced across Aden's shoulder, his face freezing in place. It seemed like he had stopped breathing.

Aden looked up, followed his gaze.

Imogen was emerging from her office, her face curled up in concentration. Beside her, his arms folded across his thick chest, Steve Lowe.

Aden's heart stopped.

He glanced around, checking exits, searching for ballistic cover. Because it seemed impossible that this would end without a hail of bullets. Could feel Rhys tensing beside him. Steve was nodding as Imogen talked, her voice soft, his face hard, anger rolling off him in waves.

Aden stared at Steve, knew that he shouldn't and yet still could not help himself. Was trying to picture him in a dark hoodie, the hood pulled up tight around his face, a gun nestled in his fingers. Standing outside his son's ward, trying to steel himself for what had to come next. He thought of Carla Lowe, the bruise, her words: 'Do you know what he said to me? He said that it would be better if he'd died. That Dylan would be better off dead.'

Aden had stopped walking, could no longer force his feet forward. Because it seemed to him now that all of the answers had unfurled before him, that what had happened – what would happen – had all now become inevitable. His hand moved towards his gun.

Then, after hours or moments, Imogen looked up. Saw Aden, Rhys. A flurry of emotions drowned her face. Then she gave a small, decisive nod, touched Steve on the arm and, with a slight inclination of her head, steered him down the corridor, away from them.

'I think this way is quicker,' Aden heard her say. 'Come on, I'll walk you.'

Imogen glanced back at them, a swift smile, a conspiratorial nod. And then they were gone.

Aden and Rhys stood for a moment, trapped in disbelief.
'Shit!' breathed Rhys.

'Yeah.' Aden's hand was still resting on his sidearm. Waiting.

Rhys gestured back towards the way they had come. 'This way?'

Aden watched Steve Lowe's retreating back. Nodded slowly.

'What?'

'You think that it's him?'

'Do I think what's him?'

'The gunman? He's about the right size, shape.'

Rhys was studying him, his forehead creased into a frown. And Aden's insides shifted, the uneasy feeling that he had said too much. 'Why would he be hanging around his son's ward with a gun? That makes no sense.'

And of course Aden couldn't tell him what Carla Lowe had said, couldn't say that he'd seen her eyes, thick with tears, as she told him that Dylan's father believed he'd be better off dead. Couldn't say any of it, because Aden shouldn't have been there at all. 'Yeah. I guess. Just getting paranoid.'

'Ade. Are you okay?' Rhys was still watching him, concerned, like he thought that at any moment Aden would crack apart.

Aden nodded, forced a smile. 'I'm fine. No worries.'

30

Imogen: Thursday 28 August, 5.27 p.m.
Three days before the shooting

Imogen slid her bare feet into the cool water. It was cloudy, dark with sand, lapping up against the broad steps on which she sat. A shiver raced through her, the water shockingly cold against her hot skin. Imogen dipped her fingers in, lapping the water against her ankles, her bare thighs. Tucked her skirt in between her knees. The sun had begun to sink in the sky. A breeze had picked up, sweeping in across the bay, raising the hairs on her arms. She raised her head, turned her face towards it.

The sunseekers had gone, for the most part, driven away by the encroaching tide. It was full in now, the water drowning the sand, tugging at the discarded bottles and wrappers, pulling them back out with it, so that they swam, waterlogged and bulbous, like plastic jellyfish. The people would be back tomorrow, though, drawn out by the heat of the day, with their once-a-year beach towels and their insubstantial swimsuits. Imogen glanced along the sea-front. A group of teenagers sat on the promenade a few hundred yards away. She couldn't see them, but could hear them, their overblown laughter fuelled with stolen cigarettes and White Lightning. She wouldn't stay long. Had just thirsted to dip her hot feet into the cold water and pretend, for a moment, that everything was as it should be.

Amy had nearly died this time. Had spun from 'doing well, soon to be released' all the way around to 'almost didn't make it'. That was what the doctors had said. The seizure – the one that had come crashing down from the clear blue sky – had ripped at her, her breath stoppered up in her chest, lodging there, so that when they got to her, with their resuscitation tools and their ruthless determination, she was all but gone. It had taken long moments. Long enough that there were many amongst them who doubted the outcome. But then it had come, so quiet it was almost impossible to detect: a quick ragged breath. Then another, then another. That was close, they had said.

And Imogen hadn't been there. Had been in session. Had turned her phone off; it was the professional thing to do. She had escorted Steve Lowe out of his session, her stomach clenching as she glanced up, saw Aden and Rhys, and for a moment she had felt a flood of panic, quickly calmed. Had steered Steve away. Had walked him, all the way to his car. Are you going to see Dylan? He hadn't looked at her, had shaken his head. Not today. It was only as she watched him drive away that she had thought to turn her phone on.

Mara had been on the floor when she arrived. Imogen had found her wedged in between the armchair and the wall, her hands over her head, wailing. She had thought Amy was dead. Imogen had run to her sister, had dropped to the floor, tugging her into a tight embrace, had felt her own tears running freely. A certain sense that the inevitable had at last happened.

Then a doctor, an older man, one with whom Imogen had passed the time again and again, turned from the bedside. Had frowned down at them. 'Your daughter is alive. Barely.'

Imogen couldn't make out the words; seemed that he must have been speaking Dutch, or some other kind of language that sounds enough like English that you think you should be able to understand it, even though you can't. Had stared at him. 'You mean, she's not . . .'

'She's breathing. She was lucky.' His words were brusque, and Imogen had wondered obliquely if he had always seemed this cold.

Mara, it seemed, had not heard him. Was still wailing, a sound like the breaking apart of the earth's crust. Imogen placed her hands on the sides of her face, forced her head up. 'Mara. Listen to me. Listen. She's okay. She's going to be okay.'

Seemed like her sister wasn't there, though, like she had left her body, just popped out for a while. Mara had stared at her, uncomprehending.

'Mara. Look. Amy's okay.' Imogen had turned her sister's head, forcing her to look at the little girl stretched across the bed.

And that was it. That was enough. Mara had scrambled then, pushing past Imogen and the remaining doctors.

'She is, isn't she?' Imogen grabbed the doctor's hand. 'She's going to be okay?'

He had studied her, his face flat. 'She seized, she stopped breathing. She came very close to dying. That should not have happened. We must . . . She's going to be with us for a good while longer.'

213

'But wait, so you still don't know why . . .'

'Dr Elliott-Lewis. She's a little girl. This should not be happening. I'm ordering more tests; there'll be blood tests. We will be keeping a very close eye on her, you can be assured of that.' He moved off, flanked by an array of younger doctors – a mother swan and her cygnets – and left her standing there, an uneasy feeling in her stomach.

The teenagers were shouting. Imogen turned her head towards the sound. Were they arguing? Or laughing? So hard to tell these days, when anger seemed to sound just like joy. She shook her head, looking back down at her feet. Could barely make them out now, but still swirled them in uneven circles.

Amy would be okay. She would be okay. Was basing that on the simple premise that anything else was unconscionable. But then, she allowed, the unconscionable happened every day. Thought of Steve. He hadn't wanted to come and see her, had made that abundantly clear. Had been appropriately guided by one of the nurses, after she had walked in on Steve and Carla screaming at each other in the middle of the ward. She had called Imogen, ostensibly to set up an appointment for him, but in truth to offer a courtesy warning. He's tightly wound. We don't see him here very often and, to be honest, I don't think he's coping with what's happened to his son. I told him he needs to see you. Made it sound like it was policy, cos you know what men are. That's okay, isn't it?

He had come into her office, a man before the firing squad, and one who was willing to go down fighting. Had sat in the comfy chair, had folded his arms, glared at her, daring her to attempt to dabble in his psyche.

He can't seem to accept it, the nurse had said on the phone. Refuses to accept his son's condition.

'Would you like to talk about your son?'

Steve had fixed her with a look, a Rottweiler baring its teeth. 'You know what happened then? You know what those murdering bastards did?'

Murdering bastards. But that was the crux of it, wasn't it? We tell ourselves the stories that we can handle, the ones that turn our world from what it is into what we need it to be to survive. These jeans shrunk in the wash. My fiancée is working late. My niece will be fine.

'I was told that your son has been diagnosed with a persistent vegetative state. That must be incredibly difficult for you and your wife.'

'You know they're back on the job, don't you? The pigs. Like nothing ever happened. Killed my kid and then, nothing. All right for some, isn't it?'

Stories were fine. But sometimes you needed someone to pull the curtain down, reveal the great and powerful Oz for the scared little man he is. 'Dylan, he survived, though, didn't he?'

He had stared at her. 'That's not surviving. Have you been up there? You seen him? He's gone. There's nothing left of him. He'd have been better off if they'd finished the job. Leaving him like this – it's worse than death. Fucking criminal, this is.' He was pointing at her, sharp jabbing motions that cut through the air.

Imogen had wondered if he even realised he was crying.

There were voices, footsteps on the sea-front right above her, and Imogen started, looking up. An elderly couple dressed in thick wool coats, the man wearing a flat cap, a terrier tugging on a lead between them. Couldn't make out

215

what they were saying, just the gentle swaying of the conversation. She caught the woman's eye. Smiled. Would have to be going home soon.

She had stayed with Mara. Had called her parents. She should let them know what had happened. It seemed the right thing to do. Had tried to ignore the knot in her stomach as she dialled. We're on our way, her mother had said. I want to be there, when it happens again. Imogen had closed her eyes, had thought how clumsy her mother's language was, how unconscious of the way in which it would settle upon a listener's ear.

They had sat, waiting for their parents, the chaos they would inevitably bring; had listened to Amy sleep. The door was propped open, could hear the nurses' voices, but not what they were saying. Imogen had rubbed her eyes, thought how much she missed her bed.

'I called him.' Mara's voice was low, but seemed too loud against the quiet.

'Who?'

'Jack. I told him she's got worse. He's booked a flight. He'll be here tomorrow.'

'That's good,' said Imogen.

A long silence, and then Mara said, 'I know what you're thinking.'

'I'm not thinking anything.'

'You are. You're thinking about him. The other one. You know. You're thinking that I'm a slut.'

Imogen had, in fact, been thinking about her sister's affair. About the jacket thrown so carelessly in a house where it didn't belong. The shoes, slotted into a life that wasn't theirs. Had thought, time and time again, how lucky her sister was. It had been plain, from the very beginning, that Jack adored her, had looked at her in a kind of wonderment, stunned that his own meagre presence could bring towards it this gem. Imogen got that, had often felt the same around her twin. It was tempting to be angry with Mara, to unleash the wellspring of frustration that had remained stoppered up for as long as she could remember. To shout at Mara for throwing away what she had, when it was all that Imogen had ever wanted.

But that wasn't fair.

Everyone's lives are different, everyone's relationship playing out to a slightly different tune.

And still, it was hardly surprising that Mara and Jack had hit troubled waters, when you really thought about it. He had idolised her, had adored her. But that, surely, is unsustainable? One cannot last for ever in a relationship believing that one's spouse hung the moon. There are irritations, mundanities that have to be fulfilled, in any relationship. And you could see it happening – the soft warping of their relationship as they settled into a marriage, a family. You could see that Jack got busier as he moved up through the ranks, from sergeant to inspector to chief inspector, more and more of his time taken up with his job, completing those portions of the adult life that were his to complete. And you could see Mara begin to wilt, a flower that had been moved into the shade for too long. And then, of course, Dubai.

'I don't think you're a slut,' Imogen said, quietly.

Mara nodded, chewed slowly on the words. 'He's been calling me. The other one.'

Imogen had studied her sister. 'What does he want?'

'He says that he wants me back. That he loves me.'

'What are you going to do?' Imogen could feel the irritation, a swirl of it beginning to rise in her insides.

Mara folded her hands across her stomach, gave a small wince. 'I don't know, Im.'

Then it erupted. Quietly, because they were in a hospital room and Amy was sleeping, but an eruption nonetheless. 'Mara, for God's sake. You're married. You can't keep doing this. You can't keep being so selfish. This isn't just about you and Jack, and whatever the hell his name is. This is Amy's family. You have to stop thinking about yourself and put her first. You owe her that.'

The tears began then, big and fat, rolling down Mara's cheeks. 'But, Im . . .'

'No. No "But, Im . . . " anything. You are being selfish.' What a relief the words seemed. So long of hardly thinking them, let alone saying them, only to have them tumble free of her, glowing in the twilight air. 'You have to stop this, Mara. For Amy's sake, if for no one else's.'

Her sister didn't look at her, stared ahead, the tears coursing over her cheeks. Then a shift, a slight nod of the head. 'Okay. Okay, I will.'

A wash of water slapped against Imogen's legs now, a surprise wave, bigger than those that had come before it, the cold of it jarring her. She pulled her legs up. Pushed herself up to standing. It was time to be going home. To Dave. She suppressed a sigh, praying to herself that his anger of yesterday would have abated, that the argument had blown itself out.

Imogen had studied her sister's face, Mara's hair loose, swathed around her shoulders, her eyes downturned. Had thought that she would love to be as effortless as her twin. 'Mara?'

'Yes?'

'Who is he?' Imogen had been surprised by the sudden

need she felt, the desperate thirst to know. She had watched her sister, the quick, fleet-footed flight of emotions across her face. Imogen's heart beating a little faster as she recognised one of them. Was it guilt?

Mara had shrugged. 'It doesn't matter now. Like I said, it's over.'

31

The Shooter: Saturday 30 August, 9.45 p.m.
Day before the shooting

It is late now. The road around is silent and dark, the rain bouncing from the road top. Puddles of orange street lights puncturing the blackness. I stare into the darkness, am fooling myself that I can see Mara's house, that the shaped shadows mean something to me. I don't know what it is I am waiting for.

I loved Mara. I can say that now. I felt something for her that, in spite of everything, I had never felt before.

I trod carefully, afraid to make a move in case it was the wrong one. But it seemed that was okay, that she was prepared to lead so that I might follow. We moved quickly, perhaps too quickly. But we left the waiting room together – Imogen forgotten now – got into my car and drove to her home. I steered the car, barely noticed the road, watching instead the trickle of rain that snaked its way down Mara's neck, slipping between her breasts.

Mara let us in through the front door, stepping aside to let me through and then closing it softly behind us. I saw nothing. I only had eyes for her, the layers of clothes that she began to peel off almost before the front door had shut, the wool and the cotton that formed puddles at the bottom of the stairs. The look that she gave me, instructional and appraising. Me pawing at my own clothes, my hands useless and overlarge, like it was the first time I had ever been tasked with undressing. Stumbling at the stairs, Mara's laughter like the shattering of glass, and suddenly she was standing above me, a higher step on the stairs, unzipping my jacket, allowing it to drift to the ground, pulling at my T-shirt. I remember the cold, burning against my skin, the sudden, startling realisation that she was wearing a bra, panties, nothing else, and that thought taking my breath away, so that then I was even more useless.

The memories of what came next are splotchy. All smooth skin, and hair that hangs like a curtain in my face, so that I can't breathe, but knowing that if I'm going to die, this is the way I want to go. Her on top of me, beneath me, surrounding me so that I can't see anything else apart from her. The taste of her, so sweet that it seems like chocolate, and knowing that no matter how much I have, it will never be enough.

A building and a building and then, just like that, it was over. And me flopping back and Mara rolling off me, reaching up, adjusting my arm so that it served as a pillow and snuggling into me so tight that I thought I must have died.

I knew then that I was in love.

I didn't say it. You don't do you? But I loved her.

Thoughts of my own demise receded into a dim and dark history, and were replaced by life, and softness and her. Something else – a presence that I'm not sure I'd ever felt before. Hope. That thought that life is not just out to screw with you, and that things could work out. We lay there, talked quietly. Well, Mara talked, a swell of words that

221

washed over me, rocked me like a mother singing a lullaby to her child. I just listened. And hoped.

I knew it wouldn't be easy. I knew that from the beginning. There would be obstacles. There would be things that must be overcome. But I also, for the most vapid of reasons, believed that they would be overcome. That here, with her, was where I was finally meant to be.

I look down at the phone where it rests on the passenger seat, picking it out in the darkness. Then I take a breath, hit Call. I raise the phone to my ear, listen as it connects, as the ringing starts. I am not expecting her to answer. I am expecting to be swept away on the wave of silence that will follow. But instead there is a click, a breath.

'Hello.'

'Hi.' My heart sits in my throat, seems like it is stopping my voice.

'Hi.' She is whispering, so softly that I can hardly hear her above the sound of the rain.

'I've really wanted to speak to you.' I'm shaking, my hand vibrating the phone against my head. 'I needed it.'

There is a long silence in which I think she has gone. Then, 'I'm sorry. I couldn't.'

Then I don't know what to say. So I sit, listening to her breathe.

'Listen, I have to—'

'No, Mara. Please.'

I hear her sigh. 'What is it?'

'I love you.' The words come out all in a rush. 'I know what you said. About . . . everything. But I love you.'

Mara cuts across me, leaves my mouth hanging open, my words cut off at the source. 'I'm sorry. I just can't.'

32

Charlie: Thursday 28 August, 5.55 p.m.
Three days before the shooting

'Hey.'

'Hi.' Aden sounds surprised. Like he didn't think he'd be hearing from me again. 'How are you?'

I glance around the hospital car park, at the smokers and the sick, the visitors scurrying around them like rats in a maze. 'Great. What about you?'

'Oh, you know. Fine. Look, I'm—'

'Don't worry about it.' I speak quickly, my words tumbling one after the other.

'No, but . . .'

'Listen, I shouldn't have taken you there, I knew it at the time. I was just interfering, sticking my nose in where I shouldn't. But then,' I let out a laugh that comes out more like a squawk and grit my teeth slightly, 'I'm a journalist, so you know how us hacks are.'

He doesn't laugh. I console myself that it wasn't that funny anyway.

'You were just trying to help. Because you care.' He phrases it oddly, with a little up-tick at the end, like it is a question, and I feel that old familiar sense of panic begin to build up.

'Yeah, well. Anyway, it's fine. I just wanted to call and say – well, I'm not sure what I wanted to say. Just thought, um . . . I'll see you tomorrow? At the pool?' I ask, sounding like a teenager.

I can hear him smiling. Git!

'Promise?' he asks.

I nod, forget that he can't see me. 'I promise. Got to get my chlorine on.' Shake my head because now I sound like a lunatic. 'Okay, see you tomorrow then. Bye.' Hang up the phone in a rush, drop my head, wonder what the hell is wrong with me.

See, it's always been a little this way with Aden. There's always been that something, the gentle hum that lies just beneath the surface. The awareness that seems to spike whenever he is around, the illusion that he is looking at me, that his gaze hangs around for longer than it should. We've never talked about it. Because, I mean, please. And I could be entirely imagining it. But it has just seemed to me for the longest time that there is some connection there that cannot easily be explained by the – let's face it – short amount of time we spend together.

I slip my phone into my bag, slot myself into the slip-stream of a group of visitors, to navigate the shoal of smokers. The sun is sinking in the sky, the heat of the day slowly beginning to abate. I ease my way past the visitors as they stop to study the stand of twenty-pence books parked in the lobby, walk, looking more confident than I feel.

I don't know when it happened. Aden didn't burst out at me, didn't melt me with his eyes or leave me a weeping puddle at the side of the pool. He was . . . there. Every day. He was there. And then, in a shift I didn't notice happening, I started to look for him to be there. And then there was the night of the shooting, and me holding a busted-up umbrella over his head and, after that, the conversation just seemed to spill, like someone had pre-scripted it, arranging all of the words so that each player in the scene gets their equal share.

I stop, scan the signs quickly. Ward 12. Upstairs, turn towards the stairwell, because I have neither the patience nor the claustrophilia required to make me think that lifts are a good idea. I take the steps two at a time, check my watch. Still visiting time. Still a chance that there will be bundles of people, that I will be able to slip in amongst them, the sneak attack of the hack. I reach the top of the stairs, pull at the door. It is quieter here, footsteps more subdued. It seems like everyone is just waiting, wondering who death is going to come for next. Ward 12 is right ahead. I hang there, my forward progression suddenly halted.

I shouldn't be here – not according to my editor at least. But then where's the surprise in that? Seems that I am always where I shouldn't be. I considered, briefly, going to see Lydia again. Throwing myself on my journalistic sword. But it would have been pointless. The afternoon was spent waiting. Lydia didn't open her office door. We could hear the voices within the office: hers, the owners who have swept in with their long-reaching gazes, the sound rising and falling, the occasional burst of anger. The newsroom waiting, trying to look busy, because the last thing you want to do when there are redundancies on the table is look like you have nothing to do. Resolute punching of keyboards, an over-focused stare at computer screens, and then, because it really is impossible to resist, a breakaway glance towards the blindfolded office, where the future is being written. So I did my job, quietly, resolutely, my gaze flicking up towards Dave. He wasn't doing anything, was just sitting there, not even pretending that his time here was well spent. Like he had already given up.

I should just keep my head down. Do exactly what I am told. But over and over again I heard Emily's mother's words. The pleading that this would not be how her daughter was to be remembered.

I sat at my desk. I kept my head down. Watched as the clock ticked to five, five-ten, five-twenty. Everyone staying later than they should. Trying to show willing. A last, silent plea. At five-thirty-five the exodus slowly began, a drifting, reluctant creep, rich with backward glances towards Lydia's office door. I stood up, threw my bag over my shoulder. Dave still sat there, staring. I should have said something, had hung there, considering. But in the end I simply left.

It would be in my own time. After work. No one could criticise that. I could root around, in my own time. Just see if there was anything there that could make a mother feel better.

I study the door to Ward 12. A security guard, one that I don't recognise, stands before the door, his arms folded across his chest, a dark tattoo snaking from underneath his short sleeves. He glances at me, a quick, appraising look, then stares off again into the middle distance. I wonder if he is modelling himself on the guards at Buckingham Palace.

I try a smile. 'Hi. I, ah . . . I need to go in there.' I gesture to the door behind him.

He looks at me, more intently now, scans my hands, my waist. I have a sudden flash that he's going to want to strip-search me. But then he shrugs and, reaching over his shoulder, pushes his thumb into the buzzer.

I smile a thank-you, but he has looked away again. Is still studying that patch of flecked paint on the opposite wall. Must really like magnolia.

A figure appears behind the glass. A nurse studying me, her face folded up into a frown. Then her arm moves, the intercom sparking to life. 'Can I help you?' She stares at me, young, thick-waisted, big-busted, her blonde hair knotted into an elaborate series of plaits. Her eyes look heavy, red-rimmed.

'My name is Charlotte Solomon. I'm with the *Swansea Times*, and I was wondering if I could have a chat with you about Emily Wilson?'

Her face slides into some expression that I cannot identify, and I fight back the urge to slip into a jabbering explanation. Sometimes the hardest part of this job is keeping your mouth shut. I think she is going to tell me to piss off, can almost see her mouth form the words. Then she glances around over her shoulder, her lips moving in silent conversation.

Dammit. I cringe. Waiting for the spark of sound, the intercom bouncing back to life, the nurse telling the security guard to throw me the hell out. But instead there is a buzz, a click, and the door swings open.

'I'm going on my break.' The nurse stands in the doorway. She doesn't smile. Up close, she has that look about her, the one that people get when they have been crying, but have stopped, the redness faded, leaving behind slack, exhausted muscles. 'I'm going to the canteen.'

'Oh. Right,' I say. I can't help but look over her shoulder, through the open ward door. It is quiet inside. A tension hanging in the air, so thick it is visible. Visitors huddle around beds, nomads around campfires, for the most part talking quietly amongst themselves, as those they have come to visit lie inert. You can see the fear in them, those who hold the hands of the sick. It is written plain across their faces, even though they are trying to hide it.

Then, beyond that, there is a room, just past the nurses' desk. The door is standing wide open. Dylan Lowe is lying prostrate across the bed, his mother Carla seated by his side. She is holding his hand. I can see the movement of her fingers, stroking the skin. A book lies open on the bed, propped up against Dylan's legs. I can't see what it is, but I can hear the soft climb and fall of his mother's voice. Occasionally her tone drops, becoming almost a growl as she morphs into a character. And I can't not smile. I take a step forward, not thinking what I am doing. Can see Dylan. His hair is damp, looks like it is freshly washed. His eyes, open. He is staring at the ceiling. I wonder what it is that he is seeing. Carla pats her son's hand, turns a page.

'Are you coming?' The nurse's voice startles me, snapping me out of my reverie. She pulls the door closed behind her with a snap and, without a glance at the security guard, marches out into the corridor.

I turn and follow.

The canteen is quiet, the metal shutters pulled down. They have stopped serving food – nothing available but what can be scavenged from the row of amusement-arcade machines. The nurse marches towards a boxy drinks machine, pushes coins into the slot. 'Tea?'

I nod. 'Thank you.'

She hands me a paper cup, the liquid inside a burnished orange colour. And nods towards a table by the window. 'Shall we sit? Sorry. The tea's not very nice.'

I smile. 'It'll be fine.' I pull out a chair, slip into it. The nurse wears an engagement ring, a narrow band, the kind of diamond that would most generously be described as a chip.

'She wasn't like that, you know.'

'Wasn't like what? I'm sorry, I don't know your name?'

She studies me, seems uncertain. Then, 'It's Chloe. Emily wasn't a party girl, someone who got plastered all the time. I know what people are saying. I hear the rumours, that she must have been drunk to have ended up . . . where she ended up. And yes, occasionally she would have a drink. But she wasn't a drinker. She'd have one, two at the most. She just . . . she wasn't like that.' Her voice tails off, a quick hard-eyed glance at me, as if daring me to disagree.

I hesitate, then, 'I know.'

She looks at me, seems startled. I wait for her to ask, but she doesn't. She's waiting for me to take the lead.

'You knew her well?' I ask.

'She was one of my best friends,' says Chloe.

I sip the tea. It truly is awful. 'Can I ask: when did you see her last?'

She is looking out of the window, her face spasming like she's in pain. 'The day before . . . you know. But the thing is,' a gulping breath in, 'I should have met her that night. We were going to have a girls' night. It was my first, since I had my baby.'

'So what happened?'

'They asked me to do an extra shift. Up on the ward. And the thing is, with the baby – and my other half doesn't make much – we need the money. So I called her, told her I couldn't go.' She leans forward, staring into her cup, black tears spilling. 'She was already in the bar.' A laugh that she doesn't really mean. 'Emily was always early. She was great about it, so understanding. But that was Emily. She was always so understanding.' She shakes her head. 'And, to be honest, I kind of forgot all about it. What with all the fuss that night – that man with a gun, and the police and everything. It was . . . it sounds awful to say "exciting", doesn't it? But it kind of was. So I forgot about Emily. And then I found out that she had died.' Her voice breaks, words swallowed in a sob.

I turn, look out of the window. The sun is beginning to sink, spilling heat into the canteen.

'I'm sorry.'

'It's okay.' I hesitate for a moment. 'Chloe, how did Emily get to the restaurant that night? Her parents said her car was in the garage.'

'A cab. That's what she said she would do, anyway.' Chloe shakes her head. 'Thing is, you've got to understand . . . Something happened to her, that night. She would never, ever have got drunk on purpose, certainly not drunk enough to have wandered onto the M4.'

I look down, nod. 'I know. I think you're right.'

That seems to calm her. She sits back, studying me again. 'Did you know her?'

'A long time ago. She was . . . a wonderful girl.'

'Yes. Yes, she was.'

'Chloe, can I ask: her mum, she said that Emily seemed down that day, that she wasn't herself. Do you have any idea why that might be?'

The nurse bites her lip, not looking at me. 'It had been a rough shift, the night before. We lost a patient – someone that Emily had taken care of for a long time – so, I mean, of course that's always rough. And then there was that other thing. The man with the gun.'

'Emily saw the gunman?'

Chloe nods. 'She was the first one. Said that she was going through notes at the nurses' station and just had that kind of feeling, you know, like she was being watched. She said that she looked up and saw this figure holding a gun in his hand, standing there, watching her.'

'Did she say anything else about it? I mean, did she recognise him at all?'

The nurse shakes her head. 'He had his face hidden. That was what she said.'

'Was there anyone who might have had a problem with Emily? Someone who may have wanted to hurt her?'

As soon as the words are out of my mouth I curse myself, because they have come out clumsy, awkward, and I can see Chloe recoil, her eyes widening in alarm.

'No. Why? What do you mean? I thought . . . it was an accident, what happened to her. That's what the police said, right?'

I nod, try to look soothing. 'Yes. Of course. I was just curious. You know, about the man that she saw. That's all.'

Chloe nods slowly, unconvinced. Then pushes her chair back. 'I should go.' She drains her cup, grimacing. 'I need to get back to the ward.'

I stand with her, hold out my hand to stay her. 'I'm sorry. One more question. The bar where you were supposed to be meeting Emily? Where was that?'

33

Aden: Friday 29 August, 10.12 a.m.
Two days before the shooting

The range was breathless, had pulled in heat from another
relentlessly hot day, sucking it into its breeze-block walls,
its aluminium roof. The officers hung around in packs, in
this way really not that different from school. The young-
sters, the ones new to firearms, who still carried their guns
with a certain swagger, thinking they were big men now.
The old-timers, who sat on overturned buckets, boxes, had
been doing this long enough to know that it's just another
job, just another day to get through before you can go
home, put your feet up. And the shooters. Aden and Tony
and Rhys. How, Aden wondered, was it that he had come
to be classed like this? He who had not shot at all. But it
was obvious, in the way the room split itself up, the other
firearms officers stepping around them, like now they had
graduated into a class that was entirely their own. Aden
leaned back against the breeze-block wall, watching as the
trainers set up the targets, could feel sweat pooling under
his collar. They had been predicting storms. For more than
a week now they had been warning and prophesying that

the heat could not continue, that it would break soon into electric skies, would deluge rain. But the skies remained relentlessly blue, the earth parched and cracked.

'Gum?'

Aden nodded, reached out and accepted the small square that Rhys passed him. 'Cheers.' He should have been off today, should have been still in bed. But operational pressures had led to the cancellation of their rest day, and so here they were, stuck on the clammy range, the atmosphere thick with a feeling of heaviness unrelated to the weather.

'Yeah.'

'Fucking hot.'

'You're not kidding.' Rhys leaned against the wall beside him, ran a hand through his hair.

They didn't say anything, made no formal agreement, but both in unison turned to watch Tony. He was standing alone. Not standing, pacing. A steady tromp, backwards and forwards. Aden thought of the tigers at the zoo, marking out the steps of their cage, enraged by their captivity. Tony filled up the dead space – the one that had formed between the shooters and the others. He walked with his shoulders thrown back, a strut like he had just walked off a film set. But every now and again his gaze would trickle back to the knotted men and women. Aden watched him: three long strides, a turn, three long strides. Another look. Was he looking to see if they were watching him, seduced by his own hero mythology? Or was he looking, waiting for them to call him in – the isolation of being different finally beginning to wear him down?

Aden's glance shifted towards the other firearms officers. The old-timers were listening to Kate tell some story about her dog, the extortionate vet bills. The newcomers, they would glance over occasionally, then quickly look back down, cowed by the shooters in their midst. Aden shook his head, would have laughed if it wasn't so fucking absurd. Too cool for one group, too lame for the other. Poor Tony.

'So, you see Charlie this morning?' asked Rhys.

Aden nodded. Resolutely not looking at his partner. 'Yup. Swimming.'

He had got there early. Had changed and then hung out at the side of the pool. Waiting. Charlie had shown up on time, exactly when she had said she was going to be there, had looked at him, a quizzical frown, wondering what the hell he was doing wandering back and forth in his swimming trunks. You okay? Yeah, just, ah . . . waiting for you. Oh. Okay. They had stood there for a moment, and even though it was the same pool they used every day, with the same people and the same sounds, everything was different. Aden had opened his mouth. Had no idea what he was going to say, just knew that there were words piling up and they had to come out or he would lose his mind. But there was a splash, someone misjudging a tumble-turn, and it pulled Charlie's attention away, and then the moment was gone. Now they were just two people standing at the side of a pool, wearing very little. Charlie had turned, pulling her goggles on as she went. Come on then. Race you!

Iestyn was done with the targets now, walking back down the range towards them with long, even strides.

'All right, let's get going. We'll have an eight-round shoot from twenty yards. Glocks first, if you please. We've got a full house today, so let's do it five people at a time. First five, line up.' He turned towards Aden, gestured with his head. 'Ade? A second, please.'

Rhys took the hint, pushed himself away from the wall to join the others waiting to shoot.

'You, ah . . . you thought any more about it?' The sergeant wasn't looking at him, had turned, folded his arms across his thick chest and was staring down-range, where the first five were finding their positions.

'It?'

'The FTU. Only closing date's coming up.'

'Yeah, I . . . I'm still thinking.'

'Think fast,' said Iestyn. 'This is a good opportunity for you. I'd like to see you on that team.'

'Okay. Sarge? The Mount Pleasant Hospital thing . . .'

'Yeah.' Iestyn shook his head. 'Looks like we'll be pulling back on that one. No sightings since Tuesday. Powers that be are going to reduce firearms patrols. Just don't have the manpower to hang about when there's no sign of trouble.'

Aden felt his stomach flip. 'Well, I mean, I'm a little concerned – you know, what with the Lowe boy being there. And, ah . . . his father, Steve Lowe. You know that he has access to weapons, right? That Dylan's grandfather has a firearms licence for a shotgun.'

The sergeant gave him a long look. 'Why the hell would Steve Lowe want to go after his own kid? Do you have any reason to think he was actually the gunman?'

Aden hung in indecision. He couldn't repeat what Carla had said, because technically he was never there.

'Yeah,' said Iestyn. 'That's what I thought. Look, I don't like the guy either, but without evidence . . . Besides, don't you think we're unpopular enough with the Lowes right now? If there's anything concrete we'll take another look, but for now I'd say put it out of your head. There's still plenty of security at the hospital, we'll still be doing patrols for the time being, just the numbers of them reduced is all. Anyway,' he clapped Aden on the shoulder, 'let me know about the FTU, okay?' He turned, striding away.

Tony had pushed his way through the throng, had taken the centre spot. Was standing there now, with wide legs. Waiting. Rhys beside him, looking tired, like he hadn't slept again. Aden had wondered if he should ask Imogen about Steve Lowe, what he was doing seeing her. Perhaps she would know more, would recognise what it seemed that only Aden saw: that Steve was capable of killing his own son. But Imogen wouldn't talk to him about it. Stupid. Of course she wouldn't – that was her job. Aden had an image of Steve Lowe sitting on her sofa, weeping into his tattooed knuckles. He shook his head, dislodging the image, because somehow that picture was worse than the other one, the one where Carla Lowe wept over the inert figure of her son. Then, of course, he was thinking about Carla again, and didn't want to do that, either. So he didn't see a gun in the boy's hand, or thought he didn't – because who could tell how genuine these memories were, when everyone knew how easy it was for memories to be corrupted? It could have been in his belt or hidden, or anything.

'Ear-defenders on. Ready. Take aim. Fire.'

The sounds bounced around the range, the dull echo of them carrying through the thick ear-defenders, boom, boom, boom.

Aden tried to concentrate on the shooting. Tried not to think about Steve Lowe or Carla Lowe or Charlie. Then the yawning silence after the sound.

'All clear? Right, holster your weapons. Let's go.'

They walked down towards the butts, the clean paper

targets now pockmarked with bullet holes grouped in the torso. Tony striding towards his target, glancing left and right to see if anyone else was looking. Rhys slower, dragging behind. Iestyn, his hands on his hips, scanned the targets.

'Nice grouping there, Tone.' He ran his finger across the paper figure. The bullet holes were grouped in the torso, one sitting in the shoulder. 'One wild one, but the rest are lovely.'

Tony let loose a bark of laughter. 'Yeah, looks just like that kid did, when I shot him.'

Aden felt a thrill of fury. The air chilled, plummeting a dozen degrees in a microsecond. The firearms officers – the new, the old – looking at one another, so many silent conversations that it felt like they were screaming. Rhys's face hardened, his arms folding.

'All right, Tone.' The sergeant shifted, uncomfortable; you could see that he was trying to work out the best way to deal with this.

Tony shrugged. 'Just sayin'.'

Aden could feel it, the rage building up. How the fuck was it so easy for him? How could Tony brush it off? This fucking wanker, who had pulled the trigger when Aden had failed, and now could laugh about the kid lying senseless in a hospital bed. Could feel Rhys beside him, vibrating. How was it that they could feel it, could see that night over and over again, so that they couldn't sleep, could barely eat, and this prick could joke about it?

'Tony. Shut the fuck up, there's a good boy,' Aden said.

They had all turned now, were looking at him, from him back to Tony, like it was some kind of tennis match. Aden stared at Tony as the expressions billowed across his face.

'Right, that's enough. Back up to twenty yards, please.

Aden, grab a spot.' Iestyn held his arms out, steering them like a sheepdog with a flock.

'Yeah,' Tony muttered, 'if you think you can actually pull the fucking trigger this time.'

There was a low, rippling breath. Everyone looking at Aden, waiting.

Aden walked steadily back to his position, waited for the others to join him, could feel the heat of their stares on his face. Waited for the sergeant to call the shoot, pulled his gun out, landed eight rounds – each and every one perfect within the centre of the torso – holstered his gun.

Knew that Tony was watching him; that he was waiting too, to see how far he could push Aden.

Waited until the ear-defenders were off. Turned to face him. 'Tell me something, Tone,' said Aden.

'What's that?' Tony was spoiling for a fight; you could see it in him, the way his feet were set wide so that he had balance, the way his fingers kept balling up, like they were itching to punch something.

'Just how small is your dick? The way I see it, must be pretty damn tiny, the way you jerk off over that gun.' That was it, the moment. Aden had known it would be, had seen it coming, but had sallied forward anyway, because he was on fire and the thoughts and the anger and all the other shit just wouldn't go away, and for once it felt good to let them out. He watched as Tony's face went slack, as he processed the words and then the blaze of light. Aden saw his shoulder pull back, knew that Tony was going to hit him, waited, feeling the sweet relief of pain before the punch ever lands.

But instead Tony's hand flew to his holster. He pulled out his gun.

Aden stared down the barrel of the Glock.

Time had ceased. There was no sound. All that there was in the world now was this small black hole, sucking everything else into it.

He should have asked Charlie out.

Then it quivered, a small movement, but it was enough to break the spell. Sound leaked back in, the sergeant bellowing, 'Holster that weapon. Holster that weapon, now.' Tony's face, split with fear as he realised just what it was he had done. Then the gun dropping away, hitting the floor with a clang, and Aden wincing, a reaction that came too late to the party. His gaze settling on Tony, and Tony's gaze on him, and then a movement that he didn't see fast enough to react to – Tony's fist flying from nowhere and connecting with his eye socket in an explosion of pain.

34

Imogen: Friday 29 August, 5.01 p.m.
Two days before the shooting

Traffic was thick, cars lining bumper-to-bumper along the sea-front road. Imogen sat, the windows rolled down, waited as an uneasy driver attempted a U-turn in the clogged roadway before her. A tourist, no doubt. It was always busy in Mumbles at this time of year, people flooding to the beaches. She leaned her head back, breathed in the salt air. Tried to stop her brain from working.

She had wandered through today's sessions, had done her best to listen to her clients. But she couldn't shake off the look on Mara's face, the way her eyes slid, down and away. Imogen could always tell when her sister was lying. It had hung over her that day, the feeling that prickled the air like there was an electrical charge in it, a thunderstorm about to break. The knowledge that there was something there, something that neither one of them was saying. The fear of what that might be.

A green light, a swell of relief from the idling cars and, finally, movement. Imogen flicked her indicator on, pulling the car into a hard right up the steep hill.

Mara had always drawn people to her. Not just men, women too. Their mother always said that Mara had an electric personality, that people just seemed to want to be around her. There were always knots of people fighting for her attention.

Wasn't that how Imogen had met Dave? Dave had been one of Mara's friends, to begin with, part of a knot of admirers who seemed to follow in her wake wherever she would go. And, of course, wherever she went, there too was Imogen. Mara had laughed at Dave. *He's such a geek. He's nice enough, I suppose, but really.* She had pulled a face, and Imogen had laughed at her, trying to ignore the splash of guilt. *He's nothing to look at, is he?*

Imogen would wonder, in her darker moments, if this was where it had been born. If she had fallen for Dave because he, too, sat in her sister's shadow, invisible.

She climbed slowly through dense traffic, the evening sun at her back. People wandered into the roadway; it seemed like for them there was no segregation: pavement, road, all the same. The Renault in front honked its horn, a loud angry parp, then a roar as the accelerator raced. It always amazed her the way in which people seemed surprised by the crowds, the density of it all, as if they believed they were the only ones who would ever have thought to come here to this place, where the village spilled down into the sea. She took a right, creeping around a blind bend.

Two years. Two years of being invisible, of Dave not seeing her as anything other than her sister's matching pair. And then the second-year ball. It would be a big event, everyone had said. White tents littering the field, wooden boardwalks that tried – and failed – to hide the mud that

241

squeezed its way through the slats, seeping into hemlines, coating the soles of the unlikely sandals for which she had paid far too much. Some band was playing, a thrumming, thundering beat; a scraggly, indie-looking conglomerate that everyone claimed to be fans of, but no one seemed to know. Imogen had bought a new dress. Dave would be there. They would all be there. And, in the quiet, dark corners of her mind, Imogen had hoped that tonight he would notice her. She had never admitted this to Mara, and afterwards she would take solace in this. That her sister couldn't have been expected to know. Not *know*-know. Not really. Imogen had let her daydreams idle, let conversation spill onto other things the way it so inevitably did with Mara, so that, in the end, her feelings for Dave could be called a secret. And you can't criticise someone for not knowing your secrets, can you?

It had been loud and sticky, all thumping bass and bumping bodies, and in the dark gloom of the tent a smell of must and mud, and she had wondered why she had gone to so much effort. Just what the point had been. Dave had arrived, a little after ten, his gaze bleary, stance unsteady. Hadn't looked at her. Which shouldn't have surprised her. Not really. She had drunk more than she should have, had drowned her sorrows in the cut-price, cut-quality tequila, so that soon her head was swirling, her footsteps awkward and uneven. Hadn't really thought to look for Mara. Not for a while. She had said that she had her eye on some Scottish lad, the captain of the fencing team. Imogen had drunk, slowly, steadily, and hadn't even stopped to ask herself where her sister was.

But she wasn't a competent drinker. Her stomach had heaved, her head spun and she had run, with awkward, slip-slidey steps, to the exit. Had barely made it before her stomach emptied itself, the vomit pooling into the mud.

Then she had seen them. Mara and Dave were tucked towards the back of the tent, seemingly ignorant of the rain that had begun to fall around them. Had their arms wrapped around each other, their bodies locked together, moving in an unsteady, out-of-beat rhythm to the music.

Imogen had stood there for impossibly long moments, watching, her brain spinning, trying to work it out, and cursing the tequila for making it so damned difficult. Because surely, if she stared long enough, there would be an explanation. She had watched as Dave's hand snaked across her sister's back, working its way down so that it rested, cupped around her buttock. Had watched as her sister looked up, smiled.

Then Imogen had turned and run, an awkward movement, her thin, strapped shoes sliding on the uneven boardwalks. Telling herself that it didn't matter, that they were both single, that they could get together if they wanted. And after all she hadn't told Mara what she was feeling, not really; had kept it all tucked up in herself the way she always did, so that her sister couldn't be expected to know. And you couldn't blame Mara for that. It was Imogen's own fault. She had got into bed and had closed her eyes and waited, until a little after three, when the front door screed open and ragged laughter was carried up the stairs and through the walls, until it seemed like it was everywhere. And then footsteps, a door closing, the sounds of a bed creaking. Imogen had cried herself to sleep.

Imogen slid the car into an empty space, at the top of the hill. Looked at their house through her rear-view mirror. Dave's car sitting outside. She sat, stared at it. Wanted to cry.

She had awoken, on the morning following the ball, and for a moment hadn't known what had woken her. Then heard the low thrum of voices through the walls. Her sister's voice, low, insistent. 'It was a mistake. You need to go. Before . . . look, just go.' Another voice – a man's – lower, almost whispering, and no matter how much she had strained, she couldn't hear the words, could just make out the tone of it, the need. Then footsteps. A door slamming.

Had lain there, had stared at the ceiling, had felt something that seemed strangely like relief. She couldn't tell who the man was, she hadn't heard him well enough. He could have been someone else. In all likelihood, would have been. The captain of the fencing team, probably, that Scottish guy. Because he was the one Mara had wanted, and Mara always got what she wanted. She didn't want Dave. She didn't even like him, not really. It would have been someone else.

Imogen pulled the keys from the ignition, cradled them in her hand. Watched the sun sinking low in the sky. She could see the sea from here, a burst of blue that snaked its way in between the houses.

She didn't see him again that year, not for months and months and months. Not until the summer had moved into autumn and then into winter, and even then it was an accident, a chance meeting: him walking into the library, her walking out. A quick recoil, him thinking that she was her sister, and then, when he realised that it was in fact her, a smile. Hanging in the doorway, getting in everyone's way, because he wanted to talk to her.

Telling herself that it was okay, because everyone makes mistakes.

Imogen had never asked Mara. She had never asked

Dave. Because there are some things that you are just better off not knowing.

Imogen pushed at the car door. She stood there in the sunlit evening street. Looking at the keys in her hand, then across her shoulder at the sea. It would be all right. Everything would be all right. She slammed the door behind her and walked with quick steps, slipping her key into the lock. Upstairs the shower was running.

She would change. Shake off the worries of the day, start the evening fresh. She would do them something nice for dinner. A steak, perhaps. Imogen ran softly up the stairs.

Afterwards, Imogen would wonder what it was, what made her do it. But, for that moment, there was no thought. The bathroom door was closed, the sound of water thumping, a typhoon in a teacup. The bedroom door standing open. Was it the wardrobe door? Was that what did it? A little half-inch of space, where usually there was a seal, just beckoning Imogen inside. Afterwards, all Imogen would remember was that it had seemed as natural as breathing, that she had walked into the bedroom and then, without thinking, it seemed, crossed the floor to Dave's wardrobe. Afterwards, it would seem that it had called to her, that somehow she had heard it, and that was why she opened the wardrobe door.

Imogen stood there, staring into the dark depths of the wardrobe. At first it seemed that all she could see was clothes, misshapen mounded piles. The sensible thing to do would be to accept that, to walk away. Imogen plunged her hand in, through dense fabric, reaching, reaching. She did not know what she was looking for, and yet somehow it seemed that she knew exactly what it was that she would find.

Her fingers gripped something cold.

There are moments when the world seems to lay itself out before you, showing itself for what it is. It seemed to Imogen that this was one of them. Her stomach lurched, felt like she would vomit.

She pulled the rifle free.

It was surprisingly light for something that could do so much damage.

She weighted the gun, staring into the wardrobe, into the hole in the fabric that she had just made. A box of ammunition.

'What are you doing?'

Imogen started, spun; hadn't heard the shower stop, Dave's footsteps. Dave stood on the threshold to their bedroom, a towel slung around his waist, hair hanging wet. Looked from her to the gun, back.

'I . . .' There was a speech, there were things she should be saying. But she wasn't saying any of them. Instead she was standing in their bedroom, holding a gun. 'Dave . . .'

'Give me the gun.'

'Why is it here? What are you . . . ?'

'Imogen, just give me the damn gun.' He leaned into her, drowning her in an overwhelming smell of soap and anger.

Now, suddenly, Imogen was afraid. She stared at him, no idea suddenly who he was, where it was he had come from. She should have given him the gun, should have just handed it right back to him. But her body had taken over, had dethroned her brain, and she was clinging to the gun like a life-raft in a choppy sea. A single thought that seemed to come from out of the pure blue sky: if I give him the gun, he's going to kill me.

So Imogen stood there, holding onto the weapon like

she would have any idea what to do with it anyway. And then Dave was leaning into her, as if he was going to kiss her, but his face curled up into an expression that she just didn't recognise, his fingers reaching for the gun. And she wasn't sure how it happened, whether it was his pulling or her pushing, but somehow she was falling, an impossibly long way, falling for ever, and he was grabbing for her, and then a crack as her head hit the wall behind her. Then nothing.

35

The Shooter: Saturday 30 August, 9.50 p.m.
Day before the shooting

I sit on my bed. I don't remember the drive home or when I finally made the decision to leave, to cast one last look at Mara's house, start my engine – my fate final. I don't remember if there was traffic, or whether the steering was light on the slick roads. I am damp, my clothes sticking to me like they have been glued there, but I don't remember getting wet. I don't remember picking up the gun. But there it sits in my hand, heavy and full of promise. I stare at it distantly. In my other hand, my mobile phone. I don't know why. Because it is already too late, the decision has been made, the path before me inevitable. But still I cling to it. Like there is still a part of me that is waiting to be saved.

We lasted longer than I could have expected, Mara and I, although still not as long as I would have hoped. I couldn't tell you now how long it was, because it seems that my entire life began and ended with her. Although I suppose in some ways that's true. I loved her. And then she was gone.

The end happened suddenly. Looking back now, I know

I should have expected it, seen it coming. With all of the baggage that we carried, it never was going to last for ever. And with all such things there is an inevitability about their ending. That the universe will once again re-establish itself, reminding you that you are irretrievably alone.

But still the ending of it took me by surprise. We were eating together, a process that involved a certain amount of subterfuge. But where she was careful, I was careless, in the truest sense of it. I didn't care. I wanted everyone to know. She was quieter than normal, seemed to have sunk in on herself. So I spoke for both of us. Seems now that I spoke more in those few months than I have ever spoken in my entire life. I talked about my day, I complained about the traffic, all the while congratulating myself on the normality of it all. Watched her as she pushed the curry across her plate, movements listless.

'You okay?' I asked.

'I'm fine.' Mara didn't look at me when she spoke. It was only afterwards, when I replayed it, that I would hear the impatience in her voice, would see her posture – that slight turn in her shoulders, the ever so subtle lean away from me – would tell myself that I should have seen it coming.

Then she had pushed her plate away, her movements electric-shock sudden, had hurried from her seat, her hand clasped across her mouth. And me staring after her like a moron. Could hear her, in the downstairs bathroom, the retching. My first thought that there must have been something wrong with the food, but then how could that be, when she had eaten so little of it anyway? Then came my second thought, slower to arrive than my first, its progress dragged down by its weight.

I stood up. Stared at the closed bathroom door.

It took minutes or hours for her to emerge, her face ashen. She wouldn't look at me. I should have known then what would come next.

'You're pregnant.' The words tasted strange in my mouth, like peppermint when you expect orange.

Mara's gaze had snapped up then, fixing me in its spotlight. She had opened her mouth, closed it. A child caught throwing stones. She looked down and away, and I could see it, that she was struggling to think up a palatable lie.

'You are, aren't you? You're pregnant?'

In those moments, short though they were, I had already written our future. A house with a garden. A dog perhaps. A swing-set. Us together, naturally. Our child. Someone of my own, someone of my blood. I had never met anyone to whom I was related. Not since I was three years old. But this child would make all that different. Would be an extension of me, something to anchor me to the rest of the world. This child would change everything. It seemed impossible and inevitable, all at once.

Then Mara shook her head. 'Don't worry about it.'

That stopped me, pulled me up short, as I'm sure it was meant to. 'What do you mean?'

'I'm not keeping it anyway.'

Now the future that had, in the space of seconds, become set in stone in my head began to crumble, a brick at a time. I stared at her, trying to make sense out of her words, hoping and hoping that I was going crazy, that what I had heard wasn't what she had said, wasn't what she meant. But she was looking back at me with a flat stare, one that she'd never used on me before. An expression of impatience on her face, like she was irritated with me.

'It's done,' Mara said. 'I've already booked the abortion. It's all been arranged.'

There are things I should have said, words I should have used that would have changed her mind. But I was too slow, too stupid to find them. And I simply stood there, stared at her.

It was already too late. Her mind, she said, was made up. No matter that I begged her, that I pleaded, got down onto my knees, grabbed at her fingers like a child. That I needed this – that I needed her, needed our child, to tie me to the human race, to keep me from drifting off into space as had seemed inevitable before, as seemed increasingly inevitable now. She looked down at me, her face a struggle of pity and disgust. No. It's my body. It's my decision. But, I will take care of you, I had said. You can divorce him. You can ring Jack right now, tell him that it's over. I'll take care of you. I'll take care of Amy. I love you.

Mara had looked down at me, looked through me. I'm sorry. I can't. See, the thing is, I just don't love you. Not the way that you love me. I'm sorry. And the baby, I understand how you feel, I do, I really do. Please don't think that I'm a bitch. But I just can't keep it. It's just too inconvenient.

Inconvenient.

The truth of my existence.

I have always been simply inconvenient.

To the mother who dumped me, who left me sodden and wandering, a child adrift, in the grounds of Mount Pleasant Hospital. So inconvenient that she leaves me there and then climbs to the top of a multi-storey car park and throws herself onto the concrete below.

To the siblings, the two pairs. The natural ones, so alike one another that it is painful to see, who look at me from some great distance, that now-familiar cocktail of sympathy and disdain. The adopted ones, with their rough edges, sticking together like they are the only two remaining pieces in a jigsaw, no room for anyone else in there because they watch the world with a suspicious eye, and they know the danger that outsiders can bring.

To the father, never there. Because he has five kids to support on a meagre pay cheque, and he could just about manage the four, but it was the mother who pushed for this fifth and final cuckoo in the nest, and it tipped the balance, in their finances, in their marriage. So that when he is there, he is there with a face puckered by frowns, and a sharp tongue that only gets sharper when he sees me, the beginning of their end. And then, after thirty years of marriage, one day he is simply gone, dead from a cerebral aneurysm, a vanishing so total and complete that it seems like he has never been.

To the mother – the other mother – who has taken on more than she can possibly handle, and who tries, and you can see the trying carved into the lines in her face, but there is only so much of her to go around, so she divides her attention between the loud and the wicked and then there is simply none left over.

To Mara. To Mara, whom I loved above anyone. With whom I would have built a future. Had a family, a life. For whom I would have lived.

I am an inconvenience.

I am invisible.

36

Charlie: Friday 29 August, 5.06 p.m.
Two days before the shooting

I slip in through the propped-open doors, unnoticed. It's quiet in here. The ceiling fans swing wildly, moving the hot air around until it whips past my skirt, a cyclone of limited proportions. There are voices, dim and clattering, coming from the 'outdoor seating area' – a beer garden in everything but name. Few people would choose to sit inside the restaurant on a day like today. There are a couple, though. A man and a woman, tucked away on an island for two, half-hidden behind a fake-ficus. They are holding hands, every now and again glancing over their shoulders. Affair. On the table by the window, in the full blaze of midday sunshine, a middle-aged woman. She is wearing a crocheted cardigan, drinking tea and sweating. About as British as they come.

My feet are sticking to the floor, a faint sheen of alcohol pulling the soles of my feet earthwards. Delizioso is one of those split-personality kind of places: Italian restaurant by day, upmarket bar by night. All hardwood floors and soft lighting. The kind of place that everyone says they frequent,

253

but no one can quite pronounce. I walk towards the bar, try not to stare at the couple hiding in the greenery.

The temperatures have reached new highs today. Thirty-five degrees. A hot and gluey night, one where you sleep in fits and starts, waking with the feeling that you are underwater. I got up early, gave up, told myself that I wanted to get a jump-start on the day anyway.

The bartender is stocking the shelves that run the length of the bar. Young, his hair surfery, falling into his eyes. He hefts the glasses, brushing the hair from his eyes with an impatient flick that looks studied. Glances sideways at me, back down, like this glass is the most interesting thing he has ever seen, then turns, bending so that his perfect little arse is in full view. I roll my eyes. I'm sorry, I just can't help it. Dump my handbag on the bar with a clatter.

'Well, hello.' He turns, apparently satisfied that the arse-view will have served its purpose, fixes me with a smile designed to wilt my heart. His teeth are crooked.

'Hi.' Remind myself to play nice, that I am looking for favours. Give him a smile. Try to mean it.

'Get you a drink?' He scans me as he says it, eyes flitting quickly across my face, settling on my cleavage.

'Diet Coke.'

'Aw, come on. Nothing stronger?' He's leaning on the bar, a studied move, tilts his head to one side.

He must have really generous mirrors in his parents' house. Be nice. Be nice. You have to talk to him, not marry him. I let out a tittling laugh, tilt my head so that we look like a matching pair of lunatics. 'Oh, I'm working, I'm afraid. Will have to stick to the soft stuff.'

He pulls a glass free, slipping it under a tap. 'What do you do?'

'Oh.' I draw coy rings on the condensation that shimmers on the bar, don't look at him. 'I'm a reporter.'

'Oh, you are? That's cool.'

Shrug.

'What are you working on?'

A heavy sigh. 'Oh, it's nothing really. It's just a thing about this girl. Did you hear about her? The one that got killed on the M4?'

He looks at me blankly, shrugs.

'Right, well, yeah. I'm just getting, you know, some background stuff. It's really boring.'

He holds out his hand. 'My name's Luke.'

I take it, shake it. Can feel the sweat on his palm, the grasp that lasts too long. 'Charlie. Nice to meet you.'

'You too, so are you . . . ?'

'Yeah, see the thing is, my editor, she's all over me about this story. I don't . . . I don't suppose you'd remember her? Emily. The girl who was killed.' I reach into my handbag, pull a photograph free, lay it flat on the bar between us. 'Apparently she was in here on Monday, twenty-fifth. Were you here that night?'

Luke frowns, looks confused, a look that I'm prepared to bet is not new for him. 'Um . . .' Sticks his hand into his pocket and pulls out his mobile. 'I'm not . . . Oh, hang on, I was working. Let me see that.' Picks up the picture, holds it an inch or so from his nose, squinting.

I suppress a smile, wonder how much more difficult he makes his life by refusing to wear the glasses he needs.

'I remember her.'

'You do?'

He nods. 'Quiet night.' A coy look, a wink of understanding. That he was prowling and there was no one else, so she would do, until his prospects improved. Any port in a storm.

I can feel a thrill of irritation, my jaw clenching, and I turn it into the rictus of a smile. Nod. Sip my drink. Try not to choke on it.

'Yeah. I remember her. She was in early, like – I don't know – six-thirty. Seven maybe.'

'Okay?'

'She sat in the corner over there, by the window.' He gestures to where the middle-aged woman is sitting. She has set down her tea now. Is knitting. 'On her own. I thought she must have been stood up.' His gaze shifts towards the table and he stares. The woman glances up, her attention drawn by the frankness of his study, and she shifts, uncomfortable.

What about Emily? What would she have done? How would she have felt under Luke's overt scrutiny?

I can feel my blood pressure climbing. Study him. He is uselessly young, nineteen maybe, pretending to be older. His long, perfectly unstyled hair is thinning on the crown, his fingers thick and short, awkward-looking. I think he was here that night, maybe looking to get laid, maybe slipped a little shot into her drink – a double where she had asked for a single, just a little nudge towards compliancy. Maybe it got busy, she got away from him, leaving him looking in dismay at the empty table that had previously seated his sure thing. Maybe she found her way onto the M4 and died.

I study him, trying to get a feel, temporarily kidding myself that you can discern the bad guys just by looking.

But then the familiar thought: you never can tell who the bad guys are, even when you know them. Even if you've known them all your life. I look down at the rings on the bar, try not to think about Aden, and then, inevitably, about my father. I was different then, before it all changed. I was softer, easier. I believed in people. And then my father vanished. I tell myself that the bad things only make you stronger, but to be honest, I don't know if I believe that. They make you harder, they turn you into an island. Sometimes I think it would have been better had I never found out and, in those moments, I have to acknowledge my mother, the fact that she tried to hide it, tried to protect me. Even though I hated her with the kind of passion only a teenager can feel, even though I called her evil, shocking names, still she was shielding me, trying to protect me from the truth that would leave an ugly, jagged scar. My mother begged me not to go to my father's funeral. I thought she was being a bitch. Told her I was going, with her or without her.

They were standing at the front. A black-haired woman with olive skin, a bulbous bump of a belly. She wept into her hands, a wail that cut through the low music, a moaning, wrenching cry. And me? I wondered if she had gone to the wrong funeral. I looked at her, at the little girl – two, three maybe – who clung to the hem of her skirt, her oddly familiar face creased into confusion and fear, and thought they had made a mistake. But my mother's expression gave it away. I get my poor bluffing skills from her. Had I followed my father, I discovered, I would have been an excellent liar.

His new family. The ones he left us for. The daughter he had hidden, another one on the way.

You can't assume that you know anybody. Ever.

'She was drinking white wine. Small.'

'What?'

'The girl.' Luke stabbed at the picture with a thick finger. 'What did you say her name was? She was drinking white wine.'

I stare at him. 'You have a remarkably good memory.'

He shrugged. 'Not really. I just remember cos of what happened after.'

'What happened after?'

'Well, like I said, it was quiet when she came in, when I gave her the wine. She seemed to be taking it pretty slowly. I offered a refill – oh, couple of times – but she always said no. Then a hen party came in. You know how it is, mad bunch. So I didn't really see her for a while, you know, I was running back and forth.' A grin that says that he'd found a more interesting port. 'Anyway, when I noticed her later on, there was a guy with her.'

'Did you get a good look at him?'

'Nah, I don't swing that way.' Another grin. 'They seemed to be talking, I don't know; like I said, I didn't really see. Frank, the other barman, was on by then too, so I don't know whether he saw them.'

'And where's Frank now?'

'Off on holidays. Ibiza for two weeks.'

'Of course he is.'

'Yeah. So, right, I saw her again then, when she was leaving. Maybe, like, ten or so. I was collecting glasses. She was steaming.'

'Drunk?'

'Yeah. I'm telling you, she couldn't stand. She was hanging all over this bloke, like he was having to carry her out.'

'But you didn't see her buying any more drinks?'

'I didn't see her, but I know that the guy she was with came up to the bar a couple of times.'

'Any idea what he ordered?'

'Nah, but like I said, you'd need to ask Frank.'

'And Frank is in . . .'

'Ibiza, yeah.'

'Right. So, now, the guy. Do you remember anything about him? Tall, short, black, white, Asian?'

'He was white. Definitely white.'

'Hair colour? Build?' Now I'm thinking of the figure on the security cameras, the man pacing the hospital hallways with a gun. Or was this just some random guy? Someone who happened across Emily when she was alone, vulnerable?

Luke shrugs. 'Sorry.'

I nod. 'I don't suppose you noticed if she was wearing a necklace, did you? Gold chain, word "Emily" on it?'

Luke thinks for a moment, then frowns. 'Yeah, you know what, actually she was. I remember noticing it when I took the drinks over. My sister's name is Emily, see, that's why I remembered.'

I nod. Glance the length of the bar. The couple are leaving, the man throwing a note down onto the table. They stand there for a moment, a quick squeeze of hands, then self-consciously split apart, allowing the space to blossom between them. Definitely an affair. My gaze tracks up. 'You have a camera?'

'Huh?'

I point at the camera that hangs beneath the eaves, trained on the bar. 'You have a camera.'

'Oh, that. No. That hasn't worked in months. Sorry.' He looks up at it, frowning. 'Oh, but, there is one outside, though. Would that help?'

37

Aden: Friday 29 August, 8.06 p.m.
Two days before the shooting

Aden pushed his way through the press of bodies. The faces were familiar, by and large. The Harrow, a small local, tucked in amongst a copse of trees, had become a popular police hangout, had been for as long as Aden could remember, all low beams, highly polished wood and a low tolerance for trouble. Rhys was sitting at the end of the bar, his shirt open at the collar, and looked to be in easy conversation with an attractive PCSO.

'Ade.' Del stood at the bar, waving with the sweeping gesture of one who has already had a few. 'What you having, mate?'

'I think I should be buying you.' Aden squeezed closer. 'Congratulations, Daddy.'

Del grinned. 'Aw, mate. She's a little corker. Six pounds eight ounces. And she's got her daddy's nose.'

'Poor little sod.'

'I know, right?'

'You got a name yet?'

'Phoebe. Phoebe Hope.'

Aden smiled, clapped Del on the arm. 'I'm chuffed for you, mate.'

Del shook his head. 'I'm telling you, it was tough. My missus, she was a bloody Spartan. Terrible seeing her like that. But she's doing all right now, and so is Princess Phoebe. Oi, pint of Carling when you're ready, love.' This to the middle-aged woman behind the bar. 'I'm glad you could come, mate. Looks like we've got a good turnout. Iestyn is supposed to be here, but he's stuck dealing with the fallout from Tony's little episode. Speaking of which, nice shiner.'

There had been a burst of pain, a firework-explosion of stars, shouting, hands reaching for him. Rhys, half-holding him up, half-holding him back, in case he launched himself at Tony. Tony was still shouting, his fury a hurricane that had only been fed by the first punch. But now they were on him, the other AFOs, pulling him back, someone removing his gun, a few leading him – no, dragging him – out of the range. Could hear him shouting out into the hallway, up the stairs, voice shrieking and strained.

And then, nothing. Everyone standing on the big empty range, stunned into silence. Aden's eye pulsing, his hands beginning to shake as the adrenaline dispersed. Someone handed him an ice-pack. He still wasn't sure who.

It had hung like that for a little while, as everybody took stock. Then the words had started, and once they started, seemed like they couldn't stop. Fuck, I thought you were dead. Did you see him, he's a bloody lunatic. He'll lose his firearms cert for this, no doubt. Only Aden and Rhys staying silent.

Then, slowly, they began to trickle back into the armoury. No official order. No instruction. Just a silent collective agreement that it would be best if everyone was unarmed for the time being. Into the cage, smelling of metal and grease and sweat, everyone slipping guns out of holsters, and something different in the air. Like what had just happened had changed everything, and they had suddenly realised the power they carried, and how, with a quick flick of the wrist, that power could be turned on one of your own.

Aden had slipped the magazine out, pulled back the slide, checking that it was free from bullets. Had felt his eye pulsing, his brain racing. A feeling settling in his stomach. Guilt. He had pushed Tony. He had taken him to the edge. Had made it almost inevitable that he would throw himself over it.

'It wasn't your fault.' Rhys's voice had been low, only for Aden to hear. 'Tony, he . . . he was going to blow, sooner or later.'

Aden looked up at the younger man, giving him a quick, effortful smile. 'Come on, Rhys. We both know I lit the fuse.'

Rhys shrugged. 'Yeah, well, he pushed you, you pushed back, he flipped. The guy . . . he's got problems.' He had glanced across his shoulder, his voice dropping further. 'We all handled it differently, the shooting. But the thing is, it got to all of us. Even Tony. This has been a long time coming for him.'

Aden nodded slowly, guilt still nuzzling at him.

The conversation thrummed, bouncing off the metal door. What would happen to Tony? Would he be fired? Arrested? Aden had kept his head down, pulling a cleaning kit closer to him, focusing on the gun, its narrow alleyways, the ease of its slide. Pulled a thin-bristled brush free.

'Ade.'

He half-turned. The AFO was older than him, by a considerable number of years, had been in Firearms longer than anyone could remember; thick-waisted, a red-blond beard that hid his age. A hard man with a sharp humour, a sharper aim. 'All right, Bob?'

Bob wasn't looking at Aden, was studying his Glock, the movement of his brush as he cleaned it. 'That guy, Tony. He's a prick.'

Aden nodded, slowly.

'Sarge tell you FTU is looking for someone?' Bob ran the Tactical Unit, had done for years.

'He mentioned it.'

Bob nodded. 'You need to apply. We want you on the team.'

Fed the brush through, pulled it back. Fed the brush through, pulled it back. 'Thanks. Yeah. I'm thinking about it.'

Aden had glanced at Rhys, his dark head ducked, trying hard to pretend he wasn't listening. Aden had given the younger man a quick smile, one that came a little easier.

They had cleaned their guns and stowed them back in the armoury. Had, as one, begun the slow trooping up the stairs.

Then Tony's voice, washing along the breeze-blocked hallway. 'You can't fucking do this to me.'

Another voice – Iestyn's, lower, just a soft bass this time, with no words in it.

'No. I've got nothing left. I've got nothing fucking left.' Tony's voice barely recognisable, warped and twisted. 'Thanks to that fucking kid and that bastard Aden McCarthy. I've got nothing.'

The barmaid, all spandex, top cut low to make the most

of her bulbous cleavage, set the pint down on the bar with a clatter. Wasn't looking at Aden or Del, her attention snagged on Rhys. Aden gave a little laugh, shook his head.

'So, tell me.' Del took a long pull of his pint. 'What's the news with you and Charlie?'

Aden didn't answer, sipped his lager. He had wanted to call her. Why, he didn't really know. Had wanted to hear her voice so badly that it had felt like a thirst. But he hadn't, because it wasn't her problem, was it? So he had sat at home and thought about her and thought about her, so that in the end it almost felt like he had spoken to her.

'No news.'

'So, are you like – y'know?'

Aden laughed, shook his head. Took another sip so that he wouldn't have to look at Del. Couldn't now remember a time when she wasn't in his head, when his days didn't run from one swimming session to the next. The truth of it was, he didn't even like swimming all that much.

'Well, why the hell not, mate?'

'We're just friends. That's all.'

Del was watching him. That uncomfortable feeling settling on Aden, like he had said more than he had intended to say.

'She's a good girl, is Charlie. I've known her a long time. There's nobody better to have around you in a pinch.' Del took another pull, shrugged. 'Crusty exterior – like, tends to make it hard work – but once she trusts you . . .' He looked at Aden across his pint. 'You should ask her out.'

Aden didn't answer, looked down at his glass, the snowy-white foam. There was something about someone knowing the worst of you, having seen you at your very weakest.

Where did you go from there? And Charlie, she was . . .
she could have anybody.

Del upended his glass, draining the remnants. 'I'm telling
you, mate. Ask her out. She's not going to hang around
for ever.'

38

Imogen: Saturday 30 August, 8.13 a.m.
Day before the shooting

Imogen walked along the hospital corridor, quiet in the morning haze. Her head swaying, seemed like the linoleum floor was bucking, rising up to meet her. She concentrated, putting care into every step, fearing that if she didn't, then she would fall again. There was a dull throbbing in the back of her head, a pulse like house-music heard through a wall.

Had she passed out? Imogen wasn't really sure. She remembered the argument, the fall (was it a fall or a push? she didn't know and, at the moment, the distinction seemed to be one that mattered), and then lying on her bedroom floor, staring up at the ceiling, thinking obliquely that there were cobwebs, that she really should dust the light. Then a heat and pressure building inside her, rising with a force so irresistible that it was all she could do to contain it. She had crawled on all fours across the landing to the bathroom, still airless and thick with steam, the thought of standing more than she could bear. Then a wrenching, and ripping, the vomit only just making the toilet basin.

Imogen remembered crying. Remembered the heat of the tears, the salt of them cutting through the acid in her mouth. She remembered knowing, although not knowing how she knew, that Dave was gone, that he had vanished somewhere in between the fall and the crack and the darkness.

She had cradled the toilet, had let her stomach empty itself, her head thumping with pain. Then, after a minute or an hour – who could tell? – she had managed to ease herself up. Walking, unsteady, her hands trailing against the buttery paintwork of the walls, back to the bedroom. Tumbling onto the still-made bed. And, before she fell asleep, passed out, whichever one it was, thinking that the gun, like her fiancé, had vanished.

Then she had slept and slept and slept.

Imogen pressed the button for the lift, waited, leaning against the wall. Beads of sweat pricked her forehead, more than just the heat of the day. The doors slid open with a ping and she stepped inside carefully, struggling to focus on the buttons.

She had awoken hours later, had slept straight through into the early-morning light. Had come to with that easy, soporific drift, the kind where life is painted in a soft palette, everything murky, a little unclear. Then she had remembered. Had sat up sharp, even though her head had throbbed, the world swirling around her.

Dave hadn't returned. Everything was as it had been. But Dave and the rifle were gone.

The lift shuddered to a halt, its doors opening with a groan that cut through her. She wanted to see Mara, needed to. And hadn't it always been this way; that when the worst of all things had come to pass, it was her sister's arms she craved. Like being back in the womb, wrapped, one within the other. Imogen moved out of the lift, along the corridor.

The doors to Ward 11 were in sight and Imogen felt a swell of relief. The young security guard with the tattooed arms leaned against the opposite wall, texting. Then the doors to Ward 11 flung open, the speed of them hitting against the wall, and there was Mara, her steps quick, her face set into a kind of fury. Imogen stopped, struggling, wondered if she knew, how it was possible that she could know.

'Mara?'

'Oh, thank God, Im. Look, I've got to go upstairs. The bloody doctors – they're insisting they need to see me; and I said: well, come down here. I mean, I've got a sick child. What the hell they think they're doing I just don't know.'

'Why . . . ?'

'I have no idea, but apparently it's life-or-death. Look, Amy's in there. She's asleep, but she's on her own.'

'No, I . . . I'll stay with her.' Imogen answered slowly, trying to coax her brain around this new thing that had to be dealt with. 'Mar . . .'

'I've got to hurry, Im. I don't like leaving her. Will you . . . Shit!' Mara wasn't looking at Imogen, was questing in her handbag. 'Dammit.'

'What?'

'I've brought Doggie with me. Shit! If Amy wakes up and he's not there . . . Oh God, and all of her other bits. Look, just take my bag in with you, will you? I'll be as quick as I can.' Mara leaned over, hooked the overlarge bag onto Imogen's shoulder and, just like that, she was gone.

It took a moment. Imogen's head was swirling, and the

bag was heavy, and she could smell her sister's perfume –
all of her that was left behind – and now she wanted to
cry. She had wanted Mara so badly. But Amy was waiting,
and there were things that had to be done. Imogen pushed
herself forward, pulled at the door.

She had barely got inside, the door still straining at its
hinges, when Mara's bag began to ring. Imogen started,
glanced over her shoulder, the dim thought that she could
call her sister back. But it was too late and she was gone.
Not thinking, Imogen reached in, pulled the phone free.

The caller display was lit up. The ringtone jangling. Dave
calling.

Imogen stood, staring at it. A feeling like her worlds
were colliding. Didn't answer, didn't do anything, just stared
at it and stared at it, and finally the ringing stopped and
the screen went dark again. A feeling worked its way
through the headache and the vague sense of nausea: that
something she had always known was creeping its way
forward. She opened her sister's call history.

Dave. Dave. Dave.

It seemed that she was looking at the phone down a
long tunnel.

Imogen leaned against the door to Amy's room, thinking
to get away, to where it was quiet and dark and she could
think. She pushed the door open, her heart thumping,
thinking about her sister's gaze, the one that would not
stick, but slid down and away, the one that meant she was
lying. Thinking about Dave's late nights, his phone never
leaving his fingers, the computer that was now password-
protected. Thinking about a night so long ago that it was
easy to pretend it never happened, and a man's voice heard
only through walls, but now it is undeniable that it was

Dave's voice. Thinking about the boots. The ones that sat beside Mara's couch.

Wanting to be sick so badly that it seemed like there was nothing else in the world.

Imogen pushed open the door, expecting only Amy, sleeping.

She was met instead with a small 'Oh!' of surprise. Imogen started, struggling to locate the sound.

'Imogen. I didn't think . . . I mean, I thought . . .' Natalie was standing beside Amy's sleeping form, had a look on her face, something that seemed almost like guilt.

'Natalie. What's going on?' It shouldn't have been strange, should it? The nurse caring for her patient. But it was. There was something, in Natalie's expression, her movements, something that screamed out to Imogen.

'Oh, nothing. Just checking Amy's breathing . . .'

'Her breathing?'

'Yes, well, after the heart-trace . . .'

'What about the heart-trace? Mara said it was fine.'

'Oh, yes. Sure.'

Sometimes it seemed to Imogen that lies came with a neon sign. This was one of those times. 'What was wrong with it? There's something wrong with her heart?'

'Um, well . . . no, not wrong.'

'So?'

Natalie's expression shifted then, guilt moving into a collapse of will, the look of one who has been caught. 'I can't talk about it, Imogen. I'm—'

'NO. You tell me now.' Imogen's voice wasn't her voice any more, but a roaring, seething tide of anger. 'What the hell is going on?'

Natalie stared at her, caught in indecision. Then with a

heavy sigh, a glance at Amy, still curled up asleep in the bed, 'Look, Im.' A quick glance towards the door. 'I could get into so much trouble for telling you this and, I mean, I wouldn't, if it was anyone but you. But the thing is, social services are involved now.'

'What? Why? What the hell are you talking about?'

Natalie folded her arms. 'It's your sister. We think Mara has been hurting Amy.'

39

Charlie: Saturday 30 August, 1.15 p.m.
Day before the shooting

It has happened, finally. The weather has broken. The torpid heat giving way to grey-cotton clouded skies, rain that spears the ground, hitting, rebounding back upon itself. I tug my cardigan tight around me, tuck my chin into the collar and shiver, cold for what seems like the first time ever. Watch the rain as it hits the newsroom window, a steady thump, thump, thump. Seems the few of us here today – the ones unlucky enough to pull the Saturday shift – are all doing the same thing, all gazes hooked on the steel skies. It's like we aren't British, like we've never seen rain before. The office is quiet. Three, maybe four of us in today. We are sitting at our desks trying to look busy, like good little worker bees; no one is saying anything. We can all feel it. It's in the air.

I glance at the clock. Fifteen minutes until this endless shift is done. Fifteen minutes until I can go home.

Dave looks ill. His normally pale skin has lightened three shades paler, a corpse pallor, his eyes rimmed with red, face slack. I glance at him, back down at my computer, stare at the blank screen, but my gaze won't stick, keeps pulling up to Dave. He lets loose a small sigh and for a moment I am afraid that he is crying. I fight the urge to run away and lock myself in the toilet.

'You okay?' I ask.

He doesn't answer, is just staring into space, and it occurs to me to wonder if he is drunk.

'Dave?'

His gaze snaps up to me then, and I recoil. He looks now like someone I have never met before. Is staring at me, and I spare a moment to wish that I'd kept my damn mouth shut.

'Are you? Okay, I mean? Only you look . . . tired.' This is me at my most diplomatic, thinking that tired sounded better than 'like death'.

He looks down then, mumbles, 'Didn't sleep.'

I nod, try to think of something else to say. Fail spectacularly. I look back at my computer. There are things that I should be doing, stories I should be working on. But I confess that none of them has my full attention. That got snagged, left behind in Delizioso, with the bartender with his flickering gaze, and Emily, drinking a small white wine until she can barely stand.

'You have CCTV outside? That would be great. Can I see it?' I had remembered to put on my best smile for the barman, might even have flirted a little, reasoning to myself that it was all in a good cause, that I could have an extra-long shower later.

'Oh, sorry. I don't have the key.'

I had stopped flirting then. 'You don't have the . . .'

'The key. It's in the manager's office. The CCTV, I mean. You'll need to speak to the manager.'

'And the manager is . . .'

'Oh, she's away. She's been in Crete for a fortnight.'

'Of course she is.' I had dropped my head, vaguely remember counting to myself. Then tried again for a smile. 'When will she be back?'

'Ah, Sunday. Yeah. Sunday.' He had leaned in, had given me a well-practised smile. 'Gives you an excuse to come back and see me again.'

Dave has moved now. Has his phone in his hands, is cradling it like it's a newborn infant. I wonder distantly who he's calling. Reason that it's probably Imogen. I wonder if he knows what is coming?

Then Lydia's door opens. The Saturday crowd takes a collective breath, heads spinning like they are on platters, until the entire room is looking at Dave. It's impossible to keep a secret in a newsroom.

'Dave?' Lydia's voice is piano-wire tight. 'Could I speak to you for a second?'

No one moves. No one breathes.

For a moment it seems that Dave will ignore her, that his last act of defiance here will be a refusal to be fired, a blatant two fingers up to the establishment. How would that work, I wonder? Will they have to get the police to come in, drag him out? But, after long moments, he looks up. Stares at Lydia as if he's never seen her before. Then begins to stand. It is excruciating. It is like watching the earth's crust tear itself apart. Dave pushes back the chair, slowly, painfully, then just stands there, like he has no idea what to do next. Then he begins to lean, and for one bizarre moment it looks like he is going to take in with him the gym bag that he keeps tucked under the desk. I wonder what he's thinking? If his reasoning is that he wants to make a clean break for it, once the axe has fallen. Then he stops, thinks better of it, and turns towards Lydia, movements treacle-slow.

We are all staring, open and frankly now, and Lydia glances around the office. 'All right, thank you. Everyone feel free to get on with your work.'

She steps back, allowing Dave to pour past her, then closes the door firmly behind them.

And now we are left. Waiting.

There are little breaks of conversation, whispers, the occasional laugh, quickly hidden away.

I watch the office door. I hate this.

Then a parp of sound, my mobile phone lighting up. A text from my mother. *Was wondering if you fancied meeting me for lunch tomorrow? Just the two of us.* I stare at it. Thinking. It would be easier to say no. We are what we are. What is the point of pretending that we are otherwise? I study the words, the shape of them on the small screen. How cautious they look. How unsure. And I think of Carla Lowe and of Emily's mother, and how much they would give to be able to do this, even to be awkward and strained with their children. But that is gone for them now, will never come back.

I move my thumb quickly across the keypad. *Sounds lovely.*

I have just pressed Send when the phone rings, startling me. For a moment I think it is my mother, that she has seen the reply, is calling to work out the details. Then I see the name. Steve Lowe.

Shit! I don't want to talk to him today. I really don't want to talk to him today.

I stare at it, taking a moment to wonder how the hell he got my personal number. I should answer, because no matter what else he is, he is still a father who has lost his son. And I'm about to, I swear, when Lydia's office door opens.

I reject the call.

Dave has aged, in the intervening minutes, looks like he has been crying. He walks out with a shuffling gait – dead man walking – back to his desk, pulls out his gym bag and with a broad reach gathers up the paraphernalia that has gathered across the table top, dumping it into the bag.

'Dave?'

They are all watching him, the entire newsroom a bunch of meerkats peering at their fallen brother. The silence is thick, seems to fill up your lungs.

He looks up at me, gives me an uncomfortable smile. 'He did it, anyway.'

'Who?' I ask, even though I'm fairly sure I already know the answer.

'Steve Lowe. He complained to the owners. I'm out.'

'Dave, I . . .' I cast around, looking for something useful to say, but he waves me off.

'Forget it.' Dave jams the zip closed on his bag and turns towards the door. Doesn't look back.

I sit there, sharing in the stunned silence. I've never liked the guy, not really, not if I'm being totally honest. But I feel sorry for him. I watch as his figure vanishes behind the warped glass, imagine that I can hear his footsteps heavy on the stairs. I push myself up. I never liked him, but no one should be all alone at a time like this.

I don't look around, even though I know that Lydia is standing there, can feel her eyes on me. Hurry to the door, pull it open. Can hear the downstairs door slam. I take the steps quickly, wondering what the hell I'll say to him if I do catch him. I'm useless at this. I'm at the bottom and pulling the door, scanning the street, and then I stop.

Aden is standing on the other side of the road. Is sheltering under the outer porch of the glass-fronted offices, his jacket done up to his chin.

I stare at him, trying to make my mind piece this together. See him see me. Give a half-hearted wave. Now I can't remember what I came out here for, because all I can see is Aden, standing there, waiting for me. I hang in the doorway and think that I don't have my coat with me, that I can't go out there because I'll get soaked. I think about my father, and I think how people are never what you think and how you have to be careful, otherwise they'll hurt you, and I look at Aden and I know exactly why it is he is here. And I stand there, and I think: what is it you are going to do? Are you going to spend the rest of your life running from your father's lies? Is that going to dictate the shape of the rest of your life? And the stubbornness, the iron, rises up in me, and now I am out of the door and down the steps, the rain battering against my skull so hard that it hurts, winding its way under my collar. I cross the street, sloshing through the standing water with my insubstantial pumps. And Aden is standing there, waiting, a fist-shaped bruise wrapping itself around his eye, looking so afraid he looks like he might cry, and that thought makes me want to laugh. So I stand on my tiptoes and I kiss him.

40

Imogen: Saturday 30 August, 5.53 p.m.
Day before the shooting

Imogen sat on the sofa in her office, had pulled her knees up into her, her head dipped low. Stared at the lavender walls. A sudden thought, that she hated lavender. She was swaying, was only dimly aware of it, her attention more drawn by her position, wondering if this was the shape she had formed in the womb. But then, surely not, not when there were two of them. Surely Mara, for all her tiny stature, her weak heart, took up the lion's share of the space. That was how it had been afterwards anyway, so why would it have been any different then? She unfolded her legs.

Her office door was closed. Imogen stared at it. She was aware that she was staring a lot, but it seemed there was little else to do. She had come here, had fled Ward 11 before Mara's return, had come here because she had nowhere else to go.

It must be getting late now. The thought was dim and distant, and she glanced around vaguely, as if expecting a window to have miraculously appeared in this room that was a cupboard in everything but name. She used to think it was cosy in here. Now it seemed absurd, airless.

Natalie's words had frozen her, had stoppered up time. *We think Mara has been hurting Amy.* Imogen had stood, glued to the ground, even though it seemed that the ground was moving beneath her.

They were wrong. There was no other possible interpretation. They were simply wrong.

Imogen had been aware of movement, of feeling starting to trickle back into her hands, her feet. A backing away. 'That's bullshit.' The word tasted strange in her mouth. She had tried it again, a tiny thrill at the power of it. 'That is utter bullshit.'

'Please,' said Natalie. 'Look, sit down.'

'I don't want to sit.'

All sotto voce, Amy still curled up, breathing soft sleeping breaths. Imogen had looked at her, had felt her heart squeeze itself in her chest.

'Please, I understand what this must look like. But you need to listen to me.' Natalie had taken hold of her hand, held it fast. 'We have been concerned for a little while. Originally the doctors were looking at encephalitis or meningitis, yes? But her symptoms, they just aren't what we would expect to see . . .'

'So, based on that, you're assuming my sister is an abuser?'

'No, not based on that. Look, Amy had her initial seizure and was admitted, yes? Now, after the seizure, what we saw was that she didn't settle as we would have expected her to. Her temperature was fluctuating, her breathing erratic, she seemed agitated. We wanted to run blood tests, but your sister was reluctant. So the doctors backed off – but I've got to tell you, Im, that raised some eyebrows: a mother not wanting the tests that could provide answers for her child.'

'She said the doctors didn't want them,' said Imogen.

'They did. But we didn't want to jump to conclusions, thought: okay, she's worried about Amy getting stuck, unnecessary pain. Not too unusual. So we ran a heart-trace instead, and what we saw were spikes that were broad, way broader than they should have been. It suggested one of two things – a cardiac defect . . .'

'Or?'

'Or that she had been given some form of medication. So we ran toxicology. And we asked Mara: was there any way Amy could have got hold of medications, antidepressants maybe?'

'Okay . . .'

'Your sister didn't like that question at all. In fact, she got pretty angry. Said there was no way, that no one in the family was on anything like that. And after that she got strange, jittery. Wouldn't leave Amy's side, even to go to the toilet.'

'She's a good mother, her daughter is sick.'

'I checked Amy myself, at about eleven o'clock. Everything was fine, she was perfectly stable. I left the room. I left Mara alone with her, and five minutes later she crashed.'

'But you can't predict a seizure. You don't know when it's going to happen.'

'No, fine. But after the seizure – bearing in mind that this one was a bad one, that we nearly lost her – after they stabilised her, the doctors got the toxicology results back. Imogen, they found amitriptyline in Amy's bloodstream.'

Imogen had reached out, had gripped the metal frame of Amy's bed.

'There is no earthly reason why Amy should have an anti-depressant in her bloodstream. None at all. Her symptoms, the temperature, seizures, the erratic breathing – all of these things are consistent with an overdose of amitriptyline.' Natalie was still holding her hand, holding her up now. 'Imogen, your sister's patterns of behaviour, the drug in Amy's bloodstream, it's suggesting that we may be looking at Factitious Disorder by proxy.'

It seemed that the words wouldn't come, that they had lodged in Imogen's throat, cut off the air. 'Munchausen's by proxy?'

'We think so,' said Natalie. 'Now, obviously, we can't take any steps until we're sure, hence the cameras. But, I mean, you're a psychologist. Have you seen any signs of this? Anything?'

Imogen wanted to cry. She leaned her head back against the sofa, stared at the walls of her box-like office, those stupid lavender walls, and willed the tears to come. But there was nothing, just this dull ringing in her ears. She was trying to think, trying to unravel it all. Because surely, there at the heart of this twisted ball of yarn was the answer. But it seemed that her brain simply would not work. There was a memory, sitting just out of reach – the feeling of a hand flat on her back – but she just couldn't get to it, couldn't get beyond swimming in this sea of lavender in this airless room.

Then the door opened.

Imogen looked up. Saw Dave standing in the doorway.

There was a spike of something then, the return of the pain in the back of her head, the crack as it had landed against the wall, and a jolt of fear. She pushed herself up, further into the sofa, as if that way she could crawl away from him. But there would be no crawling away. There were no windows in her small room. Only a door. And he was standing in it.

Dave was watching her, a look in his eyes that she simply didn't recognise, and Imogen stared at him as at a stranger, spared a moment to wonder where he had gone, the man she had slept next to for the last eight years. Had he vanished – poof! – in a puff of smoke, or had it been slower, a gradual decline to this, and she had simply missed it? He wasn't saying anything, was just watching her, and Imogen could feel her heart beating out of her chest. And then she felt something else.

Anger.

Anger for the pain in her head, and for the years of living on wafer-thin ice. For the lies, so many lies that it seemed she no longer knew which way was up and which was down. For his name on her sister's phone, again and again. For making her afraid.

Imogen pushed herself up to standing.

'Are you going to kill me this time?' She seemed to have grown taller, her voice different from normal, all spikes and hard edges.

Dave took a step back. Was staring at her, like now he didn't know her. 'What? I, no, of course not – no. I'm . . . sorry. I'm so sorry, Im.' He gestured to her head, a useless flapping motion. 'I can't believe what I did. I didn't mean to. I really didn't. It was an accident. I haven't slept. I just . . . I don't know what came over me. I'm so sorry.'

Imogen stared at him, not speaking.

'I just . . .' He was crying, slender diamond tears slipping down his cheeks. 'I don't know what's wrong with me. I try. I do, I swear. I'm trying to make this work, but I just don't know how.'

It was shifting, the shape of the room. The towering figure

of him diminishing, slipping into nothing, Imogen growing taller.

She studied him. 'You're in love with Mara, aren't you?'

Imogen waited for the lie, the prevarication, the looking from side to side, shifting from toe to toe. That would, if nothing else, suggest that he had not given up on them entirely.

He didn't look at her. He bowed his head. 'Yes.'

Imogen pulled in a deep breath, felt a blast of cold like a chill Siberian wind. The truth will set you free. How long had she known? Had she always known? She didn't say anything, not for a long time, because what was there to say? And hadn't she been complicit in her own downfall? Picking up her sister's cast-offs because it was safer than trudging out on her own into unexplored territory. A feeling settled on her of karma coming home.

They stood there, a pair of mannequins. Steeped in silence. She should cry now. Surely? But inconveniently there were no tears, just a certain sense of inevitability and, perhaps, relief. 'What was I? Was I the stand-in? The one that would do, because you couldn't have the twin you wanted?' The words came out sounding bitter, and Dave flinched, spiked by the barbs in them. But, in truth, all that she felt was tired. A certain sense of mile twenty-four in a marathon. You're almost there. Might as well get to the finish line, even if you have to crawl there.

'I'm sorry,' said Dave. 'I'm so sorry. I wanted . . . I really wanted us to work. I thought that, given time, it would change, it would get better. I thought that I would stop—'

'Loving her?'

'Yes.'

The world was unknitting itself, had begun to pool in a

cottony puddle at Imogen's feet. 'Mara isn't going to leave Jack. You know that, don't you?'

Dave looked down. Nodded.

'She values his status too much, his job, his money.' Imogen felt something, the chill of crystal clarity. 'That kind of thing – people looking up to her, paying attention to her – all of that kind of stuff is important to Mara. You know that's why she broke it off with you, don't you?'

She didn't know now: was she trying to hurt him or warn him? Seemed like the two motives had knotted themselves together, one indistinguishable from the other.

But Dave was looking at her, frowning. 'What?'

'The affair. I know about the affair. And I know that she broke it off with you.'

Dave shook his head. 'Im, I swear. Nothing has happened. Not since we were in uni. I'm not having an affair with Mara.'

41

Aden: Saturday 30 August, 10.34 p.m.
Day before the shooting

The doorbell rang, loud and insistent, and Aden hurried down the hallway, padding in bare feet. Pulled open the door without looking. The rain was coming down in sheets now, driving hard against the pavement outside, sweeping past the darkened figure on the front step into the hallway.

'All right, mate? Pizza?' The man was buried, face hidden by a hooded raincoat, drops running from the front of it in a waterfall.

'Yeah, ta.' Aden reached out, grabbed the box, suddenly very aware that he was wearing nothing but a T-shirt, boxers. He slipped the tip into the man's damp fingers. 'Good luck out there.'

'Yeah.' His voice was all but lost to the rain. 'Cheers.'

Aden ducked back inside, pressing his back against the front door to close it. Clutched the pizza box tight, took the stairs two at a time.

Charlie was still in his bed. Had pulled a sweatshirt from the clean laundry pile, slipped it on, so big that it puddled around her wrists, her waist. Her hair stood up at odd angles, make-up barely there now.

She grinned. 'Thank God, I'm starving.'

Aden set the box on the bed, leaned in, kissed her. Felt like he had done this a thousand times before, their lips already finding the groove of one another.

It had come to him in a moment of sparkling clarity. The knowledge that if he had felt like a coward before, there would be nothing more cowardly than letting Charlie slip through his fingers now. He had waited in the rain outside her office for an hour. Would have waited all day, if he had to.

Charlie was tugging at the box, pulling a slice of pizza free, the cheese sliding across the crust.

Aden had called the training sergeant, on his way to Charlie's office. Had felt the anxiety chewing at his insides, but had done it anyway. I want the Tactical Unit spot. I want to apply. The sergeant hadn't said much, but you could hear the grin. Assessment is next week. Pop by, we'll chat about it.

Aden picked up a slice of pizza, the heat of it burning his hands; thought about looking forward instead of looking back. After all, what did it all matter, when you came right down to it? The shooting had happened. He couldn't make it unhappen. All he could control was where he went from here on out. He watched Charlie, carefully balancing a slice of pepperoni on a corner of pizza, felt himself grin. 'So . . .' he said. 'Maybe tomorrow night we could, I don't know, do something?'

Charlie didn't look at him, took a bite of pizza. 'Yes. Tomorrow night would be good.' Then she glanced up with a smile and a wink.

Aden felt something stir.

Then a ringing, breaking from inside Charlie's bag.

'Dammit.' Charlie pushed back the covers, padded with bare feet across to where her stuff lay abandoned on the floor. Her shirt there, her trousers there, her bra.

Aden took another bite of pizza. Smiling.

'Oh God, not again.' Charlie sighed.

'Who is it?'

She pulled a face. 'Steve Lowe.'

She made no move to answer, just waited until the ringing stopped, until the voicemail message had beeped, then had hit a button, dialling up her voicemail. Hit the speaker. 'It's constant with him now. He's just calling me all the damn time.'

A disembodied voice filled the room. 'It's Steve Lowe. I've been trying you. I need you to get back to me, all right? The doctors, we've been up the hospital. They've done tests and stuff, on my boy, and they said . . . they're now saying it's permanent. Permanent vegetative state. They're saying there's nothing they can do for him. There's no hope.' His rough-edged voice cracked.

Aden laid down his pizza again. Rubbed at his eyes. Thinking of Carla Lowe, her thin arms, her tired eyes. Dammit.

'I think we have to let Dylan go. He'd be better off. Carla, she's not . . . she won't listen.'

Charlie was standing, biting her thumbnail, her face pale.

'But, anyway, at least I'm going to get those murdering bastards this time. They're going to pay for murdering my son.' A sob, crinkled and static-filled. 'I thought you'd want to know, anyway. Thanks.'

Aden dipped his head. Could feel heat building up behind his eyes.

'Shit!' said Charlie.

'Yeah.'

She climbed back onto the bed, slotted herself alongside him, her head sliding into the angle of his neck, hands snaking their way through to grip his. A long silence where there was nothing but the sound of the rain. Then she said, 'You still think there's a problem with the shooting?'

Aden half-turned, kissed her on the forehead. 'I really don't know. I mean, Tony flipping out the way he did . . . I don't know. Or maybe that's just what I want to think. You know, to justify the fact that I didn't shoot.' He thought for a moment. 'You know, the thing is, I just can't do this any more. I can't keep looking back. I want to look forward now. What about your friend? Emily. What are you thinking now?'

Charlie shrugged, her hair brushing against his chin. 'I don't know. I went to the bar, but to be honest, I didn't find anything that Traffic hadn't already found. I don't know what I was expecting. The bartender said Emily met someone, that she left with him. She seemed to be drunk, the bartender said she could barely stand. I'm going to go in tomorrow, take a look at their CCTV.'

Aden glanced at her, and Charlie rolled her eyes.

'I know, I know. I'm like Nancy friggin' Drew.'

'Did the Traffic boys go over the CCTV?'

'Apparently not. The camera system is in the manager's office, manager's been on holiday, someone lost the spare key . . . you know the song. I guess Traffic were satisfied with what they had. I mean, it all seems to hang together – the fact that she was drinking, could barely stand when she left the bar. Makes sense that she wouldn't be thinking, could have wandered onto the M4 by accident.'

'But you don't think so?'

Charlie sighed. 'I don't know, maybe it was an accident. But I just can't make it fit in my head, you know? And her necklace – the one she always wore – what the hell happened to that?'

More silence. A breeze had picked up now, clambering its way in through the open window, wrapping itself around them. Aden glanced towards the window, catching sight of his mobile phone lying between them on the bed. He picked it up. Studied it for a moment and then, with a quick movement, switched it off. If there was going to be trouble from Steve Lowe, he didn't want to hear about it tonight.

'It's Carla I feel sorry for.' Charlie's voice was quiet, heavy.

'Me too.'

Would she be at the hospital now? Sitting by her son, watching him, trying to make herself believe that he was only sleeping, that at any minute he would wake up, come back to them. Knowing that he never would.

Charlie shivered.

'You cold?'

'A little.'

Aden pushed himself up, crossed the room in three long strides. The rain was thundering, had formed rivers in the gutters. They were building up, lapping at the kerb stones. It would be a tough day tomorrow, if the weather stayed like this. All of this water, it would bring who knew what kind of debris to the surface. He reached out, pulled at the window. Barely paid any attention at all to the car parked across the street.

42

The Shooter: Saturday 30 August, 10.34 p.m.
Day before the shooting

I hold the gun, cradle it in my fingers, its weight reassuring. It feels now like an extension of my hand, like it was always meant to be there. I am tired. I am so tired. I have nothing left. I cannot fight any more. I simply want to sleep.

I sit on the bed still. It has occurred to me that the bullet will blow my brains across the bedroom, will spatter blood across the wall, that at the end of this no one will want to live here ever again. There is some small satisfaction that comes from that – having made that much of an impact at least.

I sit, my finger on the trigger.

The window is open. I can hear voices on the street, mingled in amongst the drumming of the rain; can smell the salt from the sea. There are footsteps, quick, almost a run, a burst of laughter that sounds like it comes from those who are young, for whom life is an adventure, who haven't yet learned just how much damage it can do. I wonder if they will hear the gunshot. If they will stop, frozen in fear. If they will call the police. Or will my death be lost amongst the roar of their laughter?

I sit. Listen.

The footsteps move further away, the voices quieter, until they are gone and I am alone again. I look down at the gun. I don't know why I haven't done it yet. I mean, I have waited for this, survived only because of the promise of this. And now it is here. So why haven't I done it?

A feeling shifts in me, old and familiar. Anger. I look at the gun. I get it, why people love them. They give you power. They give you control. You see these shootings on TV – Columbine, Virginia Tech, Hungerford – and no one understands who they are, why they did what they did. With their trench coats and their army fatigues, and their hanging heads, their pulsing anger. But I understand them. I understand what drives them, the anger that rolls inside them, which they just can't find a way to let out, and so they storm a school, a village, a mall, and people fall like trees before them. I understand that need, as intense as the need for oxygen, to finally be noticed, to finally matter. What's that they say about kids? It doesn't matter if it's good attention or bad attention. All they want is attention.

I think about the hospital, about the insatiable pull of it that drags me back, again and again like an unexpected ocean current. You can see it from here. I stand, pull the curtain aside. It glows on the skyline like a beacon, each window a tiny burst of light. It seems to me now that my entire life has been about this hospital, that it has formed the heart of my very existence – whatever that is worth. And I study it, saying my goodbyes.

Yet still I can't do it. I can't pull the trigger.

I cradle the gun. Let my fingers run across its shape, its form. And, as I stand there, gazing out over the lights of life being lived, I realise that it will not happen. That my finger will not move for me, because something is off. This is not as it should be.

I look back to the hospital again. Find the dot of light: second floor, third window across. Feel the tug of that ocean current.

Then I catch sight of my phone. It lies on the bedside table now. I stare at it, even though I know no one will call, and for a moment my mind plays tricks on me, and I think that I see the screen light up, a burst of sound. And I think that it is Mara. That she has sensed something, that somehow the universe has delivered her the message that I simply cannot live any more, that the burden is too heavy, and that she is reaching out to me, to save me. I lunge for the phone, movement so fast that I make myself dizzy. But there is nothing. Just an empty screen.

My insides plummet. What was I looking for? A reprieve?

I hold the phone in one hand, gun in the other, and before I am fully aware of what I am doing, my fingers are moving across the keypad, dialling. I don't know why. I hit Call.

I do know why. I don't want to die this way. I don't want to be alone.

I raise the phone to my ear, and I pray. Please pick up. Please pick up. I don't know what it is that I will say. My tongue has long since forgotten how to form words. I listen as the network races to make a connection, and I think it instead. Help me.

Then a click and an answerphone.

43

Charlie: Sunday 31 August, 9.02 a.m.
Day of the shooting

I step out of the front door, hang there for a moment. The sky is blue today, that crisp blue that you get after a storm. The street is still damp, tarmac soaked by last night's rain, but the temperatures are already beginning to climb and it will not be long before the heat comes. A cool breeze blows across the sea, whipping at my hair, and I feel my lungs expanding with it. You can see the sea from here. I didn't notice that yesterday. But then, yesterday, I didn't notice anything much. Just Aden, Aden, Aden, his fingers, his lips, the way our hands wrapped around one another as if they had been designed to do just that, two halves of a matching pair. I stand, watch a sailing boat out in the bay, the white of it bowed and billowing. It is a perfect day.

'So, tonight?' Aden is standing in the doorway, is wearing a towel and a smile. 'We could go out, get some dinner, go to the cinema?'

I smile, lean in. 'We could stay in?'

He kisses me, tastes of toothpaste. I really don't want to leave.

'I have to go.' I pull back before I get carried away. 'And you have to go to work. But tonight. Definitely tonight.'

'Definitely tonight.'

Another kiss, and I can't believe we haven't done this before, that he's been right here, waiting, for so long, and we've never done this; and I think that I am a moron, and that I am lucky my time didn't run out, that I didn't leave it until it was too late. Then I turn, hurry down the steps.

I will get to my mother's house early. She isn't expecting me for lunch for a couple of hours, but she will be happy that I have turned up, that I have made the effort.

I am in the car, have started the engine, have pulled out – one last wave at Aden still standing, wrapped in his towel. Grinning. I suppress a grin of my own. Fight the urge to turn around and say: screw families and work, let's hop back into bed. There is a grey Mondeo parked three doors down, something about it familiar, tugging at me, and I am turning to look when my mobile begins to ring. I glance down, thinking to ignore it. Then I see the caller ID.

Lecherous bartender.

I'm fairly sure the guy had a name, even though I couldn't tell you for the life of me what it was. My heart beats a little faster, and I angle the car hastily into a parking space.

'Hello?'

'Hiya, is that Charlie?'

'Yes.' What the hell is his name?

'It's Luke from Delizioso.'

Luke. Of course. 'Hi, Luke. How are you?'

'I'm good. Look, my manager, she's just come in. If you were still wanting to see that CCTV, she's here now. Says it'll be fine if you want to watch it.'

I drum my fingers on the steering wheel. Shit! I'm about

to say no, honestly I am; I'm about to say that it will have to wait, because I'm going to see my mother, and today I have big plans to actually make some kind of an effort with her. Unfortunately, no one informed my mouth of these plans.

'I'm on my way.'

I hang up. Shit! What the hell is wrong with me? I sit there for a moment, debating. But I can't shake the image of Emily's mother, her face old with grief, not knowing why her daughter died. And somehow that image merges, and now I'm thinking of Carla Lowe, her relentless resilience, faith betrayed. Thinking that I can't help the latter, there is nothing I can do to save her son. But I may be able to do something to help the former.

I drive faster than I should, along Oystermouth Road, up into the town. It's quiet at this time of day – just me, the street cleaners, a couple of drunks from the night before. I pull up right outside Delizioso, ignore the No Parking sign, dash inside.

Luke is waiting for me.

His hair is slicked back today, his collar pulled wide at the chest to reveal a tuft of black hair. 'Hi, you came. Stacey, Charlie's here.'

The manager is younger than I was expecting her to be, is far younger than me, early twenties maybe. Her hair is bleached white, shaved at the sides, the top of it curling over itself like a wave. She is sheathed in black – a black crêpe blouse, black skinny trousers – a tattoo on her neck, climbing up to her jaw, a snake, its fangs protruding. She nods at me, her look appraising.

'Charlie wanted to see the CCTV footage. It's about that girl, the one who died. Remember I told you?'

'All right, Luke.' Her tone is hard, makes me think of

rolled-up newspaper across a dog's nose. 'You want to come through?' This last to me. She turns, doesn't wait to see if I'll follow. 'It was the 25th August, yeah?'

'That's right.'

She pushes open a door marked Private, lets it swing shut behind her. I catch it just in time. The office is chaos, a narrow cupboard of a room, the desk barely able to support itself under the weight of the paper piles that stagger unevenly across its surface. She turns towards a small screen in the corner, typing something onto a keyboard. Looks like the one I had with my Amstrad. She sighs, low and breathy, and I smell something. Wonder if it's pot.

'There it is. You'll have to scan through it yourself. I've got stuff to do.' She looks me up and down. 'You're not going to tell anyone about this, yeah?'

I shake my head quickly. 'No, absolutely not.' Think that I wouldn't bloody dare.

She studies me, then nods, turning sharply on spiked heels.

There is no chair, so I stand, leaning over the desk until I am almost nose-to-nose with the monitor. I watch people flood past, visible only by the tops of their heads, and I can feel something sinking inside me, wonder how the hell I'm going to find her in this. The time-stamp says 10.02. I watch as unkempt figures wander by, watch as one man stops, vomits into the gutter. Thank God I didn't have breakfast. I am starting to think this was a waste of time. Then I see her.

In truth I wouldn't have known her, not if I hadn't been looking for her. Emily's hair is down, different to what I have seen before, but what throws me is the expression, slack-jawed from alcohol. Her head is tilted back, so that she's looking dead onto the camera, but her gaze is vacant, far-away. I look, can see a glint of gold around her neck. The missing necklace. The barman was right. She can barely walk, one leg seems to be dragging behind her, and she is leaning – being carried almost – by the man beside her. I look at him. He is looking dead ahead. So I can't see his face, can just see dark hair, can see that he is taller than her, slender, but because of the angle I can't see by how much. Can feel my insides sinking.

Then he looks up, looks straight at the camera.

I know him.

44

Aden: Sunday 31 August, 9.15 a.m.
Day of the shooting

Aden pulled the front door closed behind him, stepped out onto his front step and breathed in the sea air. It was lighter now, that heavy heat worn away, replaced by an easy warmth, a careless breeze. He checked the lock, turned. Felt like whistling, but that was such a cliché. He hummed instead, a quiet, easy tune. Was thinking about Charlie. Had a feeling that he would be thinking about little else for the foreseeable future. He could still smell her on him, beneath his own cologne, could still feel the curves of her, the way her body slotted into his. He took the steps quickly. Was thinking about tonight, was ticking off how long he had until he saw her again. Was thinking how everything had changed in these few small hours, life righting itself for the first time since the alleyway and the gunshots. He was happy.

But happy people are often not observant people, and perhaps that was why he didn't see it coming.

Aden was at his car, his keys in hand. Would later dimly remember the sound of footsteps, a quick, urgent step.

Would remember his body beginning to turn, because, even in love, he was a police officer, with a police officer's sense of danger.

Then the world shifted and he was falling.

Aden hit the ground, hard, the impact jarring through his elbow, pain racing up his arm, into his neck. Trying to orient himself, but all he could see was dark-flecked tarmac, a gob of chewing gum that had stuck itself to the kerb beside his head. His heart thumping, a ringing in his ears. He pushed himself up, his right arm screaming with pain. Turned, the world spinning around him.

Then the knife. It cut through the air, like it would cleave the sky in two, the sunlight catching on it until it appeared to be made of silver. Aden's arm moved, seemingly unconnected to his mind, knocking into something solid, a body mass. The knife staggered as if it was drunk, veering away from him. There was a smell: booze, sweat, old cigarettes. Then something solid – an arm, it appeared – rebounded on itself, the knife coming at him. Aden stepped back, leaning as far as his spine would allow.

His gaze lost its grip on the knife and settled instead on the one holding it.

Steve Lowe's face was balled up into a childish fury, his eyes squinting so that it seemed impossible he could see from them. He seemed to have grown in the time since Aden had seen him last, swollen up, so that now he was a roaring wave of anger. He shifted, an unsteady dance from foot to foot, and then lunged again, holding the knife level with Aden's heart, driving forward, letting loose a roar. It seemed inevitable that the knife would find its target, but then Aden's training took over, his left hand snaking out, gripping Steve Lowe's wrist, a feeling of pressure, like trying to hold back the sea. Aden shifted, taking a step back, then bringing his foot forward. It was a wild swing, one that connected by pure luck, the sole of his boot flat against Steve's knee.

There was a crack.

Then Steve was falling, tumbling downwards and hitting the tarmac with a smack, the knife falling away from him, spinning in its own private orbit. He curled in upon himself, cradling his knee, letting loose a wrenching, twisting kind of sob.

'You killed my son. You killed my son.'

And Aden stood there for a moment. Staring.

There were footsteps from somewhere nearby, someone shouting, but Aden ignored it. Reached down, pulled Steve's hands behind his back, twisting his wrist so that his hand ran parallel to his spine. Then Aden knelt, digging his knee into Steve's wrists; could feel his own heart thundering, shook his head, trying to get his vision to come back to normal, the world to unblur. With one hand, he pulled his mobile free. Dialled.

'Nine-Nine-Nine. What is your emergency?'

'This is Officer Four Nine Two. I am on Churtsley Avenue. I have been attacked by a man with a knife. I have him restrained, requesting urgent back-up.'

Steve lay beneath him, had given up the fight. Thick, fat tears coursing down his red cheeks. Aden dimly heard someone acknowledge him, heard some mention of back-up on its way, waited for the relief to flood. But nothing, just the shifting, sliding feeling of another shoe about to drop. He hung up the phone, shifted his weight, leaned in towards Steve.

'How did you know who I was? How did you get my address?'

Steve shook his head. Aden could smell the alcohol on him now, thick and pungent; incredible that he could walk, let alone anything else, with those fumes. He dug his knee in harder.

'Was it you? At the hospital? Was it?'

Steve let loose a low moan, shifted beneath him.

'How did you know where I was?'

'Some bloke. Some bloke rang me. Told me he knew where I could find the fucker that killed my boy.'

'Who? Who rang you?'

There was a new sound now, sirens – one set, two – cutting through the air. The tearing of brakes, car doors, and heavy footsteps, running.

'I don't fucking know. I don't fucking know. Some bloke. Some . . . he didn't say. Just, he was really Welshy.'

Hands are on Aden's now, a flash of metal as cuffs are clamped around Steve's wrists, then more hands, pulling Aden back, patting him down, a voice: you okay? You injured?

But Aden didn't answer, because all he could think of was a voice on the phone, a fist thundering through the air, a thick Welsh accent.

Tony.

45

Imogen: Sunday 31 August, 9.15 a.m.
Day of the shooting

Imogen stood in the hallway of Mara's empty house. Sunlight flooded in through the glass front door, everything still, quiet, dust motes dancing in the air. She hadn't gone home, had spent the night curled on the sofa in her office, hadn't slept. She had locked the door, though. She hadn't spoken to her sister, even though Mara had called her more times than she could remember. In the end Imogen had shut the phone off. Had lain on the sofa, staring into the silence.

She was alone. More alone than she had ever felt before. Because for as long as she could remember, she had always been one half of a pair. There had been her and there had been Mara. Mirror-images of one another. The person that you knew inside and out.

Imogen stood in her sister's hallway, wondered if she had ever really known her at all.

It was impossible – a jigsaw piece that simply wouldn't fit, that had been transposed from a different puzzle into this. Because this was her sister. This was her twin. Imogen stood in the hallway, stared at the relentlessly cream walls, the heavy wool carpet. What exactly was her sister capable of? They said that she had hurt Amy, but she couldn't have. She just couldn't have. And who was it that Mara was sleeping with? She had gambled her marriage away, on what? On whom?

Dave had stood, limp and listless in the doorway of her office. Had let his gaze drop, the pressure of her fury more than he could bear. 'I haven't, Im. I swear. I haven't slept with her.'

'But you wanted to?'

A long, loaded silence, then a tear rolling down his cheek. 'I was calling her. I thought, you know how she is, I thought that maybe there was a chance – you know, that she felt something for me.' He shook his head. 'I was wrong. I'm so sorry.'

Imogen had studied him, was dimly aware that she should perhaps feel pity for the man she had planned to marry, but there was none there, just the sensation of a book nearing its final pages. 'The gun?'

'What about it?'

'Why did you have the gun? You brought it home from the gun club? Why?'

He wouldn't look at her. His hands were shaking. 'I was going to . . .' Then words failed, cracking under the weight, and he looked up, pleading. 'I didn't want to go on any longer. I didn't want to live.'

Imogen ran her hands now across the smooth walls of Mara's house, seemingly glued to the spot. And Amy? Her brain bucked and fought against the thought. It was not possible that a mother could hurt her child. Was not possible that her sister, her twin, could hurt Amy. It wasn't.

But then, why was she here? Why had she come to her sister's house, used the key that she kept on the key chain, beside her own?

Imogen had told herself that she was looking for vindication, something that would prove the doctors wrong. But now she was here, and the world was reshaping itself around her, and now it seemed that all bets were off.

Imogen hurried up the stairs, pushed open Mara's bathroom door. They had a jacuzzi tub, a shower with a dizzying array of functions, an expensively tiled floor. She stood there, sensing her sister everywhere. Then the phone, ringing in her bag, and she didn't need to look to know who it was, could sense it, call it the twin-thing. That somehow maybe her sister knew where she was, what she was doing.

The ringing stopped, leaving a denser silence in its wake.

Imogen pulled open the bathroom cabinet. Scanned the bottles and jars.

It shouldn't be possible. It couldn't be possible. But her brain was raging against itself, thinking of the little girl Mara, so small and slight, backwards and forwards into hospital so much that their entire childhood had been sheathed in a white coat. Then, in the end, it seemed this was the only place that she felt at home. And that was understandable, surely? That she had spent so much time at the hospital that it felt natural to her. The day the doctors had told their parents that Mara was fine, that she could go home and be happy and healthy and normal, Mara had cried and cried, as if her heart would break.

Imogen thought of the missed schooling that followed; all those days, all those illnesses that the doctors just never seemed to be able to figure out; the fact that it was always something with Mara, some reason why she was sick. And then, as naturally as night would follow day, the MRIs, the CTs, the ultrasounds – anything to find out what was wrong with Mara, why she was so sick. Until in the end all that was left was investigative surgery. Everyone around her had baulked, saying didn't that seem like an awfully long way to go? But Mara had put a brave face on it, saying that she'd rather, because she wanted to get to the bottom of this, that it was the only way. And afterwards the doctors with their guarded expression, the sense that something had changed, the forced joviality: we found nothing, you're fine. Go home.

Mara crying, saying that it was because she thought they were going to fix her.

Imogen ran her fingers across the bottles, turning them so that the labels faced outwards. Looking for amitriptyline. Nothing.

Then had come university and Jack and, it had seemed, a miraculous recovery, one that came from nowhere. No one had questioned it, the world just breathing a sigh of relief that finally, finally, it was over. But then had come marriage and the long, slow establishment of routine that comes with setting up a life. And then Amy. Amy had brought along with her a new fear. Mara had scurried the baby back and forth to the GPs, again and again, everyone saying that it was because she was a first-time mum, she worried – it was natural. Then the raging, Mara's face hard with fury. We're changing surgeries. Those GPs couldn't find their arse with a map.

Imogen closed the cabinet, crossed the landing with quick steps, into Mara's bedroom. The bed was unmade, the quilt pooling onto the floor. Into the en suite, snapped on the light.

Now time had flip-flopped again. And they were in their parents' garden, Amy in her pink-striped swimsuit, as healthy a child as you could ever hope to see. Imogen ducking into the house to get a glass of water, because her mother had been serving home-made lemonade that was sticky and bitter and so, so sweet. Hearing a voice in the living room, knowing it was her sister, and Imogen thinking that she should go out again, that she shouldn't be here listening, because from the tone of it – the climb at the edges – Mara was angry.

'Why can't you come home, Jack? No. No. I know what you said. I don't care. It's not all about you. There's me too. And you can't just . . . No. I need you home. I want you home. Amy. She needs you.'

Imogen had taken a step closer to the door, not meaning to listen, not really, but not being able to help herself, pulled by the hysteria in her sister's voice.

'Okay, fine. Fine. You know what? Fuck you! Let's just hope that you don't live to regret putting us second.'

Imogen tugged at the bathroom cabinet, now swamped with the feeling that she was no longer looking for an absence, that the search had mutated somehow between the front door and here, that now she was looking for a presence. She scanned the cupboard. Half-empty: cotton buds, some shampoo and tampons. A sinking feeling in her stomach.

She stepped back into the bedroom, not bothering to turn off the light. She stood, staring at the unmade bed, the pile of clothes that staggered against the wardrobe door. Wanting to stop, wanting to stop more than she wanted to breathe, because if she stopped now, then they were wrong and she could have her sister back, and she'd already lost her fiancé and surely losing both a sister and a fiancé was more than anyone should be expected to bear.

But she couldn't stop.

Imogen spun on her heel, stalked towards the bedside cabinet on her sister's side of the bed. A hardback book waiting. Unread. A slender Tiffany lamp. She pulled open the drawer, running her hands through the contents. Paracetamol. A solid case for her reading glasses. A packet of condoms. And there, right at the back, a small, round plastic bottle.

She knew what it was before she read the label: Amitriptyline, 75 mg.

Imogen sat down hard on the bed. Now another memory, one that she had fought so hard to redraft. Their childhood home, the not-a-castle castle, just visible on the crest of the hill. The smell of smoke, the crackle of fire from their father's bonfire. Their mother's voice: 'Be careful there.' Imogen standing on the edge, because she wanted to see what the ants were doing, the way they lined up, a black parade of them, a series of ellipses. Looking, but still being careful, because she was the good girl. Then soft footsteps behind her and knowing it was Mara, because she was her twin and didn't she know everything about her? A low giggle, the kind she did when she was about to do something bad. Then Imogen feeling small hands being placed flat against the centre of her back, and a flood of knowledge about what was about to happen, but being powerless to stop it. Then falling and falling.

Imogen cradled the bottle of drugs and remembered the hospital. How they said she was lucky. Remembered her sister at her bedside, her eyes bright, and then the low whisper, just out of their mother's reach. 'You won't tell anyone, will you? Mammy says you're supposed to look after me. You won't tell, Im, will you?'

Imogen sat on the bed, a feeling like all of the energy had leached out of her, seeping into the mattress. She could sleep now. She could lie on this king-sized bed and she could sleep. That was all she wanted to do. Close her eyes. Forget. But she couldn't, because this wasn't about her, wasn't hers to forgive or to hide, not this time. This time it was Amy.

She pushed herself up, ran down the stairs. She pulled open the front door, out onto the path, tugging the door closed behind her. Wasn't looking where she was going, was studying the bottle.

It wasn't a sound that she should have heard. Not in the normal run of things. But perhaps her senses had been wired, thrust into overdrive by the barrelling adrenaline, because she did hear it, a sound like the soles of shoes shifting on tarmac.

Imogen looked up.

He was in amongst the leaves, a figure obscured by the green of the trees. He saw her seeing him. Stepped out into the path.

It took her a moment to place him. Another moment to wonder why it was that he was here.

It was only then that she saw the gun.

He was staring at her, his face puckered into something like hatred, the gun hanging at his side. Then he pulled it up, a movement that seemed to consume his whole body. Levelled it at her.

Time stopped.

There were surely things that she should be doing, actions that she should take. But all that came to Imogen was an unravelling feeling of inevitability, that of course it should end this way. She stared at him, at the barrel of the gun, the two of them merged into one now. Wanted to ask him why.

Then there was a sound. A crack.

It was less of a sound than one would expect, and the insignificance of it took her by surprise. She looked down, a distant curiosity more than anything else. Could see the dark-red flower of blood blossoming through her white blouse. Strange, she thought. Surely there should be pain.

Then another crack.

Imogen's legs gave way beneath her, as if the bones had simply gone, and she buckled, sliding down to the cobble-stone path. Her cheek was cold, pressed against the stones. She was surrounded by redness, darkness. Could dimly hear a dull clicking sound, a curse, the sound of footsteps running. Then the pain came, a burning, searing, punching pain. Then, mercifully, the darkness.

46

The Shooter: Sunday 31 August, 9.10 a.m.
Day of the shooting

I sit behind the wheel. The car had steered itself back towards Mara's house, seemed like I barely needed to touch the wheel. I have texted her. I have asked her to meet me there. I don't know why, but I know that she will come. Maybe because it is destiny.

Mara will be the first. This is the way it should always have been.

I sit, watching the house, am about to reach for the door handle, step out into the morning light, when something catches my eye, a fleck of gold in the darkened footwell. My stomach lurches, but it is a dim and distant feeling, one that seems unreal somehow. Without my guidance or my consent, my fingers reach down, pluck at the fine gold thread. I lift it up, hold it in the sunlight. It is a fine gold chain, narrow and delicate. That is probably why it snapped. Dangling from the end of it is a word in cursive writing: *Emily*.

On the night that I met her I was looking to get drunk, roaringly, obliteratingly drunk. It was after Mara. After the betrayal, after the news that she was going to murder my child, that she was done with me. But, I think, it was before my final decision had been made, before the final tipping over that plunging edge. I had wanted to get drunk, to tip a magic liquid down my throat, obliterate the memories. It was all I could think of, until I thought of the final thing.

Delizioso was loud when I got there. A hen party with their sashes, their blow-up penises, and I almost turned around, walked back out.

I wonder now how differently things would have played out, had I done that. Would I just have gone home, put a gun in my mouth and pulled the trigger? A quiet, violent end.

I had paused in my step, my mind – or what was left of it – weighing up my options, checking the competing pulls of temporary and permanent oblivion. Then I saw her. She was talking on the phone, voice lost amongst the rest of the sound. Watching me. She looked down when she saw that I had seen her. But it was like magic, that sense of being seen. I stood there for long moments. I stared at her. She wasn't in all honesty a pretty girl, with too-round cheeks, hair that was neither blonde nor brown, a little too much weight. But she had seen me. Under her eyes, I had become visible again. And that, at that moment, meant more than anything else.

I crossed the crowded bar to her table.

She set down her mobile, looked up, looked nervous, shifting in her seat. Gave me an uneasy half-smile. I did my best to respond. I don't know what I was hoping for, now when I look back on it. I wasn't looking for love. I don't think at that point I was capable of it. But as I vanished into nothing, there, on that night, I just wanted to be seen.

I asked her if I could sit.

She said yes, a shake in her voice.

She looked nothing like Mara, not in the downturn of her eyes, the wide splay of her breasts. She wasn't wearing make-up. Or if she was, it was only the merest suggestion of it. But there, on that night, that was a good thing. Because all I wanted to do was forget.

We talked for a little while, about this and that. All the while her head ducked, her fingers moving awkwardly on the cardboard coaster, plucking at a torn edge of it, pluck, pluck. The movement began to grate on me, after a while.

I drank a little. A beer or two.

Not enough. But then, I wondered, how much would ever be enough?

Her eyes. It was her eyes that did it. The way they kept flicking upwards, looking at me, then not looking at me. But it was like this constant reminder. I see you. I see you. I drained my glass. I wanted to fuck her. Not her. Her eyes. I wanted to fuck someone who saw me, someone for whom I wasn't an inconvenience, someone who would wash clean the taste of Mara.

I opened my mouth. Didn't know how I was going to say it, how it would play out. But then a roar of laughter burst from the hen party, stuffing the air with sound, and I lost my nerve. Because if I asked, then she would say no, and then I would be worse off than when I began.

I volunteered to go up to the bar, get us some more drinks. She was drinking white wine, a small glass that she had cradled all evening. I nodded towards it. 'Another?' A pause, then a nod, a too-grateful smile.

'Please. But just a small one.'

I ordered her a small white wine. A beer for myself. And vodka shots. I waited, while the bartender took my money, his attention entirely focused on the big-breasted woman beside me, then tipped the shots into the wine. I remember my heart thumping. Because you would taste it, right? I carried the glasses back to the table, the whole while walking on a tightrope, knowing that she would take one sip, that she would know. Would she throw the drinks in my face? Would she scream? I could feel the adrenaline coursing, and felt something like alive for the first time in days. I set the glasses down on the table, tried not to watch her as she reached for it, as her thin lips closed across the rim.

She never noticed. Later I would wonder if it was because she wasn't used to drinking – that was what she had told me anyway. If the taste of alcohol, any alcohol, was so unfamiliar to her it was impossible to discern one from the other. Whatever the cause, it became easier after that, her tongue loosening, her gaze slipping, the drinks sliding down her without question. I could see her slipping away from herself, a boat, its moorings loosed.

After more drinks than I can now remember, I gripped her by the hand, pulled her up. Thinking that I just wanted to forget.

She didn't resist, muttered something about taxis, about her car in a garage. But she slumped against me, heavier than I expected her to be, a dead weight against my shoulder, and I struggled, guiding her out of the bar, past a puddle of yellow vomit, into the dimly lit car park.

I had vague thoughts that we could have sex on the back seat of my car. But there were people, seemed like there were people everywhere. So instead I eased her into the passenger seat, slid the seatbelt around her.

I would take her home, back to mine. I would fuck her. Then I would take her wherever she needed to go.

Such was my plan, if you could call it that.

But something happened.

It was the window, I think. I should never have had the window ajar. I did it for myself, because the world was slip-sliding and unsteady and I needed to drive, didn't want to get pulled over, so I opened the window, thinking that the salted air would help me, would sober me up. We were on the M4, were doing eighty, when it all went wrong.

She had been slumped, her cheek resting against the passenger window, when all of a sudden she started. Sat up. Looked at me. But this time it was a look of fear, cold hard dread. Then she began to scream. Again and again and again, the sound painfully loud in the confines of the car. She was a thing possessed, was fighting against the seatbelt, fighting against my hand as I tried to calm her, fighting against the locked passenger door.

I don't remember her necklace coming off. I was trying to drive, trying to restrain her. But, as I hold it up in the cool sea air, I think this must have been when it had happened.

That was when I lost my temper.

I slammed the brakes on, stopped the car on the fast lane of the M4, flicking the central locking switch.

'Get the fuck out!'

She had the door open before the sentence was even finished, was gone before I knew what had happened. I leaned over, pulled the door closed, stamped on the accelerator. Then I was gone.

I had driven almost all the way home, had been sucking

in breaths of cool air, trying to calm myself down, trying to let the rage settle. I had pulled off the M4, was idling at a red light, when it hit me what I had done. Something washed over me, a swathe of guilt. She had simply been a way of forgetting, something to distract me from my life. The light turned to green and I took the roundabout in a fast sweep, turning back on myself onto the M4, now travelling the opposite way. I would pick her up. I would take her home. It would be the right thing to do.

I knew before I knew. Something in me piecing together what my conscious mind could not. Blue flashing lights. I had known then. I slowed. Saw the police cars. The ambulance. Nobody hurrying, no sirens. I put my foot down, sped away, trying not to vomit.

I turned on the television the next morning and saw her photo, with its rounded cheeks, its undecided hair. The newscaster's face suitably sombre, as her cerise lips formed the words: Swansea-born woman, Emily Wilson, was killed last night on the M4.

I stare at Mara's house. At its promise and its potential, all now gone to waste. And I reach down, pushing open the driver's door. The gun is in my hand. But then, where else would it be? Because now it feels like it has become an extension of me. I stand for a minute, studying the silent street. And then I open my fingers and allow the gold necklace to slide from my hand, landing with a small splash in a waiting puddle.

47

Charlie: Sunday 31 August, 9.55 a.m.
Day of the shooting

I sit in my car, just one amongst a sea of others. I watch police headquarters. He will be here today, I feel it in my gut. I watch the guard-house, the high walls, watch as people flood in, suited, uniformed, ready to start their working day. I wait.

I can't shake it, can't get the image from my mind. Emily, her head thrown back, gaze open, vacant. Her necklace catching in the street light. And then him, marching her onwards with a thousand-yard stare. I see it now, how it unfolded, just as if it had happened in front of me. I see Emily, sitting waiting, probably a little cowed by the noise and the booze, waiting for a friend who will never show up. I see him, selecting her, making his way towards the table in the window. Was she already drunk? Or did that come later? Did he help her with that, plying her with drinks, so that in the end she had no idea how much she'd had? Perhaps he was thinking she would make an easy lay, so soft, so unassuming. Escorting, half-carrying, her out of the bar, down the busy street, then putting her into a car

– his car? – and driving, and maybe she comes to, maybe she starts to fight back, his plan crashing down around his ears. So he gets rid of her, letting her out in the centre of the M4. Telling himself that it is okay, that he didn't actually kill her.

My phone begins to ring and I look down at it, see my mother's number. I let it go to answerphone.

I have to see him. I have to talk to him.

There is a dim and distant part of me that recognises the danger in this. There is a part of me that knows I am running into a firestorm. But I cannot stop myself. Cannot shake the image of Emily lying dead under a tarp, of her mother crying, her father listless and stunned.

The thought crosses my mind that I should call Aden. Or Del. Or, hell, just 999. But what would I say? That I saw him, on a crowded night-time street; that he was helping a woman who had drunk too much? I need to talk to him. I need to understand.

I watch the gate, staring so intently that my eyes begin to pool with tears. And it is then that I see him, slipping out as others are going in. He is wearing uniform, a jacket that looks too warm for the weather. Isn't looking at the people as they pass him, is coming out into the car park, his gaze fixed.

My hand goes to the door handle.

But something stays me. For a moment I sit there, staring at him, trying to understand what it is that I have seen.

He is carrying a gym bag on his shoulder. It looks to be heavy, the weight of its strap denting the jacket, leaving behind a knot of creases. I stare at the bag. What is it? What's wrong with this picture? The fabric is straining, has been packed to its limit. A shape juts out of the side of it, warping the bag, and I stare at it and stare at it, trying to piece it all together.

What is that?

Then he reaches his car, slides the bag off his shoulder onto the ground, and the movement changes its shape, changes the way the shadows fall. And then, in that one heart-stopping movement, I know exactly what it is he is carrying.

48

Aden: Sunday 31 August, 9.55 a.m.
Day of the shooting

Aden studied his reflection, the yellowing knot above his eye, the fresher, bluer bruise that snaked its way along his forearm. He reached out with the fingers of his opposing hand, touched it, even though he knew he shouldn't. Was rewarded with a sharp spike of pain. Shit! The locker room was quiet, smelled of stale sweat. Shift change had come and gone, and everyone had left now, out on patrol. Just Aden remaining behind, nursing his bruises.

He broke away from his reflection, pulling on his bullet-proof vest.

It was a thousand years ago that he had woken with Charlie beside him, a thousand years since he kissed her goodbye.

He patted his pockets, would ring her. But then the pain shot through his arm again and he stopped. No, he'd wait. He would tell her tonight. It would be best if he didn't worry her. The locker-room door swung inwards, bringing with it a breath of air into the pungent room.

'Ade, you all right?' Del was already in his uniform, his

jacket pulled on. Squinted at Aden's arm. 'Shit, mate. Got you a good 'un.'

'Yeah. I'll live. Any luck?'

Del grimaced, shook his head. 'Went round to Tony's house – nothing. His car is gone. You really think he gave your information to Steve Lowe?'

Aden slid a clip of ammunition into his vest. 'Yeah. Yeah, I do.'

'Well, we're going to keep looking. Everyone knows to keep their eyes peeled for him.'

Then a silence, in which they're both thinking the same thing.

'You don't think he'd have . . .'

'Mate,' Aden fixed Del with a look, 'I think I can confidently say I've got no clue what the hell Tony is going to do next.' Then something else, a thought that had been sitting at the back of his mind, unnoticed. 'Hey, you seen Rhys?'

Del started then, looking at him. 'No. Why?'

'He should be in by now. He didn't partner with somebody else?'

'No, I saw the teams leaving when I came in. He wasn't with them.'

Aden stood there for a second, a sinking feeling in his insides. Pulled out his phone and dialled Rhys's number. A pause. Then the answerphone. 'Shit!'

Del stared at him. 'I'll go round to his house. You're thinking Steve got to him first?'

Aden slipped his phone back into his pocket, moving quickly. Long strides towards the door, everything seeming unreal to him. 'I hope not.' Then a parp of sound, his mobile phone ringing. He started, fumbled for it. But before he could unravel it from the knot of fabric, the door flew open, knocking him off-balance. A police officer, young, fearful-looking. Aden dimly recognised him as Del's partner. His face was grey, eyes red, looked like he'd been crying.

'Did you hear?'

'Hear what?'

'They found the armourer. Dead.'

49

The Shooter: Sunday 31 August, 9.38 a.m.
Day of the shooting

I pull open the car door, duck inside so quickly that I bang my shoulder against the frame. The child is still watching me, his nappy hanging low, his finger now resolutely jammed into his left nostril. The Lowes' house is still in silence. The curtains are still closed. They do not know that I am here. My heart is hammering so loudly that I can hear nothing else. I should have done it. Irrespective of the child and its wide-open gaze, I should have set the gun against the lock on the Lowes' front door, pulled the trigger, moved into the house, up the stairs to where the parents lay asleep.

But now, under the scrutiny of a three-year-old child, my hands are shaking like leaves, and I can taste blind panic. My fingers go to the keys in the ignition. It's okay. It will be okay. They will go to the hospital. They are parents and that is where their child is. They will go there. And I will go there.

I pull away from the kerb, steady, deliberately not speeding. I steer the car down the hill, can see the sea from here, sparkling blue. But still I am surrounded by the boxed council houses, the abandoned cars of Harddymaes in all its glory. I glance in the rear-view mirror. I can see the off-licence, the alleyway.

Whenever I think of that night, I remember the rain. The way it drove down, sweeping across the pavement. The grip of the car on the road, seemed to be painfully light, like at any minute it could be swept away. The call, shots fired, permission to arm. Out of the car, the rain beating against my head, so hard that it hurt. Loading the weapons.

I didn't tell anyone about the other gun. The one I kept in the ankle-holster, hidden beneath my uniform trousers.

Then flying along, towards Harddymaes, sirens blaring. The adrenaline starting to course through my veins, and there's no feeling like it in the world. Like riding the world's greatest roller coaster, again and again and again. Then seeing the off-licence. The figures running.

I had found the gun – my gun – months previously. Had been doing a raid on a house. This old guy, done for threats to kill. There'd been talk of weapons, people saying that he was a hoarder, one of those end-of-days apocalyptic types. We swept through the house, black-booted locusts, the old guy shouting, telling us to fuck off, then bursting into tears. I found the gun under his mattress. It was a nice little Browning HP – single-action, 9 mm. I should have turned it in, should have put it into evidence along with all of the other shit we turned up that day. But I didn't.

It wasn't the first time I had taken things from a scene. It had developed over time into a habit, the collection of souvenirs. There was never any rhyme or reason to the things I took, just little pieces, things that caught my eye. A picture. A pen. A gun.

Then I was out of the car, the rain pounding, and I mean

pounding. I was running on a surface as slick as sheet-ice. Into that alleyway – not a patch of light, just the sound of footsteps, somewhere ahead.

I don't know why I started carrying the gun. It wasn't like I was struggling for weaponry, not in work at least. But there was something about having it, this secret source of power that no one knew about. I started taking it with me wherever I went, tucked into my ankle-holster. It was my protection; a talisman, I suppose.

And that night, running and running, my heart just pounding like it would beat out of my chest, so much adrenaline that I was giddy with it. And then I saw something, or I thought I saw something.

I would wonder about that later on. Was it my mind, drowning in chemicals, struggling to make sense of a world that made no sense at all? Was that why I did what I did?

Before I knew what I was doing, my gun was up. My finger was moving, locking itself around the trigger. And the gun was kicking back, the darkness rent with the light of the muzzle-flash. And up ahead, a soft 'Oof'.

Then there was more light, more sound, from beside me, behind me – all around me, it seemed.

Then nothing.

I reached Dylan Lowe first, my back shielding him briefly from view. I think now that I must have known, even then, what I had done. I reached him, and the blood was spilling out from the hole in his chest and my eyes were racing, up his body, down his body, looking for the gun that I know he had. That he must have had.

But there was nothing there. Just a boy lying on the floor. Dying.

I pulled the gun from my ankle-holster. Placed it in his hand.

There seemed to be no other way.

I know now that this was the beginning of the end. That the night would never leave me. That it would haunt my dreams, dominate my waking hours, so that in the end everywhere I turned, there was Dylan Lowe. I could not talk about it, seemed no way for the thoughts to be translated into words, just clumsy pieces of sound and smell and touch. Instead they crawled over me, oozing until they became a second skin, until there was no way to be rid of them. No way but this.

I sit for a moment, the car engine idling, my gaze caught in the rear-view mirror. For a fleeting second it seems that once again I can see Dylan Lowe, that he is standing before the wide-eyed window of the off-licence, watching me. I cannot move. I cannot breathe. I stare into the rear-view mirror. Blink. Now there is nothing. Dylan Lowe is gone.

50

Charlie: Sunday 31 August, 10.17 a.m.
Day of the shooting

I drive behind him, an undercover cop in a bad movie, leaving two cars between us. I follow him as he drives into Swansea. I follow him as he pulls into the hospital car park.

My hands feel like they don't belong to me, my feet someone else's. This isn't real. So I follow him, like I am caught on a thread, because I cannot believe that what I know is happening *is* actually happening.

I dialled Aden, as we crawled in end-of-holiday traffic along Fabian Way. I held the phone in one hand, the wheel in the other. Waited to hear his voice, for him to talk me down, tell me that I'm nuts. But it just rang and rang.

I pull into a space, watch him watch the hospital. Realise that my hands are shaking so badly they seem to be vibrating against the steering wheel. He isn't doing anything. He's just sitting there. Staring.

I've got carried away. It isn't what I think it is. It can't be. But what the hell is he doing?

His head is tilted, he is studying the fascia of the hospital,

326

and I follow his line of sight, my eyes trailing up the building. Second floor. Look back at him, back to where he is staring. Second floor.

I watch him, am thinking of Emily and I can't . . . I don't understand what it is that he is doing here, what will come next. Then something shifts and I think further back than that, to the boy who was there when this began. And I could kick myself for my blindness. I have been so focused on Emily, so determined to find out what happened to her, that I failed to see that there may have been other motives. Other people he could target.

Dylan Lowe.

It's like those stereograms – those visual illusions you had when you were a kid – when you stare and stare and there's nothing there, just a bunch of shapes and colours that mean nothing. And then something changes. And then everything becomes clear.

The second floor is Ward 12. The second floor is where Dylan Lowe is.

He is going to kill him.

I grab for the phone. This time I dial 999. 'Come on, come on!'

'Which service, please?'

'Police.'

There is movement in the other car; he is shifting, changing position.

'Police, what is your emergency?'

My voice has got higher, there is a hysterical twinge to it. 'There's a man at Mount Pleasant Hospital.' He is out of the car now, lifting the bag, hefting it onto his shoulder, and here, in this light, it seems breathtakingly obvious that the shape within it is a gun. 'He's got a gun. You have to

327

send someone here. He's going to kill Dylan Lowe.' The words tumble out of me, nonsensical almost, and I wish that I could be clearer, wish I could make them understand, but it seems the words are stoppered up, that there is a bottleneck now between my brain and my mouth. The operator is saying something to me, but I don't hear it, because everything I have is focused on him. He stands beside his car, looks up, his gaze fixed on the second floor. I think of Carla, sitting there, saying goodbye to her son. And then he is moving, and the thread is a chain, connecting me to him, and I hear myself say, 'Please, hurry'. And even though I know it is not enough, I drop the phone, throw open the car door so hard that it hits the Fiat beside me and I'm out.

I can smell the sea air. The sky is blue. It seems unthinkable that anything bad could happen on a day like today.

He is a couple of hundred yards in front of me, moving through the knotted smokers, in through the sliding doors. I take off at a run, calling his name. Push past a stick-thin man with his cigarette and his IV bag, the curl of smoke hitting my lungs, choking me. In through the doors. To the lobby.

I stand there, gasping like I have just run a marathon. Feels like I have run from one world into another. Because there's nothing – no sound, no fear – just people moving about as they always do. And I can't see him. He has come in and vanished, and the panic is rising in me, so fast I can't speak. Part of me registers Ernie, standing in a queue in the coffee shop. But I cannot think, speak. My gaze is darting around the lobby. I must find him.

A couple walk towards me, the woman achingly thin, her hair cropped down to the tightest of curls, the man patting her arm, talking to her in a low voice. They walk towards me and then past and out through the doors. Then I see him.

He is standing at the edge of the lobby.

He is staring at Imogen.

She is staring at him, a mobile phone held forgotten in her hand. They are frozen.

Then Rhys pulls out the gun.

Time truly stops then.

He levels it at her, pointing it so that it is level with her heart. And she isn't moving, she's just staring at him, at the gun. And my brain won't work, and my feet are stuck. Without thinking, I open my mouth.

'Rhys!' It comes out like a scream.

But even whilst the sound hangs in the air, there is a boom that reverberates through my body and she falls to the floor, the blood spraying out in a thick shower behind her.

Rhys stands there, a dark shape in his firearms uniform, such a common sight in the hospital now that he would have been all but invisible as he marched in, bearing death. He stares down at her, the gun still level with where she should have been. Then he pirouettes, and I see him full-on now. Only I've never seen *this* Rhys before. The dark hair is askew, the deep-brown eyes – the ones that women go so wild over – are empty. He tracks the gun around the lobby. Then stops.

I look, I don't want to look, but I have to look. Ernie is holding his coffee. Is staring at Rhys, at the gun, like his brain simply cannot understand what it is that he has seen.

Boom!

There are screams. I'm watching the gun, watching it

slide round the room, watching it find another target. The old woman is walking with laborious steps, her head down; it doesn't look like she has even realised she is about to die.

Boom!

She slips to the floor like she is dissolving, puddling against the linoleum.

I have to move. I have to get towards him. Get to the gun. But I can't. My feet are glued, watching the barrel of the gun circle like the hour-hand on a clock. It finds a man in a shirt and tie. He looks like he has had a job interview. He stares at Rhys. Lifts up his hands in an empty gesture of surrender.

Boom!

Then the gun slides around. Finds me.

51

Aden: Sunday 31 August, 10.28 a.m.
Day of the shooting

Aden flew through the traffic, his foot flat on the accel-erator. His heart thundered in his chest. Trying to breathe, trying to tell himself that it was just another job, but he couldn't. Because it wasn't Steve; it hadn't been Steve all along. Because Steve was in custody and, if Steve was in custody, that only left Tony, with his fury and his pain. The call had come over the air, gunman at the hospital, and with a startling clarity Aden had known. Today it wouldn't just be a story, where the gunman appeared and then disappeared as if he was never there. Today would be different. He yanked the car over hard into the car park, mounting the kerb as he took the corner too sharp. There were people up ahead, running. They flooded out of the doors, billowing towards him in a shoal, separating so that they surrounded the Armed Response Vehicle, then rejoining. Running. All running.

Aden threw open the car door. Grabbed the G36.

He could see bodies. There, through the sliding glass doors, were lifeless limbs, scattered across the floor. He felt his brain slow, struggling to piece it together, that Tony would be capable of this. A man hobbled past him, all skin and bone, dragging behind him a metal IV stand, sucking on a cigarette so hard that it seemed his face would turn inside out.

Aden raised the weapon and began to run towards the doors.

The dark figures lay stark against the light floor. The blood had pooled, had made a sea in the centre of the lobby. Aden scanned, left to right, could feel the gun, steady in his hands.

His hands steady as a rock.

Then he saw them.

They stood, carved in stone. Charlie – his Charlie – her stance wide, her chin up, daring death to take her. And Rhys.

The gun in Aden's hands sank, his mind struggling to catch up. Because this wasn't the way he thought it was going to go. Not at all. And now it all seemed slightly ridiculous, like some joke that had gone wrong.

'Rhys?'

Charlie started, looked at him, and he could see the courage flushing out of her, the tears springing to her eyes. She looked from him to Rhys and back. Was mouthing something. It looked like sorry.

'Rhys, what have you done?'

Rhys didn't answer, didn't look. His face was slack, eyes dead. Aden's gaze tracked over him, at the gun, the jacket just slightly open, the body armour visible at the neck. Aden waited for Rhys to turn, to look at him, for his face to change, the colour and the life to flood back in, to say that it wasn't the way it seemed, that it was all some kind of elaborate ruse. But there was nothing. Just Rhys, staring through his sight at Charlie.

Aden raised his handgun.

'Rhys. Drop the gun.'

Rhys didn't move, didn't seem like he was even breathing.

'I will shoot you. Drop the gun now.' Aden was surprised to hear his voice, had expected to hear a break in it, was surprised at how much like iron it sounded. 'Don't make me kill you, mate.'

That was it. Those were the words. Something happened then, a change sinking its way across Rhys's features and he shifted, looked up. His eyes locked on Aden's and for just a moment there was something that looked a lot like a smile.

'I need it to end, Ade.' The words were soft, a whisper.

Then he turned, the gun swinging, off Charlie, onto Aden.

And Aden's finger, the one that had refused to move before, was moving now, pulling the trigger. An explosion of sound, the gun slamming into his palm, and then pain – more pain than should come from the kickback. But there wasn't time, not right now.

The shot was a good one. It hit Rhys in the forehead, and he dropped to the ground.

Aden stared at him, still holding the gun up, tracked the muzzle across the fallen man. But there was no doubt about it. Rhys was dead.

Aden lowered the gun, was aware of Charlie turning towards him. Dimly heard her say something, although the words had been drowned out now by the pounding in his head. Then his legs buckled beneath him and he fell.

52

Imogen: Sunday 31 August, 10.30 a.m.
Day of the shooting

There were pieces of light, shards of it puncturing the darkness. The strangest of sensations, a weeping, a lightening. There was no pain. Not now, just a sinking dullness, as if she had drunk a strong sleeping potion and was now drifting in some dark hinterworld.

Imogen, if that was who she was now, considered dying. It seemed, when one thought about things rationally, to be a highly likely proposition at this point and, if she was being utterly and totally honest, not an entirely unpleasant one. There was a comfort in the thought: that one could simply let go, unknot one's raft from the harbour and drift away. It would certainly be easier.

She lay on the cobblestone path or on a feather-filled bed – she was unsure which – and thought about giving in. Her body was already halfway there, she could feel it. Her skin, her blood, her bones, all of it just aching to yield. All that was required now was for her mind to join in the 'abandon ship'.

Then a thought, clearer than all the others, piercing the blackness. Amy.

Imogen thought of the dimpled hands, the pixie-fine hair, the hospital bed, the seizure gripping and dropping Amy. And then another thought, just as distinct. That she did not want to die today.

She began to swim back towards herself. Amy. Amy. Sounds beginning to sweep in now: a shout, footsteps, hands, not on her back this time, but gripping her arms, stroking her head. A voice she didn't recognise. It'll be okay. It'll be okay.

Wanting to believe that more than she had ever wanted to believe anything.

Now the pain, waiting for her just beyond the darkness. It hit her like a wall, a visible force, and she rebounded off it, the urge to let go never stronger. But she had remembered and now she could not forget. Amy. Amy needed her.

Imogen opened her eyes.

A woman was kneeling beside her. Another voice, a little further away. The words 'ambulance' and 'hurry'. Pain in her stomach and her arms and her legs and her back. The woman speaking to her, words she could barely piece together, but they sounded soft, like a lullaby. And the sunlight. It seemed like it came from nowhere, hitting her suddenly, warmth billowing against her skin.

Imogen shifted, looked up so that she could see the sky. It was beautiful. An unblemished blue. It was, she thought, going to be a lovely day.

53

Charlie: Sunday 14 September, 2 p.m.
Two weeks after the shooting

I walk slowly, feels like each step is heavier than the one before, moving with the slow tide of people. We are all dressed in black, must look like a thundercloud drifting slowly through the hospital grounds. The doors of the chapel have been thrown open, the bulbous sound of organ music drifting out to meet us. But I can tell from here that we won't be going in, that the hospital chapel already houses as many as it is capable of holding. And that's okay. I'm content to stand in the garden, with the smell of roses, the cool sunlight on my skin. In fact, it is better this way.

I can see the hospital lobby from here. There is a part of my brain – a major part – that wants to look away. But I won't let it. Because isn't that my job? To catalogue tragedies, to write about them so that nobody can forget. So I let my gaze rest on the still boarded-up window, the quiet trickle of people who move in through the sliding lobby doors and out, their heads inexorably pulled to where we stand, the grieving masses. I can hear them thinking it: thank God it wasn't us.

Aden squeezes my hand. I glance up at him. Smile, or at least move my mouth into a facsimile of a smile. He was released from hospital a couple of days ago. The bullet wound in his shoulder has not entirely healed yet. The doctors say there will always be some scarring, some issues with his range of movement, but that he will, for the most part, recover. They told him he shouldn't be alone, that there should be someone at home to take care of him. At least, that's what he told me. I'm not entirely sure I believe him. But I'm happy to go along with the subterfuge. His house is nicer than my flat anyway.

The memorial service is beginning, the pastor's voice – Welsh and as dense as bread pudding – rolling over the loudspeakers that have been set up outside. I confess that I am not really listening. Instead I watch the people. They, like me, have come to say goodbye to the casualties. Or maybe we are the casualties, the hidden ones whose lives must continue on beyond this event. I'm not sure how it is that we will do that. I simply know we have no choice.

The sunlight catches on red hair, somewhere hidden within the crowd, and for a moment my heart stops and I am back in the lobby, staring at the red hair, at Imogen lying dead. And then the crowd moves and I see her and, seeing her, I wonder how I could ever have mistaken her for her twin. They really were quite different. Perhaps it was their manner, the way they carried themselves. Whatever it was, there is no doubt in my mind that Imogen is before me, standing beneath a thick-spread oak tree, the hand of a small child tucked into hers. She looks pale, thinner than before, like one strong gust and she will be over. Even from this distance, I can see the tears. Then the little girl, with her black velvet dress, the black bow in her ponytail, looks up at her, says something that is lost to the distance and the boom of the pastor, and Imogen smiles.

I look at the man beside her, dark, thick-built, his expression that far-off look of the terminally shell-shocked, and I wonder who he is. I see him nod, think for a moment that he is nodding to me, then realise it is Aden that he is addressing. I glance up at him, a questioning frown.

'That's Chief Inspector Jack Lewis. Imogen's brother-in-law,' Aden murmurs. 'He's a good man.'

Then I hear a name, and my attention snaps back to the pastor's voice.

'There were many casualties on that day. We gather today to say our farewells to them. To Ernie Dewer, security guard for forty years.'

Father of four, wife to Margaret, grandfather to seven. Loved chocolate-digestive biscuits.

'Lester Hockney, the police armourer. A well-respected officer.'

Lester had retired once, so Aden said, had come back to work because he didn't like just sitting around and doing nothing. From the information we have been able to piece together, it seems that Rhys suffered a gun-jam after trying, and failing, to kill Imogen. He must have gone to the armoury to restock on weapons, but something in his manner, or what he said, made Lester suspicious. He refused to give Rhys the key to the gun-safe. Lester died from a bullet wound to the chest. His wife had passed away six months previously.

'Maggie George, aged seventy-two. Grandmother and mother. Stephen Philips, aged twenty-four, just starting out in life.'

Maggie George, a fiercely active member of her community,

someone who had just overcome breast cancer. Stephen had been at the hospital that day interviewing for a job in the radiology department and had come out ahead of the pack, although he never got the chance to know that.

I know what name will come next, and even though I want to look away, I cannot take my eyes off Imogen as she stiffens. She knows it too.

'And Mara Elliott-Lewis, aged thirty-two. Mother to Amy, wife to Jack.'

He had killed Mara in front of me. Must have been stalled by surprise, the belief that he had already killed her once. Of course it hadn't been Mara at the house. Mara had remained at the hospital, only to die there later than intended. They didn't find Imogen until a little later – fortunately, minutes rather than hours. A neighbour walking her dog had come across her, a middle-aged woman stunned by the scene of destruction before her. Imogen had been shot in the stomach on Mara's front path, and had suffered extensively from her wounds. It is a miracle that she survived; a miracle brought about by the gun-jam. Of course wrapped within this miracle was also another tragedy. Had the gun not jammed, he would never have gone to the armoury.

'There is evil in this world, and sometimes it walks amongst us, and we do not see it until it's too late.'

I look at Aden, see him look down, shake his head, and I know exactly what it is he is thinking. That Rhys was a boy. A desperately sad, desperately desperate boy in a man's body. The experts have come out of the woodwork – they always do after things like this. Everyone wants to throw their hat into the ring, be the one to explain how he could do what it was he had done. A lot of the explanations make me want to roll my eyes. But there is one that sticks with me. That Rhys wanted to be seen, wanted to matter, even if the reason he mattered was because he had committed a terrible deed; to his damaged psyche, that would seem better than never to have mattered at all. I think of Rhys – deeply handsome Rhys – walking through a room, think how head after head would turn to follow his progress, and I want to weep. That he was so seen in life, and never could recognise it.

I don't know how long we have been standing here. I have drifted off, lost in my own thoughts, but then there is a blast of organ music that makes me jump, and slowly, steadily the crowd begins to move. It seems that we are done. I look to Imogen, tug on Aden's hand.

'Come on.'

We move through the press of bodies to where she is standing, still beneath the oak tree. I glance at Jack. The tear-tracks are clear on his face. He makes no effort to wipe them away, but reaches out, grasps Aden by the hand.

'Thank you. For what you did.'

Aden shakes his head, uncomfortable now. 'I'm sorry. I wish I could have been earlier. I wish . . .'

I wish I could have saved your wife for you.

Jack grips his hand, tighter now. 'You did what you could. You saved a lot of lives. Thank you for that.'

I look to Imogen, her gaze fixed beyond me, on what remains of the hospital lobby.

'How are you?' I ask.

She snaps her head back, seems vaguely surprised to see me before her. 'Oh, you know. They just released me. From the hospital. So, I'm . . .' She glances down at the little girl. 'Amy, honey, stay with Daddy for a second, okay. I'm going to have a chat with Charlie.'

The little girl bites her lip, nods. You can see it in her eyes, the fear that her aunt too will leave and not come back.

'How is she doing?' I nod towards Amy as we move away.

Imogen shrugs. 'She keeps asking when her mother is coming back. She doesn't understand. But then,' she said quietly, 'who does?'

I reach out and take her hand within mine.

'I should have known.' The words fall out of Imogen in a hurry, like she has to say them fast or she won't say them at all. She looks at me. 'I should have seen it in him. Rhys . . . I knew that he had problems, I could see there was more than he was willing to tell me. But I should have . . .'

I squeeze her hand. 'What? Seen the future? You couldn't have foreseen this. No one could.' I look back at Aden, still talking softly with Jack. Think of him crying on my shoulder, the same words coming from him. I should have known. 'Rhys was a man who needed help, but he was too good at putting on a brave face, and simply didn't have the words to ask. What he did – the choices he made – they are his responsibility. Not yours.'

Imogen nods, brushes away a tear. 'Did you hear about Dylan Lowe?'

They removed his feeding tube. He passed away yesterday morning.

I nod. 'At least the family can begin to grieve now.' Carla was at the hospital, the morning Rhys came for them. Steve was waiting to kick the crap out of Aden, the younger children were with their grandparents. For a dreadfully unlucky family, they were lucky that day. It was only because the neighbour saw Rhys drive away that we ever knew he was there at all.

'Yes.'

'A'tie Im?' Amy has broken away from her father, is watching us, fearful.

'I'm coming, my love. I should go.' This last to me. She gives my hand a squeeze. 'You take care. Both of you.'

I stand and watch her walk away from me, through the slowly flowing crowd, watch her take Amy by the hand.

'You ready?'

I glance up at Aden and smile. 'Can we just do one more thing?'

The chapel is almost empty now. The organist still plays and I wonder if someone should stop her, remind her that her duty is over, that she can go. I move along the pews, to the alcove that sits beneath the stained-glass window. Candles dance a flickering orange, leaving specks across my vision. I hang there awkwardly for a moment. There is probably a prayer that I should say, but I don't know any. So instead I settle for slipping a coin into the box, picking up one of the tea-lights and lighting it carefully, on the shimmering flames. I set it down in the front row and then step back.

I glance up at Aden. 'For Emily.'

ACKNOWLEDGEMENTS

Writing can be a terrifying foray into an unknown world. This book, however, truly was a labour of love, and there are so many people who have eased its path into this world.

First and foremost, to all those at the Darley Anderson Literary Agency. You're all just ridiculously lovely. But especially to the always spectacular Camilla Wray. Both my agent and my friend, you have guided, cheered and supported me through my second book as only you can. Truly none of this would be possible without you.

To the wonderful team at Arrow – thank you so much for being, as ever, an absolute joy to work with. Particular thanks to Jenny Geras for your incredible insight, guidance and support. Thank you to Francesca Pathak for your perceptive editorial guidance. Thank you to Joanna Taylor for picking up the reins so seamlessly, and to Philippa Cotton for bringing *Hidden* to the attention of readers. And to Becke Parker, whose drive, humour and unfailing brilliance have made my first forays into the world of publicity seem almost effortless.

I sought advice from many people in my efforts to keep *Hidden* as true to life as possible. Thank you to Jason Evans of the *South Wales Evening Post* for your fascinating insight into the world of crime-reporting. Also to Dr Catherine Atkins, for taking time out of your very busy schedule to sit down with me and check my understanding of all things medical.

To Donna Llewellyn, for advising me on any and all police matters, for making me copious amounts of tea, and for never failing to listen to my complaining and my worries with patience and affection. I never fail to consider myself privileged to have you as my dearest friend.

To my husband Matthew, for helping me get my facts straight, being willing to drive me ridiculous distances just so that I am not doing it alone and, quite simply, being your wonderful self. For you, my love, thank you will never seem quite enough.

I hope that I have done justice to the expertise of these brilliant people, and any mistakes that you may find are, I confess, well and truly mine.

To my family – to Mum and Dad, Ma & Pops, Cam & Deb – thank you for your unfailing support and for being the greatest cheerleaders a girl could ever have.

And finally, to my sons, Daniel and Joseph. Thank you simply for being you.